Dear Friends,

Welcome to Seattle! This volume, *Home in Seattle*, is the compilation of two books I wrote in the late 1980s and early '90s. *The Playboy and the Widow* holds a special place in my heart, as it was the first of my books to make the highly touted Waldenbooks bestseller list. Actually, the title was an experiment for me. I'd been keeping close track of that list and discovered there were key words in the titles that attracted a reader's attention. Words like *wife, husband, baby* and—yup—*playboy* and *widow*. I remember waiting with great anticipation for the release of that title to see if I'd keyed into a little-known detail (at the time), and by heaven, I had. The book hit the #10 slot on the list. Encouraged by what I'd discovered, I continued with these key words, and my titles continued to climb up the bestseller lists from that point on.

Later, I gave a series of workshops at writers' conferences explaining my findings. So if you've read *Cinderella's Cowboy Baby* or any other story using one of the long list of key words in the title, I'm pretty sure you can thank (or curse) me.

The second book in this set is *Fallen Angel* and another of the books I wrote early in my career, long before cell phones or iPads or many of the more recent advancements in technology. I've refreshed both books as best I can.

As always, I derive a great deal of pleasure hearing from my readers. You can find me on Facebook or leave me a note via my webpage at debbiemacomber.com. Or write me at P.O. Box 1458, Port Orchard, WA 98366.

I appreciate your ongoing support. And all best wishes for the new year!

Debbie Macomber

DEBBIE MACOMBER

Home in Seattle

ISBN-13: 978-0-7783-1678-7

Home in Seattle

Copyright © 2014 by Harlequin Books S.A.

The publisher acknowledges the copyright holder of the individual works as follows:

The Playboy and the Widow
Copyright © 1988 by Debbie Macomber

Fallen Angel
Copyright © 1990 by Debbie Macomber

Recycling programs
for this product may
not exist in your area.

Printed in U.S.A.

www.Harlequin.com

Also by Debbie Macomber

Blossom Street Books

The Shop on Blossom Street
A Good Yarn
Susannah's Garden
Back on Blossom Street
Twenty Wishes
Summer on Blossom Street
Hannah's List
The Knitting Diaries
    ("The Twenty-First Wish")
A Turn in the Road

Cedar Cove Books

16 Lighthouse Road
204 Rosewood Lane
311 Pelican Court
44 Cranberry Point
50 Harbor Street
6 Rainier Drive
74 Seaside Avenue
8 Sandpiper Way
92 Pacific Boulevard
1022 Evergreen Place
Christmas in Cedar Cove
    (*5-B Poppy Lane* and
    A Cedar Cove Christmas)
1105 Yakima Street
1225 Christmas Tree Lane

Dakota Series

Dakota Born
Dakota Home
Always Dakota
Buffalo Valley

The Manning Family

The Manning Sisters
The Manning Brides
The Manning Grooms

Christmas Books

A Gift to Last
On a Snowy Night
Home for the Holidays
Glad Tidings
Christmas Wishes
Small Town Christmas
When Christmas Comes
    (now retitled *Trading Christmas*)
There's Something About Christmas
Christmas Letters
Where Angels Go
The Perfect Christmas
Angels at Christmas
    (*Those Christmas Angels* and
    Where Angels Go)
Call Me Mrs. Miracle
Choir of Angels (*Shirley, Goodness
    and Mercy, Those Christmas Angels*
    and *Where Angels Go*)
5-B Poppy Lane in
    Together for Christmas
    (with Brenda Novak, Sheila Roberts
    and RaeAnne Thayne)

Heart of Texas Series

VOLUME 1
(*Lonesome Cowboy* and *Texas Two-Step*)
VOLUME 2
(*Caroline's Child* and *Dr. Texas*)
VOLUME 3
(*Nell's Cowboy* and *Lone Star Baby*)
Promise, Texas
Return to Promise

More books by Debbie Macomber listed on page 6

Midnight Sons

VOLUME 1
(*Brides for Brothers* and
   The Marriage Risk)
VOLUME 2
(*Daddy's Little Helper* and
   Because of the Baby)
VOLUME 3
(*Falling for Him,
   Ending in Marriage* and
   Midnight Sons and Daughters)

This Matter of Marriage
Montana
Thursdays at Eight
Between Friends
Changing Habits
Married in Seattle
   (*First Comes Marriage* and
   Wanted: Perfect Partner)
Right Next Door
   (*Father's Day* and
   The Courtship of Carol Sommars)
Wyoming Brides
   (*Denim and Diamonds* and
   The Wyoming Kid)
Fairy Tale Weddings
   (*Cindy and the Prince* and
   Some Kind of Wonderful)
The Man You'll Marry
   (*The First Man You Meet* and
   The Man You'll Marry)
Orchard Valley Grooms
   (*Valerie* and *Stephanie*)
Orchard Valley Brides
   (*Norah* and *Lone Star Lovin'*)
The Sooner the Better
An Engagement in Seattle
   (*Groom Wanted* and *Bride Wanted*)
Out of the Rain
   (*Marriage Wanted* and *Laughter in the Rain*)

Learning to Love
   (*Sugar and Spice* and
   Love by Degree)
You...Again
   (*Baby Blessed* and
   Yesterday Once More)
Three Brides, No Groom
The Unexpected Husband
   (*Jury of His Peers* and
   Any Sunday)
Love in Plain Sight
   (*Love 'n' Marriage* and
   Almost an Angel)
I Left My Heart
   (*A Friend or Two* and
   No Competition)
Marriage Between Friends
   (*White Lace and Promises* and
   Friends—And Then Some)
A Man's Heart
   (*The Way to a Man's Heart* and
   Hasty Wedding)
North to Alaska
   (*That Wintry Feeling* and
   Borrowed Dreams)
On a Clear Day
   (*Starlight* and
   Promise Me Forever)
To Love and Protect
   (*Shadow Chasing* and
   For All My Tomorrows)

*Debbie Macomber's
   Cedar Cove Cookbook*
*Debbie Macomber's
   Christmas Cookbook*

CONTENTS

For Jon and Bonnie Knopp

THE PLAYBOY
AND THE WIDOW

One

"Mom, I don't have any lunch money."

Diana Collins stuck her head out from the cupboard beneath the kitchen sink and wiped the perspiration from her brow. "Bring me my purse."

"Mother," eight-year-old Katie whined dramatically, "I'm going to miss my bus."

"All right, all right." Hurriedly Diana scooted out from her precarious position and reached for a rag to dry her hands.

"We're out of hair spray," Joan, Katie's elder sister, cried. "You can't honestly expect me to go to school without hair spray."

"Honey, you're in fifth grade, not high school. Your hair looks terrific."

Joan glared at her mother as though the thirty-year-old were completely dense. "I need hair spray if it's going to stay this way."

Diana shook her head. "Did you look in my bathroom?"

"Yes. There wasn't any."

"Check the towel drawer."

"The towel drawer?"

Diana shrugged. "I was hiding it."

Joan frowned and gave her mother a disapproving look. "Honestly!"

"Mom, my lunch money," Katie cried, waving her mother's purse under Diana's nose.

With quick fingers, Diana located a few dollars and promptly handed them to her younger daughter.

Five minutes later the front screen door slammed, and Diana sighed her relief. No sound was ever more pleasant than that of her daughters darting off to meet the school bus. The silence was too inviting to resist, and Diana poured herself a cup of coffee and sat at the kitchen table, savoring the quiet. She grabbed her laptop and, automatically went in search of part-time position. It was tempting, although Diana wanted to wait until the girls were a bit older. Before Stan had died, there'd been few problems with money. Now, however, they cropped up daily, and Diana was torn with the desire to remain at home with her children, or seek the means to provide extra income. For three years Diana had robbed Peter to pay Paul, juggling funds from one account to another. Between the social security check, the insurance check and the widow's fund from Stan's job, she and the girls were barely able to eke by. She cut back on expenses where she could, but recently her options had become more limited. There were plenty of macaroni-and-cheese dinners now, especially toward the end of the month. Diana could always ask for help from her family, but she was hesitant. Her parents lived in Wichita and were concerned enough about her living alone with the girls in far-off Seattle. She simply didn't want to add to their worries.

"Pride cometh before a fall," she muttered into the steam rising from her coffee cup.

A loud knock against the screen was followed by a friendly call. "Yoo-hoo, Diana. It's Shirley," her neighbor called, letting herself in. "I don't suppose you've got another cup of that."

"Sure," Diana said, pleased to see her friend. "Help yourself."

Shirley took a cup down from the cupboard and poured her own coffee before joining Diana. "What's all that?" She cocked her head toward the sink.

"It's leaking again."

Shirley rolled her eyes. "Diana, you're going to have to get someone to look at it."

"I can do it," she said without a whole lot of confidence. "I watched a YouTube online that tells you how to build a shopping center in your spare time. If I can repair the outlet in Joan's room, then I can figure out why the sink keeps leaking."

Shirley looked doubtful. "Honey, listen, you'd be better off to contact a plumber..."

"No way! Do you have any idea how much those guys charge? An appointment with a brain surgeon would be cheaper."

Shirley chuckled and took a sip of her coffee. "George could check it for you tonight after dinner."

"Shirley, no. I appreciate the offer, but..."

"George was Stan's friend."

"But that doesn't commit him to a lifetime of repairing leaking pipes."

"Would you stop being so darn proud for once?"

Funny how that word "pride" kept cropping up,

Diana mused. "I'll call him," she conceded, "but only in case of an emergency."

"Okay. Okay."

Diana closed her laptop. "Let me save you the trouble of small talk. I know why you're here."

"You do?"

"You're dying to hear all the details of my hot date with the doctor I met through Parents Without Partners."

"Not many women have the opportunity to have dinner with Dr. Benjamin Spock."

A smile touched the edges of Diana's soft mouth. "He's a regular pediatrician, not Dr. Spock."

"Whoever!" Shirley said excitedly, and leaned closer. "All right, if you know what I want, then give me details!"

Diana swallowed uncomfortably. "I didn't go out with him."

"What?"

"My motives were all wrong."

Shirley slumped forward and buried her forehead against the heel of her hand. "I can't believe I'm hearing this. The most ideal husband material you've met dances into your life and you break the date!"

"I know," Diana groaned. "For days beforehand I kept thinking about how much money I could save on doctor bills if I were to get involved with this guy. It bothered me that I could be so mercenary."

"Don't you think any other woman would be thinking the same thing?"

Diana's fingers tightened around the mug handle. "Not unless they have two preteens."

"Don't be cute," Shirley said frowning. "I have trouble being angry with you when you're so witty."

Standing, Diana walked across the kitchen to refill her cup. "I don't know, Shirl."

"Know what?"

"If I'm ready to get involved in a relationship. My life is different now. When Stan and I decided to get married, it wasn't any surprise. We'd been going together since my junior year in high school and it seemed the thing to do. We hardly paused to give the matter more than a second thought."

"Who said anything about getting married?"

"But it's wrong to lead a man into believing I'm interested in a long-term relationship, when I don't know if I'll ever be serious about anyone again."

"You loved Stan that much?" Shirley inquired softly.

"I loved him, yes, and if he hadn't been killed, we probably would have lived together contentedly until a ripe old age. But things are different now. I have the girls to consider."

"What about you?"

"What about me?"

"Don't you need someone?"

"I—I don't know," Diana answered thoughtfully. The idea of spending her life alone produced a sharp pang of apprehension. She wanted to be a wife again, but was afraid remarriage would drastically affect her children's lives.

Shirley left soon afterward, and Diana rinsed the breakfast dishes and placed them inside the dishwasher. Her thoughts drifted to David Fisher, the man whose dinner invitation she'd rejected at the last minute. He obviously liked children or he would have chosen a different specialty. That was in his favor. She'd met him a couple of weeks before and listened over coffee to the gory details of his divorce. It was obvious to Diana that he was still in love with his ex-wife. Although Shirley viewed him as a fine catch, Diana wasn't interested.

Not until she closed the dishwasher did Diana notice the puddle of water on her kitchen floor. The sink again! It would be a simple matter of tightening the pipes if the garbage disposal didn't complicate the job.

Unfortunately the malfunctioning sink didn't heal itself, and after Diana picked up Joan from baseball practice, disaster struck.

"Mom," Katie cried, nearly hysterical. "The water won't stop!"

When Diana arrived, she found that the pipe beneath the sink had broken and water was gushing out faster than it would from a fire hydrant.

"Turn off the water," Diana screamed.

Katie was dancing around, stomping her feet and screaming. By the time Diana reached the faucet, the water had reached flood level.

"Get some towels, stupid," Joan called.

"I'm not stupid, you are."

"Girls, please." Diana lifted the hair off her forehead and sighed unevenly. Either she had to call George or wipe out any semblance of a budget by hiring a plumbing contractor. Given that option, she reached for the phone and dialed her neighbor's number.

The male voice that answered sounded groggy. "George, I hope I didn't wake you from a nap."

"No…"

"Did Shirley mention my sink?"

"Who is this?"

"Diana—from next door. Listen, I'm in a bit of a jam here. The pipe burst under the sink, and, well, Shirley said something about your being able to help. But if it's inconvenient…"

"Mom," Katie screamed. "Joan used the *S* word."

"Just a minute." Diana placed her hand over the telephone mouthpiece. "Joan, what's the matter with you?" she asked angrily.

"I'm sorry Mom, it just slipped out."

"Are you going to wash out her mouth with soap?" Katie demanded, hands on her hips.

"I haven't got time to deal with that now. Both of you clean up this mess." She inhaled a calming breath and went back to the phone, hoping she sounded serene and demure. "George?"

"I'll be right over."

Ten seconds later, a polite knock sounded on the front door. Diana was under the sink. "Joan, let Mr. Holiday in, would you?"

"Okay."

"Mom," Katie said, sticking her head under the sink so Diana could see her. "How are you going to punish Joan?"

"Katie, can't you see I've got an emergency here!" She raised her head and slammed her forehead against the underside of the sink. Pain shot through her head and bright stars popped like flashbulbs all around her. She blinked twice and abruptly shook her head.

"Mom," Joan announced. "It wasn't Mr. Holiday."

Pushing her hair away from her forehead, Diana opened one eye to find a pair of crisp, clean jeans directly in front of her. Slowly she raised her gaze to a

silver belt buckle. Above that was a liberal quantity of
dark hairs scattered over a wide expanse of muscular
abdomen. A cutoff sweatshirt followed. Diana's heart
began to thunder, but she doubted it had anything to
do with the bump on her head. She never did make it
to his face. He crouched in front of her first. His blue
eyes were what she noticed immediately. They were
a brilliant shade that reminded her of a Seattle sky in
August.

"Who—who are you?" she managed faintly.

"Are you all right?"

Diana was ready to question that herself. Whoever
this man was who had decided to miraculously appear
at her front door, he was much too good to be true.
He looked as though he'd stepped off the hunk poster
hanging in Joan's bedroom.

Diana knocked the side of her head with her palm
to clear her vision. "You're not George!" It wasn't her
most brilliant declaration.

"No," he admitted with a lopsided grin. "I'm Cliff
Howard, a friend of George's."

"You answered the phone?" This was another of her
less-than-intelligent deductions.

Cliff nodded. "Shirley's at some meeting, and
George had to run to the store for a minute. I'm watching Mikey. I hope you don't mind that I brought him
along."

She shook her head.

Cliff was down on all fours by this time. "Now what
seems to be the problem?"

For a full moment all Diana could do was stare. It
wasn't that a man hadn't physically attracted her since
Stan's death, but this one hit her like a sledgehammer,

stunning her senses. Cliff Howard was strikingly handsome. His eyes were mesmerizing, as blue and warm as a Caribbean sea. She couldn't look away. He smiled then, and character lines crinkled about his eyes and mouth, creasing his bronze cheeks. She'd never stared at a man quite this unabashedly, and she felt the heat of a blush rise in her face.

"There's a problem?" he repeated.

"The sink," she murmured, and pointed over her shoulder. "It's leaking."

"Bad," Katie added dramatically.

"If you'd care to move, I'd be happy to look at it for you."

"Oh, right." Hurriedly Diana scooted aside, sliding her rear end into a puddle. As the cold water seeped through her underwear, she bounded to her feet, wiping off what moisture she could.

Something was drastically wrong with her, Diana concluded. The way her heart was pounding and the blood was rushing through her veins, she had to be afflicted with some serious physical ailment. Scarlet fever, maybe. Only she didn't seem to be running a temperature. Something else must be wrong—something more than encountering Cliff Howard. He was only a man, and she'd dated plenty of men since Stan, but none of them—not one—had affected her like this one.

"Does your husband have a pipe wrench?" he called out from under the sink. "These pliers won't work."

"Oh dear." Diana sighed. "Can you tell me what a pipe wrench looks like?"

Cliff reappeared. "Does he have a toolbox?"

"Yes…somewhere."

Women! Cliff doubted he would ever completely understand them. This one was curious, though; her round, puppy dog eyes had a quizzical look, as though life had tossed her an unexpected curveball. The bang on her head had to be smarting. She shouldn't be working under a sink, and he wondered what kind of husband would leave it to her to handle these types of repairs. This was a woman who was meant for lace and grand pianos, not greasy pipes.

"When do you expect him home?" he asked patiently. The flicker of pain that flashed into her eyes was so fleeting that Cliff wondered at her circumstances.

"I'm a widow."

Cliff was instantly chagrined. "I'm sorry."

She nodded, then forced a smile. In an effort to bridge the uncomfortable silence, she asked, "Does a pipe wrench look like a pair of pliers, only bigger, with a mouth that moves up and down when the knob is twisted?"

Cliff had to think that over. "Yes, I'd say that about describes it."

"Then I've got one," Diana said cheerfully. "Hold on a second." She hurried into the garage and returned a minute later with the requested tool.

"Exactly right."

He smiled at her as though she'd just completed the shopping center project. "Should I be doing something?" she asked, crouching.

"Pray," Cliff teased. "This could be expensive."

"Damn," Diana muttered under her breath, and looked up to find Katie giving her a disapproving glare. In her daughter's mind, *damn* was as bad as the

S word. "Don't you have any homework?" she asked her younger daughter.

"Just spelling."

"Then hop to it, kiddo."

"Ah, Mom!"

"Do it," Diana said in her most stern voice.

A few minutes later, Cliff climbed out from under the sink. "I'm afraid I'm going to need some parts to get this fixed."

"If you'll write down what's necessary, I can pick them up tomorrow and—"

"You don't want to go without a sink that long. I'll run and get what you need now." He wiped his hands dry on a dish towel and headed toward the front door.

"Just a minute," Diana cried, running after him. "I'll give you some cash."

"No need," he said with a lazy grin. "I'll pay for it and you can reimburse me."

"Okay," she returned weakly. The last time she'd looked, her checkbook balance had hovered around ten dollars, give or take a dime or two.

Cliff took Mikey Holiday with him, but not because he was keen on having the youth's company. His reasons were purely selfish. He wanted to grill the lad on what he knew about his neighbor with the sad eyes and the pert nose.

"You buckled up?" he asked the eight-year-old.

Mikey's baseball cap bobbed up and down.

"Say, kid, what can you tell me about the lady with the leaky sink?"

"Mrs. Collins?"

"Yeah." Cliff had to admit he was being less than subtle, but he often preferred the direct approach.

"She's real nice."

That much Cliff had guessed. "What happened to her husband?"

"He died."

Cliff decided his chances of getting any real information from the kid were nil, and he experienced a twinge of regret. He'd met far more attractive women, but this one got to him. Her appeal, he suspected, was that wide streak of independence and that stiff upper lip. He admired that.

It had been a while since he'd been this curious about any woman, and whatever it was about her that attracted him was potent. A smile came and went as he thought about her dealing with the problem sink. It was all too obvious she didn't know a thing about plumbing. Then he recalled the pair of puzzled brown eyes looking up at him and how she'd sensibly announced that he wasn't George.

He laughed softly to himself.

The knock on the front door got an immediate response from Diana. "You're back," she said, rubbing her palms together. She seemed to have a flair for stating the obvious.

Cliff grinned. "I shouldn't have any problem fixing that sink now."

"Good."

The house was quiet as she led him back into the kitchen. Diana hadn't been this agitated by a man since…she couldn't remember. The whole thing was silly. A strange man was causing her heart to pound like a locomotive. And Diana didn't like it one bit. Her life was too complicated for her to be attracted to a man. Besides, he was probably married, even though he didn't wear a wedding band. If Cliff was George's friend, and if he was single, it was a sure bet that Shirley would have mentioned him. And if Cliff was available, which she sincerely doubted, then he was the type to have plenty of women interested in him. And Diana had no intention of becoming a groupie.

"I really appreciate your doing this," she said after a long moment.

"No problem. What happened to the kids?"

"They're upstairs playing video games," she explained, and hesitated. "I thought you might work better with a little peace and quiet."

"I could have worked around the racket."

Diana nervously wiped her hands on her thighs. Then, irritated with herself, she folded them as though she were about to pray. Not a bad idea under the circumstances. This man was so virile. He was the first one since Stan to cause her to remember that she was still a woman. Five minutes in the kitchen with Cliff Howard and she thinking about satin sheets and lacy underwear. Whoa, girl! She reined in her thoughts.

"Could you hand me the wrench?" he asked.

"Sure." Diana was glad to do anything but stand there staring at the dusting of hairs above his belly button.

"I don't think I caught your first name," he said next.

"Diana."

He paused, his hands holding the wrench against the pipe. "It fits."

"The pipe?"

"No," he said, grinning. "Your name." He pictured a Diana as soft and feminine, and this one was definitely that. Her hair was the color of winter wheat. She smelled of flowers and sunshine; summer at its best. Her face was sensual and provocative. Mature. She'd walked through the shadow-filled valley and emerged strong and confident.

Self-consciously Diana placed her hand at her throat. "I was named after my grandmother."

Cliff continued to work, then altered positions from lying under the sink on his back to kneeling. "It looks like I'm going to have to take off the disposal to get at the problem."

"Should I be doing something to help?"

"A cup of coffee wouldn't hurt."

"Oh, sorry, I should have thought to offer you some earlier." Diana hurried to her antique automatic-drip coffeemaker and put on a fresh pot, getting the water from the bathroom. She stood by the cantankerous machine while it gurgled and drained. Soon the aroma of freshly brewed coffee filled the kitchen.

When the pot was full, Diana brought down a mug and knelt on the linoleum in front of Cliff. "Here."

"Thanks." He sat upright, using the cupboard door to support his back.

"Do you have children—I mean, you claimed you could work around the noise, so I naturally assumed that you…"

"I've never been married, Diana," he said, his eyes serious.

"Oh." He had the uncanny ability to make her feel like a fool. "I just wondered, you know." Her hands

slipped down the front of her Levi's in a nervous reaction.

"I was wondering, too," he admitted.

"What?"

"How long has your husband been gone?"

"Stan died in a small plane crash three years ago.
Both my husband and his best friend were killed."

Three years. He was surprised. He would have
thought a woman as attractive as Diana would have
been snatched up long before now. She was the marrying kind and…ultimately out of his league.

"I shouldn't have pried." He saw the weary pain in
her eyes and regretted his inquisitiveness.

"I'm doing okay. The girls and I have adjusted as
well as can be expected. I'll admit it hasn't been easy,
but we're getting along."

The phone rang, and before Diana could even think
to move, Joan came roaring down the stairs. "I'll get it."

Diana rolled her eyes and smiled. "That's one nice
thing about her growing up. I never need to answer
the phone again."

"It's Mr. Holiday." Joan's disappointment sounded
from the hallway. "He wants to speak to his friend."

"That must be you." The moment the words were
out, Diana wanted to cringe. She was making such an
idiot of herself!

Cliff rolled to his feet and reached for the wall
phone.

Because she didn't want to seem as though she were
eavesdropping, Diana moved into the living room and
straightened the decorator pillows on the end of the
sofa, positioning them just so. They were needlepoint
designs her mother had given her last Christmas.

Five minutes later, hoping she wasn't being too conspicuous, she returned to the kitchen. Cliff was under the sink, humming as he worked. The garbage disposal came off without a hitch, and he set it aside. Next he added a new piece of pipe.

"There wasn't anything in the video about replacing pipe—at least in the one I viewed, anyway," she explained self-consciously.

"I'm happy to do it for you, Diana," he said, tightening the new pipe with the wrench. "There." He stood and faced the sink. "Are you ready for the big test?"

"More than ready."

Cliff turned on the faucet while Diana squatted, watching the floor under the sink. "It looks worlds better than the last time I peeked."

"No leaks?"

"Not a one." She straightened and discovered they were separated by only a couple of inches. She blinked and eased back a couple of steps. Neither spoke. Sensual awareness was as thick as a London fog; Diana's blood pounded through her veins. Her gaze rested on the V of his shirt and the smattering of curly, crisp hairs. Gradually she raised her gaze and noticed that his lower lip was slightly fuller than the upper. It had been so long since she'd been kissed by a man. Really kissed. The memory had the power to stir her senses, and her hands gripped the sink to keep herself from swaying toward him. She was behaving like Joan over a new boy in class. Her hormones were barely under control. "I don't know how to thank you," she managed finally, her voice weak.

"It isn't necessary."

Feeling awkward, Diana said, "Let me write you a check for the supplies."

"They were only a few dollars."

That was a relief! He named a figure that was so ridiculously low that she could hardly believe it. She thought to question him, but recognized intuitively that it wouldn't do any good and quietly wrote out the check.

"I don't suppose I could have a refill on the coffee?" Cliff surprised himself by saying. Standing there by the sink, he'd nearly kissed her. She'd wanted it. He'd been partially amused by her obvious desire, until he'd realized that he wanted it, too.

"A refill? Of course. I don't mean to be such a poor hostess." She moved to the glass pot and brought it over to Cliff, who had claimed a chair at the table. Diana topped his cup and then her own, returned the pot and took a seat opposite him.

"Do you like Chinese food?" he asked unexpectedly, again surprising himself. It wasn't her beauty that attracted him so much as her spirit.

Diana nodded. Her stomach churned and she knew what was coming. She hoped he would ask her, and in the same heartbeat prayed he wouldn't.

"Would you have dinner with me tomorrow night?"

"I..."

"If you're looking for a way to repay me, then make it simple and share an evening with me."

"Joan's got baseball practice." Instead of looking for excuses, she should be thanking God he'd asked. "But Shirley could pick her up."

Cliff grinned, his blue eyes almost boyish. "Good, then I'll see you at six-thirty."

Diana responded to the pure potency of his smile. "I'll look forward to it."

The minute Cliff was out the door, Diana phoned her neighbor.

"Shirley, it's Diana," she said, doing her best to curtail her excitement. "Where have you been hiding him?"

"Who? I just walked in the door. What are you talking about?"

"Cliff Howard!"

"You met Cliff Howard?"

"That's just what I said. After all these months of indiscriminately tossing men at me, why didn't you introduce us earlier?"

A lengthy, strained silence followed. "I'm going to shoot George."

"Shoot George? What's that got to do with anything?"

Shirley raised her voice in anger. "I told that man to keep Cliff Howard away from you. He's trouble with a capital *T*, and if you have a brain in your head you won't have anything to do with him."

Two

"Mom, do you want to borrow my skirt?" Joan held up a skimpy piece of denim that was her all-time favorite.

"No thanks, sweetheart." Diana was standing in front of the mirror in her bathroom, wearing only her slip and bra.

"But, Mom, this skirt is the absolute!"

Diana sighed. "I appreciate the offer, sweetie, but it's about four sizes too small. Besides, I have no intention of looking like Katy Perry."

"But Cliff's so handsome."

Leave it to Joan to notice that. This year Diana had seen a major transformation take hold of her elder daughter. After one week of fifth grade, Joan had wanted her ears pierced and would have killed for fake nails. The youngster argued that Diana was being completely unreasonable to make her wait until junior high before wearing makeup. Everyone wore eye shadow and Diana must have been reared in the Middle Ages if she didn't know that. Boys were quickly becoming all-important, too. Fifth grade! How times had changed.

"Are you going to wear your pearl earrings?" Joan asked next.

The pair were Diana's best and saved for only the most festive occasions. "I—I'm not sure."

She wasn't sure about anything. Shirley seemed convinced Diana was making the mistake of her life by having anything to do with Cliff.

Her neighbor claimed he was a notorious playboy who would end up breaking her fragile heart. He was sophisticated, urbane and completely ruthless about using his polished good looks to get what he wanted from a woman, or so Shirley claimed. Next she had admitted next that she was half in love with him herself, but as Diana's self-appointed guardian, Shirley couldn't bear thinking what could happen to her friend in the hands of Cliff Howard.

After Shirley's briefing, Diana was too curious to find out to consider canceling the date.

"Mom, the earrings," Joan repeated impatiently.

Her daughter shrill voice broke into Diana's thoughts. "I don't think so."

"Do it, Mom."

"But if I wear them now, I won't have anything to razzle-dazzle Cliff with later."

Joan chewed on the corner of her lower lip, grudgingly accepting her mother's decision. "Right, but what about your hair?"

"What about it?" Diana's hair was styled the way she always wore it, parted on the side and feathered back away from her face.

Joan looked unsure. "You look so ordinary, like this is an everyday date or something."

"I don't think now would be the time to experiment with something different."

"I suppose you're right," Joan admitted reluctantly.

Diana checked her watch; she had plenty of time, but the way Joan kept suggesting changes wasn't doing a whole lot for her self-confidence. Maybe her daughter was right, and it was time to do something different with her hair and makeup. But age thirty was upon her, and no matter how she parted her hair or applied her makeup, she wasn't going to look like Stacey Q., Joan's favorite female rock star. Well, almost favorite. Stacey Q. ran a close second to Katy Perry.

When Diana came out of the bathroom, she discovered her daughter sorting through her closet. "I have what I'm going to wear on the bed."

"But, Mom, black pants and a blouse are so boring."

"The blouse is silk," she told her coaxingly.

"Men like black silk, not white."

Diana preferred not to know where Joan had gotten that little tidbit of information. The child was amazing. While Diana slipped into the pants, Joan lay across the queen-size mattress and propped her chin up with her hands.

"You know who Cliff reminds me of?" Joan asked with a dreamy look clouding her blue eyes.

"Who?"

" Christian Bale."

"Who?" Diana stopped dressing long enough to turn around and face her daughter.

"You know, the actor."

Diana sighed. "I suppose he does faintly resemble him, but Cliff's hair is dark."

"Cliff's hot stuff, Mom. He's going to make your blood boil."

"Joan, for heaven's sake. The way things are going, I may never see him again after tonight."

Alarmed, Joan bolted upright. "Why not?"

"Well, for one thing my clothes are boring, and for another I don't look a thing like Katy Perry and my hair's all wrong."

"I didn't say that," Joan returned defensively.

The doorbell chimed and Joan tore out of the room. "It's him. I'll get it."

Diana let out an exasperated breath, squared her shoulders and did one last check in the mirror. She'd dressed sensibly, hoping to be tactful enough to remind Cliff that she was a widow and a mother. According to Shirley, Cliff had previously dated beauty queens, centerfolds and an occasional actress. Diana was "none of the above." Her reflection revealed round eyes and a falsely cheerful smile. Good enough, she decided as she reached for her sweater and placed it over her arm; nights still tended to be nippy in May.

Joan came rushing back to the bedroom. "He brought you flowers," she announced in a husky whisper. "Mom," she continued, placing her hand over her heart, "he's so-o-o handsome."

As Joan had claimed, Cliff stood inside the living room with a small bouquet of red roses and pink carnations. It had been so long since a man had given her flowers that Diana's throat constricted and she couldn't think of a single word to say.

He smiled, and the sun became brighter. Shirley was right. This man was too much for a mere widow.

"You look lovely."

Somehow Diana managed a feeble thank-you.

"Mom's got terrific legs," Joan inserted smoothly, standing between Diana and Cliff and glancing from one to the other. "I keep telling her that she ought to show them off more often." She slapped her hands against her sides. "But my mother never listens to me."

Diana glared at her daughter, but said nothing. "I'll find a vase for these." As she left the room, Joan's chatter drifted after her. Her daughter found it important that Cliff know she was much too old to have a baby-sitter. Katie was over at the Holidays', but at eleven, Joan was far too mature to have anyone look after her.

"I thought you had baseball practice?" Diana heard Cliff ask.

"Normally I do," Joan explained with a patient sigh, "but I skipped today because my mother needed me."

Diana reappeared and Joan escorted the couple to the front door. It was on the tip of Diana's tongue to remind Joan of the house rules when she was alone, but one desperate glance begged her not to. Diana grudgingly complied and said everything that was needed with one stern look.

"Have a good time," Joan said cheerfully, holding the front door open. "And, Cliff, you can bring Mom home late. She doesn't have a curfew."

"I'll have her back before midnight," Cliff promised.

Joan nodded approvingly. "And don't worry, Mom, I'll take care of everything here."

That was what concerned Diana most. She kissed Joan's cheek and whispered, "Remember, bedtime is nine." Shirley would be over then to sit with the girls until Diana returned.

"Mom," Joan said under her breath, "you're treating me like a child."

Diana smiled apologetically. However, it would be just like her daughter to wait up half the night to hear the details of this date, and Diana couldn't face Joan and Shirley together.

Cliff's sports car was parked in front of the house. It was a two-seater that Diana couldn't identify. Cool. Very cool. He held open the door and helped her inside. She mumbled her thanks, feeling self-conscious and out of her element. Diana drove a ten-year-old SUV and wouldn't know the difference between a BMW and an MGB.

Cliff joined her a moment later, inserted the key in the ignition and turned to her, smiling. "Is she always like that?"

"Always. I hope she didn't embarrass you."

"Not at all." He looked more amused than anything.

"I sometimes wonder if I'm going to survive motherhood," Diana commented, her hands clenching her purse.

"You seem to be doing an admirable job."

"Thanks." But Cliff hadn't seen her at her worst. Katie called her the screaming meemie when she let loose. Diana didn't lose her cool often, but enough for the girls to know that the best thing for them to do was nod politely and agree to everything she shouted, no matter how unreasonable.

Cliff started the engine, doing his best to hold back his amusement. This daughter of Diana's was something else. He'd been looking forward to seeing this widow all day. He continued to be confounded by the attraction he felt for her. True, she was pretty enough, but years older than the women he normally dated. Diana had to be close to his age.

Several times during the day, he'd discovered his thoughts drifting to her, wondering what she was doing and what catastrophe she was fearlessly facing now. After he'd finished with her sink, he'd gone to the Holidays' and drilled George, wanting to ferret out every detail about Diana he could. Shirley arrived home then, and when she learned that he planned to take Diana to dinner, her disapproval had been tangible. She'd mumbled some dire warning about the wrath of God coming down upon his head if he ever hurt Diana.

However, it was never Cliff's intent to hurt any woman. He realized George and his other golfing friends credited him with the playboy image, but he wasn't Hugh Hefner. He wasn't even close. Oh, there'd been a few relationships over the years, but very few. It was true that most women found him attractive, and it was also fair to say he liked variety. The truth was his reputation far outdistanced reality.

When Cliff had drilled his friend about Diana, George hadn't been able to say enough good things about the young widow. To escape Shirley's threats, the two men had gone to the local pub and talked late into the night. Cliff went away satisfied that he'd learned everything George knew about his next-door neighbor.

In the car seat, Diana clasped and unclasped her purse. She was nervous. She hadn't felt this uptight since…never, she decided. A man had stepped out of the pages of *Gentleman's Quarterly* and into her life. This shouldn't be happening to her. Events like that were reserved for fairy tales and *gossip magazines.* Not widows whose money couldn't stretch till the end of the month.

Diana wanted to stand Shirley up against a wall and shoot her for filling her with doubts. One date! What possible damage could one dinner date do? The one and only time she was interested in finding out details about a man, and all Shirley could do was point out that Diana was headed down the road to destruction. Shirley claimed lesser women crumbled under Cliff's charm. He broke their hearts, but he hated to see them cry. Diana, according to Shirley, was too gentle natured to be hurt by this playboy.

Consequently Diana didn't know anything more about Cliff than she had when he'd left her house the night before.

"How do you know George?" she asked, breaking the silence.

"George and I golf together," Cliff explained.

George was a real sports fanatic.

"Do you play?" Cliff asked.

"I'm afraid not." No time. She was the room mother for Katie's second grade class, did volunteer work at the elementary school the girls attended, taught Sunday school and was heavily involved in Girl Scouts. "I used to play tennis, though," she added quickly. "Used to" being the operative expression. Every Thursday had been her morning on the court, but that was before Joan was born and...oh, good grief, that was eleven years ago. Where had all the years gone?

They arrived at the Chinese restaurant and were seated in a secluded booth. "This place isn't high on atmosphere, but I promise you the food's terrific," Cliff said.

Diana studied the menù, and her stomach growled just reading over the varied list of entrées. If the food tasted half as good as it sounded, she would be satisfied. "You needn't worry," she said, "I'm easy to please. Anything that I don't have to cook is fine by me."

The waiter appeared, and they placed their order. Diana cradled the small teacup in both hands. "I know you fix leaky sinks in your spare time, but what do you normally do?"

"I'm an attorney." His gaze settled on her mouth. "Are you a working mother?"

Diana bit back a defensive reply. A man who had never been married wouldn't appreciate the fact that *every* mother was a working mother. "Not outside the house," she explained simply. "I keep thinking I should find a part-time job, but I'm delaying it as long as possible."

"What have you trained for?"

"Motherhood."

Cliff grinned.

"I suppose that sounds old-fashioned. But you have to remember that Stan and I married only a few months after I graduated from community college. The first couple of years, while Stan worked for Boeing, I attended classes at the University of Washington, but I got pregnant with Joan and didn't earn enough credits for a degree. At one time I'd hoped to enter the nursing profession, but that was years ago."

Their hot-and-sour soup arrived. "Why don't you do that now?" Cliff wanted to know.

"I could," she admitted, and shrugged, "but I feel

it's too important to spend time with the girls. They still need me. I'm all they've got and I'd hate to be torn between attending Joan's baseball games and doing homework, or squeezing in an additional night class." She paused and dipped her spoon in the thick soup. "Maybe that's an excuse, but my children are the most important investment I have in this life. I want to be there for them."

"What if your husband were alive?"

"Then I'd probably be in nursing school. The responsibilities of raising the girls would be shared." She hesitated. She doubted that Cliff would understand any of this—a bachelor wouldn't. "To be honest, I'm not toying with the idea of getting a part-time job because I want one. Money is tight and it gets tighter every year. I suppose by the time Joan's in junior high, the option will be taken away from me, but by then both girls will be better able to deal with my being away from home so much."

"Joan seemed eager enough to have you leave tonight."

Diana nodded, hiding a smile. "That's because she thinks you look like Christian Bale."

"I'm flattered."

Diana noted that she didn't need to explain to him that Christian Bale was an actor. "I hope you don't find this rude, but how old are you, Cliff?" Diana knew she was older. She had to be—if not in years, then experience.

"How old do you think?"

She shrugged. "Twenty-five, maybe twenty-six."

"How old are you?"

A hundred and ten some days. Fifteen on others. "Thirty last September."

His grin was almost boyish. "I'm thirty-one."

The conversation turned then, and they discussed local politics. Although they took opposing points of view, Diana noted that he respected her opinions and didn't try to sway her to his way of thinking. Cliff was far more liberal than Diana. Her views tended to be conservative.

From their conversation, she discovered other tidbits of information about him. He skied, and had a condo at Alpental on Snoqualmie Pass. His sailboat was docked at the Des Moines Marina and he enjoyed sailing, but didn't get out often enough. He was allergic to strawberries.

Diana hated to see the evening end. It had been years since she'd had such a fun date. Cliff was easy to talk to, and she was astonished when she happened to notice the time. They'd been sitting in the booth talking for nearly three hours.

"How about a movie?" he suggested on the way to the restaurant parking lot.

Regretfully Diana shook her head. "Sorry, Cliff, but it's after ten. I should think about heading back."

It looked for a moment as though he wanted to argue with her, but he changed his mind. Diana was sure that most of his dates didn't need to rush home. More than likely they lingered over wine in front of a romantic fireplace, shared a few kisses and probably more. It was the "probably more" that got her heart pumping. It would be a foolish mistake to let this relationship advance beyond friendship. All right, she admitted it. She was attracted to the man. Good grief, what red-blooded female wouldn't be? But they lived in different worlds. Cliff was part of the swinging singles scene and she was like a modern day Betsy Ross, doing needlepoint in her rocking chair in front of the television.

"You're looking thoughtful," he said as they left the restaurant.

"I do?" she murmured.

Once again he opened the car door for her, and she scooted inside as gracefully as she could manage. Again her fingers moved to the clasp on her purse. For some reason she was nervous again. She liked Cliff more than any man she'd dated since Stan's death, but it went without saying that she wasn't the woman for him.

Cliff pulled out of the parking lot and was soon on the freeway heading south. They chatted easily, and Diana could see where Cliff would make a good attorney. He could be persuasive when he wanted to be. Darn persuasive.

"That was my exit," she told him when he drove past it. She jerked her head over her shoulder as though it were possible for them to reverse their direction.

"I know."

"Where are you taking me?" She was more amused than irritated.

"If you must know, I want to kiss you and I wasn't exactly thrilled to do it in front of an audience."

As Joan had predicted it would, Diana's blood reached the simmering point. A kiss would quickly accelerate it to the boiling stage.

"Joan and Katie will be in bed by now." He needn't worry about them peeking through the living room drapes.

"I was thinking more of George and Shirley," Cliff told her.

Diana laughed; he was probably right. She could picture Shirley waiting by her front window, drapes parted, staring at the street.

Cliff took the next exit to the small community in the south end of Seattle called Des Moines. "I want you to see something," he explained.

"Your sailboat?"

"No," he said softly. "The stars."

Romantic, too! She could resist anything but romance. It wasn't fair that in a few hours he could narrow in on her weaknesses and break down all her well-constructed defenses.

There were several dozen cars in the huge parking lot. A wonderful seafood restaurant was an attraction that brought many out on a lovely spring evening.

Cliff parked as far away from the restaurant as he could. He turned off the ignition and climbed out of the car. By the time he was around to her side, Diana's heart was pounding so hard it threatened to break her ribs.

With his arm draped around her shoulders, Cliff led her down onto the wharf. The night was lovely. A soft breeze drifted off the water and the scent of seaweed and salt mingled with the crisp air. The sky was blanketed in black velvet, and the sparkling stars dotted the heavens like diamonds.

"It's lovely, isn't it?" she said, experiencing the wonder of standing beneath a canopy of such splendor.

Cliff's answer was to turn her in his arms. She looked up at him, and her hair fell away from her face.

He raised his hands to touch her cheeks and stared down at her. His fingertips slowly glided over each feature. Such smooth skin, warm and silky, and eyes that could rip apart a man's heart. Slowly he lowered his mouth to hers, denying himself the pleasure for as long as he could endure it.

Their mouths gently brushed against each other's like rose petals caught in a breeze. Velvety smooth. Soft and warm. Infinitely gentle, but electric. Again he kissed her, only this time his mouth lingered, longer this time, much longer.

Diana felt her knees go weak and she swayed toward him, slipping her arms around his neck. A debilitating sensation overcame her. She couldn't think, couldn't breathe, couldn't move.

Cliff groaned and his grip tightened and moved to the back of her head. He slanted his mouth across hers, sampling once more the pure pleasure of her kiss. He'd been right; she tasted incredible of sweet-butterscotch. Hungrily, his lips devoured hers, again and again, unable to get enough of her. Diana felt the tears well in her eyes, and was at a loss to know where they came from or why. One slipped from the corner of her eye and rolled down the side of her face, leaving a shiny trail.

At first her tears were lost to him, he was so involved with the taste of her. When he realized she was crying, he stopped and drew away from her.

"Diana?" he asked tenderly, concerned.

Embarrassed, she tucked her chin against her shoulder, not knowing what to say. "Then why…"

"I don't know. I am such an idiot." She jerked her hand across her face and smudged her carefully applied mascara. "I don't know, Cliff. I honestly don't know."

He tried to hold her, but she wouldn't let him.

"Because it was good," she offered as an explanation.

"The kiss?"

"Everything. You. The dinner. The stars." She sobbed once and held her hands over her face. "Everything."

"I didn't have anything to do with making the stars shine," he teased softly. Although she didn't want him to hold her, Cliff kept his hands on her shoulders, seeking a way to comfort her.

Diana knew he was attempting to lighten the mood, but it didn't help.

"Come on, let me take you home." This wasn't what he wanted, but he didn't know what else to do.

Miserable, she nodded.

"I have to admit this is the first time my kisses have caused a woman to weep."

She attempted to laugh, but the sound that came out of her throat was like the creak of a rusty hinge. No doubt this was a switch for him. Women probably swooned at his feet. Tall, handsome, rich men were a rare species.

He draped his arm around her shoulders again as he led her back to his car. When he opened the door for her, he paused and pressed a finger under her chin, lifting her face so that she was forced to meet his gaze.

"It was just as good for me," he told her softly.

Diana longed to shout at him to stop. All this wasn't necessary. The last thing she wanted was for him to sweep her off her feet, and already she was so dangerously close to tumbling that it rocked her to the bottom of her soul. They weren't right together. Cliff was wonderful, too good to be true. His tastes leaned toward someone young and sleek, not a widow with two daughters whose lifetime goals were to grow up and succeed Katy Perry.

All the way back to the house, Diana mentally rehearsed what she planned to say at the door. He'd ask her out again, and she'd tell him in hushed, regretful tones that she had to decline. She had to! The option had been taken away from her the instant he'd pulled her into his arms. Shirley was right—this man was more dangerous than fire!

Only Cliff didn't give her the opportunity to refuse him. Like the perfect gentleman, he escorted her to the door, thanked her for a lovely evening, gently kissed her forehead and walked away.

Diana was grateful he hadn't made her say it, but her heart pounded with regret. Cliff had realized there could be no future for them, and although she would have liked to find a way, it was impossible.

A week passed, a long, tedious, week when life seemed to be an uphill battle. Joan went through two packages of press-on nails, and they turned up in every conceivable corner of the house. Katie's allergies were acting up again, and Diana spent two dreary afternoons sitting in a doctor's office waiting for the nurse to give Katie her shot.

Shirley was over daily for coffee and to reassure Diana that she'd made the right decision about not seeing Cliff again. It seemed Cliff had recovered quickly and was said to be dating Dana Mattson, a local television talk show hostess. Diana thought of Cliff fondly and wished him well. In many ways she was grateful for their one evening together. She'd felt more alive than at any other time since Stan's death. She was grateful that he'd shown her the light, but now she didn't know if she could be content with living in the shadows again.

The Thursday afternoon following their dinner, Diana planted marigolds along the edges of the flower bed in the backyard. The huge old apple tree was in bloom and filled the air with the sweet scent of spring, but Diana was too caught up in her own thoughts to notice. All day she'd been in a blue funk, depressed and irritable. Every time she saw the wilted bouquet of roses and carnations in the center of the kitchen table, she felt faint stirrings of regret. Friday there wouldn't be any choice but to toss the flowers. It was silly to allow a lovely bouquet to mean so much.

After depositing her garden tools in the garage, she stepped into the bathroom to wash her hands. Joan was standing on top of the toilet, leaning across the sink and staring in the mirror. Her young mouth was twisted in a grimace.

"What are you doing?" Diana demanded.

"I'm practicing so I look cool. See." She turned to face her mother, her mouth twisted in a sarcastic sneer that would have wilted daffodils.

"You look terrible."

"Great. That's exactly the look I'm going for."

"Joan, sweetheart," she said with growing impatience, "I just put five hundred dollars down at the orthodontist's so that you could have lovely, straight teeth."

Joan stared at her blankly.

"Do you mean to tell me I'm spending thousands

of dollars to straighten the teeth of a child who plans never to smile?"

"Boy, are you a grouch," Joan announced as she jumped down off the toilet. "What's the matter, Mom, is Aunt Flo visiting?"

It took Diana a moment to make the connection with her monthly cycle. When she did, her knees started to shake. In an even, controlled voice, she turned toward her daughter. "When did you learn about Aunt Flo?"

"A year ago."

"But…" So much for the neat packet she'd mailed away for that so carefully explained everything in the simple terms that a fifth grader would understand.

"I figured you'd get around to telling me one of these days," Joan said, undisturbed.

"Oh, dear." Diana sat on the edge of the tub.

"It's no big deal, Mom."

"Who told you…when?" Diana's voice shook as she realized that her little girl wasn't so little anymore. "Why didn't you come to me?"

"Honestly, Mom, I would have, but you think a fifth grader is too young for panty hose."

"You are!"

"See what I mean?" Joan declared, shaking her head.

"Who told you?"

"The library…"

"The Kent library?" Good grief, it wasn't safe to take her daughter into the local library anymore.

"You see," Joan explained, "we had this discussion in fourth grade that sort of left me hanging, so I checked out a few books."

"And the books told you everything?"

Joan nodded and started to speak, but was interrupted by her younger sister, who stuck her head in the bathroom door.

"I'm starved—what's for dinner?"

"I haven't decided yet."

Katie placed her hands on her hips. "Is it going to be another one of *those* dinners?"

"Can't you see we're having a serious mother-daughter discussion here?" Joan shouted. "Get lost, dog breath."

"Joan!" Diana cried, and quickly diverted an argument. "Don't call your sister that. Katie, I'm hungry, too. Why don't you check what's in the refrigerator? I'm open for suggestions."

"Okay," Katie cried eagerly, and hurried back into the kitchen.

"Are you mad?" Joan asked in a subdued voice. "I didn't tell you before, well because…you know."

"Because I won't let you wear panty hose."

Joan nodded. "You've got to remember, I'm growing up!"

Diana swiped the hair off her face. At this moment she didn't need to be reminded of the fact her elder daughter was turning into a woman right before her eyes.

Katie had emptied half the contents of the refrigerator on top of the counter by the time Diana entered the kitchen. "Find anything interesting?"

"Nothing I'd seriously consider eating," Katie said. "Can we have Kentucky Fried Chicken tonight?"

"Not tonight, honey."

"How about going to McDonald's?"

"If we can't afford KFC, we can't afford McDonald's."

"TV dinners?" Katie asked hopefully.

"Let me see what we've got." She opened the freezer door and glared inside, hoping against hope she'd somehow find three glorious flat boxes.

The doorbell chimed in the distance. "I'll get it," Joan screamed, and nearly knocked over the kitchen chair in her rush to get to the front door first.

"Oh, hi." Joan's voice drifted into the kitchen. "Mom, it's for you."

The list of possibilities ran through Diana's mind. The paperboy, Shirley Holiday, the pastor. She rejected each one. Somehow she knew even before she came into the room who was at the door. She'd longed for and dreaded this moment.

"Hi," Cliff said, smiling broadly. "I was wondering if the three of you would like to go on a picnic with me."

"Sure," Joan answered first, excited.

"Great," Katie chimed in.

Cliff's gaze didn't leave Diana's. "It's up to your mother."

Three

"I thought we'd go to Salt Water Park," Cliff said, his gaze holding Diana's. He resisted the urge to lift his hand, touch her cheek and tell her she'd been on his mind from the minute he'd left her. After their dinner date he'd instinctively realized that if he were to ask her out again, she'd refuse. The only way he could get her to agree to see him again would be to involve her daughters.

"Can we have Kentucky Fried Chicken?" Katie asked, jumping up and down excitedly.

"Katie!" Diana cried. That girl worried far too much about her stomach.

"As a matter of fact," Cliff answered, "I've got it in the car now."

"Mother," Katie pleaded, her eyes growing more round by the second. "KFC!"

"I'll get a blanket," Joan said, rushing through the living room and down the hall to the linen closet.

"I've got to change shoes," Katie added, and zoomed after her sister, leaving Diana and Cliff standing alone.

"I take it this means you're going?"

Diana decided his smile was far too sexy for his own good, or for hers. "I don't appear to have much of a choice. If I refuse now, I'm likely to have a mutiny on my hands."

Cliff grinned; his plan had worked well. A streak of dried dirt was smeared across her chin, and her blond hair was gathered at the base of her neck with a tie. Her washed-out jeans had holes in the knees. Funny, but he couldn't remember the last time a woman looked more appealing to him. She was everything he'd built up in his mind this past week, and more.

What he'd told her that night was true—he'd never had a woman respond to his kisses with tears. Unfortunately, what Diana didn't know was that he'd been equally shaken by those moments in the moonlight. He'd been attracted to her from the minute she'd stared up at him from beneath her kitchen sink and described a plumber's wrench. She'd amused him, challenged his intelligence, charmed him, but what had attracted him most was her complete lack of pretense. This wasn't a woman whose life centered around three-inch long fingernails. She was gutsy and authentic.

Over dinner, he'd discovered her wit and humor. On social issues she was opinionated but not dogmatic, concerned but not fanatical. She was unafraid of emotion and possessed a deep inner strength. All along he'd known how much he wanted to kiss her. What he hadn't anticipated was the effect it would have on them both. A single kiss had never touched his heart more. Diana had been trembling so badly, she hadn't noticed that he was shaking like a leaf himself. He experienced such a gentleness for her, a craving to protect and comfort her. He felt like a callow youth, unpracticed and green. Thrown off balance, he hadn't enjoyed the feeling.

On the way home from the marina, they'd barely talked. By then Cliff was confident he wouldn't be seeing her again. That decided, a calmness had come over him. A widow with children was no woman to get involved with, and Diana was the take-home-to-mother type he generally avoided.

Picturing himself as a husband was difficult enough, but as a father...well, that was stretching things. He'd always enjoyed children and looked forward to having his own someday; he just hadn't planned on starting with a house full. He did like Joan and Katie—they were cute kids. But they were kids. He hardly knew how to act around them.

Then why had he gone back to Diana's? Cliff had asked himself that same question twenty times in as many minutes. He'd been out a couple of times that week, but neither woman had stimulated him the way those few hours with Diana had. He heard her laugh at the most ridiculous times. A newscast had left him wondering what her opinion was on an important local issue. He'd waited a couple of days for her to contact him. Women usually did. But not Diana.

Interrupting his thoughts, Joan returned to the living room, dragging a blanket with her. The eleven-year-old was quickly followed by a grinning, happy Katie.

"You ready?" Cliff asked.

"We won't all fit in your sports car," Diana said, fighting the natural desire to be with Cliff and angry with herself for wanting it so much. She'd changed clothes and washed her face, but she still felt like Cinderella two nights after the ball.

"We can take two cars," Joan suggested, obviously not wanting anything to ruin this outing.

Palm up, Cliff gestured toward her elder daughter. "Excellent idea."

Joan positively glowed. "Can I ride with Cliff?"

Diana's brows involuntarily furrowed in concern. "I...ah."

"It's fine with me," Cliff told her, and noticed that Katie looked disappointed. "Then Katie can ride with me on the way home."

"Okay," Diana agreed reluctantly.

Diana followed Cliff to Salt Water Park, which was less than ten minutes from the house. She'd taken Joan and Katie there often and enjoyed the lush Puget Sound beachfront. On their last visit, the girls had watched several sea lions laze in the sun not more than twenty feet off the shore on a platform buoy.

When Cliff turned off the road and into the park entrance, Diana saw him throw back his head and laugh at something Joan had said. A chill went up Diana's back at the thought of what her daughter could be telling him. That girl had few scruples when it came to attractive men. But Diana was concerned for another reason. Both her girls liked Cliff, which was unusual, and although she'd dated a number of men during the past few years, rarely had she included the children in an outing. As much as possible, she tried to keep her social life separate from her family.

Cliff pulled into a space in the parking lot, and Diana eased the SUV into the spot beside him. Even though it was a school night, there seemed to be several families out enjoying the warm spring evening. Both Joan and Katie climbed out of the respective cars and rushed across the thick grass. Within seconds they returned to inform Cliff that there was an unused picnic table close to the beach.

Diana waited while Cliff took the bag of food from the trunk of his car. She felt awkward in her sweatshirt and wished she'd taken the time to change into a new pair of shorts. Had she known she was going on a picnic with Cliff, she would have washed her hair that afternoon and tried to do something different with it. That would have pleased Joan. Suddenly her thoughts came to an abrupt halt. She was traipsing on dangerously thin ice with this playboy.

"I've been meaning to ask you what kind of car this is?" she asked as he closed the trunk.

"A Lamborghini."

"Oh." She didn't know a lot about sports cars, but this one had a name that sounded expensive.

The girls were waiting at the table for them when Diana and Cliff arrived. Joan had unfolded the blanket and spread it out beneath a tall fir tree.

"Can we go looking for seashells?" Joan asked.

"I want to eat first," Katie complained. "I'm hungry."

"I bought plenty of food." Cliff said, opening the sack and setting out four individual boxes. Each one contained a complete meal.

"What's for dessert?" Already Katie had ripped open the top of her box, and a chicken leg was poised in front of her mouth.

"Ice cream cones, but only if you're good," Cliff answered.

"What he means by 'good,'" Joan explained in a hushed voice, "is giving him plenty of time alone with Mom. They need to talk."

Diana's eyes flared with indignation. "Did you tell her that?" she demanded in a low whisper.

Cliff looked astonished enough for her to believe in his innocence. "Not me."

From the corner of her eye, Diana saw him give Joan a conspiratorial wink, and was all the more upset. Rather than argue with him in front of the children, Diana decided to wait. However, maintaining her anger with Cliff was impossible. He shared the picnic table bench with Katie and sat across from Diana. He was so charming that he had all three females under his spell within minutes. Diana found it only a little short of amazing the way he talked to the girls. He didn't talk down to Joan and Katie, but treated them as miniature adults, and they adored him for it. From Diana's point of view, this man could do with fewer worshiping females.

The girls finished their meal in record time and were off to explore. While Diana tossed their garbage into the proper receptacle, she shouted out instructions.

"Don't you dare come back here wet!" she cried, and doubted that they'd heard her.

"Wet?" Cliff asked.

"Leave it to them to decide to go swimming."

"Once they find out how cold the water is, they'll change their minds," he said confidently.

Cliff had moved from the picnic table to the blanket and sat with his back propped against the tree, watching Diana as she made busywork at the picnic table.

"I'm sure the birds will appreciate your dumping

those crumbs on the ground," he said, and patted the area beside him. "Come and sit down."

Unwillingly Diana did as he asked, but sat on the edge of the blanket. It was too dangerous to get close to Cliff; such raw masculinity unnerved her. She'd been three years without a man, and this one made her feel things she would have preferred to forget.

"I wish you hadn't done this," she said in a small, quiet voice.

"What?"

"Don't play dumb with me, Cliff Howard. You know exactly what I'm talking about."

"Why are you sitting so far away from me?"

"Because it's safe here."

"I don't bite." His mouth curved up in a sensual smile that did uncanny things to Diana's equilibrium.

"Maybe not, but you kiss," she told him irritably.

His eyes held hers. "It was good, wasn't it?"

She nodded. "Too good."

His smile was lazy. "Nothing can be *too* good."

Diana couldn't find it within herself to disagree, although she knew she should. "What's this about your suggesting to Joan that they give us time together alone?"

His mouth broadened into a deeper grin. "Actually, that was her idea."

Diana rolled her eyes heavenward. That sounded exactly like something Joan would suggest.

"I like your girls, Diana," he said gently. "You've done a good job raising them."

"They're not raised yet—besides, you're seeing their good side. Just wait until they start fighting. There

are days when I think they're going to seriously injure each other."

"My brother and I were like that. We're close now,
although he's living in California." Cliff paused and
told her a couple of stories from his youth that produced
a smile and caused her to relax. "Rich and I talk at least
once a week now. Joan and Katie will probably do the
same once they leave home."

Bringing her legs up, Diana rested her chin on top
of her knees. One hand lazily picked up a long blade
of grass. It felt right to be with Cliff. Right and wrong.

"Why haven't you married?" The question was
abrupt and tactless, slipping out before she could temper the words.

Cliff shrugged, and then his answer was as direct
as her question. "I haven't found the right woman. Besides, I'm having too much fun to settle down."

"Usually, when a man's over thirty there's a reason…I mean…some men can't make a commitment,
you know." Oh, heavens, she was making this worse
every minute.

"To be honest, I've never considered marriage."
There hadn't been any reason to. That wasn't to say
he hadn't been in love any number of times, but generally the emotion was fleeting and within a few weeks
another woman would capture his attention. Once he'd
had a girl move in with him, but those had been the
most miserable months of his life, and the experience
had taught him valuable lessons. Expensive ones. He
would never again accept that kind of arrangement.

"Shirley mentioned a Becky somebody."

Bless Shirley's black heart, Cliff mused. "She lived
with me for three months."

"You didn't want to marry her?"

"Good grief, no. I was never so glad to get rid of anyone in my life."

Diana frowned. The knowledge that Cliff had lived with a woman proved that he was a swinging single, as she'd suspected. That he'd want to spend time with her was only a little short of amazing. Perplexed, she wrapped her arms around her legs and briefly pressed her forehead to her knees.

"You don't approve of a man and woman living together?" The troubled look that clouded her eyes made her opinion all the more evident.

Diana lifted her head and her eyes held his. "It isn't for me to approve or disapprove. What other people do is their own business as long as it doesn't affect me or my children."

"But it's something you'd never do?"

Her hesitation was only slight. "I couldn't. I have Joan and Katie to consider. But as I said, it's not up to me to judge what someone else does."

Her answer pleased him. Diana was too intelligent to get caught in a dead-end relationship that would only end up ripping apart her heart.

Unfortunately Cliff had been forced to learn his lessons the hard way.

"You were on my mind every day, all day, all week," he said softly, enticingly. "I thought about you getting up and taking the girls to school. Later, I remembered you telling me you wanted to plant marigolds. That's what you did today, isn't it?"

Diana nodded and closed her eyes. "I had a crummy week." She didn't want Cliff to court her. Her attraction to him was powerful enough without his telling her he hadn't been able to get her off his mind.

"The fact is, I couldn't stop thinking about you," he added.

"I filled out an application for a job with the school district this morning," she told him brightly. She was desperate for him to stop leading her on. She didn't need for him to say the things a woman wants to hear. They weren't necessary; she had been fascinated from the moment he'd walked into her house. "There's a good chance they'll be able to hire for September."

"When I wasn't thinking about you," he continued, undaunted, "I was remembering our kisses and wondering how long it would be before I could kiss you again."

Her fingers coiled into hard fists. "I'll probably be working as a teacher's aid," she said, doing her utmost to ignore him.

"Don't make me wait too long to kiss you again, Diana."

Her hands were so tightly bunched that her fingers ached. She forced herself to ignore him, to pretend she hadn't heard what he was saying. Closing her eyes helped to blot out his image, but when she opened them again, he had moved and was sitting beside her.

"How long are you going to make me wait?" he asked again, in a voice that would melt concrete.

His eyes rested on her mouth. Diana tried to look away, but he wouldn't let her. Even when he raised his hand and turned her face back to him, his gaze didn't stray from her lips. He pressed his index finger over her mouth and slid it from one corner of her lips to the other. Diana couldn't have moved to save her life.

"You don't need to tell me anything. I know what you're thinking and that you weren't able to get me off your mind, either. I know you want this."

One of his hands cupped the side of her face, and her eyes fluttered closed. His other hand slipped around her waist as he brought her into his arms. In that moment Diana couldn't have resisted him to save the world. He knew her, knew that he'd been on her mind all week, knew how much she regretted that things couldn't be different for them.

Cliff lowered his head and pressed his lips over hers. The kiss was gentle and so good, that Diana felt her heart would burst. Emotionally rocked, she trembled as though trapped in the aftermath of an earthquake.

Slowly his mouth worked its way over hers, and she opened her lips to him in silent invitation, the way a flower does to the noonday sun, seeking its warmth, blossoming. Diana groaned, and her arms curled around his torso until her hands met at his spine. Before she was aware of how it had happened, Cliff placed his hands on her shoulders and pressed her backward, anchoring her to the blanket. He raised his head, and his eyes delved into hers.

Diana sank her fingers into the dark hair at his temples and smiled tentatively. It was the sweetest, most tender expression Cliff had ever seen, filled with such gentle goodness that he felt his heart throb with naked desire. He longed to press her body under his.

"Do you feel it, too?" he asked, needing to hear her say the words.

Diana nodded. "I wish I didn't."

"No, you don't," he returned with supreme confidence. A surge of undiluted power gripped him.

"I think he kissed her."

A girlish giggle followed the announcement.

"Katie?" Cliff asked Diana.

She nodded.

Cliff levered himself off Diana and helped her into a sitting position. Self-conscious in front of her children, Diana ran her fingers through her hair, lifting it away from her face.

"We found a starfish," Joan said, delivering it to her mother and sitting on the blanket.

Diana didn't notice the proud find as much as the fact that her daughter's shoes were missing and the bottoms of her jeans were sopping wet. Chastising Joan in front of Cliff would embarrass the eleven-year-old, and Diana resisted the urge.

"Isn't he gorgeous?" Katie demanded.

"Who?" Diana blinked, thinking her daughter could be talking about Cliff.

"The starfish!" Both girls gave her a funny look.

"Yes, he's perfectly wonderful. Now take him back to the water or he'll die."

"Ah, Mom…"

"You heard me." She brooked no argument.

Joan picked up the echinoderm and rushed back to the beach. Katie lingered behind, her head cocked at an angle as she studied Cliff.

"Do you like to kiss my mother?" she asked curiously.

Cliff nodded. "Yes. Does that bother you?"

Katie paused to give some consideration to the question. "No, not really, as long as she likes it, too."

"She likes it, and so do I."

Katie's pert nose wrinkled. "Does she taste good?"

"Real good."

"Gary Hidenlighter offered me a baseball card if I'd let him kiss me. I told him no." She wrapped her hands around her neck, then, graphically pretending to strangle herself. "Yuck."

"It matters who you're kissing, sweetheart," Diana explained. A fetching pink highlighted her cheekbones at her daughter and Cliff talking about something so personal.

Having satisfied her curiosity, Katie ran toward the pathway that led to the beach and to her elder sister.

"I have the feeling that if Gary Hidenlighter had offered her Kentucky Fried Chicken, she would have gone for it."

Cliff chuckled, his eyes warm. "What do I need to trade to gain your heart, Diana Collins?"

Ignoring the question, Diana picked up the blanket and took care to fold it with crisp corners. She held the quilt to her stomach as a protective barrier when she finished.

"I asked you something."

"I have no intention of answering such a leading question." In nervous agitation she flipped a stray strand of hair around her ear.

"Can I see you again tomorrow?" he asked. "Dinner, a show, anything you want."

Diana's heart constricted with dread. Now that she was faced with the decision of whether to see him again, the answer was all too clear.

"Listen," she murmured, wrapping her arms around the blanket to ward off a chill, "we need to talk about this first."

"I asked you to go to a movie with me."

"That's what I want to talk about."

"Is it that difficult to decide?"

"Yes," she whispered.

Cliff stood and leaned against the tree, bracing one foot against the trunk. "All right, when?"

Diana was uncertain. "Anytime the girls aren't around."

"Later tonight?"

She'd never felt more unsure about a man in her life. The sooner they talked, the better. "Tonight will be fine."

"Don't look so bleak. It can't be that bad."

It was worse than bad. Shirley's warnings echoed in her ears, reminding her that she'd be a fool to date a prominent womanizer who was said to have little conscience and few scruples. Diana's insides were shaking and her nerves were shot. She was a mature woman! She should be capable of handling this situation with far more finesse than she was exhibiting.

"I—I wish you hadn't come back." Her emotions were so close to the surface that she tossed the blanket on the picnic table and stalked away, upset with both Cliff and herself.

For half a minute, Cliff was too stunned to react. This woman never ceased to astonish him. She'd wept in his arms when he'd kissed her, and when he'd told her how attracted he was to her and asked her out again, she'd stormed away as though he'd insulted her.

Driven by instinct, Cliff raced after her, his quick stride catching up with her a few feet later.

"Maybe we should talk now," he suggested softly, gesturing toward a park bench. "We can see the girls from here. If there's a problem, I don't want it hanging over our heads. Now tell me what's got you so upset."

She gaped at him. He honestly didn't know what was wrong. He was driving her crazy, and he seemed completely oblivious to the fact. Gathering her composure, Diana nodded in silent agreement and sat down.

Cliff joined her. "Okay, what's on your mind?"

You! she wanted to scream, but he wouldn't understand her anger anymore than she did. "First of all, let me tell you that I am very flattered at the attention you've given me. Considering the women you usually date, it's done worlds of good for my ego."

A frown marred his brow. "I don't know what you're talking about."

"Oh, come on, Cliff," she said in an effort to be flippant. "Surely you realize that you're 'hot stuff.'"

"So they tell me."

She expelled her breath slowly, impatiently. "A date with you would quicken any female's heart."

"I'm flattered you think so."

"Cliff, don't be cute, please—this is difficult enough."

He paused, leaned forward and clasped his hands. "I don't understand what any of this has to do with a picnic supper. I like you. So what? I think your daughters are wonderful. Where does that create a problem?"

"It just does." She felt like shouting at him.

"How?" he pressed. Women generally went out of their way to attract his attention. He found it an ironic twist that the one woman who had dominated his thoughts for an entire week would be so eager to be rid of him. Her defiance pricked his ego. "All right, let's hear it," he said, his voice low and serious.

Still, he wouldn't look at her, which was just as well for Diana, since this was difficult enough.

"I don't want to see you again," she said forcefully, although her voice shook. There—it was out. Considering the way she responded to his kisses, she must be out of her mind. Although she had to admit she didn't feel especially pleased to decline his invitation, it was for the best.

Cliff was silent.The thing was he knew she was right, but he felt he was on the brink of some major discovery about himself. Ego aside, he realized he could have just about any woman he wanted, except Diana Collins.

"I suppose Shirley told you I have the reputation of being some heartless playboy. Diana, it's not true."

Diana paused to take in several deep breaths. She'd hoped that he'd spare her this. "I think you're wonderful...."

"If you honestly felt that way, you wouldn't be so eager to be rid of me."

"Don't, Cliff," she pleaded. She wasn't going to be able to explain a thing with his interrupting every five seconds.

"What I can't understand," he said, shaking his head, "is why you're making it out to be some great tragedy that I find you attractive."

"But I'm not your...type," she declared for lack of a better description. "And if we continue to see each other, it will only lead to problems for us both."

"It seems to me that you're jumping to conclusions."

"I'm not," she stated calmly.

Cliff was losing his temper now. "And as for your

not being my type, don't you think I should be the one to decide that?"

"No," she argued. Diana could hardly believe she was telling the most devastating man she'd ever known that it would be better for them not to see each other again.

"Why not?" he shot back.

"Because."

"That doesn't make a lot of sense."

Diana clamped her mouth closed. It wasn't going to do any good to try to reason with him. He probably was so accustomed to women falling into his arms that he wasn't sure how to react when one resisted. A few years earlier she would have been like all the others, she noted mentally.

"Diana," he said after a calming minute. "I don't know what's going on in that twisted mind of yours, but I do think you're being completely unreasonable. I like you, you like me..."

"The girls..."

"Are terrific."

"But, Cliff, you drive a Lamborghini."

The car bothered her! "What's that got to do with anything?"

Diana wasn't sure she could explain. "It makes a statement."

"So does your Ford SUV."

"Exactly! What I can't understand is why a man who drives an expensive sports car is interested in seeing a thirty-year-old widow who plows through traffic in a ten-year-old bomber."

"Bomber?"

Diana's grin was fleeting. "That's what the girls call the Ford."

Cliff's gaze drifted to the two youngsters running along the rolling surf. Their bare feet popped foam bubbles with such mindless glee that he found himself smiling at their antics.

Diana's gaze followed his and her thoughts sobered. "This doesn't really have anything to do with what cars we drive, does it?"

"No," Diana admitted softly. "Shirley warned me about you."

"I'm not going to lie," Cliff murmured. "Everything she said is probably true. But of all the women I've met, I would have thought you were one to form your own opinions."

"If it were just me, I'd be accepting your offer so fast it would make your head spin," she answered honestly. "But the girls think you're the neatest thing since microwave popcorn and they're at a vulnerable age."

"Somehow I get the feeling that what's bothering you isn't any of these things. Not the car, not the girls, not the other women I date."

He read her thoughts so well it frightened her. She clenched her hands together and nodded. "I can't be the woman you want."

He frowned. "What do you mean?"

"I haven't got the body of a centerfold or the looks of a beauty queen. I've had children."

"Hey, I'm not complaining. I like what I see."

"You might not be so sure if you saw more of me."

"Is that an offer?"

Color bloomed full force in her cheeks. "It most certainly was not."

"More's the pity."

"That's another thing. I'm…not easy."

"You're telling me. I've spent the past fifteen minutes trying to talk you into a movie. After all this I certainly hope you don't intend to turn me down."

She laughed then, because refusing him was impossible. He was right; she was the type of person to make up her own mind. Shirley would have her hide, but, then, her neighbor hadn't been the sole subject of his considerable charm.

"You will go with me, won't you?"

"Where?" Katie cried, running up from behind them.

"Cliff wants to take me to a movie."

Katie clapped her hands. "Oh, good. Can Joan and I go, too?"

Four

"I hope you know what you're getting yourself into," Diana's neighbor muttered, her brow puckered. She paused and stared at the bottom of her empty coffee cup. "George told me he's seen Cliff Howard bring lesser women to their knees."

"Listen, Shirley, I'm a big girl. I can take care of myself."

Shirley snickered softly. "The last time you told me that was when you decided to figure your own income tax, and we both know what happened."

Diana cringed at the memory. In an effort to save a few dollars a couple of years back, she'd gone over her financial records and filled out her own tax forms. It hadn't appeared so difficult, and to be truthful, she'd been rather proud of herself. That was until she'd been summoned for an audit by an IRS agent who had all the compassion and understanding of grizzly bear. It had turned out that she owed the government several hundred dollars and they weren't willing to take Mastercard. They were, however, amicable to confiscating her home and children if she didn't come up with the five-hundred-dollar discrepancy. Scraping the money together on her fixed income had made the weeks following the audit some of the most unpleasant since her husband's death.

"I just don't want to see you get hurt," Shirley added in thoughtful tones. "And I'm afraid Cliff Howard's just the man to do it."

"What I want to know is why I've never seen Cliff before now?" Diana asked in an effort to change the subject. "You know so much about him, like he was a longtime family friend. I didn't even know he existed."

"George plays golf with him a couple of times a month. They meet at the country club. Until the other night, Cliff had only been to our house once." Her mouth tightened. "I should have known something like this would happen."

"Like what?"

"You falling head over heels for him."

Diana laughed outright at that. "Rest assured, I am not in love with Cliff Howard."

"But you will be," Shirley said confidently. "Every woman falls for him eventually. Some of the stories going around the clubhouse about him would shock you."

"Well, you needn't worry. I'm not going to fall for him."

"That's what they all say," Shirley told her knowingly.

Diana avoided her friend's gaze. Her neighbor wasn't saying anything she hadn't already suspected. She liked Cliff, was strongly attracted to him, but she wasn't going to fall for him. She was too intelligent to allow herself to be taken in by a notorious playboy.

But, no matter what her feelings, Diana couldn't completely discredit Shirley's advice. Her neighbor could very well be right, and Diana could be headed down the slick path to heartache and moral decay.

She paused and cupped her hands around her coffee mug. "He's been wonderful with the girls," she said, hoping that alone was excuse enough to date Cliff.

"I know," Shirley answered softly, shaking her head. "That confuses me, too. I never thought Cliff Howard would like children."

"Mikey thinks he's great."

"Yeah, but Cliff won him over early by bringing him an autographed baseball."

Shirley had a point there. Besides, Mikey was the friendly sort and not easily offended. "Joan and Katie are crazy about him."

Shirley's eyes narrowed. "Just don't make the mistake of thinking you're different from all the others women who have wandered in and out of his life."

Diana pondered her friend's words. Shirley had gone to great lengths to describe Cliff's "women." To hear her neighbor tell it, Cliff Howard hadn't so much as looked at a woman over thirty, much less shown an interest in dating one. It went without saying that he usually avoided women with children. Cliff had told her himself that she was the first widow he'd taken out. Diana didn't know what was different about her, wasn't sure she wanted to know. He seemed to honestly enjoy being with her and the girls, and for now that was enough.

"What makes you think you'll be different?" Shirley pressed.

"But I am different. You said so yourself," Diana

answered after a lengthy pause, holding her neighbor's concerned gaze.

"I don't mean it like that." An exasperated sigh followed. "Just keep reminding yourself that Cliff could well be another Casanova."

Diana laughed outright. "Unfortunately he's got his good looks."

"You're about as likely to have a lasting relationship with Cliff as you are with Casanova, so keep that in mind."

"Yes, Mother," Diana teased softly. She found Shirley's concern more touching than irritating.

"Just don't make me say 'I told you so,'" her neighbor returned, and the doubt rang clear in her voice.

Diana mused over their conversation for most of the day. Shirley wasn't telling her anything she hadn't already considered herself. She'd been playing with fire from the minute she'd agreed to that first dinner date with Cliff, and she knew it, but the flickering flames had never been more attractive. She was thirty, and it was time to let her hair down and kick up her heels a little.

For his part, Cliff wasn't stupid, Diana realized. He knew what kind of physical response he drew from her, knew she had been teetering with indecision when he had suggested they see each other again. So when Katie had piped in and asked to go to the movies with them, Cliff had jumped on the idea. By including the girls, he'd known she wouldn't refuse. How could she, with Joan and Katie doing flips over the idea? The man was a successful attorney and he'd read her ambivalence with the ease of a first grade primer. Although she'd been determined to put an end to this silliness, her well-constructed defenses had tumbled with astonishing unconcern and she was as eager for the drive-in as the girls. It was one of the last left in the country and in South King Country, in the countryside.

"Mom," Katie cried as she rushed into the kitchen the minute the school bus dropped her off. "Can Mikey go to the drive-in movie with us?"

Diana hedged. "I don't know, honey. Cliff has to agree."

"He won't care. I know he won't, and besides, he knows Mikey and Mikey's parents know Cliff." She slapped her hands against her side as though that fact alone were enough for anyone to come to the same decision, then grinned beguilingly.

Arguing with such logic seemed fruitless. "Let's wait and talk to Cliff once he arrives."

"Okay."

Diana watched in amazement as Katie grabbed an apple from the fruit basket and dashed out the front door to join her friends. Usually Diana was subjected to a long series of arguments whenever the girls were after something, and Katie's easy acceptance pulled her up short.

"Well, all right," she muttered after her daughter, still bemused.

By the time Cliff arrived, Diana was convinced that half the neighborhood was waiting. He parked his sports car in the driveway, and was instantly besieged by a breathless, excited Joan and two or three of Joan's friends. Katie and Mikey followed a second later. Both Diana's girls grabbed for Cliff's hand, one trying to outdo the other. With a patience that pleased and surprised Diana, Cliff stopped their excited chatter. He directed his first question to Joan.

Watching the humorous scene from the front porch, Diana saw her elder daughter issue an urgent plea for Cliff to allow her to invite their very best friends in all the world to the drive-in with them.

Kate started in next. Cliff's gaze went from the girls to a series of neighborhood kids who stood in the background, awaiting his reply.

From her position, Diana could clearly see Cliff's confusion. He'd asked for this, she mused, having trouble holding in her laughter.

"Hi," she greeted him, coming down the steps.

"Hi." His bewildered gaze sought hers as he motioned toward Joan and Katie and the accumulated friends. "What do you think?"

"It's up to you."

"Please, Cliff," Katie cried, her hands folded as if praying.

Cliff glanced down on Diana's daughter and released a long, frustrated sigh. He'd thought about this evening all day, and planned—or at least hoped—the drive-in movie would quickly put the girls to sleep so he could kiss Diana. Once again he'd discovered she'd dominated his thoughts most of the afternoon. His plans certainly hadn't included dragging half the neighborhood to the drive-in with him.

"I thought of a way it could work," Diana told him. "Come inside, and we'll talk about it."

Her compromise wasn't half bad, Cliff mused an hour later as he parked his sports car beside the SUV full of kids at the drive-in. They'd agreed earlier to take Diana's vehicle simply because his car wouldn't hold everyone. Diana had suggested they drive both cars and park next to each other. That way the adults could maintain their privacy and still manage to keep an eye on the kids, who were feeling very mature to have their own car. Now that he thought about it, Diana's idea had been just short of brilliant.

"How does everyone feel about popcorn?" Cliff asked once they'd situated the cars halfway between the screen and the snack bar.

"I already popped some," Diana informed him, climbing out of the driver's seat. Joan eagerly replaced her, draping her wrist over the steering wheel and looking as though she were Jeff Gordon ready for the Indy 500.

Diana sorted through something in the rear of the SUV and returned with her arms full. She handed each child his own bag of popcorn and a can of soda. "Don't eat any until the movie starts," she instructed, and was greeted by a series of harmonizing moans. "That goes for you, too," she told Cliff, her eyes twinkling.

He grumbled for show and shared a conspiratorial wink with Joan, who, he could see, had already managed to sample her goodies. He held his car door open for Diana before walking around the front and joining her in the close confines of his Lamborghini.

Diana scooted down low enough in the seat to rest her head against the back of the thick leather cushion. The contrast between them had never been more striking. She wore Levi's and a pink sweatshirt, while Cliff was fashionably dressed in slacks and a thick crewneck sweater. Diana sincerely doubted that any of his other dates had ever dressed so casually. Nor did she believe other women had six kids tagging along. Know-

ing Cliff's game, Diana considered the neighborhood
tribe poetic justice.

"This is turning into a great idea," he said, wondering how much longer it would take before it got dark.

Before Diana could answer, a Road Runner cartoon
appeared on the huge white screen. The kids in the car
next to them cheered with excitement, and even from
her position in Cliff's sports car, she could hear them
rip into their bags of popcorn.

"You're a good sport," Diana said, feeling self-conscious all of a sudden. "I mean about the kids and
everything."

"Hey, no problem."

"How'd work go?" She felt obligated to make small
talk, certain he wouldn't possibly be interested in the
cartoon.

"Good. How about your day?"

"Fine." She clenched her hands together so hard her
fingers ached. "Joan went to the orthodontist." Now
that made for brilliant conversation! She'd bore him
to death before the end of the previews.

"So she's going into braces?"

Diana nodded and reached for her bag of popcorn
so she'd have something to do with her hands. "I told
her she's enough of a live wire as it is."

Cliff chuckled. "I'm glad to hear she's going
straight."

Now it was Diana's turn to laugh. What had seemed
the perfect solution an hour before now had the feel of a
disaster in the making. Alone with Cliff, she'd seldom
been more uncertain about anything. Joan and Katie
had been her shield, protecting her from the wealth of
emotion Cliff was capable of raising within her. She

sat beside him, quivering inside, never having felt more vulnerable. He could make cornmeal mush of her life if he chose to, and like a fool, she'd all but issued the invitation for him to do so. Shirley's warnings sounded in her ears like sonic booms, and for an instant, Diana had the sinking feeling that one of Custer's men must have experienced the same sensation as he rode into battle, wondering what he was doing there. Diana wondered, too. Oh, man did she wonder.

The credits for the Lucas film rolled onto the huge screen, but Diana's thoughts weren't on the highly rated movie. The open bag of popcorn rested on her lap, but she dared not eat any, sure the popcorn would stick halfway down her desert-dry throat.

"Diana?"

She jumped halfway out of her seat. "Yes?"

Cliff's smile was lazy and gentle and understanding. "Relax, will you? I'm not going to leap on you."

If there'd been a hole to crawl into, Diana would have gladly jumped inside. "I know that."

"Then what's the problem?"

There didn't seem to be enough words to explain. She was a mature, capable woman, but when she was around him, all her hard-earned independence evaporated into thin air like an ice chip on an Arizona sidewalk. He brought back feelings she preferred to keep buried, churning emotions that reminded her she was still a young, healthy woman. When she was with Cliff, she was a red-blooded woman, and her body felt obliged to remind her of the needs she didn't want to remember. With Cliff so close beside her, the last thing on her mind was motherhood and apple pie. His proximity caused her to quiver from the inside out.

She wanted him to kiss her, longed for his touch. And it scared her to death.

"Diana?"

Slowly she turned to look at him. Her face felt hot against the crisp evening air, and Cliff's look brushed lightly over her features. He was kissing her with his eyes, and she was burning up with fever. Suddenly the interior of the car made her feel claustrophobic. She set the popcorn aside and reached for the door handle.

His hand stopped her. "You're beautiful."

He whispered the words with such intensity that Diana felt them melt in the air like cotton candy against her tongue. She wanted to shout at him not to say such things to her, that it wasn't necessary. She didn't need to hear them, didn't want him to say them. But the protest died a speedy death as he reached for her shoulders. His gaze held her prisoner for what seemed an eternity as he slowly slid his hand from the curve of her shoulder upward, until he found her warm nape. He didn't move, hardly breathed, anticipating her reaction. When he could wait no longer for an invitation, he wove his fingers into her hair and directed her mouth toward his.

Cliff's lips claimed hers in a fury of desire. His mouth slanted against hers in a full, lush kiss that spoke of fervor and timeless longing. The shaking inside Diana increased and she raised her hands to grip his shoulders just to maintain her equilibrium. Her skin was hot and cold at the same time.

Suddenly it all seemed too much. Using her arms as leverage, Diana abruptly broke away. Head bowed, she drew in ragged breaths. "Cliff, I…"

He wouldn't allow her to speak and gently directed her mouth back to his. All the resolve she could muster, which wasn't much, had gone into breaking off the kiss. When he reached for her again, unwilling to listen to any argument, there was nothing left with which to refuse him. His mouth opened wider, deepening the kiss, and Diana let him. Folding her arms around his neck, she leaned into his strength. He brought her against him possessively until her ribs ached and the heat of his torso burned its way down the length of her own. Cliff felt her body's natural response to him and he groaned. At this moment he'd give anything to be anyplace besides a drive-in. He wanted to lift the sweatshirt over her head and toss it aside. The pain of denial was strong and sharp as he buried his face in the sloped curve of her neck. With even, steady breaths, he tried to force his pulse to a slow, rhythmical beat as he struggled within himself. It had been a long time since he'd experienced such an intensity of need.

The battle that waged inside Diana was fierce. She wanted to push herself away from him and scream that she wasn't like his other women. There'd been only one lover in her life, and she wasn't going to become his next conquest simply because her hormones behaved like jumping beans whenever he touched her. But the words that crossed her mind didn't make it to her lips.

"Diana…" Cliff spoke first, his voice filled with gruff emotion. "Listen, I know what you're thinking."

"Don't, Cliff, please don't." She twisted her face away from him, unable to form words to explain all that she was thinking and feeling. She felt both tormented and compelled by what was happening to them.

Cliff tensed, and his fingers dug into her shoulders.

"What's wrong?" She lifted her head and bravely raised her gaze to meet his own.

"Don't look now, but we've got an audience."

"Joan?"

"And…others."

"How many others?"

"Five."

"All six of the kids are staring at us?" The hot flush that had stained her neck raced toward her cheeks and into the roots of her hair. She'd assured all the neighborhood parents that the drive-in movie was rated PG, and here she was giving them an R-rated sideshow.

"Six noses are pressed against the window, and six pairs of eyes are glued on us," Cliff interjected with little humor.

"Oh, no," Diana groaned, hanging her head in abject misery.

"Joan's giving me the thumbs-up sign, Katie looks shocked and Mikey's obviously thoroughly disgusted. He's decided to cover his eyes."

"What should we do?" Diana asked next, horribly embarrassed.

"Good grief, why ask me? I don't know a thing about kids."

His hold was tight enough to cause her shoulders to ache, but Diana didn't complain. She was as much at a loss about what to do as Cliff was. "I think we should smile and wave, and then casually go back to watching the movie."

"This isn't the time to be cute."

"I wasn't trying to be funny. That was my idea."

"If that's the best you can come up with, then I suggest you turn in your Mother of the Year Award."

"What?" Diana cried.

"We could be warping young minds here, and all you're doing is coming up with jokes."

"Oh, for heaven's sake, I think it's safe to assume they've seen people kiss before now," Diana said, growing more amused by the moment.

"Hey, Mom."

Joan's shout interrupted their discussion. Forcing herself to appear calm and collected, Diana twisted around, painted a silly smile on her face and rolled down the window. "Yes, sweetheart?" she answered in a perfectly controlled voice. She was actually proud of herself for maintaining her cool. She prayed her expression gave away none of the naked desire she'd been feeling only moments before.

"Why are you arguing with Cliff?"

"What makes you ask that?"

"You weren't fighting a minute ago."

"You were kissing him real hard," Katie popped in. She was leaning from the back seat into the front and sticking her head out the side window next to her sister. "Judy Gilmore's boyfriend kissed her like that the time she babysat for us. Remember?"

"Say, aren't you kids supposed to be watching the movie?" Cliff asked, having trouble disguising his chagrin.

"It's more fun looking at you," Joan answered for the group.

"Mom, I've got to go to the bathroom."

"Me, too." Three other voices chimed in from behind Katie.

"I'll take you." Diana couldn't get out of the car fast enough. Rarely had she been more grateful for the call of nature.

By the time Diana returned, Cliff's mood had improved considerably. He was munching on popcorn and staring at the screen. When she eased into the seat beside him, he glanced in her direction and grinned. "The movie's actually pretty good."

Diana suspected it wasn't half as amusing as they'd been. She had to give Cliff credit—he really was a good sport.

By the time the second feature had started, Joan, Katie and their friends were sound asleep.

"I should have waited until now to kiss you," Cliff joked, staring across at the car filled with snoozing youngsters. "Problem was, I was too eager."

That had been Diana's trouble, as well. From the minute she'd sat beside him and they'd been alone, she'd known what was bound to happen. She'd wanted it too much.

Cliff looped his arm around her shoulder and brought her head down to his hard chest. "Now that we haven't got a crowd cheering us on, do you want to try it again?" He gave her a self-effacing, enticing half smile.

Diana laughed, and although the console prevented her from cuddling up close to his side, she adjusted herself as best she could. "When I was a teenager, we used to call the drive-in the 'passion pit.'"

"Hey, I'm game. I don't know if you recognize it or not, but there's chemistry between us." He brushed the hair from her brow and pressed his lips there.

"I noticed it all right." His kiss just then was like adding water to hot grease. "It's more potent than I care to dwell on."

"I'll say."

He did kiss her again during the second movie, but more for experimentation than anything. His fingers, tucked under her chin, turned her mouth to his as his warm lips touched, stroked and brushed her. Temporarily satisfied, Cliff settled back and watched the movie for a few minutes more. He reached for her again later and nibbled along her neck. He refused to hold her tight, as aware of the danger as she of this explosive fireworks between them. A drive-in movie with a carload of kids parked in the next space was not the place to get overly romantic.

The second movie over, Cliff met her back at the house after Diana had dropped off Joan and Katie's friends. Both girls were more interested in sleeping than climbing out of the car. Finally Cliff lifted the sleeping Katie into his arms and carried her inside and up the stairs. A dreamy-eyed Joan followed behind, yawning as she went.

Diana tucked the blankets around her elder daughter. Joan planted her hands beneath her pillow and rolled onto her side. "Mom?"

"Yes, honey."

"Thank Cliff for me, okay?"

"Will do."

Joan forced one eye open. "Are you going to see him again?"

"I...don't know, honey. He hasn't asked me out."

"You should invite him to dinner. You make great spaghetti."

"Honey, I don't think that's a good idea."

"I happen to love good spaghetti," Cliff answered. Diana turned and found him standing in the doorway of Joan's bedroom. "Why don't you make up a batch and bring it sailing?"

"Sailing?"

"You and the girls." Having heard Diana's hesitation, he resigned himself to including her daughters in every outing until she learned to trust him. "We'll make a day of it."

"When?"

Cliff thought about waiting another week to see Diana again, and knew that was much too long. His schedule for the next week was hectic and he'd be lucky to find the time to spend more than an hour or two with her. He had two cases going to trial and a backlog of work awaiting his attention. "Tomorrow," he suggested.

Joan bolted upright. "Hey, that sounds great. Count me in."

Irritated, Diana glared down on her daughter. "Cliff, I don't know. I'd think you'd have had your fill of me and the girls for one weekend."

"Let me be the judge of that."

"I've never been sailing before," Joan reminded Diana, her two round eyes gazing up at her pleadingly. "And you know how Katie loves anything that has to do with the water."

"We'll talk about it later," Diana told her firmly, and walked out of the bedroom. Cliff followed her down the stairs.

"Well, what do you say about tomorrow?" he asked, standing in front of the door.

"I'm...not sure." She remained on the bottom step, so that when he walked over to her, their eyes were level.

He smiled at her then and slipped one arm around

her waist to pull her against him. In an effort to escape, Diana pried his arm loose and climbed one stair up so she rose a head above him.

If she thought he was going to let her go so easily, Cliff mused, then Diana Collins had a great deal to learn about him.

He brought her into his arms and kissed her untiel everything went still as hot, tingling shivers raced through Diana. She closed her eyes and stopped breathing.

"Tomorrow," she said in a tight, strained whisper. "What time?"

"Noon," Cliff mumbled, and dropped his hands.

Diana gripped the banister until her nails threatened to bend. "Thank you for tonight."

It was all Cliff could do to nod. He backed away from her as though she held a torch that was blazing out of control. Already he was singed, and all he could think about was coming back for more.

Five

"How long will it take before I catch a fish?" Katie asked impatiently. Her fishing pole was poised over the side of the sailboat as the forty-foot sloop lazily sliced through the dark green waters of Puget Sound.

"Longer than five minutes," Diana informed her younger daughter. She tossed an apologetic glance in Cliff's direction. He'd been the one so keen on this outing. She wasn't nearly convinced all this time together with the girls would work. Cooping the four of them up in the close confines of a sailboat for an afternoon wouldn't serve anyone's best interests as far as she could see. But Cliff had assured her otherwise, and the girls continued to swoon under the force of his charm. With such resounding enthusiasm from both parties, Diana certainly wasn't going to argue.

"The secret is to convince the fish he's hungry," Joan said haughtily with the superior knowledge of a girl three years Katie's senior.

"How do you do that?"

Diana was curious herself.

"Move your line a little so the bait wiggles," Joan

answered primly, and gyrated her hips a couple of times as an example. "That makes the fish want to check out what's happening. In case you weren't aware of it, fish are by nature shy. All they need is a little encouragement."

"All fish are shy?" Diana muttered under her breath for Cliff's benefit.

"Especially sharks," he returned out of the corner of his mouth.

"I've met a few of those in my time." Chuckling, Diana watched as he finished baiting Joan's hook and handed her the pole. Cliff could well be a shark, but if so, he was a clever one.

When he'd completed the task, he paused and grinned at her.

"What about you?" Diana asked as he settled down by the helm. "Aren't you going to fish?"

"Naw." He slouched down and draped his elbow over the side of the sloop. Squinting, he smiled into the sun and expertly steered the sailboat into the wind.

For a full minute, Diana couldn't look away. Shirley had painted Cliff in such grim tones—a man without conscience who freely used women. When he was finished, Shirley had said, he hurled them aside for fresh conquests. Looking at him now, Diana refused to believe it. Cliff was patient with the girls, and exquisitely gentle with her. Just being with him was more fun than she could remember having had in months. He appeared completely at ease with her and Joan and Katie. But, then, she reminded herself, women were said to be his forte. If Cliff were indeed the scoundrel her neighbor so ardently claimed him to be, then he'd done an excellent job bamboozling her.

"Mom, come and look," Katie called, and Diana moved closer to her daughter.

Cliff smiled. He was enjoying this outing with Diana and her family. Getting the girls occupied fishing had helped. He had them using his outdated equipment, so nothing expensive could be ruined. Actually, he was rather proud of himself for being so organized. He'd set the fishing gear the girls could use on one side of the boat and his own on the other. That way, there would be no confusion.

Now, with the girls interested in catching "shy" fish, he could soak up the sun and take time to study Diana. She was nothing like the women he was accustomed to dating. The attraction he felt for her was as much a shock to him as it apparently had been to her.

She'd finished with Katie and sat next to him. They were so close that Cliff could feel the warmth radiating from her. He longed to put his arm around her and bring her closer to his side. Okay, he'd admit it! He wanted to kiss her. Her butterscotch kisses were quickly becoming habit forming. All he'd need to do was lean forward. Their torsos would touch first, and his mouth would quickly find hers. No matter where he looked—the sky, the green water, the billowing sails, anyplace—he couldn't dispel every delicate, womanly nuance of Diana. Frustrated, he deliberately turned his thoughts to other matters.

"How's it going girls?" he called, seeking a diversion.

"Great," Joan shouted back.

Cliff was impressed with her enthusiasm.

"All right, I guess," Katie said, peering over the side. "Here fishy, fishy, fishy."

"That isn't going to help," Joan snapped, and as if to prove her point, she swung her fishing pole back and forth a couple of times, looking superior and confident.

Contented, Cliff grinned, and his gaze drifted back to Diana. She was a widow, no less. He'd always pictured widows as old ladies with lots of grandchildren, which was illogical, he realized. Diana was his own age. It wasn't that he'd avoided dating women thirty and over, he simply hadn't been attracted to any. But he was attracted to Diana. Oh yes, was he attracted! He wasn't so naive not to realize his playboy reputation had put her off. He'd give his eyeteeth to know what she'd heard—it would do wonders for his ego. Smiling, he relaxed and loosened his grip on the helm. He didn't know what George Holiday had told his wife, but apparently Shirley had repeated it in graphic detail. Luckily Diana had a decent head on her shoulders and was smart enough to recognize a bunch of exaggerations when she heard them.

Diana had never been on a sailboat before and she loved it, loved the feeling of relaxed simplicity, loved the wind as it whipped against her face and hair, loved the power of the sloop as it plowed through the water, slicing it as effectively as a hot butcher's knife through butter. Earlier, Cliff had let her man the helm while he'd moved forward to raise the sails, and she had been on a natural high ever since.

"You're looking thoughtful," Cliff said to Diana a moment later.

Her returning smile was slow and lazy. She closed

her eyes and let the wind whip through her hair, not caring what havoc the breeze wrecked. "I could get used to this," she murmured, savoring the feel of the noonday sun on her upturned face.

"Yes," Cliff admitted. He could get used to having her with him just as easily. When he stopped to analyze his feelings, he realized that she was the down-home type of woman he didn't feel the need to impress. He could be himself, relax. He was getting too old and lazy for the mating rituals he'd been participating in the past few years.

"Cliff!" Joan screamed into the wind, her shrill voice filled with panic. "I've…got something." The fishing pole was nearly bent in two. "It's big."

"Joan caught a whale," Katie called out excitedly.

"Hold on." Cliff jumped up and gave the helm to Diana.

"Here, you take it," Joan cried. "It's too big for me."

"You're doing fine."

"I'm not, either!"

"Joan, just do what Cliff says," Diana barked, as nervous as her daughter.

"But he hasn't said anything yet."

"How come Joan can catch a fish and I can't?" Katie whined. "I wiggled my hips and everything."

"Honey, now isn't the time to discuss it."

"It's never the time when I want to ask you something."

"Reel it in," Cliff shouted. The urge to jerk the pole out of the eleven-year-old's hands and do it himself was strong. The once confident Joan looked as if she would have willingly forgotten the whole thing.

Cliff watched as the fifth grader's hand yanked against the line. "Don't do that—you'll lose him!"

"I don't care. You do it—I didn't really want to kill a fish, anyway."

"Don't be a quitter," Cliff said, more gruffly than he'd intended. "You're doing fine."

"I am not!"

Exasperated, Cliff moved behind Joan and helped her grip the pole. With his hand over hers, he reeled for all he was worth, tugging the line closer and closer to the boat.

"I can see him," Katie shouted, jumping up and down.

"It's a salmon," Cliff called out as they got the large fish close to the boat. "A nice size sockeye from the look of him." He left Joan long enough to retrieve the net, then leaned over the side of the boat to pull the struggling salmon out of the water.

"Gross," Joan muttered, and closed her eyes. "No one told me there was going to be blood."

"Only a little," Diana assured her.

"I want to catch a fish," Katie cried a second time. "It's not fair that Joan caught one and I didn't."

"Don't worry about it," Joan said with a jubilant sigh. "I'll help you."

"I don't want your help. I want Cliff to show me."

"Cliff has to steer the sailboat," Diana explained to her younger daughter. She knew this peaceful afternoon was too good to be true. The girls would erupt into one of their famous fights and shock poor Cliff. He wasn't used to being around children—he wouldn't understand that they bickered almost constantly.

"I'm hungry," Katie decided next.

In order to appease her younger daughter, Diana climbed below deck to the galley, where Cliff had stored the picnic basket, and got Katie a sandwich and a can of her favorite soda.

Within a half hour, both girls were back to fishing, and serenity reigned once again.

"How much longer will it take?" Katie demanded within a few minutes. The irritating question was repeated at regular intervals.

Cliff's smile was getting stiffer by the minute. He wished he hadn't invited the girls along. He wanted Diana to himself, but he realized she would have refused the invitation if Joan and Katie hadn't been included. For the past thirty minutes, he'd been sitting watching Diana and wanting to kiss her. He couldn't do half the things he longed to do with Joan and Katie scrutinizing his every move. They were good kids, but it wasn't the same as being alone with Diana. And with Katie whining every few minutes, Cliff sorely felt the need for a little peace and quiet. His musings were interrupted by Katie's excited shout.

"Mommy, I got a fish, I got a fish!"

"I'll show you how to bring him in!" Joan yelled, and quickly moved to her sister's side, dragging her fishing pole with her.

"Hey! Watch your lines." Cliff's warning came too late, and before anyone could do anything to prevent it, the two fishing lines were hopelessly entangled.

"What do we do now?" Joan asked, tossing Cliff a look over her shoulder.

Once Cliff had assessed the situation, he shrugged and sadly shook his head. "There's nothing to do. I'll have to cut both lines."

"But my fish…"

"Honey, you can't reel him in now," Diana hastened to explain, praying Katie wouldn't be too terribly disappointed.

Cliff hated to cut the fishing lines, too, and was angry for not having warned the girls about what would happen if they didn't mind their poles. In addition to losing the fish, he was throwing away good lures and weights. Thankfully, there was nothing of real value like his— It was then that he saw his open tackle box on the other side of the boat. Cliff went stark still. He'd given both girls specific instructions to stay out of his gear. His swift anger could not be contained.

"Who got into my stuff?" he demanded, and knelt down to examine his box. His worst fears were quickly realized. "My lucky lure is missing. Who took my lucky lure?"

"Joan, Katie, did either of you get into Cliff's box?" Already Diana feared the answer. Cliff looked as though he'd like to strangle both girls for so much as touching his equipment.

"Where is my lucky lure?" Cliff repeated, his face hard and cold.

"You…you just cut it off." Katie's head dropped so low Diana could see her crown.

For a minute it looked as though Cliff would jump overboard in an effort to retrieve his silver lure from the murky green waters.

"That was my lucky lure," Cliff repeated, as if in a daze. "I caught a forty-pound rock cod with that silver baby."

"Katie," Diana coaxed, "why did you get into Cliff's equipment when he asked you not to?"

Cliff slammed the lid to his tackle box closed, and the sound reverberated around the inside of the sailboat like a cannon shot. He stood and turned his back to the three women. Diana and her girls couldn't appreciate something like a special lure. To them it was just a five-dollar piece of silver. To him it was his "sure bet." The success of an entire fishing expedition depended on whether he had that silver lure. He might as well hang up his fishing pole for good without it. A woman couldn't be expected to appreciate how much it meant. Burying his hands inside his pants pockets, Cliff muttered something vile under his breath and decided there wasn't anything he could do about it now. The lure was gone.

"Mom, I just heard Cliff swear," Joan whispered.

"Cliff, I'm sorry." Diana felt obliged to say something, although she realized it wasn't nearly enough. She felt terrible. With one look at the way the hot color had circled his ears, she knew how truly angry he was.

"It's my fault," Katie blubbered, hiding her face against her mother's stomach. "Joan caught a fish and I wanted one, too, and I thought Cliff's pretty lure would help."

"You'll replace the lure out of your allowance money," Diana said sternly.

Tears welled up in the small, dark eyes as she nodded, eager to do anything to appease Cliff.

With slow, deliberate action, Cliff returned to the helm and sat down heavily. His brooding gaze avoided Diana and the girls. "Don't worry about it," he said as calmly as possible.

"I'm sorry, Cliff," Katie whispered in a small, broken voice.

He forced his gaze to the youngster. "Don't give it a second thought," he said almost flippantly.

"I'll buy you a new silver lure just as pretty."

"I said, don't worry about it."

If possible, Katie's brown eyes grew more round. Tears rolled down her pale cheeks.

"How about something to eat?" Diana interjected, rubbing her palms together, hoping to generate interest in the packed lunch.

"We're not hungry," Joan answered for both her and her sister.

"Cliff?"

"No, thanks."

"I guess I'm the only one." She got out a sandwich and even managed to choke down a couple of bites.

Cliff's gaze drifted to Diana, who was valiantly pretending nothing was wrong. If she didn't watch it, she was likely to gag on that sandwich. Joan and Katie were huddled together, staring at him like orphans through a rich family's living room window on Christmas Eve. Joan had her arm draped over her sister's shoulders, while Katie looked thoroughly miserable. Finally Cliff couldn't stand it anymore.

"How come she loses my lure and I'm the one feeling guilty?" If there'd been a place to stalk off to, he would have done it. As it was, he was stuck on the boat with all three of them, and he wasn't in the mood for company or conversation.

"I think it's time to head back to the marina," Diana murmured, and sat beside her daughters.

Cliff couldn't have agreed with her more. He mumbled some reply and quickly tacked across the wind, heading in the direction of Des Moines Marina. Every now and then, his gaze reverted to Diana and her daughters. The three sat in the same dejected pose, shoulders hunched forward, eyes lowered to the deck, hands planted primly on their knees. The sight of them only made Cliff feel worse. All right, he'd lost his temper, but only a little. His conscience ate at him. So he shouldn't have yelled, and Joan was right, he had sworn. He'd overreacted. Talk about the wrath of Khan! But for crying out loud, Katie had gotten into his equipment, when he'd given specific instructions for her to stay out.

Diana longed to say or do something to alleviate this terrible tension. Cliff had every reason to be upset. She was angry with Katie, too, but the eight-year-old was truly sorry, and other than replacing the lure, which Katie had already promised, there was nothing more the little girl could do.

"Cliff…"

"Diana…"

They spoke simultaneously.

"You first," Cliff said, and gestured toward her, unable to tolerate the silence any longer.

"I want you to know how sorry I am." When Cliff opened his mouth, she knew before he spoke what he planned to say, and it irritated her more than an angry argument. Squaring her shoulders, she gritted her teeth and waved her index finger at him. "Please don't tell me not to worry about it."

"Let's forget it, okay?" His smile was only a little stiff. He didn't want this unfortunate incident to ruin a promising relationship. When it came to dealing with women, he did fine—more than fine. It was Joan and Katie who had placed him out of his element.

"It's obvious you're not going to forget it."

"It's just that it was a special lure," Cliff said, although that certainly didn't excuse his anger.

Katie placed her hands over her face and burst into sobs.

If Cliff had been feeling guilty before, it was nothing compared to the regret that shot through him at Katie's teary tirade. He'd lost his favorite lure; *he* felt guilty, and she was crying. He didn't understand any of this, but the one thing he did know was that he couldn't bear to see the youngster so miserable. Without forethought, he left the helm and went over to Katie. He picked her up and hugged her against his chest before turning to steer the sloop with Katie cradled in his lap. "It's all right, sweetheart," he whispered, wrapping his arms around her.

"But…I…lost…your…lucky lure," she bellowed.

"It was just an ordinary lure. You can buy me another one just like it, and then that one will be my luckiest lure ever."

"I'm…so-o-o sorry." She kept her face hidden in his shoulder.

"I know."

"I'll never ever get into your fishing box again. I promise."

She raised her head, and Cliff wiped a tear from the corner of her eye. The surge of tenderness that overtook him came as a surprise. He'd been angry, but he was over that. There were more important things in life than a silly lure, and he'd just learned that an eight-year-old's smile was one of them.

"We've both learned a valuable lesson, haven't we?"

Katie responded with a quick nod. "Can I still be your friend?"

"You bet."

Her returning grin was wide.

"You want to learn how to steer the sailboat?"

She couldn't agree fast enough. "Can I?"

"Sure."

Diana felt the burden of guilt lift from her shoulders. She enjoyed Cliff's company and liked the way he'd included the girls in their dates. He'd gone out of his way to be good to her, and she would have hated to see everything ruined over a lost lure. He had a right to be upset—she was mad herself—but anger and regret weren't going to replace his "silver baby."

Diana watched as Cliff patiently showed Katie the importance of heading the sailboat into the wind. The eight-year-old listened patiently while Cliff explained the various maneuvers. He looked up once, and their eyes happened to meet. Cliff smiled, and Diana thought she'd never seen anything more dazzling. From now on she wasn't listening to anything Shirley Holiday had to say. She knew everything she needed to know about Cliff Howard.

Remembering how good Cliff had been with Katie after she'd lost his lure made the days that followed the sailing trip pass quickly as she anticipated seeing him again. They'd left the marina, had dined on Kentucky Fried Chicken, Katie's favorite, and had headed back to Diana's house. Cliff had discreetly kissed her goodbye, invited her to dinner and promised to phone.

Joan sauntered into the kitchen, paused and glanced

at the two chicken TV dinners sitting on top of the kitchen counter. "Is Cliff taking you to dinner?"

"Good guess."

Joan wrinkled up her nose. "I hate to tell you this, but Katie's not going to eat chicken unless it's from the Colonel."

Diana opened the microwave and placed the frozen meals inside. "She'll live."

"A starving woman wouldn't eat that, either."

Diana sighed. "You'll enjoy the chicken, so quit worrying about it."

"Okay."

The phone rang, and Joan leaped to answer it as if there were some concern that Diana would fight her for it.

"Hello."

Diana rolled her eyes as her daughter's voice dipped to a low, seductive note, as though she expected Justin Bieber to phone and ask for her.

"Oh, hi, Cliff. Yeah, Mom's right here." She placed the receiver to her stomach. "Mom, it's Cliff."

Diana wiped her hands dry on a kitchen towel and reached for the phone. "Hello."

"Hi."

The sound of his voice did wondrous things to her pulse. She wouldn't need an aerobics class if she talked to Cliff Howard regularly. "The kids' dinner is in the microwave, and the girls are going over to Shirley's afterward, so I should be ready within the hour."

"That makes what I have to tell you all the more difficult." He'd been looking forward to this dinner date all week and was frustrated.

"You can't make it?" Diana guessed. She should

have known something like this would happen. Everything had gone too smoothly. The girls were going to Shirley's, she'd found a lovely pink silk dress on sale and her hair looked great, for once. Naturally Cliff would have to cancel!

"I'm sorry," he stated simply, and explained without a lot of detail what had happened. A court date had been changed and he had to prepare an important brief by morning. He wouldn't be able to get away for hours. He hated it, would have done anything to get out of it, but couldn't. Then he waited for the backlash that normally followed when he was forced into breaking a dinner engagement.

"I know you wouldn't cancel if it wasn't something important," Diana said, hiding her disappointment.

"You're not angry?"

His question took Diana aback. "Should I be?"

"I...no."

"I'm not saying I won't miss seeing you." She marveled that she was so willing to admit that. When it came to Cliff, she continued to feel as though she were standing on shifting sand. She was afraid of letting her emotions get out of control, and she didn't want to rely on him for more than an occasional date. And yet every time he asked to see her again, she was as giddy as Joan over the rock group U2.

"I'll make it up to you," Cliff promised.

"There's no reason to do that."

"How about dinner Thursday?"

Diana checked the calendar beside the phone. "The PTA is electing its officers for next year, and since I'm a candidate for secretary, I should at least make a showing."

"How about—"

"Honestly, Cliff, you don't need to make anything up to me. If you're so—"

"Diana," he cut in, "I haven't seen you or the girls in three days. I'm starting to get withdrawal symptoms. I actually found myself looking forward to watching the Disney Channel this week."

Diana laughed.

"If you can't go out with me Thursday, then how about Friday?" Now that he'd gained her trust, he felt more comfortable about having her accept an invitation without having to include her daughters.

"Cliff, listen, I'm already going to be gone three nights this week."

"Three?"

"Yes, I went to a Girl Scout planning meeting on Monday. I had a quick Sunday school staff meeting Tuesday and now the PTA thing on Thursday. I don't mind leaving the girls every now and then, but four nights in one week is too much. If you want the truth, it's probably a good thing you have to cancel tonight. I don't like being gone this much."

Cliff leaned back in his desk chair and chewed on the end of his pencil. After the fishing fiasco, he'd hoped to avoid including the girls in any more of their dates for a while. "Okay," he said reluctantly, "let's do something with the girls on Friday."

"Cliff, no."

"No?"

"Really. Both Joan and Katie have been up late every night this week. Katie's got a cold, and I really don't want to take her out again. Friday night, I planned on ordering pizza and getting them both down early." She wasn't making excuses not to see him, and prayed he understood that. Everything she'd said was the complete truth.

"Saturday night, then?" He wasn't giving up on her, not this easily.

Her breath was released on a nervous sigh. "All right."

Six

The house was still, and Diana paused for a moment to cherish the quiet. After loud protests and an argument with Joan, who seemed to think a fifth grader should be allowed to stay up and watch *MTV*, both girls were in bed. Whether they were asleep or not was an entirely different question. Peace reigned, and that was all that mattered to Diana.

She brewed herself a cup of tea and sat with her feet up, reading. In another two weeks school would be out, and then Joan and Katie would find even more excuses to put off going to bed. If it were up to those two ruffians, Diana knew they'd loiter around until midnight. Only Diana wouldn't let them. In some ways she was eager to spend the summer with the girls, and in other ways she dreaded three long months of total togetherness. Her parents had insisted on having them fly to Wichita and had even paid for their airline tickets. Diana was looking forward to those two weeks as a welcome reprieve. She missed seeing her family and in the past had briefly toyed with the idea of moving back to her hometown. That had been her original intention after Stan had died. Her parents had planned to come and help her with the move, but Diana had hedged, uncertain. Now she was convinced she'd made the right decision to stay in the Seattle area. With the loss of their father, the girls had already experienced enough upheaval in their young lives. A move so soon afterward wouldn't have been good for any of them. Although Diana dearly loved her family, she did better when they weren't hovering close by.

Her wandering thoughts were interrupted by the doorbell. She paused and checked the time. It was only a few minutes past nine, but she rarely received company this late.

Setting aside her book and her tea, she answered the door. "Cliff."

"Hi." His ready smile was filled with charm. "Did you win the election?"

Diana was more than a little surprised to see him. After their telephone conversation a couple of days before, she hadn't known what to think. She stepped aside so he could come in. "Win the election?" she repeated, not following his line of thought.

"Yes, you told me you were up for PTA secretary."

"Oh, yes. I was running unopposed, so there wasn't much chance I'd lose."

"Is that Cliff?" Katie, dressed in her pink flannel nightgown, appeared at the top of the stairs.

"Hi, Katie." Cliff raised his hand to greet the youngster, his smile only a little forced. He preferred to spend time with Diana alone tonight.

"Katie, you're supposed to be asleep."

"Can I give Cliff his lure?"

"Okay." Diana knew it would do little good to argue.

While shopping in a local store the day before, Katie had found a similar fishing lure, and they'd bought it as a replacement for Cliff's. At the time, Diana had wondered if there would be an opportunity to see Cliff again. He had asked to see her on Saturday, but she half expected him to cancel. She wasn't sure where their relationship was headed. He seemed determined to see her again, but she hadn't heard a word from him since their abrupt telephone conversation a few days earlier.

Katie flew down the stairs and raced into the kitchen. "Mom, where'd you put it?"

"In the junk drawer."

As if by magic an exasperated Katie reappeared, hands on her hips. "Mom," she said with a meaningful sigh, "all the drawers are filled with junk."

Rather than answer, Diana stepped into the kitchen and retrieved the fishing lure for her daughter.

Katie eagerly ripped it from Diana's fingers and hurried back to Cliff, who was sitting in the living room. "Here's another lucky lure," she said, her eyes as round as grapefruits. "I'm real sorry I lost yours."

Cliff's gaze sought Diana's as he accepted the lure. "I told you not to fret over it."

"But you got real angry, and I felt bad because I wasn't supposed to get into your fishing gear and I did. Mom's making me pay for it out of my allowance."

"I'd rather you didn't." Cliff directed the comment to Diana.

Before Diana could respond, Katie broke in. "But I have to!" she declared earnestly. "Otherwise I won't learn a lesson—at least that's what Mom said."

"Moms knows what's best," Cliff managed to murmur, looking uncomfortable.

Katie brightened. "Besides, I thought that if I bought you another lucky lure, then you'd take Joan and me out in your sailboat again. Next time I promise I won't get into your fishing box." As though to emphasize her point, she spit on the tips of her fingers and dutifully crossed her heart.

Before Cliff realized Katie's intention, the little girl hurled her arms around his neck and gave him a wet kiss on the cheek.

Diana smiled at his shocked look. "Tell Cliff goodnight, honey."

Without argument, Katie paused long enough to give her mother another hug and kiss, then dutifully traipsed back upstairs.

"It seems women have a way of throwing themselves into your arms," Diana teased once Katie had left the room. She hoped to lighten the mood. She didn't know why Cliff had come, especially when he looked as though he'd rather be anyplace else in the world than with her.

"I sincerely hope the trait runs in this family," Cliff teased back. He held out his arms to her, then complained with a low groan when Diana chose to ignore his offer.

Cliff wasn't exactly sure what was going on with him. After their last adventure on the sailboat, he'd decided that although he enjoyed Joan and Katie, he preferred to keep the kids out of the dating picture. It was Diana who interested him. In fact, he couldn't stop thinking about her.

She wasn't as beautiful as other women he'd seen. Her hips were a tad too wide, but where physical attributes had seemed important in the past, they didn't seem to matter with her.

When it came to women, Cliff wasn't being conceited when he admitted he could pick and choose. Yet the one woman who filled his thoughts was a young widow with two preteens. He'd been so astonished at the desire he felt for Diana that he'd phoned his brother in California and told him about her.

Rich had listened, chuckled knowingly and laughed outright when Cliff mentioned that Diana was a widow with two daughters. Then he'd made some derogatory comment about it being time for Cliff to find a real woman. Cliff had been vaguely disappointed in the conversation. Subconsciously he'd wanted his brother to tell him to wise up and stay away from a woman with children. Cliff had almost *wanted* Rich to tell him to avoid Diana and insist that a relationship with her would be nothing but trouble. Maybe that was what Cliff wanted to hear, but it wasn't what he felt.

Even if Rich had advised him to break things off with her, he doubted that he would have been able to. She was in his blood now, increasing the potency of his attraction each time they were together. That evening as he'd sat in his office, he hadn't been able to get his mind off Diana. Twice he'd picked up the phone to call her. Twice he'd decided against it. He didn't like what was happening to him. No one else seemed to notice that he was sinking fast. And there wasn't a life preserver in sight.

Sitting in the overstuffed chair beside Cliff, Diana took a sip of her tea and attempted to put some order to her thoughts. She was happy to see Cliff. More than happy. But a little apprehensive, too.

"How was your day?" she asked finally when he didn't seem inclined to wade into easy conversation.

"Busy. How about yours?"

"I went in for a job interview with the school district this morning." Cliff couldn't possibly understand what courage that had taken. She hadn't worked outside the home since Joan had been born, and had no real credentials. "I'm hoping they'll hire me as a teacher's aide. That way I'll have the same hours as the girls."

"Do you think you'll get the job?"

Diana answered with a soft shrug. "I don't know. The principal from Joan and Katie's school gave me a recommendation, since I've done a substantial amount of volunteer work there. The last school levy passed and the district's been given the go-ahead to hire ten teacher's aides. I have no idea how many applications they took or how many they interviewed."

"If that doesn't pan out, I'm sure I could find a part-time position for you in my law firm." The minute Cliff made the offer, he regretted it. Having Diana in his office two or three times a week could end up being a source of personal conflict.

"Thank you, Cliff, but, no."

"No?" This woman continued to astonish him. He'd expected her to jump at the offer. "Why not?"

"It's downtown, and I'd prefer to be as close to the girls as I can in case they get sick and need to come home…." That was the first plausible excuse to surface. Although it was the truth, Diana didn't have a great deal of choice when it came to finding employment.

She'd turned down his offer because she preferred not to work in the same place as Cliff.

"I can understand that," he said, relieved and irritated at the same time. Diana had him so twisted up in knots he couldn't judge his own emotions anymore. He shouldn't have come tonight, he knew that, but staying away had been impossible.

"I'm pleased you stopped by," Diana said next.

He was happy she was pleased, because he was more confused than ever. He had thought that if he stopped off and they talked, then maybe he'd know what was happening to him. Wrong. One look at Diana and all he wanted to do was make love to her.

"I want you to know I feel bad about our conversation the other day." Diana felt as though she were sailing into uncharted waters, her destination unknown. Their telephone conversation had gone poorly, and she wasn't sure whose fault it was. Cliff had kept insisting on seeing her again, and she had kept refusing, finally giving in. More than that, it seemed that Cliff had been expecting her to be angry because he'd had to cancel their dinner date. She hadn't been. Then Cliff had sounded as though he'd wanted to start an argument and was confused when she wouldn't be drawn into a verbal battle.

"You feel bad because I canceled dinner?" Cliff asked.

"No, because I had to turn down your offer for another date."

Cliff felt more than a little chagrined. He'd admit it—her refusal had irked him. For all his suave sophistication, he wasn't accustomed to having a woman turn him down. It had taken a fair amount of soul-searching to decide he wanted to see Diana again—without Joan and Katie. Her rejection, no matter how good her reasons, had been a blow to his considerable pride.

"You turned me down for dinner *and* Friday night," he reminded her.

"I thought I explained…"

"I know."

Diana lowered her gaze to her mug of tea, which she was gripping tightly with both hands. "You don't know how hard that was."

"Then why did you?"

"For the very reasons I told you."

His brow puckered into a deep frown.

"I like you, Cliff. Probably more than I should." She didn't know what weapon she was handing him by admitting her feelings, but she was too old for silly games, too wise to get tangled up in a web of emotion and too intelligent not to look at him with her eyes wide open. They weren't right for each other, but that hadn't seemed to matter. They'd weathered their relationship much better than she had ever imagined they would. If they were going to continue to see each other, then she preferred that they be honest about their feelings. Honest, and up-front.

"I like you, too, Diana," he admitted softly, his eyes holding her all too effectively. "I'm not sure I'm ready for what's developing between us, but I want it. I want you."

The muscles in her stomach constricted with his words. She'd asked for his honesty, and now she was forced to deal with her own reactions to it. Cliff frightened her because he made her feel again; he'd reawakened the deep womanly part of her that craved touch.

Intuitively she'd known the first time he'd kissed her how potent his caress would be. In the years since Stan had died, she'd effectively cast the hunger for love and desire from her life.

Until Cliff.

Knowing this made each minute they spent together all the more exciting. It made each date all the more dangerous.

Diana tore her gaze from his. "What are we going to do about it?"

"I don't know."

"I...don't, either."

Cliff drew in a hard breath and held out his arms to her. "Come here, Diana."

Of its own volition, her hand set the tea mug aside. She stood and walked over to Cliff and offered no resistance when he pulled her down and cradled her in his lap. Her hands rested against his shoulders as his eyes gently caressed her face. It was almost as if he were asking her to object.

She couldn't. She wouldn't. A long, uninterrupted moment passed before Cliff lifted her hair from her shoulder and tenderly kissed the side of her neck. His lips felt cool against her skin, and she turned her head to grant him the freedom to kiss her where he willed.

At the sound of her soft gasp, his tongue made moist forays below her ear. Cliff loved the scent of her. Other women relied on expensive perfumes, and yet they couldn't compare to the fresh sunshine smell that was Diana's alone.

An all-too-warm, tingling sensation raced through Diana. Against her will, she closed her eyes. Her fingers gripped his shirt collar as his lips slowly grazed a trail across the underside of her chin.

"Cliff…" she moaned. "Please…"

"Please what?"

Her throat constricted, and she felt as if she were going to cry again. When she spoke, the words came out sounding like someone trying to speak while trapped underwater. "I want you to kiss…me."

His hands covered each side of her face and directed her mouth to his. Their lips slid across each other's with sweet familiarity. Diana was eager, so eager, but the urgency was gone, leaving in its wake a pure electric, soul-stirring sensation.

She clung to him even as the tears burned their way down her face. When he paused, as though unsure, she kissed him back, her mouth parted and pliant over his. She'd come this far and she refused to let him back away from her now.

Diana's kiss was all the encouragement Cliff needed. His arms tightened around her, and he gently rocked her, unable to get close enough. He felt the moisture on her face and tasted the salt of her tears. The reason for their being there humbled him. She was opening up to him as she never had before, trusting him, granting him custody of her wounded heart.

Diana moaned as his hands roamed over her back, bringing her as close as it was humanly possible.

At her soft cry tenderness engulfed him like a tidal wave. He wanted Diana in that moment more than he'd ever craved anything in his life. The passion she aroused in him was almost more than he could bear. He tried to tell her what she did to him by kissing her again and again, but it wasn't enough. Nothing seemed to satisfy the building fire within him. "Diana," he moaned, "I'm afraid if we continued like this we're going to end up making love in this chair."

The words made no sense to Diana. Cliff had transported her from limbo into heaven in a matter of moments. She had no desire to leave her newly discovered paradise. Her only response was a strangled, nonsensical plea for him not to stop.

"Upstairs," he said a minute later. "I want to make love to you in a bed."

Somehow the words made it through the thick haze of desire that had clouded her brain. He wanted to make love to her in a bed! Upstairs. Joan and Katie—her daughters—were upstairs.

"No," she managed.

"No?" Cliff echoed, shocked.

"The...girls."

"So? Aren't they asleep?"

"I...don't know. It doesn't matter."

"It matters to me," he argued. "I need you, Diana."

She didn't need to guess how much he wanted her— she was feeling the same urgency. It had been slowly building in her for three long years.

"I want you," he reiterated forcefully. Pressing his hands over her ears, he kissed her long and hard so she'd know he wasn't just muttering the words.

Diana drove her fingers into his hair and slanted her mouth over his in eager response. "I need you, too," she whispered against his lips. "Right now, I could almost die I want you so much."

"Good."

"But, Cliff, I can't. I..."

"Come on, honey, don't argue with me. We're mature adults—we both know what we want—so what's stopping you?"

"Cliff, you don't understand."

He closed his eyes and groaned. "Somehow I knew that you were going to say that."

"Joan and Katie are up there."

"They're asleep, for heaven's sake." He could argue with her if she were being reasonable, but he was defenseless against such logic. "They won't even know."

"I'll know."

His hold on her torso tightened as he buried his face in the smooth silk of her skin. He drew in a ragged breath as the battle between his conscience and his raw need raged within him. Without too much trouble, he knew he could change her mind. She wanted him nearly as much as he craved her, and all it would take to convince her of that was a few more uninterrupted minutes. He released an anguished sigh when his conscience won. There would be another chance, another place, and the next time it would be right.

"Are you angry?" Diana asked.

He thought about it a moment, then shook his head. "No."

"I feel like I've been a terrible tease."

"Then tease me anytime you want," he managed on the tail-end of a sigh. "Now," he said, easing her off his lap, "walk me to the door and kiss me good-night while I still have the power to leave you."

She rose unsteadily. The carpet under her feet seemed to buckle and sway beneath her.

Cliff held out his hand to steady her. "Are you okay?"

"I don't know," she admitted with a half smile. She

didn't know if she'd ever be the same again. Every part of her was throbbing with need, and yet all she could taste was frustration and regret.

He wrapped his arm around her and let her walk him to the front door. Their kiss was ardent, but brief. His arms continued to hold her. "Saturday night," he reminded her. "I'll pick you up at six-thirty."

It was all Diana could do to nod.

She remained leaning against the door frame long after Cliff had left. A strange chill rattled her as she realized how close she had come to walking up the stairs and making love with Cliff. It was then that she realized there was no real commitment between them, not even whispered words of love, only the pure physical response of a lonely widow to an exceptionally handsome man. Diana gripped her stomach as a wave of nausea passed over her. She felt ill and frightened.

Somehow she made it up the stairs and into bed, but that didn't guarantee sleep. Over and over again she thought about what had nearly happened with Cliff. No doubt women regularly fell into bed with him. Diana couldn't blame them; he would be a wonderful lover. Gentle and considerate. Even now, hours after he'd left, her body tingled from the memory of his touch.

She wanted him, but the situation was impossible. Her life was filled with responsibilities now. She wasn't carefree and single—she was a mother.

After twenty more minutes of tossing and turning, Diana glanced at the clock. Life wasn't simple for her anymore. Not with two daughters who watched her every move. When she'd been dating Stan, there'd been no real thought to the future. It had all been so easy.

They were in love, so they got married. Diana was burdened with obligations now on all sides. Ones she willingly accepted.

For two days, she agonized over what she was going to say to Cliff. She wanted to set the record straight, explain that what had nearly happened wasn't right for her. She couldn't deny that she desired him; he'd see through that fast enough.

When Cliff arrived promptly at six-thirty to pick her up on Saturday night, she kissed the girls goodbye and stiffly followed Cliff to his car. Although he'd told her they were going to dinner, he hadn't said where.

"You look as jumpy as a pogo stick," he said once they were seated inside his Lamborghini. He was dying to kiss her. Already he ached with the need to hold her in his arms and taste her kisses.

"I...we need to talk."

Cliff placed the key in the ignition, then leaned over to gently brush his mouth over hers. "Can't it wait until dinner?"

Diana shook her head. "I don't think so. It's about what nearly happened the other night."

"Somehow I thought you'd bring that up." His hands tightened around the steering wheel. He'd gone too fast for her, but she'd amazed him with how ready and eager she was. It hadn't been right for them Thursday, but it would be tonight—he'd make certain of that.

"I'm not ready for...it." Her face flushed with embarrassment. She'd never talked to a man this way, not even with Stan.

"Lovemaking." If she wouldn't say the word, he would. He didn't know what her problem was. The fact that she would deny what was happening between them surprised him, especially after all her talk about honesty. Their making love was inevitable. He'd known it almost from the first.

He wanted her desperately. Every time he closed his eyes, he pictured her in his bed, satin sheets wrapped around her, with her arms stretched toward him, inviting him to join her. She wouldn't need to ask him twice. These past two days without her had been hell. He wanted her so much that he felt naked and vulnerable without her, and now he was determined to have her. It hadn't felt right to walk away from her the other night. The memory of her kisses had returned to haunt him.

"All right, lovemaking," Diana echoed, her voice firm but low. "After the other night, I'm afraid I've given you the wrong impression."

Cliff reached over and squeezed her fingers. "Don't worry, honey, we're not going to do anything you don't want."

Diana should have felt better with his reassurance, but she didn't. She'd dreaded this evening from the moment he'd left her, and yet the hours hadn't gone by fast enough until she'd seen him again. She thought she knew what she wanted, but one look at Cliff and she was unsure of everything.

"You didn't say where we were going for dinner," she said, making conversation.

He smiled, and his face lit up with boyish charm. "It's a surprise."

He drove toward Des Moines and Diana was certain he was taking her to the fancy seafood restaurant the marina was famous for, but he drove past it and instead headed up the back roads to the cliff above the water.

"I didn't know there was a restaurant up this way," she confessed.

"There isn't," he told her with a wide grin. "We're going to my condo. I've been cooking all day."

"Your place," Diana echoed, and the words seemed to bounce around the car like a ricocheting bullet. Her heart slammed against her breast with dread.

"I'm a fabulous chef…wait and see."

Her responding smile was weak and filled with doubt.

Cliff parked his car in the garage and came around to help her out. He tucked his arm protectively around her waist as she climbed out of his car, then paused to gently kiss the side of her neck. His tender touch went a long way toward chasing away Diana's fears, and she smiled up at him.

Cliff was eager to show her his home and proudly led her into his condominium. The first thing Diana noticed was the flickering flames of the fireplace. The table was set for two, with candles ready to be lighted. The room was dark, and music played softly from the expensive speakers.

As she surveyed the room, a chill shimmied up her spine. "You haven't heard a word I've said, have you?"

Seven

"Of course I've been listening," Cliff insisted. He didn't know what was bothering Diana, but she'd been acting jumpy from the minute he'd picked her up.

"I told you, I'm not ready."

"For dinner?" He couldn't understand why she was so riled up all of a sudden. He'd been looking forward to this evening for days. The crab was cracked for their appetizers, hollandaise sauce simmered on top of the stove, ready to be poured over fresh broccoli. The thick T-bone steaks were in the refrigerator, just waiting to be charcoal grilled. He wanted everything perfect for tonight, for Diana. The wine was chilled—he'd seen to it all.

"In case you weren't aware of it," Diana cried, pointing a finger at her chest, "I live in this body!"

"What in the world are you talking about?"

"This." She gestured wildly with her arm toward the open space of his living room. "Tell me, Cliff, exactly what have you planned for tonight?" She flopped down on his white leather couch, crossed her legs and glared at him with wide, accusing eyes.

"A leisurely candlelight dinner. Is that a crime, or did I miss something in law school?"

Diana ignored his sarcasm. "And that's all? What about after dinner?"

He scooted the ottoman in front of the couch, sat down and leaned forward so his eyes were level with hers. "I thought we'd share a couple of glasses of wine in front of the fireplace."

"And sample a few stolen kisses, as well?" she coaxed.

Cliff grinned, relaxing. "Yes."

The lilting strains of the music from a hundred violins drifted through the room. She noticed the way the lights in the hallway that led to the master bedroom had been dimmed invitingly. The door to his room was cracked open, a ribbon of muted light beckoning to her. The romance in the condominium was so thick, Diana could hardly see the romancer.

"But you're planning on something else happening, aren't you?" she asked, her eyes effectively holding his.

Cliff opened his mouth to deny it, then quickly decided against trying to bluff his way out of the obvious. He didn't have any choice but to be honest with Diana. Before he could say anything, she cut him off.

"Don't lie to me, Cliff Howard," she declared, folding her arms defiantly around her torso. "Do you think I'm stupid? Do you honestly believe I'm so naive to not know that you've planned the big seduction scene?"

"All right. All right." He eased her arms loose and reached for her stiff fingers, holding them between his hands. "Maybe I'm going off the deep end here, but after the other night, I thought maybe..."

"Exactly what did you think?"

"That you and I had something special going for us. Something very special."

"You want to make love to me?"

"You're right I do," he murmured, and raised her fingertips to his lips. His gaze didn't leave hers, as though seeking confirmation. "And you want me, too, so don't try to deny it."

"I have no intention of doing so. You're right on target...things could easily have gotten out of hand the other night."

Cliff was beginning to feel more confident now. He realized that some women required more assurances. "Then you can understand—in light of Thursday night—why I'm thinking what I'm thinking." He raised his eyebrows suggestively, seeking a way to alter the sober tone of this conversation. Diana was becoming far too defensive over something that was inevitable. Wanting her in his bed shouldn't be considered a felony. Surely she realized that.

Diana felt incredibly guilty. She couldn't be angry with Cliff when she'd given him every reason to believe she was willing to sleep with him. Not until he'd left and her head had cleared did she realized how wrong a physical relationship with Cliff was for her. Unfortunately Cliff had no way of knowing about her sudden change of heart. The anger rushed out of her as quickly as it had come. She freed one hand from his grip and gently traced the underside of his well-defined jaw. She wasn't sure what she'd gotten herself into, but she wanted to make it right for them both.

Cliff captured her hand and held it against his cheek, needing her more and more by the minute. If she didn't stop looking at him with those incredibly lovely brown eyes, he couldn't offer any guarantee he'd be able to serve the meal he'd spent so much time preparing.

"Cliff, I feel bad about all this, but I'm simply not ready."

He stared at her for a full moment, weighing his options. She was frightened, he could see that, and he didn't blame her for acting like a nervous virgin. It had been a long time since a man had properly loved her. Thursday night she'd been as hot as a firecracker. It had hurt Cliff to leave her, both physically and mentally. She had to know him well enough to realize that he wasn't going to rush her into something she didn't want. First he had to make sure everything was right for her.

"Honey," he whispered, and leaned forward to sample her sweet lips. Their mouths clung, and when he sat back down, he closed his eyes at the bolt of passion that surged through him. "Trust me, you're ready."

Diana blinked back the dismay. Nothing she'd said had sunk into Cliff's thick skull. She tugged her hands free and clenched them together. "Answer me this, Cliff. Do you love me?"

Groaning inwardly, Cliff forced a smile. Over the years he'd come to almost hate that word. Women hurled it at him continually, as if it were a required license for something they wanted as much as he did. "I believe there's magic between us."

Diana's returning grin was infinitely sad. "Oh, Cliff, it sounds as if you've used that phrase a hundred times. I expected you to be more original than that."

She shamed him, because he *had* used that line before—not as often as she said, but enough to warrant a guilty conscience. Her look told him how much she disapproved of glib, well-worn words. To hear her tell it, he was another Hugh Hefner. Well, he had news for her—she wasn't exactly Mother Teresa. He didn't know how she could deny the very real and strong sexual tension between them. Diana was warm and loving, and confused. All he wanted to do was show her how good things could be between them, and Diana was making it sound as though he should be arrested for even thinking about taking her to bed.

She dropped her gaze and sighed. "It would be best if I went home."

Her words were as unexpected as they were unwelcome. "No!"

"No?"

"Diana, we've got something magical here. Let's not ruin it." Cliff was grasping at straws and knew it, but he didn't want her to leave.

"What we've got is a bunch of hormones calling out to one another. There's no commitment, no love!"

"You don't believe that."

"Am I wrong?" she asked with eyes that ripped into his soul. "Are you ready to offer your life to me and the girls?" She knew the answer, even if he didn't. Love preceded marriage, and although he cared for her, he didn't love her.

Commitment was another word Cliff had come to abhor. He jerked his fingers through his hair, almost afraid to speak for fear of what he'd say. "I can't believe we're having this conversation."

Already she was on her feet, her purse clenched under her arm. "Goodbye, Cliff."

He stood and crossed the room. "Why are we arguing like this, when all I want to do is make love to you?"

Dejected, Diana paused, her hand on the doorknob. "In case you haven't figured it out, that's exactly our problem."

Cliff was growing more impatient by the minute. Impatient and overwhelmingly frustrated. Okay, so she'd read his intentions; he hadn't exactly tried to cover up what he'd planned for the evening. She could be a good sport and play along, at least until after dinner. He wasn't going to force her into anything if she honestly objected. "Is wanting you such a sin?" he asked.

"No," she answered smoothly, "but I need something more than magic." She couldn't explain it any better. If Cliff didn't understand love and commitment, then it was unlikely he'd be able to follow her reasoning. And she had no intention of trying to justify it anyway.

"Come on, Diana, wake up and smell the coffee. Times have changed. Men and women make love every night."

"I know." She had no more arguments. There was nothing more to say. She twisted the knob and pulled.

Cliff's fist hit the door, closing it with a sharp thud. "I don't know what happened between Thursday night and now, but I think you're being entirely unreasonable."

"I don't expect you to understand."

His anger and disappointment were almost more than he could bear. "Please don't leave."

"I can't see any other option."

He gritted his teeth, trying to come up with some way to make her understand. "Diana, listen to me. I'm a sexual person. I haven't been with a woman in a long time. I've got to have you for the pure physical release, I…"

Her stunned look caused him to swallow the rest of what he was saying.

"Goodbye, Cliff," she said, and then jerked open the door and walked out.

Cliff stared at the closed front door for a full minute. He couldn't believe he'd said that to her, as though she and she alone were responsible for easing his sexual appetite. He couldn't have made a bigger mess of this evening had he tried.

Diana didn't know she could walk so fast. Instead of going along the sidewalk, she cut between parked cars and crossed the street. Within a few minutes she was close to the marina. A Metro bus pulled to a stop at the curb, and its heavy doors parted with a whoosh. Without knowing its destination, Diana climbed on board. She had already taken her seat, when she saw Cliff's sports car race past the bus and chase after a taxi. Her eyes followed Cliff and the taxi until they were out of sight.

Diana was able to get a transfer from one bus to another, and an hour later she walked inside her house, exhausted and furious.

"Mom, where were you? What happened?" Joan cried, running to the door to greet her. "Cliff's been calling every ten minutes."

She ignored the question and headed for the refrigerator. For the past half hour, she'd been walking. She was dying of thirst, and her feet hurt like crazy—a lethal combination. Both Joan and Katie seemed to recognize her mood and went out of their way to avoid her.

Diana had been home fifteen minutes, when the phone rang again. Joan sprinted into the kitchen to answer it.

"If it's Cliff, I don't want to talk to him," Diana yelled after her daughter.

Joan reappeared a couple of minutes later. "He just wanted to know that you got home okay."

"What did you tell him?"

"That you were mad as hops."

Diana groaned, sagged against the back of the over-stuffed chair and hugged a pillow to her stomach. That wasn't the half of it. The next time she went racing out of a man's condominium, she'd make sure she carried enough cash to take a cab home. She'd ridden on the bus with two winos and a guy who looked like a candidate for the Hell's Angels.

"Are you mad at Cliff, Mom?" Katie wanted to know, plopping down at her mother's feet.

"Yes."

"But I like Cliff."

"Don't worry, kid, I got all the bases covered." Joan sank onto the carpet beside her sister. "Cliff just phoned. I advised him to wait a couple of days, then send roses. By that time, everything will be forgotten and forgiven."

The pressure Diana applied to the pillow bunched it in half. "Wanna bet?" she challenged.

Shirley poured herself a cup of coffee and sat at the kitchen table beside Diana. "It's been a week."

"I told you I didn't want to hear from him." Diana continued copying the recipe for yet another hamburger casserole that disguised vegetables. She had only a few minutes before the girls would be home from school, then the house would become an open battlefield. Both Joan and Katie had been impossible all week. Without understanding any of what had happened between Cliff and her, her daughters had taken it upon themselves to champion his case. Diana refused to talk about him and, as a last resort, had forbidden either girl to mention his name again.

For the first few days after their argument, Diana had held out hope that things could be settled between her and Cliff, It didn't take long for her to accept that it was better to leave matters as they were. They were in a no-win situation. The bottom line was that they'd only end up hurting each other. Despite everything, Diana was pleased to have known Cliff Howard. She'd been living her life in a cooler; she'd grieved for Stan long enough. It was time to join the land of the living and soak up the sunshine of a healthy relationship again. Dating Cliff had shown her the way out of the chill, and she would always be grateful to him for that. In the past three years, she'd dated only occasionally. Cliff had helped her to see that she was ready to meet someone, pick up the pieces of her shattered life and move on.

"But I feel bad," Shirley continued, holding the coffee mug with both hands. "George told me I had the wrong impression of Cliff—he isn't exactly the playboy I led you to believe."

"Honestly, Shirley, I'd think you'd be happy. I've finally agreed to a dinner date with Owen Freeman." For two years her neighbor had been after Diana to at least meet this distant relation of hers. Diana had used every excuse in the book to get out of it. She simply hadn't been interested in being introduced to Shirley's third cousin, no matter how successful he was. Cliff had changed that, and Diana would have thought her neighbor would appreciate this shift in attitude.

"I know I should be thrilled you're willing to meet Owen, but I'm not." Shirley ran the tip of her index finger around the rim of her mug. She hesitated, as though she'd noticed the flower vase in the center of the table for the first time. It came from a florist. "Who sent the flowers?"

"Cliff."

"Cliff Howard?"

Diana nodded, intent on copying the recipe. He'd taken Joan's advice and sent the bouquet of red roses with a quick note of apology scribbled across the card. In other words, the next move was up to her. It had taken Diana several days of soul-searching to decide not to contact him. The decision hadn't been an easy one, but it was the right one.

"But if he sent you flowers, then he must be willing to patch things up."

"Maybe." Diana dropped the subject there.

Her neighbor paused. "The least you could do is tell me what he did that was so terrible. If you can't talk to me, then who can you talk to?"

Diana's fingers tightened around the pencil. Shirley wasn't asking her anything Joan and Katie hadn't drilled her about a dozen times. Both girls had been out of joint from the minute Diana informed them she wouldn't be seeing Cliff again. Katie had argued the loudest, claiming she wanted to go on his sailboat one more time. Joan had ardently insisted she liked Cliff better than anyone, and had gone into a three-day pout when Diana wouldn't change her mind. As patiently as she could, Diana explained to both girls that there would be other men they would like just as well as Cliff.

"What I want to know," Diana said, reaching for her own coffee as she studied her friend, "is why you've changed your tune all of a sudden. When I first started going out with Cliff, you were full of dire warnings. And now that I've decided not to see him again, you're keen for me to patch things up with him."

"You're miserable."

"I'm not," Diana shot back, then realized what Shirley said was true. She missed Cliff, missed the expectancy that he'd brought back into her life, the eagerness to greet each day as a new experience. She missed the little things—the way his hand reached for hers, lacing her fingers with his. She missed the way his eyes sought her out when the girls were jumping up and down at his feet, wanting something from him. She hadn't realized how lonely she was until Cliff had come into her life, and now the emptiness felt like a huge, empty vacuum that needed to be filled.

"It's best this way," Diana said after a thoughtful moment.

Shirley's hand patted hers. "Okay," she said reluctantly, "if you say so."

"I do."

Neither spoke for a long time. Finally Shirley ventured into conversation. "When are you having dinner with Owen?"

"Tomorrow," Diana answered. Now all she had to do was pump some enthusiasm into meeting Shirley's third cousin, who taught English literature at the local community college.

* * *

The following evening, Diana tried to convince herself what a good time she was going to have. She showered and dressed, while Joan followed her around the bedroom, choosing her outfit for her.

"How come you're wearing your pearl earrings?" Joan demanded. "You didn't wear them for..." She started to say Cliff's name, then hurriedly corrected herself since he was a forbidden subject. "You know who—and now you're putting them on for some guy you haven't even met."

Diana's answering smile was weak at best. She needed the boost in confidence, but explaining that to her daughter would be difficult.

When her mother didn't answer, Joan positioned herself in front of Diana's bedroom window that looked down onto the street below. "A car just pulled into the driveway."

"That will be Mr. Freeman. Joan, please, be on your best behavior."

"Oh, no."

"What's wrong?"

"He just got out of the car—he's wearing plaid pants."

Diana reached for her perfume, giving her neck and wrists a liberal spray, and rolled her eyes toward the ceiling. "It's not right to judge someone by the clothes he wears."

"Mom, he's a nerd to the tenth power." Joan sagged onto the end of the mattress and buried her face in her hands. "If you end up marrying this guy, I'll never forgive you."

"Joan, honestly!"

"Mom, Mr. Freeman is here," Katie screamed from the foot of the stairs after peeking out the living room window. She raced up to meet her mother, who was coming out of the bedroom. "Mom," she whispered breathlessly. "He's a geek. A major geek!"

Feigning a smile, Diana placed her hand on the banister and slowly walked down the stairs to answer the doorbell.

As far as looks went, the blonde won over Diana, hands down, Cliff decided. He smiled at the sleek beauty who clung to his arm, and tried to look as though he were enjoying himself. He wasn't. In fact, he'd been miserable from the minute Diana had walked out of his condominium. At first he'd been furious with her. For a solid hour he'd driven around, searching for her, desperate to locate her. Only heaven knew where she'd run off to—it was as though aliens had absconded with her.

Twice he'd broken down and phoned her house, nearly frantic with worry. Joan had assured him, on the third call, that her mother was home and safe. It was then that Cliff had decided that whatever was between Diana and him was over. She was a crazy woman. One minute she was melting in his arms, and the next she was as stiff as cement, hissing accusations at him.

Two days later, after he'd had a chance to cool down, Cliff changed his mind. He'd behaved like a Neanderthal. The remark he'd made about being a sexual person returned to haunt him. It was no wonder she was angry, but she'd played a part in their little misunderstanding, leading him on, letting him think there was a green light in her eyes where it was actually a flashing red one. He didn't possess ESP—how was he supposed to read her mind? Okay, he'd make the first move toward a reconciliation, he decided, and then leave the rest up to her. On his instructions, his secretary ordered the roses with an appropriate message. Cliff had sat back and waited.

When he hadn't heard from Diana by the end of the week, he was stunned. Then shocked. Then angry. All right, he'd play her game—he was a patient man. In time she'd come around, and when she did, he'd play it cool. If anyone was sitting home nights, alone and frustrated, it wouldn't be him. He'd make sure of that.

Hence Marianne—the blonde.

"Who are you going out with tonight?" Joan asked her mother as she sat at the kitchen table and glued on a false thumbnail.

"Not Mr. Freeman again," Katie groaned, and reached for an apple.

"He's a nice man."

"Mom, if you wanted nice, I could set you up with Mr. Rogers or Captain Kangaroo."

Diana hated to admit how right Joan was. Owen Freeman excited her as much as dirty laundry. He'd brought her candy, escorted her to a classical music concert and treated her with kindness and respect. He'd even supplied her with letters from his colleagues attesting to his character, just in case she was worried about being alone with him. Maybe Cliff wasn't so out of line to have mentioned magic. She felt it with him, but she certainly didn't with Owen Freeman. There were so many frogs out there and so few princes.

"Have you read through his references yet?" Joan asked.

"Honey, that was a very nice gesture on Mr. Freeman's part."

"He's a geek."

"Katie, I want you to stop calling him that."

Her younger daughter shrugged.

Joan spread contact cement across the top of the nail on her little finger. A pile of fake fingernails rested in front of her. "It's your life, Mom. You know how Katie and I feel about Mrs. Holiday's cousin, but you do what you want."

"Well, don't worry about it—you're not having dinner with him. I am."

Joan rolled her eyes toward the ceiling. "Lucky you."

Owen arrived a half hour later. He brought Joan and Katie a small stuffed animal each and a small bouquet of flowers for Diana. He really was an exceptionally nice man, but, as Joan had said, so were Mr. Rogers and Captain Kangaroo.

When Owen headed toward Des Moines and the restaurant at the marina, Diana tensed. Of all the places in the south end to eat, he had to choose this one.

"I understand the food here is excellent," Owen said once they were seated.

"I've heard that, as well," Diana said, looking over the top of her menu. Her heart was pumping double its normal rate. She was being silly. There was absolutely no reason to believe she would run into Cliff Howard simply because this restaurant was close to his condominium. No sane reason at all.

Owen ordered a bottle of wine, and Diana nearly

did a swan dive into the first glass. Alcohol would help soothe her jittery nerves, she reasoned. After tonight, Diana decided, she would tell Owen that it simply wasn't going to work. He was such a nice person, and she didn't want to lead him on when there was no reason to believe anything would ever develop between them. Her mind worked up a variety of ways to tell him, then she decided to take the coward's way out and leave a voice mail message after he dropped her off following dinner.

"You're quiet this evening," Owen said softly.

"I'm sorry."

"Are you tired?"

She nodded. "It's been a long week." Diana turned her head and looked out over the rows and rows of watercraft moored in the marina. Without much trouble, she located Cliff's forty-foot sloop.

"Do you sail?" she asked Owen, without taking her eyes from Cliff's boat.

"No, I can't say that I do."

"Fish?"

"No, it never appealed to me."

Diana pulled her gaze away. Owen was forty, balding and incredibly boring. Nice, but boring.

"I did go swimming once in Puget Sound," he said, his voice rising with enthusiasm.

Diana's smile was genuine. No doubt, Owen saw himself as a real daredevil. "I did, too—once, by accident."

"Really?"

She nodded, and the silence returned. Finally she said, "I enjoy picnics."

Owen's forehead puckered into a brooding frown. "I don't get much time for outdoor pursuits."

"I can imagine...with school and everything."

"Bridge is my game."

"Bridge," Diana repeated, amused. Owen Freeman was really quite predictable. "I imagine you're good enough to play in tournaments."

The literature professor positively gleamed. "As a matter of fact, I am. Have you ever played?"

"No," she admitted reluctantly.

The hostess escorted another couple to the table across from their own. Diana didn't pay much attention, but the blonde was stunning.

"I would thoroughly enjoy teaching you," Owen continued. "Why, we could play couples."

"I'm afraid I don't have much of a head for cards." Except when it came to her VISA or Mastercard. Then she knew all the tricks.

"Don't be so hard on yourself. You've just lacked a good teacher, that's all. I promise to be patient."

Diana felt someone's stare. She paused and looked around and didn't recognize anyone she knew. Taking another sip of her wine, she relaxed. "Is it warm in here? Or is it just me?" she asked Owen.

"It doesn't seem to be overly warm," Owen responded, and turned around as though to ask the opinion of those sitting at the table closest to their own.

Feeling feverish, Diana frantically fanned her face. It was then that she saw Cliff. The voluptuous blonde she'd noticed a few minutes before sat beside him, her torso practically draped over his arm. Diana's hand froze in midair as her breath caught in her lungs. Her worst nightmare had just come true. Cliff was dating Miss World, and she was with Captain Kangaroo.

Eight

"Katie, will you kindly come down from that tree!" Diana yelled as she jerked open the sliding glass door that led to the backyard. It seemed she was going to have to cut down the apple tree in order to keep her younger daughter from climbing between its gnarled limbs. The girl seemed to think she was half monkey. Two days into summer vacation, and already Diana was beginning to sound like a banshee.

"Mom..."

"Katie, just do it. I'm in no mood for an argument." She slammed the door, furious with herself for being so short-tempered and angry with Katie for disobeying her. A rush of air escaped her lungs as she slouched against the kitchen wall and hung her head in an effort to get a firm grip on her emotions.

"Mom?"

Diana lifted her eyes to find Joan standing on the other side of the room, studying her with an odd look. She frowned. "What?"

In answer to her mother's question, Joan pulled out

a chair and patted the seat. "I think it's time for us to have another of our daughter-mother talks."

If her preteen hadn't looked so serious, Diana would have laughed. Not again! Diana had only just recovered from the first such conversation. Joan had spoken to her about the importance of not doing anything foolish—such as marrying Owen on the rebound from Cliff.

"Again, Joan?" she asked, her eyes silently pleading for solitude.

"You heard me."

Diana rolled her eyes toward the ceiling and seated herself. While Diana waited, Joan walked around the counter and brewed a cup of coffee. Once she'd delivered it to her mother, she took the chair across from Diana and plopped her elbows onto the tabletop, her hands cupping her face as she stared at her mother.

"Well?"

"Don't rush me. I'm trying to think of a diplomatic way of saying this."

"I've been a grouch. I know, and I apologize." Diana could do nothing less. She'd been snapping at the girls all week. School was out, and it took time to adjust. At least, that was what she told herself.

"That's not it."

"Is it Owen? You needn't worry. I won't be seeing him again."

In a spontaneous outburst of glee, Joan tossed her hands above her head. "There is a God!"

"Joan, honestly!"

"So you're not going to date Owen anymore. What about…" She paused abruptly. "You know…the one whose name I've been forbidden to mention."

"Cliff."

Joan pointed at her mother's chest. "He's the one."

"What about him?" Diana asked, ignoring her daughter's attempt at humor.

The amusement drained from the eleven-year-old's dark eyes. "You still miss him, don't you?"

Diana lowered her gaze and shrugged. She preferred not to think about Cliff. Ever since the night she'd seen him with that bimbo clinging to him like a bloodsucker, Diana had done her best to avoid anything vaguely connected with Cliff Howard. It was little wonder they hadn't been able to get along. Obviously, Cliff's preference in women swayed toward the exotic. Their breakup had been inevitable. He might have been satisfied with apple pandowdy for a time, but his interest couldn't have lasted. Not when he could sample cheesecake anytime he wished. Diana had been intelligent enough to recognize that from the first, but she'd been so flattered—all right, attracted to Cliff— that she'd chosen to ignore good old-fashioned common sense. Joan was right, though. She did miss him. But more important, she'd gotten out of the relationship with her heart intact. No one had been hurt; she'd been lucky.

"Anyway, Katie and I have been thinking," Joan continued.

"Now that's dangerous." Diana took a sip of her coffee and nearly choked as the hot brew slid down the back of her throat. Joan had made it strong enough to cause a nuclear meltdown.

"Mom, Katie and I want you to know something."

"Yes?"

"Whatever Cliff did, *we* forgive him. We think that you should be big enough to do the same."

* * *

Marianne batted her thick, mascara-coated lashes in Cliff's direction, issuing an invitation that was all too obvious. He pulled her into his arms and kissed her hard. Harder than necessary, grinding his mouth over hers, angry with her for being so transparent and even angrier with himself for not wanting her.

The woman in his arms moaned, and Cliff obliged by kissing her again. He didn't need to be an Einstein to realize he was seeking something. Every time he kissed Marianne, it was a futile effort to taste Diana.

The blond wound her arms around his neck and seductively rubbed her breasts over his torso. Cliff couldn't force any desire for her, and the realization only served to infuriate him.

His hands gripped Marianne's shoulders as he extracted himself from her grasp.

She looked up at him, dazed and confused. "Cliff?"

"I've got a busy day tomorrow." He offered the lame excuse, stood and reached for his jacket. "I'll give you a call later." He hurried out the door, hardly able to escape fast enough. Once inside his car, he gripped the steering wheel with both hands and clenched his jaw. What was happening to him? Whatever it was, he didn't like it. Not one bit.

Diana stood at the sliding glass door and checked the sleeping foursome on the patio. In an effort to make up for her cranky mood, and in a moment of weakness, she'd agreed to let the girls each invite a friend over for a slumber party. Now all four were sacked out in lawn chairs, with enough pillows, blankets, radios and stuffed animals to supply a small army. They'd talked, laughed, carted out half the contents of the kitchen and had finally worn themselves out. Peace and goodwill toward men reigned for the moment.

Diana had just poured herself a cup of decaffeinated coffee, when the doorbell chimed. Surprised, she checked her watch and noticed it was after ten. She certainly wasn't expecting anyone this late.

Setting aside her coffee, she moved into the entryway and pressed her eye to the peephole in the front door. Her gaze met the solid wall of a man's chest—one she'd recognize anywhere. Cliff Howard's.

There wasn't time to react, or time to think. Her heart hammered wildly as she unbolted the lock and gradually opened the door.

"Hi," he said awkwardly. "I was in the neighborhood and thought I'd stop in. I hope you don't mind."

He was dressed in a dinner jacket, his tie was loosened and the top two buttons of his shirt were unfastened. Cliff didn't need anyone to tell him he looked bad. That was what he felt like, too. So the dragon lady wasn't going to come to him. Fine, he'd go to her, and they'd get this matter settled once and for all. Hard as it was to admit, he missed her. He even missed Joan and Katie. It hadn't been easy swallowing his pride this way, and he sincerely hoped Diana recognized that and responded appropriately.

"No, I don't mind." Actually, she was pleased to see him now that she'd gotten over the initial shock. They hadn't exactly parted on the best of terms, and she wanted to clear the air and say goodbye without a lot of emotion dictating her words. "I'd just poured myself a cup of coffee. Would you care for some?"

"Please." He followed her into the kitchen, sat down,

noticed the open drape and pointed toward the patio. "What's going on out there?"

"School's out, and the girls are celebrating with a slumber party."

He grinned and nodded toward the large pile of blankets. Only one hand and the top of a head were visible. "I take it the one with the six-inch bright red fingernails is Joan."

Grinning, Diana delivered his cup to the table and nodded. "And the one clenching sixteen Pooh bears is Katie." As she moved past Cliff, she caught a whiff of expensive perfume and the faint odor of whiskey.

"It's good to see you, Diana." The fact was, he couldn't stop looking at her.

"There wasn't any need to tear yourself away from a hot date to visit, Cliff. I'm here most anytime." Her words were more teasing than angry, and she smiled at him.

He smiled back. "The least you could do is pretend you're happy to see me."

"But I am."

She really did have the most beautiful eyes. Dark and deep, wide and round. They were capable of tearing apart a man's heart and gentle enough to comfort an injured animal. He remembered how their color had clouded with passion when he'd kissed her, and wondered how long it would be before he could do it again. He longed for Diana's kisses as much as he missed her quick wit.

Diana settled herself in the chair across from him, not wanting to get too close. Cliff had that look in his eyes, and she was beginning to recognize what it meant. If she gave him the least amount of encouragement, he would reach for her and cover her mouth with his own. Then everything she'd discovered about herself these past days without him would be lost in the passion of the moment.

"Why did you come? Did your dinner companion turn you down?"

She didn't know the half of it, he thought to himself.

Diana grinned into her coffee cup. "Was she the same girl as the other night?"

"Yes," Cliff admitted sheepishly. "Unfortunately all her brains are situated below her neck."

"Now, Cliff, that was unkind." So her own estimation of Miss World had been right on; the blonde was a bimbo. It was tacky to feel so good being right about the other woman. Tacky, but human.

"Well, your date certainly resembled William F. Buckley."

Diana was unable to hold back her laugh. "He brought me references."

"What?"

"He's Shirley's third cousin, and apparently he thought I needed to know something more about him. Honestly, Cliff, I thought I'd die. He'd had someone from Highline Community College write up a letter telling me what a forthright man he is, and there was another letter from his dentist and a third from his apartment manager."

They laughed together, and it felt incredibly good. Diana wiped a tear from the corner of her eye and sighed audibly. "Joan and Kate were scared to death I'd marry him."

"How have the girls been?"

"They're great." Actually, Diana was grateful both

her daughters were asleep; otherwise they might have launched themselves into Cliff's arms and told him how miserable their mother had been without him.

"And you?"

"Good. How about yourself?"

"Fair." Cliff didn't know the words to describe all that had been happening to him. Nothing had changed, and yet everything was different. He'd dated one of the most sought-after women in Seattle, and she'd left him feeling cold. His little black book was filled with names and phone numbers, and he hadn't the inclination to make one phone call.

"Actually, I'm glad you stopped by," Diana said, wading into the topic they'd both managed to avoid thus far. "I owe you an apology for running off on you that way."

"Diana, honestly, I still don't know what I did that was so terrible."

"I realize that."

"I thought we had something really good going. I didn't mean to rush you—I assumed—falsely, it seems—that you were as ready for the physical part of our relationship as I was."

Diana lowered her gaze, and her hands tightened around the mug. "I wish I could be different for you, but I can't."

"You wanted me. I knew that almost from the first."

She still did, but that didn't alter her feelings. "Unfortunately I need something more than magic."

"What?" If he could give it to her, he would.

Her eyes were infinitely sad, dark and soulful. "You know the answer to that without my having to spell it out for you."

At least she had the common sense not to say it: love and commitment. He wasn't pleased at the thought of either one.

"Listen," she said, slowly lifting her eyes to capture his. "I'm glad you're here, because we do need to talk. A lot of things have been going through my mind the past couple of weeks."

"Mine, too."

"I like you, Cliff. I really do. It would be so easy to fall in love with you. But I'm afraid that if I did, we'd only end up hurting each other."

Feeling confused, he frowned darkly at her. "How do you mean?"

"When we first started going out, you automatically included the girls—mainly because I had them gathered around me like a fortress, and you recognized that you had to deal with them in order to get to me."

He grinned because she was right on target; that had been his plan exactly.

"Later, after the fishing fiasco, you realized that having the girls around wasn't the best thing for a promising relationship. I can't say that I blame you. There's no reason for you to be interested in children— a ready-made family isn't for you, and children do have a tendency to mess things up."

Cliff opened his mouth to contradict her, then realized that basically she was right. After the sailing trip, he had more or less decided the time had come to wean Diana away from her girls. To be honest, he'd wanted her all to himself. Oh, he'd planned to include Joan and Katie occasionally, but he was mainly interested in Diana. Her daughters were cute kids, but he could easily have done without them, and as much as possible, he'd hoped to keep them in the background of anything that developed between him and Diana.

"You make me sound pretty mercenary." Actually, when he thought about what he'd been doing, he realized that his actions could be construed as selfish. All right, so he'd been selfish!

"I don't mean to place you in a bad light."

"But it's true." It hadn't been easy for him to admit that, and he felt ashamed.

"Herein we have the basic problem. I can't be separated from the girls. You may be able to ignore them, but I can't. We're one, and placing me in the middle and asking me to choose between you and my daughters would only make everyone miserable."

Cliff's smile was wry. "You know, you would have made a great attorney."

"Thanks."

"The way I deal with Joan and Katie could change, Diana." His gaze continued to hold hers. She was right; he'd been thinking only of himself, and he'd been wrong. But now that the air had been cleared, he was more than willing to strike up a compromise.

"Perhaps it could change." She granted him an A for effort, and was pleased that he cared enough to want to try. "But there's more."

"There is?"

"Cliff, for some reason you have a difficult time making a commitment to one woman. I suspect it has a lot to do with the girl who lived with you. Shirley told me about her."

"Becky." He didn't even like to think about her or the whole unfortunate experience. It had happened a long time ago, and as far as he was concerned, the whole affair was best forgotten.

"You might not be thrilled with this, but I think you cared a great deal for Becky. I honestly believe you loved her."

Unable to remain seated, Cliff stood and refilled his coffee cup, even though he'd taken only a few sips. "She was a selfish bitch," he said bitterly, his jaw tight.

"That makes admitting you loved her all the more difficult, doesn't it?"

"Who do you think you are? Sigmund Freud?"

"No," she admitted softly. "Believe me, I know what you went through when she moved out. Although the circumstances were different, I was unbelievably angry with Stan after he died. I'd take out the garbage and curse him for not being there to do it for me. I'd never been madder at anyone in my life. As crazy as it sounds, it took me months to forgive him for dying."

"Stan's death has absolutely nothing in common with what happened between me and some airhead. Becky wandered in and out of my life several years ago and has nothing to do with the here and now."

"Perhaps you're right."

"I know I am," he reiterated forcefully.

"But ever since then, you've flitted in and out of relationships, gained yourself a playboy reputation and you positively freeze at the mention of the word love. I'd hate to think what would happen if marriage turned up in casual conversation."

"That's not true." He felt like shouting now. Diana hadn't even known Becky. He was lucky to have gotten away from the two-timing, schemer. Diana had it all wrong—he was planning on falling in love and getting married someday. It wasn't as if he'd been soured on the entire experience.

"I understand how you feel, believe me. Loving someone makes us vulnerable. If we care about anyone or anything, we leave ourselves wide open to pain. Over the years, the two of us have both shielded our hearts, learned to keep them intact. I'm as guilty as you are. I've wrapped my heart around hobbies. You use luxuries. The only difference between the two of us is that I have Joan and Katie. If it hadn't been for the girls, they might as well have buried me in the casket with Stan. It would have been safe there—airless and dark. Certainly there wouldn't have been any danger of my heart getting broken a second time. You see, after a while the heart becomes impenetrable and all our fears are gone."

Standing across from her, Cliff braced his hands on the back of the chair. He said nothing.

"I guess what I'm trying to say is that I finally understand the reason I couldn't sleep with you. Yes, you were right on target when you said I was physically ready, but emotionally and spiritually I'm miles away. You were right, too, when you claimed there was magic between us. After dating Owen, I recognized that isn't anything to sneeze at, either." She paused, and they shared a gentle smile. "But more than that, I realized that without love, without risking our hearts, the magic would fade. A close physical relationship would leave me vulnerable again and open to pain." She dropped her gaze to the tabletop. "It hurts too much, Cliff. I don't want to risk battering my heart just because something feels good."

When she'd finished, the silence wrapped itself around them.

Diana was the first one to speak. "But more than anything, I want you to know how grateful I am to you."

"Me? Why?"

"You woke me up. You made me feel again."

"Glad to oblige, Sleeping Beauty." Cliff hadn't liked what she'd said—maybe because it hit to close to the truth. She was right; he had changed after Becky, more than he'd ever realized. He wasn't particularly impressed with the picture Diana had painted of him, but the colors showed through all too clearly. She was right, too, about surrounding himself with luxuries. The sailboat, the fancy sports car, even the ski condo— they were extravagances. They made him feel good, made him look good.

After a long moment, Cliff moved away and emptied his coffee cup into the sink. "You've given me a lot to think about," he said with his back to her.

She'd given them both a lot to think about. Diana walked him to the front door and opened it for him. "Goodbye, Cliff."

He paused for a moment, then reached for her, folding her in his arms, pressing his jaw against the side of her head. He didn't kiss her, didn't dare, because he wasn't sure he would still be able to walk away from her if he did.

Diana slowly closed her eyes to the secure warmth she experienced in his arms. She wanted to savor these last moments together. After a while, she gently eased herself free.

"Goodbye, Diana," he whispered, and turned and walked away without looking back.

"Hey, Cliff, how about a cold beer?"

"Great." He stretched out his hand without disturbing his fishing pole and grabbed for the Bud Light. Holding the chilled aluminum can between his thighs, he dexterously opened it with one hand and guzzled down a long, cold drink.

"This is the life," Charlie, Cliff's longtime fishing buddy, called out. His cap was lowered over his eyes to block out the sun as he leaned back and stretched out his legs in front of him. The boat rocked lazily upon the still, green waters of Puget Sound.

"It doesn't get much better than this," Cliff said, reaching for a sandwich. The sun was out, the beer was cold and the fish were sure to start biting any minute.

The weather forecast had been for a hot afternoon sun. It was only noon, and already it was beginning to heat up. Charlie and Cliff had left the marina before dawn, determined to do some serious fishing. Thus far neither man had had so much as a nibble.

"I'm going to change my bait," Charlie said after a while. "I don't know what's the matter with these fish today. Too lazy, I guess. It looks like I'm going to have to give them reason to come my way."

"I think I'll change tactics, too." Already Cliff was reeling in his line. It was on days like this, when the fish weren't eager and the sun was hot, that he understood what it meant to be a fisherman. Once he had his pole inside the boat, he reached for his tackle box and sorted through the large assortment of hand-tied flies and fancy lures. A flash of silver stopped his search.

His replacement lucky lure. His fingers closed around the cold piece of silver as his thoughts drifted to Katie. She was rambunctious and clever, and whenever she walked, the eight-year-old's pigtails would bounce. Grinning, he remembered how she'd leaned over the side of his sailboat and called out to the fish, trying to lure them to her hook before her sister's. His grin eased into a full smile as he recalled the girls' antics that Saturday afternoon.

"You know what I've been thinking?" Charlie mumbled as he tossed his line over the side of the boat.

Cliff was too caught up in his thoughts to care. He'd done a lot of thinking about what Diana had said the other night. In fact, he hadn't stopped thinking about their conversation. He hadn't liked it, but more and more he was beginning to recognize the truth in what she'd had to say.

"Cliff?"

Sure, he'd missed Diana, regretted his assumptions about their casually drifting into a physical relationship. But he missed Joan and Katie, too, more than he'd ever thought he would. The instant flare of regret that constricted his heart at the sight of the lure shocked him. He was beginning to care for those two little girls as much as he did for their mother.

"Cliff, good buddy? Are you going to fish, or are you going to kneel and stare into that tackle box all day?"

There was a reason Diana hated Monday mornings, she decided as she lifted the corner of Joan's double bed and tucked the clean sheet between the mattress and the box spring. She hated changing sheets, and once a week she was reminded of the summer job in her junior year of high school. She'd been a hotel maid and had come to hate anything vaguely connected with housekeeping.

When she finished with the girls' sheets, she was going to wash her hair, pack a picnic lunch and treat Joan and Katie to an afternoon at Seahurst beach in Burien, another South Seattle community. She might even put on a swimsuit and sunbathe. Of course, there was always the risk that someone from Greenpeace might mistake her for a beached whale and try to get her into the water, but she was willing to chance it.

Chuckling at her own wit, Diana straightened and reached for a fresh pillowcase. It was then that she heard a faint, but sharp cry coming from outside, and recognized it immediately as something serious. It sounded like Katie. She tossed the pillow aside and started out of Joan's bedroom. The last time she'd looked, both girls were in the backyard playing. Mikey Holiday had been over, as well as a couple of other neighborhood kids.

"Mom!" Joan shrieked, panic in the lone word. "Mom! Mom!"

It was the type of desperate cry that chills a mother's blood. Diana raced down the stairs and nearly collided with her elder daughter. Joan groped for her mother's arms, her young face as pale as the sheet Diana had just changed.

"It's Katie…she fell out of the apple tree. Mom, she's hurt…real bad."

Nine

Diana walked briskly down the wide hospital corridor. Katie was at her side, being pushed in a wheelchair by the nurse who'd met her at the emergency entrance. The eight-year-old sobbed pitifully, and every cry ripped straight through Diana's soul. She hadn't needed a medical degree to recognize that Katie had broken her arm. What did astonish Diana was how calmly and confidently she'd responded to the emergency. Quickly she had protected Katie's oddly twisted arm in a pillow. Then she'd sent Joan and Mikey over to his house with instructions for Shirley to contact Valley General Hospital and tell them she was on her way with Katie.

"You'll need to fill out some paperwork," the nurse explained when they reached the front desk.

Diana hesitated as the receptionist rose to hand her the necessary forms.

Katie sobbed again and twisted around in her chair. "Mom…don't leave me."

"Honey, I'll be there as fast as I can." It wasn't until Katie had been wheeled out of sight and into the cubical that Diana began to shake. She gripped the pen between her fingers and started to complete the top sheet, quickly writing in Katie's name, her own and their address.

"Could...I sit down?" Now that her hands had stopped trembling, her knees were giving her problems. The entire room started to sway, and she grabbed the edge of the counter. She was starting to fall apart, but couldn't. At least not yet, Katie needed her.

"Oh, sure, take a seat," the woman in the crisp white uniform answered. "There are several chairs over there." She pointed to a small waiting area. A middle-aged couple was sitting there watching the *Noon News*. Somehow Diana made it to a molded plastic chair. She drew in several deep breaths and forced her attention to the questionnaire in front of her. The last time she'd been in Valley General was when Stan had been brought in.

Her stomach heaved as unexpected tears filled her eyes, blurring her vision as she relived the horror of that day. Three years had done little to erase the effects of that nightmare. Her throat constricted under the threat of overwhelming sobs, and again Diana forced her attention to the blank sheet she needed to complete.

But again the memories overwhelmed her. She'd been contacted at home and told that Stan had been in an accident. Naturally she'd been concerned, but no one had told her he was in any grave danger. She'd left the girls with Shirley and rushed to the hospital. Once she'd arrived, she'd been directed to the emergency room, given a multitude of forms to complete and told to wait. There'd been another man who'd just brought his wife in with gallbladder problems, and Diana had even joked with him in an effort to hide her nervousness. It seemed they kept her sitting there waiting for hours, and every time she inquired, the receptionist told her the doctor would be out in a few minutes. She asked if she could see Stan and was again told she'd have to wait. Finally the physician appeared, so stiff and somber. His eyes were filled with reluctance and regret as he spoke. And yet his message was only a few, simple words. He told Diana he was sorry. At first, she didn't understand what he meant. Naturally, he was sorry that Stan had been hurt. So was she. It wasn't until she asked how long it would be before her husband could come home and seen the pity in the doctor's eyes that she understood. Stan would never leave the hospital, and no one had even given her the chance to say goodbye to him. Diana had been calm then, too. So calm. So serene. It wasn't until later, much later, that the floodgates of overwhelming grief had broken, and she'd nearly drowned in her pain.

Katie's piercing cry cut sharply into Diana's thoughts. Her reaction was instinctive, and she leaped to her feet. The hospital staff hadn't let her go to Stan, either.

She stepped to the receptionist's desk. "I want to be with my daughter."

The woman took the clipboard from Diana's numb fingers and glanced over the incomplete form. "I'm sorry, but you'll need to finish these before the doctor can treat your daughter."

"Please." Her voice cracked. "I need to be with Katie."

"I'm sorry, Mrs. Collins, but I really must—"

"Then give her something for the pain!" The sound

of someone running came from behind her, but Diana's senses were too dulled to register anything more than the noise.

"Diana." Cliff joined her at the counter, his eyes wide and concerned. "What happened?"

"Katie...they won't let me be with Katie."

Tears streamed down her face, and Cliff couldn't ever remember seeing anyone more deathly pale. It was then that he realized that he'd never imagined that Diana could be so unnerved. One look at her told him why he'd found it so urgent to rush here. Somehow he'd known that Diana would need him. Until a half hour ago, his day had been going rather smoothly. He'd been eating a sandwich at his desk, thinking about a case he was about to review, when his secretary had stuck her head in the door and announced that someone named Joan was crying on the phone and asking to speak to him. By the time Cliff had lifted the receiver, the eleven-year-old was almost hysterical. In between sobs, Joan had told him that Diana had taken Katie to the hospital. She'd also claimed that her mother couldn't afford to pay the bill. Cliff had hardly been able to understand what had happened until Shirley Holiday had gotten on the line and explained that Katie had broken her arm. Cliff had thanked her for letting him know, then had sat quietly at his desk a few minutes until he'd decided what he should do. After a moment he'd dumped the rest of his lunch in the wastepaper basket, stood and reached for his suit jacket. He'd tossed a few words of explanation to his secretary and crisply walked out the door.

A broken arm, although painful, was nothing to be worried about, he'd assured himself. Kids broke their arms every day. It wasn't that big a deal. Only this wasn't just any little kid, this was Katie. Sweet Katie, who had tossed her arms around his neck and given him a wet kiss. Katie who would sell her soul for a bucket of Kentucky Fried Chicken. Diana's Katie— his Katie.

He hadn't understood why he felt the urgent need to get to the hospital, but he did. Heaven or hell wouldn't have kept him away. It was a miracle that the state patrol wasn't after him, Cliff realized when he pulled into the hospital parking lot. He'd driven like a crazy man.

"Mrs. Collins has to complete these forms before she can be with her daughter," the receptionist patiently explained for the third time.

Diana's hand grasped Cliff's forearms, and her watery eyes implored him. "Stan...never came home."

Cliff frowned, not understanding her meaning. He reached for the clipboard and flipped the pages until he found what he wanted. "Diana, all you need to do is sign your name here." He gave her the pen.

"I'm sorry, but I will have to ask Mrs. Collins to fill out all the necessary—"

Cliff silenced the receptionist with one determined look. "I can complete anything else."

Diana scribbled her name where Cliff had indicated and gave the clipboard back to him.

"Take Mrs. Collins to her daughter," he stated next in the same crisp, dictatorial tone.

The woman nodded and stood to walk around the desk and escort Diana to where they'd wheeled Katie.

Cliff watched Diana leave, reached for the clipboard and took a seat. It wasn't until he read through the first few lines she'd completed that he understood what Diana had been trying to tell him about Stan. The last time she'd been in the hospital was when her husband had been brought in after the airplane accident. From the information George Holiday had given him, Cliff understood that Stan had been badly burned. On the advice of Stan's physician, Diana had never seen her husband's devastated body. One peaceful Saturday morning, Diana kissed her husband goodbye and went shopping with her daughters, while he took off in a private plane with a good friend. And she never saw her high-school sweetheart again.

Less than an hour later, Diana appeared and took a seat beside Cliff. She'd composed herself by this time, embarrassed to have given way to crying as she had.

"They're putting a cast on Katie's arm," she said when Cliff looked to her. "She's asking to see you."

"Me?"

"Yes, Cliff, you."

They stood together. Diana paused, feeling a bit chagrined, but needing to thank him. "I don't know who told you about the accident or why you came, but I want you to know how much I appreciate your…help. Something came over me when we arrived at the hospital, and all of a sudden I couldn't help remembering the last time I was here. I got so afraid." Her voice wobbled, and she bit into her bottom lip. "Thank you, Cliff."

"No problem." He was having a hard time not taking her in his arms and offering what comfort he could. His whole body ached with the need to hold her and tell her he understood. But after their last discussion, he didn't know how she'd feel about him touching her. He buried his hands in his pants pockets, bunching them into impotent fists. "I'm here because I want to be here—there's nothing noble about it."

Although he made light of it, Diana knew he'd left his law office in the middle of the day to rush to the hospital. His caring meant more than she could ever tell him. She wanted to try, but the words that were in her heart didn't make it to her tongue.

"Cliff!" Katie brightened the minute he stepped into the casting room.

"Hi, buttercup." Her face was streaked with tears, her pigtails mussed with leaves and grass and a bruise was forming on the side of her jaw, but Cliff couldn't remember seeing a more beautiful little girl. "How did you manage that?" He nodded toward her arm.

"I fell out of the apple tree," she told him, and wrinkled up her nose. "I wasn't supposed to climb it, either."

"I hope you won't again," Diana interjected.

Katie's young brow crinkled into a tight frown. "I don't think I will. This hurt real bad, but I tried to be brave for Mom and Joan."

"I broke my leg once," Cliff told her. The thought of Katie having to endure the same pain he'd suffered produced a curious ache in the region of his heart. He watched as the PA worked, wrapping her arm in a protective layer of cotton. Then he dipped thick plaster strips in water and began to mold them over Katie's forearm and elbow.

"I've missed you a whole lot," the little girl said next.

"I've missed you, too." Cliff discovered that wasn't a lie. He'd tried not to think about Diana and her daughters since the night of their talk. The past couple of days, he'd been almost amused at the way everything around him had reminded him of them. He'd finally reached the conclusion that he wasn't going to be able to forget these three females. Somehow, without his knowing how, they'd made an indelible mark on his heart. What Diana had said about Becky and him had been the truth. Funny, he'd once told Diana to wake up and smell the coffee, and yet he had been the one with his head buried in the sand.

"Mom missed you, too—a whole bunch."

"Katie!"

"It's true. Don't you remember you were cranky with me and Joan, and then you told us you were sorry and said you were still missing Cliff and that was the reason you were in such a bad mood."

A hot flush seeped into Diana's face and circled her ears. With some effort, she smiled weakly in Cliff's direction, hoping he'd be kind enough to forget what Katie had told him.

"Don't you remember, Mom? Joan thought it was Aunt Flo again and you said—"

"I remember, Katie," she said pointedly.

"Who's Aunt Flo?" Cliff wanted to know.

"Never mind," Diana murmured under her breath.

"Will you sign my cast?" Katie asked Cliff next. "The only boys who can sign it are you and Mikey."

"I'd be honored."

"And maybe Gary Hidenlighter."

"Who's he?" The name sounded vaguely familiar to Cliff, and he wondered where he'd heard it.

"The boy who offered her a baseball card if she'd let him kiss her."

"Ah, yes," Cliff answered with a lopsided grin. "I

seem to recall hearing about the dastardly proposition now."

"Kissing doesn't seem to be so bad," Katie added thoughtfully after a moment. "Mom and you sure do it a lot."

Cliff lightly slipped his arm around Diana's shoulders and smiled down on her. "I can't speak for your mother, but I know what I like."

"I do, too," she responded, looking up at Cliff, comforted by his feathery touch.

Getting Katie out of the hospital wasn't nearly as much a problem as getting her in had been since Cliff was there to smooth the way. While Diana filled in the spaces Cliff had left blank on the permission forms, he wheeled Katie up to the hospital pharmacy and had the prescription for the pain medication filled. By the time they returned, Diana had finished her task. As the two came toward her, the sight of them together filled her with an odd sensation of rightness.

"Can I ride in Cliff's car?" Katie asked once they were in the parking lot.

"Katie, Cliff has to get back to his office."

"No, I don't," he countered quickly, looking almost boyish in his eagerness. "While we were waiting, I phoned my secretary and told her I was taking the rest of the day off."

"Oh, goodie." Katie's happy eyes flew from her mother to Cliff and then back to Diana again. "Since Cliff isn't real busy, can I go in his car?"

Diana's gaze went to Cliff, who acquiesced with a short nod.

All the way into Kent, Katie chatted a mile a minute. The physician had claimed that the pain medication would make the little girl drowsy, but thus far it had had just the opposite effect. Katie was a wonder.

"I used my new lucky lure the other day," Cliff said when he was able to get a word in edgewise.

"Oh, good. Did it work?"

"Like a dream." His change in luck had astonished him and had amazed Charlie, who'd wanted to know where Cliff had bought that silver lure. Cliff had sailed back into the marina that afternoon with a good-size salmon and a large flounder, while Charlie hadn't gotten so much as a curious nibble.

Katie let out a long sigh of relief. "I was real afraid the new one wouldn't have the same magic."

"Then rest assured, Katie Collins, because this new lure seems to be even better than the old one. In fact, you might have done me a favor by losing the original."

"Really? Are we ever going to go fishing on your sailboat again? I promise never to get into your gear unless you tell me I can."

"I think another fishing expedition could be arranged, but let's leave that up to your mother, okay?" He wasn't sure Diana would agree to seeing him again, and didn't want to disappoint Katie.

"That sounds okay," Katie assented.

When Cliff pulled into the driveway behind Diana's gray bomber, it seemed that half the kids in the neighborhood rushed out to greet Katie.

They followed her into the house, and she sat them down, organized their questions and patiently answered each one, explaining in graphic detail what had happened to her. As he looked on from the kitchen, it seemed to Cliff that she was holding her own press conference.

While Katie was hailed as a heroine, Diana brewed coffee and brought a cup to Cliff. "Do you mind if I take a look around your garage?" he asked her unexpectedly after taking a sip.

"Sure, go ahead." She wondered what he was up to and was mildly surprised when he reappeared a couple of minutes later with a handsaw.

"Here," he said, handing her his suit jacket, and marched outside.

Katie noticed he was gone right away. "What's Cliff doing?"

Diana was just as curious as her daughter and followed him out the sliding glass door. She paused, watching him from the patio as he methodically started trimming off the lower branches of the backyard's lone tree.

By the time he'd finished, Cliff had loosened his tie, unfastened the top buttons of his starched shirt and paused more than once to wipe the sweat from his brow.

Grateful for his thoughtfulness, Diana started issuing instructions. Soon the neighborhood kids had gathered around him and stacked the fallen limbs into a neat pile. Diana was so busy watching Cliff and telling the kids to keep out of his way that he was nearly finished before she noticed that Joan was missing.

Diana wandered through the house, looking for her daughter. When she didn't find her on the lower level, she wandered up the stairs.

"Joan?"

She heard a muffled sob and peeked inside the first bedroom, looking past all the Justin Timberlake posters to her daughter, who had flung herself across the top of her half-made bed.

"Joan?" she asked softly. "Don't you want to come and see Katie?"

"No."

"Why not? She wants you to sign her cast."

"I'm not going to. Not ever."

Diana moved to her daughter's side and sat on the edge of the mattress. Puzzled by Joan's odd behavior, she brushed the soft wisps of hair from the eleven-year-old's furrowed brow.

Huge tears filled the preteen's dark brown eyes. She muttered something about Cliff that Diana couldn't understand.

"You phoned him at his office?"

Joan nodded. "I...I don't know why. I just did."

"Do you think I'm angry with you because of that?"

Joan shrugged in open defiance. "I don't care if you are mad. I wanted to talk to Cliff and I did...Katie was hurt and I thought he had the right to know."

The realization that both girls had turned to Cliff in the emergency was only a little short of shocking to Diana. Katie had asked about him even before Diana had had a chance to tell the youngster he was in the hospital waiting room, filling out the forms. And Joan had contacted him at his office, knowing she would probably be punished for doing so. No other man Diana had ever dated had had this profound effect on her daughters. Without trying, without even wanting to, Cliff Howard had woven himself into their tender hearts. Although it hurt, Diana understood now that she'd made the right decision to break off her relationship with him. Cliff possessed the awesome power to hurt her children, and it was her duty, as their mother, to protect them.

"Mom," Joan sobbed, straightening up enough to hurl herself into her mother's arms, "I was so afraid."

"I know, sweetheart." Fresh tears filled Diana's eyes at the memory of those first minutes at the hospital. "I was, too."

"I…thought Katie would never come home again."

Diana's own fears had been similar. In all the confusion, she hadn't considered what had been going on in Joan's mind. As the eldest, Joan could remember the day her father had died. She had only been eight at the time, and although she might not have understood everything, she could vividly remember the horror, just as Diana had earlier in the day.

"You can have my allowance if you need it…."

"I don't need your allowance, honey."

Embarrassed now by the display of emotion, Joan wiped the moisture from her cheek and gave her mother a determined, angry look. "That Katie can be really stupid. You know that, don't you?"

"Cliff cut off the lower limbs so Katie won't be able to climb into the apple tree again."

Joan nodded approvingly. "It's a good thing, because that Katie can be so stupid. Knowing her, she wouldn't learn a single lesson from this. If something hadn't been done, she'd probably break her other arm next week."

Diana hid her smile, and the two hugged each other. "Come downstairs now, and you can talk to your sister."

Joan nodded. "All right, but don't get mad at me if I tell Katie she's got the brains of a rotting tomato."

* * *

"Mom, is there room in your suitcase for my iPad?"

Diana groaned, glanced toward the ceiling and prayed for patience. "Unfortunately I need some space for my clothes," she said, and attempted to shut the suitcase one last time. It wouldn't latch. "Your iPad has low priority at the moment."

"Mom!" Katie hurried into the bedroom. "Did you tell Cliff we were going to Wichita to visit Grandma and Grandpa?"

Diana hedged, trying to recall if she had or not. She had, she thought. "Yes."

"How come he hasn't come over since he brought me home from the hospital?"

The tight, uncomfortable feeling returned to Diana's chest. "I...don't know."

"But I thought he would."

So had Diana. She'd laid her cards out on the table, and the next move was his. He'd been wonderful with Katie that day she'd broken her arm, more than wonderful. While Katie had slept during the afternoon from the effects of the medication, he'd taken Joan out shopping. Together they'd purchased Katie a huge stuffed Pooh bear. At dinnertime he'd insisted on providing Kentucky Fried Chicken, much to her younger daughter's delight. But after they'd eaten, he'd said a few words of farewell, and that had been the last Diana or the girls had heard from him.

Actually, Diana was grateful for this vacation. These next two weeks with her parents would help all three of them take their minds off one Cliff Howard.

"He didn't even sign my cast."

"I think he forgot," Diana said, sitting on her suitcase in an effort to latch it.

"I think we should call him," Joan chimed in.

"No."

"But, Mom…"

One derisive look from Diana squelched that idea.

"What is it with that man, anyway?" Joan asked next. "I don't understand him at all."

Joan wasn't the only one Cliff baffled.

"I thought he was hot for you."

"Joan, please."

"No, really, Mom. The day he brought Katie home, he could hardly take his eyes off you."

Diana had done her share of looking, too. She'd wanted to talk to him, let him know how much she appreciated what he'd done for her and the girls, but he had left before the opportunity arose, and they hadn't heard from him in four days. Now that she'd had some time to give the matter thought, she'd decided not to protect the girls from the danger of Cliff denting their tender hearts. She'd seen how wonderful he'd been with Katie and how thoughtful with Joan. He'd never intentionally hurt them.

"Cliff told me he'd take me fishing again," Katie said. Her cast was covered with a multitude of messages and names in a variety of colors, but she'd managed to save a white space for Cliff under her elbow. "But he said if we went again, it would be up to you. We can go, can't we, Mom?"

Before Diana could answer Katie, the phone rang. Joan pounced on the receiver next to Diana's bed like a cat on a cornered mouse.

"Hello," she said demurely, sat down and grinned

girlishly. She crossed her legs and thoughtfully examined the ends of her fingernails. "It's good to hear from you again."

It was obviously a boy, and Joan was in seventh heaven.

"Yes, she's recovered nicely. Katie always was the brave one. Personally, at the sight of blood, I get the vapors. It's a good thing my mother kept her wits about her."

Diana bounced hard on the suitcase and sighed when the latch snapped into place. Success at last.

"Yes, she's sitting right here. She's packing. You do remember we're leaving for Wichita tonight, don't you? You didn't? Well, that's strange…Mom claims she did tell you. Yes, of course, just a minute." Grinning ear to ear, Joan held out the phone to her mother. "It's for you, Mom. It's Cliff."

Diana's heart fell to her knees and rebounded sharply before finally settling back into place. Joan had to be joking. "Cliff Howard?"

"Honestly, Mother, just how many Cliffs are you dating?"

"At the moment, none."

As diplomatically as possible, Joan steered her younger sister out of the bedroom and started to close the door.

"But," Katie protested, "I want to talk to Cliff, too."

"Another time," Joan said, and winked coyly at her mother.

Clearing her throat, Diana lifted the telephone receiver to her ear. "Hello."

"Diana? What's this about you leaving for Wichita?"

"Yes, well, I thought I mentioned it."

A short silence followed. "How long are you going to be gone?"

"Two weeks."

Her answer was followed by his partially muffled swearing. "Listen, would it be all right if I came over right away?"

Ten

Cliff pulled his sports car into Diana's driveway and turned off the engine. For a long moment he kept his hands on the steering wheel, his thoughts heavy. Maybe Diana had told him about this trip to Wichita, but if she had, he sure didn't remember it. He'd reached a decision about himself and his relationship with Diana and her girls. The process had been painful, but now that he knew his mind, he wasn't going to let a planned two-week vacation stand in his way.

Determined, he climbed out of his car, slammed the door and headed for the house.

Diana met him on the front porch, and once again Cliff was struck by her simple beauty. Her dark eyes with their long, thick lashes searched his face. Her lips were slightly parted, and a familiar ache tightened Cliff's midsection. If everything blew up in his face today, if worse came to worse and he never saw Diana Collins again, he'd always remember her and her kisses. They'd haunt him.

"Hello, Cliff." Diana was amazed how cool and unemotional she sounded. She wasn't feeling the least bit controlled. From the minute they'd finished their telephone conversation, she'd been pacing the upstairs, wandering from room to room in a mindless search for serenity. She'd never heard Cliff sound quite so serious. Now that he'd arrived, she noted that his piercing blue eyes revealed an unfamiliar intensity.

"Hello, Diana."

She opened the screen door for him.

"Where are the girls?" he asked once he was inside the house. He kept his hands in his pockets for fear he'd do something crazy, like reach for her and kiss her senseless. He'd been thinking about exactly that for four long days. Being with her only increased his need to taste her again.

"Joan and Katie are saying goodbye to all their friends in the neighborhood. You'd think we were going to be gone two years instead of two weeks." Actually, this time alone with Cliff had been Joan's doing. Her elder daughter hadn't been the least bit subtle about suggesting to Katie that perhaps they should take this opportunity to bid their friends a fond au revoir. Katie, however, had been far more interested in seeing Cliff. Diana estimated they'd have fifteen minutes at the most, before Katie blasted into the house.

Cliff jerked a hand out of his pocket and splayed his fingers through his hair. Now that he was here, he found he was tongue-tied. He'd practiced everything he wanted to say and now he didn't know where to start.

"Would you like some coffee?"

"No, thanks, I came to talk." That sounded good.

"Okay." Diana moved into the living room. Whatever was on Cliff's mind was important. He hadn't so much as cracked a smile. She imagined his behavior was similar when he stood in the courtroom before the jury box. Each move would be calculated, every word planned for the maximum effect.

Diana lowered herself into the overstuffed chair, and Cliff took a seat directly across from her on the sofa. He sat on the edge of the cushion, his elbows resting on his thighs, and clenched his hands into tight fists.

"How's Katie?"

Diana's smile came from her heart. "She's doing great. After the first day she didn't even need the pain medication."

"And you?"

Without his having to explain, Diana understood. "Much better, I...I'm not exactly sure I know what happened that day in the hospital, but emotionally I crumbled into a thousand pieces. I was about as close to being a basket case as I can remember. I'll always be grateful you were there for Katie and me."

"Her accident taught us both several valuable lessons."

"It did?" Diana swallowed around the uncomfortable tightness in her throat. She hardly recognized the Cliff who sat across from her; he was so grim-faced and unreadable.

Cliff seemed unable to take his eyes off her. There was so much he longed to tell her, and he'd never felt more uncertain about how to express himself. Knowing she would be leaving for her parents' had thrown him an unexpected curveball. He wished he could have taken her to an expensive restaurant and explained everything on neutral ground. Now he felt pressured to clear the air between them before she left for Wichita.

"Until Katie broke her arm," he went on to say, "I'd

more or less decided, after our late-night conversation, that you were right and it was best for us not to see each other again." He sat stiffly, feeling ill at ease. "It didn't take you long to see through me— I'm definitely not the marrying kind, and you knew it. You appealed to my baser instincts and I appealed to yours, but anything more than that between us was doomed. Am I right?"

Out of nervous agitation, Diana reached for the pillow with the cross-stitch pattern and fluffed it up in her lap. "Yes...I suppose so."

"Not seeing me again was what you wanted, wasn't it?" Cliff challenged.

Regretfully Diana nodded. It was and it wasn't. A relationship with Cliff showed such marvelous promise, and at the same time contained the coarse threads of tragedy. If the only threat had been *her* heart and *her* emotions, Diana might have risked it.

At least those had been her thoughts before the accident, when she'd seen how good Cliff had been with her girls. Joan and Katie were already involved.

"I see."

Diana wasn't sure he did. If he understood all this, then there wasn't any reason for this urgent visit now. Suddenly she understood what he was getting at. Her cheeks flushed, and she stood, holding the decorator pillow to her stomach. "Cliff, I apologize."

"You do?" He was the one who wanted to ask her forgiveness.

"Yes. I had no idea Joan would contact you when Katie was hurt. I'll make sure it doesn't happen again. I don't know why she did it...but I've talked with her since and explained that she should never have made that call, and she promised she..."

Cliff stormed to his feet. "I'm not talking about that!"

"You're not?"

"No." He lowered his voice, paused and ran his hand along the back of his neck a couple of times. "Listen, I'm doing a poor job of this."

She stared at him in wide-eyed wonder, not knowing what to think.

"Sit down, would you?"

Diana lowered herself back into the chair.

Cliff paced the space in front of her as though she were a stubborn member of the jury and he were about to make the closing argument in an important trial. He couldn't believe he was making such a mess of something this basic. Talking to Diana should have been a simple matter of explaining his change of heart, but once he arrived, he felt as nervous as a first-year member of a debate team.

Diana pressed her hands between her closed knees and studied Cliff as he moved back and forth in the small area in front of her chair. It was on the tip of her tongue to tell him that if he didn't hurry, the girls would be back and then their peace would be shattered. With Katie doing cartwheels at the sight of him, there wouldn't be a chance for a decent discussion.

Perhaps, Cliff decided, it would be best to start at the beginning. "Do you remember the night I came over after work and we sat and talked?"

Diana grinned and nodded. "As I recall, we did more kissing than talking."

Cliff relaxed enough to share a smile with her, and

when he spoke his eyes softened with the memory of how good the gentle lovemaking between them had been then. "It didn't feel right to walk away from you that night."

Diana's gaze dropped to the carpet. It hadn't felt right to her, either, but there was so much more at stake than her feelings or his.

"After I left you, I decided a romantic evening alone together in my condo would be just the thing to seal our fates. Do you remember?"

She wasn't likely to forget. "Listen, Cliff, I don't know what your point is, but…"

Cliff wasn't entirely sure anymore, either. "I guess what I'm having such a difficult time telling you is that I don't bed every woman I date." Diana was special, more than special. She had never been, and never would be, a number to him—someone he'd use to boost his ego. He wanted to explain that, and it just wasn't coming out the way he'd planned.

"It's none of my business how many women you've slept with." If he was going to make some grand confession, she wasn't interested in hearing it.

"But this does involve you."

She stood again, because it was impossible to remain seated. "Listen, Cliff, if you're going to tell me you slept with that…that bimbo blonde then…don't."

"Bimbo blonde? Oh, you mean Marianne. You think I made love to her? Diana, you've got to be joking."

"No, I'm not." The unexpected pain that tightened her chest made it almost impossible to talk evenly. The power Cliff Howard wielded to injure her heart was lethal. Diana had recognized that early in their relationship and had taken steps to protect herself. Yet here he was, stirring up unwelcome trauma.

"I didn't sleep with her! Diana, I swear to you by all that I hold dear, I didn't go to bed with Marianne." His words were little more than a hoarse whisper.

She walked across the room and looked out the window. Where were the girls when she could really use them? "That's hardly my business."

"I'm trying to make a point here."

"If so, just do it," she said, and whirled around to face him, shoulders stiff. She was on the defensive now and growing more impatient by the minute.

"I want to apologize for…"

"That's exactly what I thought," she flared, resisting the urge to place her hands over her ears to blot out his words. "And I don't want to hear it…so you can save your breath."

"For the night at my condominium," Cliff continued, undaunted. "I set up that seduction scene because we both felt the magic, and I wanted you." He lowered his voice to an enticing whisper of remembered desire. "Heaven knows I wanted you." And nothing had changed.

Now it was Diana's turn to pace, and she did so with all the energy of a raw recruit eager to please his sergeant. She stopped when she realized how ridiculous she must look and slapped her hands against the sides of her thighs. "Just what is your point?"

For a minute Cliff had forgotten. "When you walked out on me that night, I can't remember ever being angrier with anyone in my life. I figured if you were into denial, then fine, but I was noble enough to be honest about my feelings."

"I wonder if there's a Pulitzer Prize for that," she murmured sarcastically, and wrapped her arms around her waist.

Cliff ignored her derision. "Later I had a change of heart and decided I could be forgiving, considering the circumstances. I gave you ample time to come to me, and when you didn't, I was forced to swallow my pride and bridge the uneasiness between us. You may be impressed to know that I don't do that sort of thing often."

A snicker slipped from Diana's clogged throat. She tightened her grip on her waist. The longer he spoke, the more uncertain she was as to how to take Cliff. He was being sarcastic, but it seemed to be at his expense and not hers.

"That night you lowered the boom and told me a few truths," Cliff continued. "Basically, let it be known that you weren't interested in falling into bed with me because of some mystical, magical feeling between us. You also took it upon yourself to point out a couple of minor flaws in my personality. As I recall, shortly afterward I was left to lick my wounds."

A smile cracked the tight line of Diana's mouth. "Was I really so merciless?"

"Wanna see the scars?"

"I didn't mean to be so ruthless," she said tenderly, filled with regret for having injured his pride, although she'd known the nature of their talk would be painful for him.

"The truth hurts—isn't that how the saying goes?"

Diana nodded.

"I've done a lot of thinking since that night." Only a few feet separated them, and he raised his hands as though to reach for her and bring her close to him. Reluctantly he dropped his fists to his side and took a step in the opposite direction.

"And?" Diana pressed.

"And I think we may have something, Diana. Something far more valuable than magic. Something I'm not likely ever to find again. I don't want to lose you. I realize I may have ruined everything by trying to rush you into bed with me, and I apologize for that. I'd like a second chance with you, although I probably don't deserve one."

His eyes softened and caressed her with such tenderness that Diana stopped breathing until her lungs ached. When she spoke, the words rushed out on the tail end of a raspy sigh. "I think...that could be arranged."

"Whatever it is between us is potent—you'll have to agree to that."

Diana couldn't deny the obvious.

"I know you have your doubts and I honestly can't blame you. But if you agree to letting me see you again, I promise to do things differently. I'm not going to pressure you into lovemaking—you have my word on that."

"I've made my share of mistakes, too, and I think it would only be fair if I came up with a few promises of my own."

He looked at her as though he hadn't had a clue as to what she was talking about.

"I have no intention of rushing you into making a commitment. And the word *love* will be stricken from my vocabulary." Feeling almost giddy with relief, she smiled warmly.

Cliff smiled in return. "I wonder if we could seal this bargain with a kiss."

"I think that would be more than appropriate."

Cliff had reached for her even before she'd finished speaking. He needed to hold her again and savor her softness pressing against him. She was halfway into his arms, when the front door burst open.

"Cliff!" Katie leaped into the living room with all the energy of a hydroelectric dam. Her pigtails were swinging, her eyes aglow. "I didn't think you'd ever get here. You forgot to sign my cast, and I saved you a space, but it's getting dirty."

Joan followed shortly after Katie. "Hi, Cliff," she said nonchalantly. She tossed her mother an apologetic look.

Cliff pulled a pen from inside his suit pocket and knelt in front of Katie.

"What took you so long?" Katie demanded as Cliff started penning his message on her cast.

"I don't know, buttercup," he answered, looking up to Diana and smiling.

"I can't get over how much the girls have grown," Joyce Shaffer, Diana's mother, said with an expressive sigh, alternately glancing between Joan and Katie.

"It's been a year, Mom." The long flight from Seattle to Wichita had left the girls and Diana exhausted. Joan and Katie had fallen asleep ten minutes after they arrived at Diana's family home. Diana longed to join her daughters, but her parents were understandably excited and wanted to chat. Diana and her mother gathered around the kitchen table, nibbling on chocolate chip cookies, drinking tall glasses of milk and talking.

"Poor Katie," her mother went on to say sympathetically. "Is her arm still hurting?"

"It itches more than anything."

Burt Shaffer pulled up a chair and joined the two women. "Who's this Cliff fellow the girls were telling me about?"

Diana hesitated, not exactly sure how to explain her relationship with Cliff. She didn't want to lead her family into thinking she was about to remarry, nor did she wish to explain that she and Cliff had reached a still untested understanding.

"Cliff and I have dated a few times." That was the best explanation she could come up with on such short notice. She should have been prepared for this. The minute the girls had stepped off the plane, Katie had shown her grandparents where Cliff had signed her cast and told the detailed story of how he'd let her ride in his car on the way home from the hospital. First Katie, then Joan, had spoken nonstop for a full five minutes, extolling his myriad virtues, until Diana had thought she'd scream at them both to cut it out.

"So you've only dated him a few times." Her father nodded once, giving away none of his feelings. "The girls certainly seem to have taken a liking to him. What about you, Rosebud? Do you think as highly of this Cliff fellow as Joan and Katie seem to?"

"Now really, Burt," her mother cut in. "Don't go quizzing poor Diana about the men in her life the minute she walks in the door. Diana, dear, did I tell you Danny Helleberg recently moved back to town?"

Diana and Danny had gone to high school together a million years ago. Although they'd been in the same class, Diana had barely known him. "No…"

"I talked to his mother the other day in the grocery

store and I told her you were flying out for a visit. She says Danny would love to see you again."

"That would be nice." Not really, but Diana didn't want to disappoint her mother.

"I'm glad you think so, honey, because he phoned and I told him to call again in the morning."

"That'd be great." Her smile was weak at best. She had hardly said more than a handful of words to Danny Helleberg the entire time they were in school together. Recounting the memory of their high-school days should take all of five minutes. It was the only thing they had in common.

"His wife left him for another man. I did tell you that, didn't I? The poor boy was beside himself."

"Yes, Mom, I think you did mention Danny's marital problems." She tried unsuccessfully to swallow a yawn, gave up the effort and planted her hand over her mouth, hoping her parents got the hint.

They didn't.

"Danny and his wife are divorced now."

Diana did her best to try to look interested. It was the same way every visit—her parents seemed to think it was their duty to supply her with another husband. Every summer a variety of men were paraded before her while Diana struggled to appear grateful.

"Tell us about Cliff," her dad prompted.

Diana's finger tightened around her milk glass. "There really isn't much to tell. We've only gone out a few times."

"What's his family like?" her mother wanted to know, looking as though she already disapproved. If Diana was going to remarry, it was her mother's opinion that the man should be from Wichita. Then Diana wouldn't have any more excuses to remain in Seattle.

"Really, Mom, I don't have any idea—I haven't met his parents."

"I see." Her mother exchanged a look with her father that Diana recognized all too well. "Cliff's an attorney," she added hurriedly, hoping that would impress her parents.

"That's nice, dear." But her mother didn't seem overly swayed by the information. "We just hope you aren't serious about this young man."

"Why?" Diana asked, surprised.

Her mother looked more amazed than Diana. "Why, because Danny Helleberg is back in town. You know how well his mother and I get along."

Diana felt like grinding her teeth. "Right, Mom."

Cliff leaned back on his leather couch and stretched out his legs in front of him, crossing his ankles. Diana's first email had arrived. Already adrenaline was pumping through him. Four days. She'd been gone only four days, and he missed her more than he thought it was possible to miss another human being. He thought about their last minutes together while he'd driven her and the girls to the airport. Diana had lingered as long as she could, seeking to delay their parting. So much had remained unsaid between them. She'd wrapped her arms around his neck and kissed him soundly. The memory of that single, ardent kiss still had the power to triple his pulse rate. It was the type of kiss men remember as they go into battle. A kiss meant to forge time and distance. She'd looked as dazed as he felt. Without saying anything more, she'd turned and left him, rushing into the airport with Joan and Katie at her side. Cliff had remained at the airport drop-off point far longer than necessary, wishing she were back in his arms. Two weeks, he'd thought. That shouldn't be so long, but the way the time was dragging, each minute seemed longer than the one before. Two weeks was an eternity.

He grinned as he read over the first few lines that told him about Joan and Katie and how Katie had told her parents about him before Diana had had the opportunity to mention his name. The smile faded when he read how her parents were pressuring her to move to Wichita so they could look after her properly. He sighed audibly as he scrolled down to the second page. Diana assured him this was an old argument and that she had no intention of leaving Seattle. She loved her parents, but being close to them would slowly, surely, drive her crazy. Cliff agreed with that. He loved his family, but they had the same effect upon him.

Cliff continued reading. Diana told him she regretted the impulsive kiss at the airport. Now all she could think about was getting back to Seattle and seeing him again. Nothing had ever been that good—not even their first kiss at the marina under the starlight.

Cliff agreed.

If she experienced half the emotion he had over that kiss, she'd call her family vacation short and hurry back to him. All he could think about was Diana coming home and his holding her again.

He left the computer and went into the kitchen to fix himself something for dinner. Five minutes later he returned, pausing over the last few words she'd written about the kiss.

On impulse he reached for the phone. If he didn't hear her voice, he'd be the one to slowly, surely, go crazy. Getting her parents' number wasn't a problem, and he quickly punched it out, checking his watch and figuring out the time difference.

"Hello."

Cliff would have staked his life savings that Joan would answer. He was right.

"Hi, Joan."

"Cliff! How are you?"

"Fine." Okay, so that was a minor exaggeration; he would be once he talked to Joan's mother.

"We went to Sedgwick County Zoo today. It was great. I saw a green snake and a black-necked swan."

She paused, and Cliff heard muffled arguing.

"Joan," Cliff called after a long pause, "are you there?"

"Yes, Cliff," she said a bit breathlessly. "It seems my darling younger sister wants to talk to you."

"Okay." Briefly Cliff wondered if he'd end up speaking to everyone in the entire household before he was able to talk to Diana.

"Hi, Cliff," Katie shouted. "I told Grandma and Grandpa all about you, and Grandpa says he's going to take me fishing here in Wichita."

"That sounds like fun. Where's your mother?"

"There was a bad storm the other night and there was lightning and thunder, and I woke up scared and Mom came in and told me there was music in the storm. Did you know that? And guess what? She was right. I went back to sleep, and in the morning I could still remember the funny kind of drums that played."

Cliff was impressed at Diana's genius. "I'm glad you're not afraid of thunder anymore."

Once again Cliff heard muffled words and then silence. "Katie? Is someone on the phone?"

"Hello, Cliff."

Joan again. "Listen, sweetheart, could I speak to your mother?"

"I'm afraid that poses something of a problem," Joan whispered huskily into the receiver, as though she'd cupped her hand over it.

"It does?"

"Yes. You see, she isn't here at the moment."

"What time do you expect her back?"

"Late. Real late."

"How late?"

"She didn't get in until after midnight last night."

Cliff grinned. "I suppose she's seeing a lot of her old high-school friends."

"Especially one old friend. A *boyfriend*," Joan said heavily.

"Oh?"

"Yes, his name is Danny Helleberg. He's not nearly as good-looking as you, but Grandma told me that looks aren't everything. Grandma insists that Danny will make an excellent stepdad. Katie and I aren't sure. Out of all the men mother's been dating—including the man with references—we vote for you."

Eleven

A week! It hadn't even taken Diana a week to forget about him. The minute she was out of Cliff's sight, she'd started dating another man behind his back. Outrage poured over him like burning oil, scalding his thoughts. He should have learned from Becky that women weren't to be trusted. He'd been a fool to allow another woman, someone he'd thought he could trust, to do this to him a second time.

Pacing seemed to help, and Cliff did an abrupt about-face and marched to his living-room window with a step General MacArthur would have praised. All along, Diana had probably planned and plotted this assault on his pride. Look at how cleverly she'd manipulated him thus far! Why, she'd had him eating out of the palm of her hand! With his fists clenched tightly at his sides, Cliff turned away from the unseen panorama before him and stepped into his kitchen, opening the refrigerator. He stared blankly at its contents, shook his head, wondered what he was doing there and closed the door. Diana was ingenious, he'd grant her that much. She had him right where she wanted him—lonely, miserable and wanting her. From the minute he'd met her, he hadn't been himself. It was as though he were out of sync with his inner self while he mulled over what this young widow and her daughters were doing in his life. He'd listened to her while she tore him apart, searched deep within himself and recognized the truth of what she'd said. And all the while she'd waited patiently for him to return to her. And he had. Diana had been so confident that she hadn't so much as tried to contact him. Not once.

Then this sweet, innocent widow had duped him into believing this two-week jaunt to Wichita was a vacation to visit her family. She was visiting all right, but it wasn't her family she'd been so eager to get home to see. Oh, no, it was some old-time boyfriend she could hardly wait to date again. While she'd been looking at Cliff with those wide, deceiving eyes of hers, she'd been scheming to hook up with this Danny whatever-his-name-was.

And another thing—some mother she turned out to be, leaving Joan and Katie this way. Both girls had bubbled over with excitement, they'd been so happy to hear from him. The poor kids were lonely. And what children wouldn't be, left in a strange house with people they hardly knew, while their mother was gallivanting around Wichita with another man?

Cliff knew one thing. If Diana was painting the town, he wasn't going to idly sit at home, pining away for her. He was through keeping the TV Guide company, through missing Diana or even thinking about her. In fact, he was finished with her entirely, he decided suddenly. He didn't need her, and it all too obvious that she didn't need him, either. Fine. She could have it her way. In fact, she could have her old high-school boyfriend. Being the noble man he was, Cliff determined that he would quietly bow out of the picture. He'd even wish the two childhood sweethearts every happiness.

Now that he'd made a decision, Cliff took out his little black book and flipped through the pages. The names and phone numbers of the women listed here would give Diana paranoia. Grinning, he ran his finger down the first section and stopped at Missy's phone number. One look at Missy, and Diana would know she was out of the running. Already he felt better. The thought of Diana comparing herself to another one of his dates and falling short was comforting to his injured ego. As he'd told himself a minute before, Cliff Howard didn't need Diana Collins.

He reached for the phone and hit the first three digits of Missy's number, then abruptly disconnected. He wasn't in the mood for Missy. Not tonight.

Determined, he turned the page and smiled again when he saw Ingrid's name. The pretty blond Swede was another one Diana would turn green over. This time, however, it wasn't the voluptuous body that would pull the widow up short, although heaven knew Ingrid was stacked in all the right places. No, Ingrid was a well-educated corporate attorney, in addition to being independently wealthy. Cliff knew how much Diana would have loved to get her college degree. Soothed by the thought, Cliff reached for the phone and punched out a long series of numbers, but he hung up before the first ring.

Diana wasn't such a terrible mother. Look at how she'd calmed Katie down in the middle of a thunderstorm. The unexpected, unwanted thought caused him to frown.

Okay, so she hadn't exactly left her daughters in the hands of strangers, but Joan and Katie hardly knew their grandparents. It seemed to Cliff that Diana would want to spend her time with her mother and father. He sagged against the back of the couch and let out his breath in a heated rush.

He didn't want to be with Missy tonight, not Ingrid, either. Diana was the only woman who interested him, and had been the only one for weeks. He had an understanding with Diana, unspoken, but not undefined. They had something wonderful going—they wanted to test these feelings, explore this multifaceted attraction. If she felt the need to date other men, then that was up to her. For his part, he'd been living in the singles world for a long time; he didn't need another woman in his arms to tell him what he already knew. His gaze fell to the black book in his hands. He riffled through the pages, stopping now and again at a name that brought back fond memories. Yet there wasn't anyone listed whom he'd like to wrap in his arms, no one he longed to kiss and love. Given a magic wand and a bucketful of wishes, Cliff would have conjured up Diana Collins and only Diana Collins. Widow. Mother. And, he added painfully, heartbreaker.

Cliff must have dozed off watching television, because the next thing he was aware of was the phone. Its piercing rings jolted him awake. He straightened, rubbed his hand over his eyes, then reached for his cell.

"Hello."

"Cliff, it's Diana."

The sound of her voice was enough to send the

blood rushing through his veins. When he spoke, he attempted to hide the sarcasm behind banter. "So how was your hot date with Danny Heartthrob?"

"That's what I called about. Listen, Cliff, I don't know what the girls told you…"

"Quite a bit, if you must know." Again he made it sound as though the entire evening had been a joke to him.

"Are you mad?"

She sounded worried and uptight, but Cliff thought it was poetic justice. "Should I be?"

"No!"

"Then why all the concern?"

Diana hesitated, not liking the condescending note in his voice. "I thought, you know, that you might have gotten upset because…well, because I'd gone out to dinner with Danny."

"Two nights in a row, according to Joan."

"I swear I don't even like him. He's a dead bore, but my mother's got this thing about my remarrying before I shrivel up and become an old woman. To hear her tell it, that's likely to happen in the next six weeks. Time is running out."

"Listen, if you want to see this Danny every night of your vacation, it's fine with me."

"It is?" came Diana's stunned response. "I…thought we had an understanding."

Cliff felt shut out and hurt, but he wasn't about to let her know that. Yes, they did have an agreement, but apparently it didn't mean a whole lot to Diana. Obviously she considered herself free to date other men, when he still hadn't recovered from the shock of not finding a single name in his black book that interested him. The only woman he wanted was Diana Collins, but unfortunately she was with another man.

"If you think I'm going to fly into a jealous rage, then you've got me figured all wrong. I'm just not the type," Cliff said, wondering exactly what this bozo Danny looked like. "The way I see it, you're on vacation and you're a big girl. You can do what you want."

Diana pondered his tone more than his words. She'd been sick when Joan and Katie had told her Cliff had phoned. He wouldn't understand that she'd gone out with Dan to appease her mother. These two dates had been part of a peacekeeping mission.

"You mean you're honestly not angry?"

"Naw."

"If the circumstances were reversed, I'm not sure I'd be as generous." She made an impatient, breathy sound, then burst out, "I know this is none of my business, but maybe you're being understanding about this because you've been seeing someone...since I've been in Wichita?"

Cliff would have loved to let her think exactly that, but he wasn't willing to lie outright. Misleading her, however, was an entirely different story.

"I'm sure there's been ample opportunity," Diana added, feeling more miserable by the minute.

"Well, as a matter of fact..."

"Forget I asked that," she insisted. "If you're going out with Bunnie or Bubbles or any of the other girls listed in your bachelor directory, I'd rather not know about it."

"Do you doubt me?" he asked, trying to sound casual. She had a lot of nerve. He was the one sitting home nights staring at the boob tube while she was flirting with everything in pants on the other side of the Rocky Mountains.

"It isn't a matter of trust," Diana answered after a long moment.

"Then what is it?"

"I'm not sure." The frustration was enough to make her want to cry. "We had so little time together before I had to leave. I'd been looking forward to this trip for weeks and then I didn't even want to go. There was so much I wanted to tell you, so much I wanted to say."

A pulsating silence stretched between them.

"It's ten-thirty here," Cliff said at last, checking his watch and figuring the time difference. It was past midnight there. "Did you just get in?"

"About twenty minutes ago."

"Did you have a good time?"

"No."

Naturally she'd tell him that, and just as naturally he believed her, because it hurt too much for him to think otherwise.

"I will admit that I was a little bit jealous when I first talked to Joan." He didn't like telling her that much; it went against his pride. But letting her know his feelings would help.

Diana relaxed and closed her eyes.

"But it wasn't anything I couldn't work out myself," he added magnanimously. "I didn't like it one bit, if you're looking for the truth, but beyond anything else, I trust you."

The line went quiet for a moment. "Oh, Cliff, I've been so worried."

"Worried," he repeated, realizing Diana was close to tears. "Whatever for?"

"After what happened with you and…Becky, I had this terrible feeling that you'd think I was…I don't know, cheating on you."

"You haven't even cheated *with* me yet."

Her soft laugh was like a refreshing sea mist on a hot, humid afternoon. Cliff savored the sweet musical cadence of her voice.

It struck him then, struck him hard.

He was in love with Diana. No wonder he'd reacted like a lunatic when Joan had told him her mother was out with an old high-school flame. He'd been a blind fool not to acknowledge his feelings before now. He'd been attracted to her physically almost from the first, and the pull had been so strong that sharing a bed with her had been the only thing on his mind. Her reaction to that idea had left him reeling for days. She wanted more, demanded more. At the time he hadn't learned that the physical response she evoked in him only skimmed the surface of his feelings for her.

"I can't tell you how boring tonight was," Diana went on. "Dan doesn't like women who wear Levi's. Can you believe that, in this day and age? I spent the entire evening listening to his likes and dislikes, and I'm telling you—"

"Diana," Cliff interrupted her.

"Yes?"

The need to say it burned on his tongue, but he held back. A man didn't tell a woman he loved her over the phone. "Nothing."

The line went completely silent for a moment. "I'm not seeing him again. I made that perfectly clear to Dan tonight." She could deal with her mother's disappointment more readily than she could handle another date with a fuddy-duddy thirty-year-old.

"Don't let me stand in your way," Cliff returned almost flippantly. He was still shaking with the realization that he loved Diana. When a man cared this deeply for a woman, he shouldn't need those kinds of reassurances.

Suddenly angry, Diana frowned at the receiver. "That's a rotten thing to say."

"What is?"

"Oh, don't play stupid with me, Cliff Howard. I hadn't planned on seeing Dan again, but since you have no objection, then fine."

He could feel the heat of her anger a thousand miles away. Her words were hurled at him with the vehemence of a hand grenade. "What's made you so mad?"

"You. Do I honestly mean so little to you?"

"What on earth are you talking about?"

"That...that last statement of yours about my dating Dan, as though you couldn't care less and..."

"I couldn't care less," he echoed, and feigned a yawn.

"Fine, then."

Cliff couldn't so much as hear her breathe. It was as though they'd been caught up in a vacuum, both struggling to find an escape, but discovering they were trapped.

She'd do it, too. Diana would go out with this clown again just to spite him. Women! He'd made a major concession on her behalf, and she didn't have the good sense to appreciate it. "Okay, you want me to say don't go out with Dan...then I'm saying it."

It was exactly what Diana had needed to hear five minutes before. Unfortunately his admission had come too late. "You've got no claim on me. I can see anyone I please, and you…"

"The hell I don't have a claim on you."

"The hell you do!"

"I love you," he shouted. "That must give me some rights."

"You don't need to shout it at me!"

"How else am I supposed to get you to listen?"

"I…I don't know." If she had felt like crying before, it was nothing compared to what she was experiencing now. "You honestly love me?" Her voice was little more than a whisper.

"What's wrong now?" True, he hadn't planned on telling her like this, but he expected some kind of reaction from her. What he'd honestly hoped she'd do was to burst into tears and tell him she'd been crazy about him from that first night when he'd repaired her sink.

"Why did you tell me something like this when I'm a thousand miles away?"

"Because I couldn't hold it inside any longer. Are you going to keep me in suspense here? Don't you think you should let me know what you feel toward me?"

"You already know."

"Maybe, but I'd still like to hear you say it."

"I love you, too." The words were low and seductive, rusty and warm.

"How much longer are you going to be gone?" he asked, having difficulty finding his voice.

"Too long."

Cliff couldn't have agreed with her more.

* * *

"Will Cliff be at the airport?" Joan wanted to know, returning the flight magazine to the pocket in the seat in front of her.

"Yeah, Mom, will he?" Katie asked, tugging on Diana's sleeve.

Diana nodded. "He said he would."

The Boeing 737 was circling Sea-Tac airport before making its final approach for landing.

Joan and Katie had been far less impressed with flying on the return trip from Wichita, and Diana felt mentally and physically drained after coming up with twenty different ways to keep the pair entertained.

Cliff had promised he'd be waiting in the airport when they landed. Although Diana was dying for a glimpse of him, she almost wished she had time to take a shower and properly touch up her makeup before their reunion. She felt haggard, and it wasn't entirely due to the long flight.

Diana had made the mistake of admitting to her parents that she was in love with Cliff. She'd been honest in the hope that her mother would understand why she didn't want to date anyone else while she was in Wichita. Instead the announcement had been followed by a grueling question-and-answer session. Her mother and father had demanded to know everything they could about Cliff and his intentions toward her and the girls. Diana couldn't reassure them since she didn't know herself. Instead of being pleased for Diana, her parents seemed all the more concerned. Consequently, her last week in Wichita had been strained and uneasy for everyone except the girls.

"You talked to him lots."

"Who?" Diana blinked, trying to listen to Katie.

Her younger daughter gave her a look that told Diana she was losing it. "Cliff, of course. Every time I turned around, you two were on the phone."

"We spoke a grand total of six times."

"But for hours."

"Yeah," Joan piped in. "The first week we were there, you hardly mentioned his name. In fact, you got mad at Katie for telling Grandma and Grandpa about him and then the second week you hogged the phone, talking to him every minute of the day."

"I did not hog the phone!"

"Someone could have been trying to get through to me, you know," Joan said defensively.

"Who?"

"I...don't know, but someone, maybe a boy."

"Is Cliff going to marry you?" Katie asked. "I think I'd like it if he did."

Oh, no, not the girls, too. First her parents wanted to know his intentions, and now Joan and Katie. It was too much. "I have no idea what's going to happen between Cliff and me," Diana answered forcefully. It was little wonder that Cliff hated the word *commitment*— she was beginning to have the same reaction herself.

"I, for one, think it would be fabulous to have a father who looks like Cliff," Joan said, tilting her head in a thoughtful pose.

"Speaking of rock stars," Diana said pointedly, her gaze narrowing on her elder daughter, "did you really tell the boy who carried out Grandma's groceries that we're a distant relation to Phil Collins?"

Joan's bemused gaze slid to the other side of the plane. "Well, I'm sure we must be related one way or another. Just how many Collinses could there be? It is a small world, Mother, in case you hadn't noticed."

The plane landed on the runway with hardly more than a timid bounce, then the taxi to the receiving gate took an additional ten minutes. By the time the 737 had pulled to a stop and passengers were starting to disembark, Diana's nerves were frayed. The girls were right; she had talked to Cliff nearly every night. But now that they were home, she was skittish and self-conscious. She wished she'd done something glamorous with her hair before they'd left Wichita, but at the time, she'd been so eager to get on the plane and back to Seattle that she hadn't planned ahead.

Joan and Katie tugged at her arms, urging her to hurry as they briskly walked down the narrow jetway. It seemed as if everyone was hurried toward baggage claim, and although Diana didn't readily see Cliff, she knew he was there.

"Diana."

She'd just made it past the first large group crowding around the carousel.

"Over here."

Before Diana could think, Joan and Katie had left her side and hurled themselves at Cliff as though they'd just spent the past ten years in boarding school.

He crouched to receive their bear hugs and nearly toppled when he looked up and smiled at Diana.

"Welcome home," he said, straightening. Lightly he wrapped his arm around her shoulder and brushed his lips over hers. He paused to inhale the fragrance of spring that was hers alone and briefly closed his eyes in gratitude for her and the girls' safe return.

"Do you want to see my suntan?" Joan asked.

"Sure." Cliff was so glad to have them back that he would have agreed to anything.

"I got another Pooh bear from Grandma."

Cliff grinned down on Katie, and would have willingly given her a whole warehouse full of her favorite bear. Oh yes, it was good to have them back.

"What about you?" Cliff asked, slipping his arm around Diana's waist. "Is there anything you want to show me?"

"Maybe."

"Later?"

"Later," she agreed with a soft smile.

They weren't back in the house five minutes before Joan and Katie were out the door, eager to let their friends know everything about Wichita.

Cliff had just finished delivering the last suitcase to Katie's bedroom. He paused at the top of the stairs and waited for Diana to meet him.

"If I don't get to properly kiss you soon, I'm going to go crazy." He held his arms out to her. "Come here, woman."

Without hesitation, Diana walked into his arms as though she'd always belonged there. It didn't matter to her that the front door was wide open, or that the girls were likely to burst in at any minute. All that concerned her was Cliff.

His hands knotted at the base of her spine as his gaze drifted hungrily over hers. "Did you see any more of Danny-boy?"

"You know I didn't."

"Good, because I was insanely jealous." His mouth found hers in an expression of fiery need, and he poured everything he'd learned about himself into the kiss. Everything he'd learned about what was right for them. Nothing had gone according to schedule while Diana was away. Every second, every minute of their separation had only heightened his need to have her back. Again and again he kissed her, needing her and showing her how much. His lips branded her and cherished her, and his tongue dipped into the secret warmth of her mouth.

Fire streaked through Diana's veins, and a delicious throbbing ache spread through every part of her body. The Boeing aircraft had landed in Seattle, she had even carried her suitcases into the house, but she hadn't been home until exactly this minute. The realization of how much Cliff had come to mean to her in such a short time was both powerful and frightening. She slid her arms around him, needing the reassurance of his closeness. Her hands traced his back, slowly playing over his ribs and the taper of his spine. She savored the feel of this man who held her and loved her and needed her as much as she needed him.

Diana's breathing became raspy when Cliff's mouth moved from her lips to the side of her neck. She trembled and snuggled closer in his embrace.

"Welcome home, Diana." His own breathing was shaky.

"If I go to the grocery store, to the dentist, to the bank, anywhere, promise you'll greet me this way when I return."

"I promise." His grip on her shoulders relaxed, but he didn't release her. Not yet.

"Oh, I nearly forgot." She broke away and hurried into her bedroom. "I brought you something."

Cliff followed her inside. "You did?"

Already Diana had tossed her suitcase on top of the mattress and was sorting through a stack of neatly folded clothes for the T-shirt.

"Diana?"

"It's right here. Just hold on a minute."

"Listen, I know this is soon and everything…"

"It's blue—the same color as your eyes." When she'd first seen the T-shirt, her heart had almost broken, she'd missed him so much.

Cliff buried his hands in his pockets. This wasn't exactly how he planned to do this, but he'd done a lot of thinking while Diana had been away and seeing her again proved everything he thought to question. "Diana…"

"It's here. I know it is." She paused and twisted around. "I may have tucked it in Joan's suitcase." Determined to find it, she hurried into her daughter's bedroom, paused and whirled around. "I'm sorry, Cliff, what were you saying?"

"Nothing." He felt like a fool.

"Okay." Diana went back and started rooting through the suitcase. The shirt was perfect for Cliff, and she was eager to give it to him.

"Actually, I had some time to mull over our relationship while you were away, and I was thinking that maybe we should get married."

At last Diana found the shirt, lifted it out and turned to face him, her eyes wide with triumph. The excitement drained from her as quickly as water through a sieve.

"What was it you just said?"

Twelve

"Mom, what do you think?" Joan paraded in front of her mother as though the eleven-year-old were part of a Las Vegas floor show. She wiggled her girlish hips and demurely tucked her chin over her shoulder while placing her hands on bended knee. "Well?"

Diana successfully squelched a smile. "You look at least fifteen, if not older."

Joan positively glowed with the praise.

"How come we have to wear a dress?" Katie grumbled, following her sister into the living room. Diana's younger daughter wasn't the least bit thrilled at the prospect of a dinner date with Cliff if she had to wear her Sunday clothes. "How come Cliff can't just bring over KFC? I like that best."

"Hey, dog breath, I want to eat in the Space Needle," Joan blasted her.

In a huff, Katie crossed her arms and glared defiantly at her sister. "I think it's silly."

The dinner date with the girls to announce their engagement had been Cliff's suggestion. He'd wanted to take Joan and Katie someplace fancy and fun and

had chosen the famous Seattle landmark from the 1962
World's Fair.

"Come on, girls," Diana pleaded, "this night is special, so be on your absolute best behavior."

"Okay," the two agreed simultaneously.

Cliff arrived ten minutes later, dressed in a crisp
pin-striped three-piece suit and looking devilishly
handsome. The minute he walked in the house, the
girls burst into excited chatter, gathering around him
like children before a clown. Although he was listening to Joan and Katie, his eyes sought out Diana's and
were filled with warmth and gentle promise. One look
confirmed that his wild imagination hadn't conjured
everything up out of desperation and loneliness. She
did love him, and heaven knew he loved her.

Seeing Cliff again made Diana feel nervous, impatient and exhilarated. She'd only arrived back in Seattle
the day before, and her whole world had been drastically changed within a matter of a few hours. The
memory of Cliff standing on the other side of Joan's
bedroom from her, looking boyish and uncertain as he
suggested they get married, would remain with Diana
all her life. Anyone who knew this man would never
have believed the confident, sophisticated Cliff Howard could be so unsure of himself. In that moment,
Diana knew she would never again doubt his love. She
didn't recall how she'd answered him. A simple yes or
a nod—perhaps both. What she did remember was the
joy of Cliff crushing her in his arms and kissing her
until they'd been forced to part when Joan and Katie
returned.

"Can I order KFC at the Space Needle?" Katie asked
a second time, breaking into Diana's musings.

"Every restaurant serves chicken, dummy," Joan inserted. "Personally, I'm going to order shrimp."

If dishes were wishes, Cliff would order two weeks alone in a hotel room with Diana. He dreamed about making love to her, about lying in bed and experiencing the feel of her skin brushing against him. He thought about waking up with her in the morning and falling asleep with her at night. Night after night, day after day. The mere suggestion excited him, filled him with anticipation for the good life that lay before them. The physical desire he felt for her was deep, honest and powerful. On the twenty-minute drive into Seattle, both Joan and Katie were excited and anxious and kept the conversation going, bantering back and forth, then squabbling, then joking.

The elevator ride up the 605-foot Space Needle left Joan and Katie speechless with awe. Diana treasured the brief silence. She didn't know what had gotten into her girls lately, but they seemed either to be constantly chattering or else endlessly bickering.

The hostess seated them by a window overlooking Puget Sound and the Olympic mountain range. The two girls sat together, and Cliff sat beside Diana. Once they were comfortable, they were handed huge menus. Diana's eyes skimmed over her own, and when she'd made her decision, she glanced in the girls' direction.

"Katie," she whispered, both embarrassed and amused, "honey, the napkin's not a party hat. Take it off your head."

"Oh." Katie's dark eyes were filled with chagrin.

Joan smothered a laugh, which only proved to embarrass Katie more.

"How was I supposed to know these things?" Katie demanded.

Joan opened her mouth to explain it all to her younger sibling, but Diana interceded with a scalding look that instantly silenced her oldest daughter.

Cliff set his menu aside when the waitress appeared, and after everyone had made their selection, he ordered champagne cocktails for the adults and Shirley Temples for the girls. While waiting for their drinks to arrive, Cliff placed his arm around Diana, cupping her shoulder. She raised her hand and linked her fingers with his. His touch was light, almost impersonal, but Diana wasn't fooled. Cliff was as nervous about this evening as she was. So much rested on how Joan and Katie reacted to their news.

"Cliff and I have something we'd like to tell you," Diana said softly after the waitress had placed a drink in front of each one of them. She knew how much the girls liked Cliff, but she wasn't sure how they'd feel about him becoming a major part of their lives. It had been just the three of them for a long time.

Joan took a long sip of her Shirley Temple. Her eyes were raised, but her head was lowered. She looked like a crocodile peering at them from just above the waterline. For her part, Katie was busy spreading out the linen napkin across her lap.

Diana resisted the urge to shout at them both that this was important and they should pay attention.

"Cliff and I are trying to tell you something," Diana said forcefully, gritting her teeth with impatience.

"What?"

The fact that they'd decided to get married wasn't something to be blurted out without preamble. Diana had hoped to start off by explaining to her daughters how she'd come to love Cliff and how her love would affect Joan's and Katie's life.

"Cliff and I have discovered that we love each other very much." Diana's fingers tightened around his. Just being able to say the words and not having to hide them in her heart produced a special kind of joy.

"So?" Katie murmured, lifting the tiny, plastic sword from her drink and shoving both maraschino cherries into her mouth at once.

"I already knew that," Joan said knowingly.

"So," Diana said slowly, and expelled her breath, "Cliff and I were thinking about getting married."

"And we wanted to know your feelings on the matter," he inserted, studying both Joan and Katie. He was as uptight about this evening as Diana. But the girls seemed more concerned about sucking ice cubes than listening to what their mother had to say.

Joan shrugged. "Sure, if you want to get married, I don't care."

"Me, either," Katie agreed, and juice from the two cherries slid down the side of her chin.

"Oh, gross," Joan cried, and pointedly looked in the opposite direction.

Diana's patience was quickly wearing thin. "Girls, please, we're not talking about what we're going to have for breakfast tomorrow morning. If Cliff and I do get married, it's going to be a major change in all our lives." She was about to relay that the marriage would mean they'd be moving and the girls would be changing schools, but Joan interrupted her.

"Will I get a bigger allowance?"

"Can I have a new bike?" Katie asked on the tail end of her sister's question.

"Can I tell people we're going to be rich?" Joan asked without guile.

"If we're going to be rich, then I should be able to get a new bike, shouldn't I?"

"We are not going to be wealthy because I'm marrying Cliff," Diana cried, raising her voice and doing a poor job of hiding her disappointment in her daughters. She wasn't sure what she'd expected from Joan and Katie but it certainly hadn't been indifference and greed.

"Gee, Mom, why are you so mad?" Joan asked, studying her mother with a quizzical frown. "Katie and I already knew you were in love with Cliff. We couldn't help but know from the way you've been acting all summer."

Both girls seemed to want an answer.

"I see," Diana answered softly, briefly regaining a grip on her emotions.

"Then neither of you has any objection to our getting married?" Cliff asked.

Diana was as tense as a newly strung guitar. What upset her most was the way the girls were behaving; the entire dinner was about to be ruined.

Joan and Katie shared a look and answered his question with a short shake of their heads.

"I think it'd be great if you married Mom," Joan answered. "But if it's possible, I'd like to be able to get my ears pierced before the wedding." Briefly she fondled her thin earlobe. "What do you think, Cliff?"

As an attorney, Cliff was far too wise to get drawn

into those mother-daughter power games. "I think that's up to your mother."

"And you already know my feelings on the matter, Joan!"

"Okay. Okay. Sorry I asked."

Any further argument was delayed by the waitress, who delivered their order, and for a brief time, all dissension was forgotten. Katie dug into her crispy fried chicken, while Joan daintily dipped her jumbo shrimp in the small container of cocktail sauce.

"Mom, will Cliff be my father?" Joan asked a minute later, cocking her head in a thoughtful pose.

"Your stepfather."

Joan nodded and dropped her gaze, looking disappointed. "But would a stepfather be considered a real enough father for the banquet?"

It took Diana only a moment to understand Joan's question. The Girl Scout troop Joan had been involved with throughout the school year was sponsoring a father-daughter dinner at the end of the month. Diana had read the notice and not given the matter much thought. Unless someone from church volunteered to escort them, the girls generally didn't attend functions that involved fathers and daughters.

"I'm sure a stepfather will be acceptable," Cliff answered. "Would you like me to take you to the banquet?"

"Would you really?"

"I'd be more than happy to."

It seemed such a minor gesture, but a feeling of such intense gratitude filled Diana's heart that moisture pooled in her eyes. She turned to Cliff and offered him a watery smile. "Thank you," she whispered. She wanted to say more, but speaking was quickly becoming impossible.

His eyes held hers in the most tender of exchanges, and it took all the strength and good manners Cliff could muster not to kiss Diana right there in the Space Needle restaurant. His insides felt like overcooked mush. He was ready for a wife, more than ready, and he was willing to learn what it meant to be a father.

It wasn't his intention to take the memory of Stan away from Joan and Katie, nor would he be the same kind of father they'd known. He was sure to make mistakes; he wasn't perfect and this father business was new to him, but he loved Joan and Katie and he planned to care for them as long as he lived. Somewhere along the way to discovering his feelings for Diana, her daughters had neatly woven strings around his heart.

"It's because of me, isn't it?" Katie asked, waving a chicken leg in front of Diana's and Cliff's nose as though it were a weapon.

"What is?" Diana asked.

"That you and Cliff are going to get married."

"How come?" Joan asked sharply, reaching for her napkin. "I think it's because of me."

"No way!" Katie cried. "I was the one who broke my arm and Cliff came back to Mom because of that!"

"Yeah, but I was the one who called and told him you were in the hospital—so it's all my doing. If it hadn't been for me, we could have ended up with Owen, or worse yet, Dan from Wichita, as our new dad."

"Will you girls kindly stop arguing?" Diana hissed. Embarrassment coated her cheeks a shade of hot pink.

People were turning around to stare at them. Diana was certain she could feel disapproving looks coming their way from the restaurant staff.

"Who did it, then?" Katie demanded.

"Yeah, who's responsible?"

Both girls stopped glaring at each other long enough to turn to look at their mother.

"In a way you're both responsible," Diana conceded, praying the two would accept the compromise.

"Ask Cliff." Once again the chicken leg was waved under their noses.

"Yeah, Cliff, what do you think?"

"I think…"

"Drop it, girls," Diana insisted in a raised voice the girls readily recognized as serious. "Immediately!"

The remainder of the dinner was a nightmare for Diana. Whereas Joan and Katie had chattered all the way into Seattle, they sat sullen and uncommunicative on the drive home to Kent. A couple of times Cliff attempted to start up a conversation, but no one seemed interested. Diana knew she wasn't.

Back at the house, Joan and Katie went upstairs to their rooms without a word.

Diana stood at the bottom of the stairs until they were out of sight and then moved into the kitchen to make coffee. Cliff followed her and placed his hands on her shoulders as she stood before the sink.

Miserable and ashamed of her children's behavior, Diana hung her head. "I am so sorry," she whispered when she could speak.

"Diana, what are you talking about?"

"The girls—"

"Were exhausted from a two-week vacation with

their grandparents. You haven't been back twenty-four hours, and here we are hitting them with this." Gently his hands stroked her bare arms. He felt bad only because Diana did. "I love you, and I love the girls. Tonight was the exception, not the norm. They're good kids."

She nodded because tears were so close to the surface and arguing would have been impossible. Cliff must really love her to have put up with the way Joan and Katie had behaved. Diana couldn't remember a time when her daughters had been worse. After all these years as a single mother, Diana had prided herself on being a good parent and in one evening she'd learned the truth about her parenting skills.

"Diana," Cliff whispered, "put that mug down. I don't want any coffee. I want to hold you."

The mug felt as if it weighed a thousand pounds when Diana set it on the counter. Slowly she turned, keeping her eyes on the kitchen floor, unable to meet his gaze.

His arms folded around her, bringing her against him. He didn't make any demands on her, content for the moment to offer comfort. His chin slowly brushed against the top of her head, while his hands roved in circles across her back. The action had meant to be consoling, but Cliff had learned long before that he couldn't hold Diana without wanting her. Diana looped her arms around his neck and directed his mouth to hers. The kiss was possessive, filled with frustration and undisguised need. Diana shuddered as the wild, consuming kiss.

Cliff was pacing outside the gates of heaven. He loved this woman, needed her physically, mentally, emotionally—every way there was to need another human being. But she was driving him crazy The drugged kiss went on unbroken, and so did the way she moved against him. "Diana," He pulled his mouth from hers and buried his face in her shoulder while he came to grips with himself.

They remained clenched in each other's arms until their strained, uneven breathing calmed. Gathering her courage, Diana tilted back her head until she found his eyes.

Cliff smiled at her, bathing her in his love. His thumb brushed the corners of her mouth, needing to touch her.

Little could have gone worse tonight, and Diana felt terrible. "You don't have to go through with it, you know."

He frowned, not understanding.

"With the wedding... After tonight, I wouldn't blame you if you backed out. I think if the situation were reversed, I'd consider it."

Cliff's frown deepened. She had to be nuts! He'd just found her and he had no intention of doing as she suggested. He saw the doubt in her eyes that told him of her uncertainty. He met her gaze steadily, his own serious. "No way, Diana," he whispered, and cupped her face, tilting her head upward to meet his descending mouth. The kiss was deep and long, warm and moist. When he broke away, his shoulders were heaving and his breathing was fast and harsh. He didn't move a muscle for the longest moment. Then, slowly, regretfully, he dropped his arms.

"I'd better go," he said with heavy reluctance. It was either go now or break his promise to her.

Diana wanted him to stay, needed him with her, but she couldn't ask it of him. Not tonight, when everything else had gone so wrong. Wordlessly she followed him to the front door.

He paused and lifted his hand to caress her sweet face. Diana placed her own over his and closed her eyes.

"I'll call you tomorrow."

She nodded.

"Mom, when will Cliff be here?"

Diana finished removing Joan's hair from the hot curler before glancing at her wristwatch. "He's due in another hour."

"Do you think he'll like my dress?"

"I'm sure he'll love it. You always did look so pretty in pink."

"Really?"

Diana couldn't remember Joan ever being more anxious for anything. The Girl Scout banquet was a special night for her daughter and for Cliff. The wedding was set for the second week of August; they'd found a house near Des Moines that everyone was thrilled with, and they planned to make the big move before the first day of school. Diana had already started some of the packing.

Her parents were flying out for the ceremony, as were Cliff's. His brother, Rich, and his wife and family were driving up from California. But for Joan, the wedding and all the planned activities that went along with it ran a close second to the father-daughter banquet. Cliff had told her he was ordering an orchid for

Joan, and out of her allowance money Joan had proudly purchased a white rose boutonniere for Cliff.

The phone pealed in the distance, and a minute later Katie stuck her head in the bathroom door. "It's for you, Mom. It's Cliff." Katie paused and glanced at her elder sister. "Wow, you look almost grown up."

"You really think so, Katie?"

Smiling, Diana hurried into the upstairs hallway and picked up the telephone receiver. "Hi, there. Oh, Cliff, you wouldn't believe how pretty Joan looks. I've never seen her—"

"Diana, listen…"

"She's more excited than on Christmas morning—"

"Diana." This time his voice was sharp, sharper than he'd intended. He was in one heck of a position, torn between his job and his desire to be with Joan for her special night. He didn't mean to blurt it out, but there didn't seem to be any other way to say it. "I can't make it tonight."

Diana was so stunned she sagged against the wall and closed her eyes. "What do you mean you can't make it?" she asked after a tortuous moment when the terrible truth had begun to sink in. Surely she'd misunderstood him. She hoped there was some kind of mix-up and she hadn't heard him right.

"The senior vice president has asked me to take over a case that's going to the state supreme court. I just found out about it. The first briefing is tonight."

"But surely you can get out of one meeting."

"It's the most important one. I tried, Diana."

"But what about Joan?" This couldn't be happening—it just couldn't. The new dress, Joan's first pair of panty hose, her hair freshly permed and set in hot rollers. "What about the father-daughter banquet?"

Cliff couldn't feel any worse than he already did. "I phoned George Holiday, and he's agreed to take her. There will be other banquets."

"But Joan wants to go with you."

"Believe me, if I could, I'd take her. But I can't." He was growing impatient now, more angry at the circumstances than with Diana, who couldn't seem to believe or accept what he was telling her.

"But surely they'd have let you know about something this important before now."

"Diana, I'll explain it to Joan later. I've got to get back to the meeting. I'm late now. Honey, believe me, I'm as upset about this as you are."

"Cliff," she cried, "please, you can't do this to her." But it was too late, the line had already been disconnected. When she turned around, Diana discovered Joan watching her with wide brown eyes filled with horror and distress.

"Cliff's not going, is he?" she asked in a pained whisper.

"No...he's got an important meeting."

Without a word, Joan turned and walked into her bedroom and closed the door.

The minute it was feasibly possible, Cliff prepared to leave the meeting. He shoved the papers into his briefcase and left with no more than the minimal pleasantries. He felt like a heel. His conscience had been punishing him all night. Okay, okay, it wasn't his fault, but he hadn't wanted to disappoint Joan. His only comfort was that he'd be able to take her to the father-daughter banquet the following year and the year after that. Surely she'd understand this once and be willing to look past her disappointment.

The porch light was on at Diana's, and he hurriedly parked the car. To his surprise, Diana met him at the front door. She looked calm, but she didn't fool him; he knew her too well. Anger simmered just below the surface. He'd hoped she would be more understanding, but he'd deal with her later. First he had to talk to her daughter.

"Where's Joan?"

"In her room. She cried herself to sleep."

"Oh, no." Cliff groaned. He moved past Diana and up the stairs into the eleven-year-old's bedroom. The room was dark, and he left the light off and sat on the corner of her mattress. His heart felt heavy and constricted with regret as he brushed the curls off her forehead.

"We need to talk," Diana whispered from outside the doorway. Her arms were crossed over her chest and her feet were braced apart, as though to fend off an attack.

"How did the banquet go?" he asked as he followed her down the stairs.

Diana shrugged. "Fine, I guess. Joan hardly said a word when she got home."

"Honey, I'm sorry, I really am. This kind of thing doesn't come up that often, but when it does, there's nothing I can do."

"You broke her heart."

Cliff didn't need Diana piling on any more guilt than what he already had. It wasn't as though he'd deliberately gone out of his way to disappoint Joan.

He certainly would rather have spent the night with Diana's daughter than cooped up in a stuffy, smoke-filled office.

"I know a banquet with an eleven-year-old girl isn't high on your priority list..."

"Diana, that's not true—"

"No...you listen to me. You want to break a date with me, then fine. I'm mature enough to accept it. But I can't allow you to hurt one of my children. I absolutely refuse to allow it."

Cliff ran his fingers through his hair and angrily expelled his breath. "You're making it sound like I deliberately planned this meeting just so I could get out of the banquet."

"All I know," Diana said, holding in the anger as best she could, "is that if it had been Stan, he would have been here!"

Stan's name hit Cliff with all the force of a brick hurled against the back of his head. He reeled with the impact and the shock of the pain. "Are you going to throw his name at me every time something goes wrong?"

"I don't know," she murmured. "All I know is that I don't want you to hurt Joan and Katie."

"You're making it sound like I'm looking for the opportunity."

"I've had all night to think about what I want to say," Diana confessed, dropping her gaze, unable to meet the cutting, narrowed look he was giving her. "All of a sudden I'm not so sure marriage would be the best thing for me and the girls."

Cliff knotted his hands into tight, impotent fists. "Okay, you want to call off the wedding, then fine."

His willingness shocked her. "I don't know what I want."

"Well, you'd better hurry up and decide."

A horrible silence stretched between them like a rolling, twisting fog, blinding them from the truth and obliterating the love that had once seemed so strong and invincible.

"I'll give you a week," Cliff announced. "You can let me know then what you want to do." With that, he turned and walked out the front door.

Thirteen

"Are you making poached eggs again?" Joan whined when she came down the stairs for breakfast.

"Yes," Diana said. "How'd you know?"

"Oh, Mom, honestly." The preteen plopped down at the kitchen table and shook her head knowingly. "You always make poached eggs when you're upset. It's a form of self-punishment—at least, that's what I think. Katie says it's because you still haven't made up with Cliff." She paused to study her mother. "Katie's right, too. You know that, don't you?"

Mumbling something unintelligible under her breath, Diana cracked two raw eggs over the boiling water. A frown gently creased her forehead. "Just how many times this week have I served poached eggs?"

"Three," Joan came back quickly. "Which is exactly as many days since you and Cliff had your big fight."

"We didn't have a big fight," Diana answered in a calm, reasonable voice.

Joan shrugged and took a long drink of her orange juice before answering. "I heard you. You and Cliff were shouting at each other—well, maybe not shouting, but your voices were raised, and I could hear you all the way upstairs." She paused as though considering whether to add a commentary. "Mom, I think you were wrong to talk to Cliff that way."

Diana groaned and scraped the butter across the top of the hot toast. "This isn't a subject I want to discuss with you, Joan."

"But I saw Cliff when he came into my bedroom, and he felt terrible about missing the banquet."

"I thought you were asleep!"

"I wasn't really...I had my eyes closed and everything, but I was peeking up at him through my lashes. He felt really bad. Even I could see that."

Diana wielded the butter knife like a sword, waving it at her daughter. "You should have said something then."

Looking guilty, Joan reached for her orange juice a second time. "I was going to, but you started talking and saying all those mean things to Cliff, and I was glad because I was still angry with him." She paused and sighed. "Now I wish I'd let him know I was awake. Then maybe I wouldn't be eating poached eggs every morning."

Diana served her daughters breakfast, but she didn't bother to eat any herself. She didn't need a week to decide if she wanted to marry Cliff. Within twenty-four hours after their argument, she recognized that she'd behaved badly. Joan and Katie were far more than willing to confirm her suspicions about the way she'd acted. Diana was forced into admitting she'd been unreasonable. More than anything, she deeply regretted throwing Stan's name at Cliff. Beyond whatever else she'd said, that had been completely unfair. She owed

Cliff an apology, but making one had never come easy to her—the words seemed to stick in her throat. But if she didn't do it soon, she'd have a mutiny on her hands. Already Katie had hinted that she was going to move in with Mrs. Holiday if she had to eat poached eggs one more morning.

The girls went swimming that afternoon, and while they were at the pool, Diana paced the kitchen floor, gathering up the courage to contact Cliff. With a stiff finger, she punched out the number to his office as she rehearsed again and again what she planned to say.

"Hello," she said in a light, cheerful voice. "This is Diana Collins for Cliff Howard."

"I'll connect you with one of his staff," the tinny receptionist's voice returned.

Diana was forced to ask for him a second time.

"Mr. Howard's in a meeting," his secretary explained in a crisp professional tone. "Would you like to leave a message?"

"Please have him return my call," Diana murmured, defeated. She was convinced Cliff had given his secretary specific instructions to inform her that he was out of the office. The suspicion was confirmed when, hours later, she still hadn't heard from him. He'd said a week, and he seemed determined to make her wait that long, Diana mused darkly after Joan and Katie were in bed asleep. He wanted her to sweat it out. Either that, or he'd decided to cut his losses and completely wash his hands of her.

Depressed and discouraged, Diana sat in front of the television, flipping channels, until she stumbled upon an old World War II movie. For an hour she immersed her woes in the classic battle scenes and felt tears course down her cheeks when the hero died a valiant death. The tears were a welcome release. Once she started, she couldn't seem to stop. Soon there was a growing pile of damp tissue on the end table beside her chair.

The doorbell caught her by surprise. There was only one person it could be. Cliff. Loudly she blew her nose, then quickly rubbed her open hands down her cheeks to wipe away the extra moisture. With her head tilted at a regal angle, she moved into the entryway, her heart pounding at a staccato beat.

"Hello."

Cliff took one look at her and blinked. "Are you okay?"

She nodded and pointed to the television behind her. "John Wayne just bit the dust, but he took the entire German army with him."

Cliff stepped inside the house. "I see."

He looked good, Diana thought unkindly. The very least he could do was show a little regret—a few worry lines around the mouth. Even a couple of newly formed crow's-feet at his eyes would have satisfied her. At the very least, he could say something to let her know he'd been just as miserable as she. Instead he was the picture of a man who had recently returned from a two-week vacation in the Caribbean. He was tan, relaxed, lean and so handsome he stole her breath.

"I understand you called the office," he said stiffly.

Diana nodded, but couldn't manage to get the practiced apology past the clog in her throat.

"You wanted something?"

Again she nodded. His expression was tightening— she was losing him fast. Either she had to blurt out how sorry she was, or she was going to let the most fantastic man she'd ever met silently slip out of her life.

"Is it so difficult to tell me?"

Confused, she nodded, then abruptly shook her head.

Cliff released a giant sigh of frustration and impatience, then reached for her, gripping her shoulders. His fingers dug deep into the soft flesh of her upper arms. "I'm not letting you go this easily."

"What?" She blinked at the shock of his harsh treatment.

"I know what you're going to say and I refuse to accept it."

She slapped her hand over her heart, her eyes as round and as wide as full moons. "You know what I'm going to say?"

In response, he nodded, released her shoulders and instead captured her face. If she'd wished to witness his pain and regret, she saw it now. It filled his face, twisting his mouth and hardening his jaw. "I love you, Diana." With that, he lowered his mouth to hers in a punishing kiss that robbed her of her breath and her wits.

Cliff groaned, and Diana slipped her arms around his neck, melting her body intimately against his. "Cliff." Reluctantly she broke away, lifting her soft brown eyes to capture his. Her hands bracketed his face as a slow, sweet smile turned up the corners of her mouth. "I love you so much. I'm so sorry for what happened— I was unreasonable. Forgive me. Please."

Shock and disbelief flickered briefly across his taut features.

"You can't honestly believe I'm going to cancel the

wedding," she whispered, humbled by this man and his love for her. "The reason I called you today was to tell you how much I love you." The moisture that brightened her eyes now had nothing to do with the emotion brought on by the sentimental movie. These tears came all the way from her heart.

Cliff looked for a moment as though he didn't believe her. He kissed her again because he couldn't remain with his arms wrapped around her and not sample her familiar sweet taste. He felt weak with relief and, at the same moment, filled with an incredible, invincible strength.

Cliff's kiss filled Diana with desire, left every muscle in her body quivering. Her passion matched his. Cliff pressed his lips over hers in mounting fervor, and Diana rose onto her toes to align herself more intimately with his body.

"Diana." He groaned and tore his mouth from hers. "We…we have things to settle here."

"Shh." She kissed him hungrily, slanting her mouth over his as she wove her fingers through his thick hair, savoring the feel and taste of him.

Cliff could refuse her nothing. The golden glow of a crescent moon outlined her beautiful face. Cliff released a deep sigh of awe at the priceless gift she was granting him—herself, without restraint, without restriction.

"Let's go upstairs," she whispered.

Cliff blinked and raised his hands to capture her face, holding her steady so he could look into her passion-drugged eyes. When he spoke, his voice was husky and deep. "Aren't the girls up there?"

"Yes, but…?"

Their breaths warmed each other's mouths. "I can't believe I'm doing this," he groaned, and closed his eyes to a silent agony.

"Doing what?"

"Refusing you."

"Cliff, no." Diana couldn't believe it, either. After all the times he'd tried to seduce her, now he was turning her down. "Why?" she choked. "I want you."

"Believe me, honey, I want you, too—so much it hurts." He spoke through clenched teeth, his hands gripping her upper arms. Diana went still in his arms, and he relaxed as though a great tension had eased from him.

"Not the first time we make love," he murmured into her hair, his voice low and raw. "Not like this. We'll be married in ten days. I can wait."

"I don't know that I can," she complained.

"Yes, you can. The loving is going to be very good between us."

If it was going to be like it had been tonight, Diana didn't know if she'd survive the honeymoon.

It took Cliff almost an hour to find the headstone. He'd wandered around the graveyard in the early morning sunlight, intent on his task. Today was to be his wedding day. Friends and relatives crowded around him at every turn. His sane, sensible mother had become a clucking hen. His father kept slapping him across the back, smiling and looking proud. Even his brother seemed to follow him around like a pesky shadow, just the way he'd done in their youth. There were a thousand things left to be done on this day, but none so important as this.

Now that he'd located the place, Cliff wasn't sure what had driven him here. He squatted and read the words engraved with such perfection into the white marble: STANLEY DAVID COLLINS, HUSBAND, FATHER. The date of his birth and death were listed. No epitaph, no scripture verse, just the blunt facts of one man's life.

Slowly Cliff stood and placed his hands in his pockets as he gazed down at the headstone. His heart swelled with strong emotion, and in that space of time, he knew what had driven him to this cemetery on this day. He hadn't come to seek solitude from all the hustle and bustle, nor had he sought escape from the people who had suddenly filled his home. He didn't need a graveyard to be alone. He'd come to talk to Stan Collins. He'd come because he had to.

"I wish I'd known you," he said, feeling awkward, the words low and gruff. "I think we would have been friends." From what he'd learned from George Holiday and the information he'd gleaned from Diana and the girls, Stan had been a good man, the type Cliff would gladly have counted as a friend.

Only silence greeted him. Cliff wasn't sure what he'd expected, certainly no voice booming from heaven, no sounds from the grave. But something— he just didn't know what.

"You must have hated leaving her," he said next. He didn't know much about Stan's death, only bits and pieces he'd picked up from Diana the day he'd gone to the hospital when Katie had broken her arm. Between Diana's nonsensical statements and her panic, he'd learned that she hadn't been able to see Stan when they'd brought him into the emergency room. There'd been no time for goodbyes. The realization twisted a tight knot in Cliff's stomach. "I know what thoughts must have been in your mind." He bowed his head at the grim realization of death. "I would have been filled with regrets, too."

A strange peace settled over Cliff, a peace beyond words. He relaxed, and a grin curved his mouth. "You'd be amazed at Joan and Katie. They're quite the young ladies now." Diana was letting both girls stand up with her today as maid of honor and bridesmaid. She'd sewn them each a beautiful long pink dress with lace overlays. Joan had claimed she looked at least fourteen. Heels, panty hose, the whole nine yards. Katie was excited about getting her hair done in a beauty shop. Cliff laughed out loud at the memory of the eight-year-old insisting they serve Kentucky Fried Chicken at the wedding reception. Joan had been thrilled with the prospect of having an extra set of grandparents at Christmastime. Within minutes both girls had had his parents eating out of their hands. They'd been enthralled with Diana's two daughters from the minute they'd been introduced.

"You'd have reason to be proud of your girls," he said thoughtfully. "They're fantastic kids."

The humor drained from his eyes as his gaze fell once more to the engraved words on the headstone. The word *father* seemed to leap out at him. "I guess what I want to say is that I don't plan on trying to steal you away from Joan and Katie." Stan would always be their father; he had loved his children more than Cliff would ever know until he and Diana had their own.

Now Cliff would be the one to raise Joan and Katie and love and nurture them into adulthood, guiding them with a gentle hand. "I know what you're thinking," he said aloud. "I can't say I blame you. I'm new to this fatherhood business. I can't do anything more than promise I'll do my best."

Now that he'd gotten past the girls, Cliff was faced with the real reason he had come. "I love Diana," he said plainly. "I didn't expect to, and I imagine you'd be more than willing to punch me out for some of the things I've tried with her. I apologize for that." His hands knotted into tight fists inside his pants pockets. "I honestly love her," he repeated, and sucked in a huge breath. "And I know you did, too."

The sun had risen above the hills now, bathing the morning mist with its warm, golden light so that the grass glistened. After a long reverent moment, Cliff turned and traced his steps back to the parking lot.

He took a leisurely drive back to his condominium and found his brother parked outside waiting for him.

"Where have you been?" Rich demanded. "I've been all over looking for you. In case you've forgotten, this is your wedding day."

Undisturbed, Cliff climbed out of his car and dropped the keys into his pants pocket.

Still Rich wasn't appeased. "I didn't know what to think when I couldn't find you." He checked his watch. "We were supposed to meet Mom and Dad ten minutes ago."

"Did you think I'd run away?" Cliff joked.

"Yes. No. I didn't know what to think. Where the blazes did you go that was so all-fired important?"

Cliff smiled into the sun. "To talk to a friend."

* * *

"Mom, I've got a run in my panty hose," Joan cried, her young voice filled with distress. "What am I supposed to do now?"

"I don't like the feel of hair spray," Katie commented for the tenth time, bouncing her hand off the top of her head several times just to see what would happen to the carefully styled but stiff curls.

"I've got an extra pair of nylons in the drawer," Diana answered Joan first. "Katie, keep your hands out of your hair!" Her mother was due any minute, and Diana didn't know when she'd been more glad to see either parent. Surprisingly, she wasn't nervous. She was more confident about marrying Cliff than any decision she'd made in the past three years. He loved her, and together they would build a good life together.

"You're not wearing your pearl earrings," Joan said with astonishment, and loudly slapped her sides. "Good grief, is any date more important than this one?"

Diana wrinkled her brow. "What do you mean?"

"Don't you remember? Honestly, Mom! I wanted you to wear the pearls the first night you went to dinner with Cliff, and you told me you wanted to wait for something festive to impress him."

Diana smiled at the memory. "I think you're right," she said, and traded the small gold pair for the pearls. "Nothing's more important than today." Her knees felt weak, not with doubts, but with excitement, and she sat on the corner of the mattress. "How do you girls feel?" she asked, watching her two daughters carefully.

"We're doing the right thing," Joan said with all the confidence of a five-star general. "Cliff's about the best we're going to do."

"What?" Diana asked with a small, hysterical laugh.

"Really, Mom," Katie came back. "For a while, I thought we'd get stuck with that Danny fellow from Wichita."

"Or Owen," Joan added. Both girls looked at each other and made silly faces and cried, "Oou!"

"Who's Owen?" Diana's mother asked as she stepped into the bedroom.

"He's the major geek I was telling you about who brought the references," Joan explained before Diana had the chance. He really was a dear man and someday he'd find the right woman. Fortunately, according to Joan and Katie, it wasn't her.

"Ah, yes," Joyce said, sharing a secret smile with her daughter. "You look lovely, sweetheart."

"Thanks," Joan answered automatically, then looked and gave her grandmother a chagrined smile. "Oh, you mean my mom."

"All three of you look beautiful."

Joan and Katie beamed at the praise.

"Watch, Grandma," Katie said. Tucking her arms close to her side, Katie whirled around a couple of times so the hemline of her dress flared out.

"Stop behaving like an eight-year-old," Joan cried. "You're supposed to be mature today."

"But I am eight!"

Joan opened her mouth to object, then realized she'd already lost one of her press-on fingernails. For a wild minute, there was a desperate search for the thumbnail. Peace ruled once they located it.

"Mother, would you check Katie's hair?" Diana asked. "She can't seem to keep her fingers out of it."

"Sure. Katie," Joyce called to her granddaughter, "let's go into the ladies' room."

Three hours later, Diana stood in front of the pastor who had seen her through life and death in the church where she sat each Sunday morning. Her parents, Cliff's family and a small assortment of close friends were gathered behind them. Joan and Katie stood proudly at her side.

The man of God warmed them all with a rare, tranquil smile. Diana turned, and her gaze happened to catch Cliff's. He did love her, more than she'd ever dared to dream, more than she'd ever thought possible. He stood tall and proud and eagerly held her eyes, his love shining through for her to read without doubt, without question. He was prepared to pledge his life to her and Joan and Katie. The commitment she sought he was about to willingly vow.

Witnessing all the love in Cliff's eyes had a chastising effect upon Diana. The man she'd once considered an unscrupulous womanizer had chosen her to share his life. He was prepared to love her no matter what the future held for them, prepared to raise her daughters and guide their young lives. Out of all the beautiful women he'd known, Cliff had chosen her. Diana didn't know what she'd done to deserve such a good man, but she would always be grateful. Always.

The minister opened his Bible, and Diana focused her attention on the man of the cloth. Her heart was full. Happiness had come to her a second time when she'd least expected it.

When the moment came, Cliff repeated his vows in

a firm, assured voice, then silently slipped the solitary diamond on her finger. Diana prepared to do the same.

Her pastor's words echoed through the church. When he asked her if she would take Cliff as her lawfully wedded husband, she opened her mouth to say in an even, controlled voice that she would. However, she wasn't given the chance.

Joan spoke first. "She does."

Katie chimed in. "We all do."

Fourteen

So much for the small, intimate wedding party, Cliff thought good-naturedly several hours later. Everywhere he looked, there were family and friends pressed around him and Diana, shaking his hand, kissing Diana's cheek and offering words of congratulations. Each wished to share in their day and their happiness, and Cliff was pleased to let them. If it wasn't their guests pressing in around them, then it was Joan and Katie. The two popped up all over the hall, jostling gaily around the room like court jesters. Every now and again Cliff captured Diana's gaze, and the aching gentleness he saw in her eyes tore at his soul. Beyond a doubt, he knew that she was just as eager to escape as he was.

Other than their meeting in the church, Diana hadn't had more than a moment to talk to this man who was now her husband. They stood beside each other in the long reception line and were so busy greeting those they loved that there wasn't an opportunity to speak to each other.

When there was a small break in the line of relations and friends, Cliff leaned close and whispered in her ear, but she scarcely recognized his voice. His aching whisper was filled with raw emotion. "I adore you, Mrs. Howard."

Her eyes flew to his as the shattering tenderness of his words enveloped her. So many things were stored in her heart, so much love she longed to share. Because she couldn't say everything she wanted to, Diana moved closer to Cliff's side. Very lightly she pressed her hip against his. Cliff slipped his hand around her waist, drawing her nearer and tighter to him. For the moment at least, they were both content.

Hours later they arrived at the hotel room, exhausted but excited. A bottle of the finest French champagne, a gift from Cliff's brother, awaited them, resting in a bed of crushed ice.

Cliff gave the champagne no more than a fleeting glance. He wasn't interested in drinking—the only thing he wanted was his wife. He wrapped his arms around Diana and kissed her hungrily, the way he'd been fantasizing about doing all afternoon. He was starving for her, famished, ravished by his need.

Diana eagerly met his warm lips, twining her arms around his neck and tangling her fingers in the thick softness of his dark hair. She luxuriated in the secure feel of his arms, holding her so close she could barely breathe. She smiled up at him dreamily and sighed.

"I didn't think we were ever going to be alone," she whispered, her voice shaky with desire. Pausing, she pressed her face against the side of his strong neck.

"Me, either." His voice wasn't any more controlled than hers. His gaze fell on the bed, and the desire to make love with Diana wrapped itself around him like a fisherman's net, trapping him. He didn't want to rush Diana—he'd hoped their lovemaking would happen naturally. It was only late afternoon. They should have a drink and a leisurely dinner first, but Cliff doubted that he could make it through the first course. "Shall we have a drink?" he asked, easing her from his arms. Over and over again, he silently told himself to be patient, to go slow. There was no reason to rush into this when they had all the time in the world.

"I don't want any champagne," Diana answered in a husky whisper.

"You don't?"

Smiling, she shook her head. "I want *you*. Now. Don't make me wait any longer."

Cliff's knees went weak with relief, and he turned to face her. His heart pounded like a giant jackhammer in his chest.

"Oh, Cliff," she murmured, holding out her arms in silent invitation. "I don't think I can wait a minute more. I love you so much."

His eyes glowed with the fire of his passion as he reached for her. He kissed her once, twice, hardly giving her a chance to breathe. Their bodies strained against each other, needing and giving more.

Wildly Diana returned his kisses, on fire for her husband, desiring him in a way that went beyond physical passion.

In response to Diana, Cliff wrapped his arms around her, bringing her close to him so she would know beyond a doubt how much he longed to make her his. Somehow, while still kissing, they started to undress each other. Deftly Diana loosened his necktie, rid him of his suit jacket and unfastened the buttons of his shirt.

When she splayed her hands over his bare chest, she sighed and reveled in the firm, hard feel of him.

With some difficulty, Cliff located the zipper in the back of Diana's dress and fumbled with it. Diana sighed into his mouth and reluctantly tore her lips from his. She whirled around, sweeping up the hair at the base of her neck to assist him and resisted the urge to stamp her foot and demand that he please hurry.

Their clothes were carelessly tossed around the room one piece at a time. By the time they'd finished, Diana was breathless and weak with anticipation. She'd thought to hide her imperfect body from Cliff, eager to climb between the sheets and hide, but he wouldn't allow it.

Cliff broke away long enough to study Diana. His sharp features, hardened now with excitement, softened with indescribable tenderness. Just looking at her made the breath catch in his throat and the blood surge through his veins in a violent rush. His senses were filled with the sight of her as his eyes swept her body in one long, passionate caress. His breath was labored when he spoke. "You're so beautiful."

"Oh, Cliff." Tears pooled in her eyes. Her body carried the marks of childbirth, but her husband saw none of her flaws. He viewed her with such a gentle love that he was blinded to her imperfections. Her heart constricted with emotion, and Diana was certain she couldn't have loved Cliff Howard more than she did at that precise moment.

His self-control was cracking, Cliff realized as he pulled back the sheets from the king-size bed and tossed the pillows aside. He wanted Diana so much his breath came quickly, no matter how hard he tried to slow it, and his heart beat high in his throat. He kissed Diana again and pressed her back against the mattress. After the lovemaking their arms and legs remained tangled as they lay on their sides facing one another. Cliff was trapped in the web of overpowering sensation. He saw her tears and felt his chest tighten with such a tender love that he could have died at the moment and not suffered a regret. Everything in his life until this one moment seemed shallow and worthless. The love he shared with Diana was the only important thing there would ever be for him. He'd found more than a wife; he'd found his life's purpose, his home.

Murmuring her love, Diana slipped her arms around his neck and pulled his head to hers. Her kiss was full, holding back nothing. Again and again Cliff kissed her. They were soft, nibbling kisses; the urgency of their lovemaking had been removed. They both slept and woke late in the evening. While Diana soaked in a hot bathtub, Cliff ordered their dinner from room service. Her stomach growled as the smell of their meal wafted into the large pink bathroom. She was preparing to climb out of the water, when Cliff came to her, holding a fat, succulent shrimp.

"Hungry?" he asked.

Diana nodded eagerly. It'd been hours since she'd last eaten—morning, to be exact—and at the time she'd been too excited to down anything more than a glass of orange juice.

"Good." He plopped the shrimp in his mouth and greedily licked the sauce from the ends of his fingers. Darting a glance in her direction, he laughed aloud at her look of righteous indignation.

He left the room and returned a couple of moments

later with an extra shrimp, taking delight in feeding it to her. Diana hurriedly dried off and dressed in a whispery soft peignoir of sheer blue. The lacy gown had been a gift from Shirley Holiday, with instructions for her to wear it on her wedding night.

When she reappeared, Cliff had poured them each a glass of champagne. He turned to hand her hers and stopped abruptly when he viewed her in the sheer nightgown, his eyes rounding with undisguised appreciation.

"Do you like it?" she asked, and did one slow, sultry turn for effect.

Cliff only nodded; to speak was nearly impossible.

Diana took a sip of the champagne and pulled out a chair. One by one, she started lifting domed lids to discover what he'd ordered. "Oh, Cliff, I'm starved."

He dragged his gaze from the dark shadow of her nipples back to their meal. His gaze fell to the table. Food. Their dinner.

"Filet mignon," Diana said, and sighed her appreciation. "I can't believe how famished I am." She looked up to discover her husband's eyes burning a trail over her.

Cliff moistened his lips. Diana's gown teased him with a soft cloud of thin material that fell open to reveal her thigh and the top of her hip. He found he couldn't tear his eyes off her. Wistfully he cast a glance at the bed. He dared not suggest it—not so soon after the last time. Diana would think he was some kind of animal.

"Cliff?" Diana whispered.

He squared his shoulders and forced a smile.

"Cliff Howard." Although he made a gallant effort

to disguise what he wanted Diana knew. This man was a marvel. "Now?"

He looked almost boyish. "Do you mind?"

She glanced longingly at her dinner, grabbed a second shrimp and smiled. Standing, she reached for his hand and led him toward the bed.

"Married life seems to agree with you," Shirley Holiday commented three weeks later, after Cliff and Diana had returned from their honeymoon.

There'd been some adjustments, Diana mused. They'd recently moved into their two-story house, situated between Des Moines, and Salt Water State Park and were still unpacking. The girls had settled into their new school and were learning to adjust to sharing their mother, which was something they hadn't realized would happen once she and Cliff had married.

"It has its moments," Diana agreed. Like the first night they were in their new house! Cliff had just started to make love to her, when Katie burst into the bedroom, crying because of a bad dream. Cliff murmured something about having a nightmare of his own, while Diana scrambled for some clothes. The first thing the following morning, Cliff had put a lock on the bedroom door. Then, later in the same week, Diana and Shirley had planned on hitting a sale at Nordstrom's, when Cliff had shown up at the house unexpectedly. She'd thought, at first, that he'd come to take her to lunch, but he'd had other plans. Giggling, Diana had phoned her friend and said she'd be a few minutes late.

"I can't remember the last time I saw you this happy," Shirley said with an expressive sigh. "You know, I feel responsible for all this."

"For what?" Diana asked, joining her friend at the kitchen table.

"For the two of you getting together."

It took a supreme effort on Diana's part not to remind her former neighbor that she had done everything within her power to discourage Diana's relationship with the known playboy and womanizer, Cliff Howard.

"So when do you start your college classes?" Shirley asked while Diana poured them each a second cup of coffee.

The bride glanced in the direction of the kitchen calendar that hung beside the phone. "In a couple of weeks." After the wedding, Cliff had insisted Diana give up her job with the school district. As far as her future was concerned, Cliff had other plans.

"I think it's wonderful the way Cliff's encouraging you to go back to school. How long will it take you to get your nursing degree?"

Grinning, Diana propped her elbows on top of the oak table. "About ten years, the way we plan it."

Shirley's eyes widened with surprise. "That long—but whatever for?"

"I plan to take a couple of long breaks in between semesters."

"But, Diana, that doesn't make sense. This is a golden opportunity for you. I'd think…"

"Shirley!" Diana stopped her. "We're planning on me having a baby as soon as possible." And another the following year, if everything went according to their schedule. From the way Cliff had been working at the project, Diana believed she was bound to be pregnant by the end of the month. Not that she was complaining. The lovemaking between them was exquisite, just as she'd always known it would be. Each time her husband reached for her, she marveled at how virile he was. And how gentle.

The conversation between the two women was interrupted by Cliff, George and the girls, who came through the front door, returning from a golfing match.

"We're back," Cliff said, leaning over the chair and kissing Diana's cheek.

"Cliff let me drive his golf cart," Joan announced proudly as she entered the kitchen. "It's only a few more years, you realize, till I'll be old enough for my driver's permit."

"All Cliff let me do was steer," Katie complained, plopping herself down in the seat beside her mother.

"Next year you can drive the cart," Cliff told her.

Katie responded by folding her arms and pinching her lips together in a pretty pout. "It's not fair. Joan gets to do everything."

"The older one always does," Joan answered with a superior air.

"Are you going to let her talk to me that way?" Katie demanded. "Just what kind of a mother are you?"

"Girls, girls," Cliff said, without raising his voice. Joan and Katie stopped arguing, but when they didn't think he could see, Katie stuck her tongue out at Joan, and Joan eagerly reciprocated.

Cliff did his best to disguise a smile. He was smiling a lot lately. Marrying Diana and taking on the responsibility for Joan and Katie had changed him. There'd been so many wasted years when he'd drifted from one meaningless relationship to another, seeking an elusive happiness, finding himself chasing after the pot of gold at the end of the rainbow. But now he'd found real love, experienced it firsthand, and it had altered the course of his life.

That night, Diana fell asleep in her husband's arms. A loud clap of thunder woke her around midnight. She rolled onto her back and rubbed the sleep from her face.

"I wondered if the storm would wake you," Cliff whispered, raising himself up on one elbow in order to kiss her.

Diana kissed him back and looped an arm around his neck. "Have you been awake long?"

"About five minutes." Once more, his mouth tenderly grazed hers. "Have I told you lately how much I love you?"

"You *showed* me a couple of hours ago!"

He nuzzled her neck and the familiar hot sensation raced through Diana, and she sighed her pleasure.

Cliff kissed her in earnest then, wrapping her in his arms. "What have you done to me?" He growled the question in her ear. "I can't seem to get enough of you."

"Do you hear me complaining?" Completely at ease now with his body, she touched and kissed him in places she knew would evoke a strong reaction.

"You little devil," Cliff whispered raggedly.

"Want me to stop?"

"No," he answered on a low growl. "I'm crazy about you, woman."

Diana stiffened and turned her head toward the bedroom door.

Cliff was instantly aware of the change in her mood. "What is it?"

"Katie."

"I didn't hear her."

"She's frightened of storms." Already Diana was freeing herself from his arms.

Mumbling under his breath, Cliff rolled onto his back and swallowed down the momentary frustration. "I'm beginning to relive a nightmare of my own. When are you going to be back?"

"In a minute." Diana climbed out of the bed and reached for her robe.

"Give me a kiss before you go," Cliff insisted, then yawned loudly. "Wake me if I go back to sleep."

Diana willingly obliged. "I shouldn't be long."

"Hurry," he coaxed, and yawned a second time.

Diana was gone only a matter of minutes, but by the time she returned and slipped between the sheets, Cliff was snoozing.

"Sweetheart," she whispered, gently shaking him awake.

He rolled over and automatically reached for her.

"Honey," Diana murmured.

"Just a minute," he whispered sleepily. "I need to wake up." He nibbled softly on her earlobe.

"It's Katie," Diana told him.

"What about her?"

"She's frightened by the storm."

"I'm frightened, too, but I understand—go ahead and go back to comfort Katie."

Diana pushed the hair from his face and gently kissed the side of his jaw. "She doesn't want me—she requested you."

"Me?"

"You."

A slow, easy smile broke out across Cliff's handsome features. Comforting his daughter in a storm. It was exactly the kind of thing a father would do.

* * * * *

FALLEN ANGEL

One

The least it could do was rain! What was the use of living in Seattle if it wasn't going to so much as drizzle? And Amy was in the mood for a cloudburst.

She bought herself an order of crispy fried fish and chips simply because she felt guilty occupying a picnic table in the tourist-crowded pier along the Seattle waterfront. The mild June weather had refused to respond to her mood and the sun was playing peekaboo behind a band of thin clouds. No doubt it would ruin everything and shine full force any minute.

"Excuse me—is this seat taken?"

Amy glanced up to discover a man who looked as though he'd just stepped out of a Western novel and was searching for Fort Apache standing opposite her. The impression came from a leather band that was wrapped around his wide forehead and the cropped-waisted doeskin jacket.

"Feel free," she said, motioning toward the empty space opposite her. "I'll be finished here within a couple of minutes."

"It doesn't look like you've even touched your meal."

"I couldn't possibly eat at a time like this," she said, frowning at him.

His thick brows shot upward as he lifted his leg over the wooden table and sat opposite her. "I see."

Amy picked up a fat French fry and poised it in front of her mouth. "I've been home exactly two weeks and it hasn't so much as rained once. This is Seattle, mind you, and there hasn't even been a heavy dew."

"The weather *has* been great."

"I'd feel better if it rained," she returned absently. "It's much too difficult to be depressed when the sun is shining and the birds are chirping and everyone around me is in this jovial, carefree mood."

The stranger took a sip of his coffee, and Amy suspected he did so to cover a smile. It would be just her luck to have a handsome stranger sit down and try to brighten her mood.

He set the cup on the picnic table and leveled his gaze at her. "You look to me like a woman who's been done wrong by her man."

"That's another thing," Amy cried. "Everything would be so much simpler if I'd been born a male."

Her companion's brown eyes rounded. "Is that a fact?"

"Well, of course, then I wouldn't be in this mess... well, I would, but I'd probably be happy about it."

"I see."

Feeling slightly better about the situation, Amy tore off a piece of fish and studied it before popping it into her mouth. It tasted good, much better than she'd anticipated. "It wouldn't be nearly this difficult if I didn't have the most wonderful father in the world."

His dark eyes softened. "Then you shouldn't need to worry."

"But it just kills me to disappoint him." Amy took another bite of the battered fish. "After all, I am twenty-three—it's not as though I don't know what I want."

"And what *do* you want?"

"How would I know?" she muttered. "No one even asked me before."

Her newfound friend laughed outright.

Amy smiled, too, for the first time in what seemed like years. "If I'm going to be spilling my guts to you, I might as well introduce myself. I'm Amy Johnson."

"Josh Powell." He held out his hand and they exchanged quick handshakes.

"Hello, Josh."

"Hello yourself," he returned, grinning broadly. "Are you going to be all right, Amy Johnson?"

She expelled a harsh sigh, then shrugged. "I suppose." Another French fry made its way into her mouth. When she reached for the fish, she noted that Josh had stopped eating and was studying her.

"Is there a reason you're wearing that raincoat?" he asked.

She nodded. "I was hoping for a downpour—something to coordinate with my mood."

"I thought you might have heard a more recent forecast. An unexpected tropical storm or something."

"No," she admitted wryly.

"Frankly, I'm surprised by the weather myself," Josh stated conversationally. "I've been in Seattle several days now, and the sun has greeted me every morning."

"So you're a tourist?"

"Not exactly. I work for one of the major oil companies, and I'm waiting for government clearance before I head for the Middle East. I should fly out of here within the week."

Her father owned a couple of oil wells, but from what Amy could remember they were in Texas and had been losing money for the past few years. If her father was experiencing minor financial problems with his vast undertakings, then it was nothing compared to what was bound to happen when *she* stepped into the picture. He had such high hopes for her, such lofty expectations. And she was destined to fail. It would be impossible not to. She had about as much business sense as Homer Simpson. Her college advisers had repeatedly suggested she change her major. Personally, Amy was all for that. She worked hard and even then she was considered borderline as to whether she would be accepted into the five-year joint BA and MBA program. She'd been number three on a waiting list. Then her father had donated funds toward a new library, and lo and behold, Amy and everyone else on the list had been welcomed into the prestigious school of business with open arms.

"I'm impressed with what I've seen of Seattle," Josh went on.

"It's a nice city, isn't it?" Amy answered with a soft smile. She leaned forward and plopped her elbows on top of the picnic table. "Do you think it would work if I feigned a fatal illness?"

"I beg your pardon?"

"No," she said, answering her own question. "It wouldn't." Knowing her father, he would call in medical experts from around the world, and she'd be forced into making a miraculous recovery.

Josh's amused gaze met hers.

"I'm not making the least bit of sense, am I?"

"No," he admitted dryly. "Do you want to talk about it?"

Supporting her cheek with the palm of one hand, she stared into the distance, wondering if discussing the matter with a stranger would help. At least he would be unbiased.

"My father is probably one of the most dynamic men you'll ever meet. Being around him is like receiving a charge of energy. He's exciting, vibrant, electric."

"I know the type you mean."

"I'm his only child," Amy muttered. "You may have noticed that Dad and I don't share a whole lot of the same characteristics."

Josh hedged. "That's difficult to say—we only met a few minutes ago, but from what I've seen, you don't seem to lack any energy."

"Take my word on this, Dad and I aren't anything alike."

"Okay," he said, then gestured toward her. "Go on."

"I recently acquired my MBA—"

"Congratulations."

"No, please. If it had been up to me I would have hung around the campus for as many more years as I could, applied for a doctorate—anything. But unfortunately that option wasn't left open to me. According to my father, the big moment has finally arrived."

"And?"

"He wants to take me into the family business."

"That isn't what you want?"

"Heavens, no! I know Dad would listen to me if I had some burning desire to be a teacher or a dental assistant or anything else. Then I could talk to him and explain everything. But I don't know what I want to do, and even if I did, I'm not so certain it would matter anyway."

"But you just said—"

"I know, but I also know my father, bless his dear heart. He'd look at me with those big blue eyes of his, and I'd start drowning in this sea of guilt." She paused long enough to draw in a giant breath. "I'm the apple of his eye. According to him, the sun rises and sets on my whims. I can't disappoint him—Dad's got his heart set on me taking over for him."

"You've never told him this isn't what you want?"

She dropped her gaze, ashamed to admit she'd been such a coward. "Not in so many words—I just couldn't."

"Perhaps you could talk to your mother, let her prepare the way. Then it won't come as any big shock when you approach your father."

Once more Amy shook her head. "I'm afraid that won't work. My mother died when I was barely ten."

"I see—well, that does complicate matters, doesn't it?"

"I did this to myself," Amy moaned. "I knew the day was coming when I'd be forced to tell him the truth. It wasn't like I didn't figure out what he intended early enough. About the time I entered high school, I got the drift that he had big plans for me. I tried to turn the tide then, but it didn't do any good."

"Turn the tide?" Josh repeated. "I don't understand."

"I tried to marry him off. The way I figured it, he could fall in love again, and his new wife would promptly give birth to three or four male heirs, and then I'd be off the hook. Unfortunately, he was too busy with the business to get involved with a woman."

"What if *you* married?"

"That wouldn't..." Amy paused and straightened as the suggestion ricocheted around the corners of her brain. "Josh...oh, Josh, that's a brilliant idea. Why didn't I think of that?" She nibbled on her lower lip as she considered his scheme, which sounded like exactly the escape clause she'd been wanting. "If my father would be willing to accept any excuse, it'd be something like that. He's a bighearted romantic, and if there's one thing he wants more than to see me in the business—it's grandchildren." Her blue eyes flashed with excitement as she smiled at Josh. Then it struck her, and she moaned. "There's one flaw to this brilliant plan, though." She raised her fingers to her mouth and stroked her lips while she gave the one weakness some thought.

"What do you mean there's a flaw?" Josh repeated, sounding impatient.

"I'm not in love."

"That's not such a difficult hang-up. Think. Surely there's one man you've met in your life that you like well enough to marry?"

She considered the list of men she'd dated and her shoulders sagged with defeat. "Actually, there isn't," she admitted reluctantly. "I dated in college, but only a little, and there was never anyone I'd seriously consider spending the rest of my life with."

"What about the boys who attended high school with you? Five years have passed, and things have changed—perhaps it's time you renewed those old friendships."

Once more Amy frowned, then regretfully shook her head. "That won't work, either. I attended a Catholic girls' school." She closed her eyes, prepared to mentally scan through a list of potential men she might consider marrying. Unfortunately, she couldn't think of a single one.

"Amy," Josh whispered, "are you all right?"

She nodded. "I'm just thinking. No," she said emphatically, as the defeat settled on her shoulders like a blanket of steel, "there's no one. I'm doomed."

"You could always have a heart-to-heart talk with your father. If he's as wonderful as you claim, then he'll be grateful for the honesty."

"Sure, and what exactly do I say?"

"The truth. You might suggest he train someone else to take his place."

Despite the fact that Josh was serious, Amy laughed a little. "You make it sound so easy...you couldn't possibly realize how difficult telling him is going to be."

"But necessary, Amy."

The second to the last thing Amy needed was the cool voice of reason. The first had been a handsome stranger introducing himself to her. When a person is depressed and miserable, she decided, everything seems to fall apart!

"Talk to him," Josh advised again.

As much as Amy wanted to argue with him, he was right. Her eyes held on to his as if she could soak up his determination.

"The sooner you get it over with the better," he added softly.

"I know you're right," she murmured. "I should do

it soon…before I find myself behind a desk, wondering how I ended up there."

"What's wrong with *now?*"

"Now?" Her startled gaze flew to Josh.

"Yes, now."

Her mouth opened to argue with him, but she realized there really wasn't any better time than the present. The corporate headquarters was within walking distance, and it would be best to face her father when she was charged with righteous enthusiasm. If she delayed the confrontation until dinnertime, she might chicken out.

"You're absolutely right. If I'm going to talk to my father, I've got to do it immediately." In a burst of zeal, she charged to her feet and offered Josh her hand. "Thank you for your advice."

"You're most welcome." He smiled and finished his coffee. "Good luck."

"Thanks, I'm going to need it." Securing the strap of her purse over her shoulder, she deposited what remained of her lunch in the trash and marched toward the sidewalk in smooth strides of military precision. When she reached the street, she turned to find Josh watching her. She raised her hand in a gesture of farewell, and he did the same.

An hour later, Amy sat in the back row of the Omnitheater at the Seattle Aquarium, slouched down as far as she could in her seat without slipping all the way out of it and into the aisle. Her hand covered her eyes. A documentary about the Mount St. Helen's disaster was about to start.

Disasters seemed to be the theme of Amy's day. Following her trip to the Rainier Building on Fifth Avenue, she'd walked to the waterfront area where her car was parked. The thought of returning home, however, only added to her misery, so she'd opted for the documentary.

Her bravado had been strong when she reached the fifty-story structure that housed Johnson Industries. She'd paused on the sidewalk outside and glanced up at the vertical ribs of polished glass and concrete. About half of all the people inside were a part of the conglomerate that made up her father's enterprise.

Her mistake had been when she'd started working with the figures. Calculating two hundred people per floor, that came to twenty thousand workers inside the Rainier Building—when full—of which a possible ten thousand were Johnson employees.

Of all those thousands, very few would stand equal to or above Amy in the capacity her father had chosen for her.

She wasn't exactly stepping into an entry-level position. Oh, no, she'd been groomed for a much loftier point on the corporate scale. Her father's idea had been to place her as a director, working her way through each of the major sections of the company until the most important aspects of each department had been drilled into her. Naturally, Harold Johnson planned to stay on as president and chief executive officer until Amy had learned the ropes, but "the ropes" felt too much like a hangman's noose to suit her.

The lights lowered in the Omni-theater, and Amy heard someone enter the row and sit next to her.

"I take it the confrontation with your father didn't go well."

Amy's hand flew away from her face. It was Josh. "No," she whispered.

"What happened?"

She flopped her hands over a couple of times, searching for a way to start to explain. "It's a long story."

The man in front of them twisted around and glared, clearly more interested in hearing the details of the natural disaster than Amy's troubles.

"I've already seen the movie once," Josh said. "Do you want to go outside and talk?"

She nodded.

As she suspected, the sun was shining and the sky was an intense shade of blue. Even the seagulls were in a jovial mood.

"Do you want some ice cream?" Josh asked when they reached the busy sidewalk. He didn't wait for her reply, but bought them each an enormous double scoop waffle cone, then joined her in front of the large, cheerful water fountain.

Amy sat on the edge of the structure, feeling even more pathetic than she had earlier that afternoon.

"I take it you talked to your father?"

"No," she muttered. "I didn't get past Ms. Wetherell, his executive assistant." She lapped at the side of the cone, despite everything enjoying the rich, smooth taste of the vanilla ice cream. "I don't think I've ever really looked at that woman before. She reminds me of a prune."

"A prune?" Josh repeated.

"She might have been a pleasant plum at one time, but she's been ripened and dried by the years. I think it might be the fluorescent lighting." Amy knew she would look just like Ms. Wetherell within six months. She was going to hate being trapped indoors with no possibility of escape.

"The prune wouldn't allow you to talk to your own father?"

"He was in an important meeting." She turned to Josh and shrugged. "I was slain at the gate."

"Amy..."

"I know exactly what you're going to say, and you're absolutely right. I'll talk to my dad tonight. I promise you I will."

"Good."

He looked proud of her, and that helped. "How'd you happen to be in the Omni-theater?" she asked. It had to be more than coincidence.

"I saw you go inside and was curious to find out what happened."

He'd removed the leather jacket and draped it over his shoulder, securing it with one finger. His eyes were deeply set, his nose prominent without distracting from his strong male features. His ash-blond hair was longer than fashionable, but well kept. It seemed to Amy that calendar and poster manufacturers were constantly searching for men with such blatant male appeal. Men like Josh.

"Is something wrong?" he asked her unexpectedly.

"No," she said, recovering quickly. She hadn't realized she'd been staring quite so conspicuously.

"Your ice cream is melting," he told her.

Hurriedly, she took several bites to correct the problem. The green-and-white ferry sounded its horn as it approached the pier. It captured Josh's attention.

"Did you know that Washington has the largest ferry

system in the United States and the third largest in the world?" Amy asked, in what she hoped was a conversational tone.

"No, I didn't."

"When you consider someplace like the Philippines with all those islands, that fact is impressive." Amy realized she was jabbering, but she wanted to pull attention away from herself and her problems. "Our aquarium is the one of only a few in the world built on a pier," she said, adding another tour-guide fact. "Have you been up to the Pike Place Market yet?"

"Several times, and I've enjoyed it more each visit."

"It's the largest continuously operated farmers' market in the nation."

"You seem to be full of little tidbits of information."

She smiled and nodded. Then she closed her eyes and expelled her breath in a leisurely exercise. "I really do love this city."

"It's home," Josh said quietly, and Amy sensed such a longing in his voice that she opened her eyes to study him.

"Would you like to walk with me?" he asked her unexpectedly. Standing, he offered her his elbow.

"Sure." She tucked her arm around his, enjoying the feeling of being connected with him. Josh had been a friend when she'd needed one. They barely knew each other—they'd exchanged little more than their names—and yet she'd told him more about her problems than she had anyone. Ever. Even her closest college friends didn't know how much she dreaded going to work for her father. But Josh Powell did. A stranger. An unexpected friend.

It took them forty minutes to walk from the waterfront area to the Seattle Center on Queen Ann Hill. They stood at the base of the Space Needle, which had been built for the 1962 World's Fair and remained a prominent city landmark. Feeling it was her duty to relay the more important details, Amy told him everything she could remember about the Space Needle, which wasn't much. She finished off by asking, "Where's home?"

"I beg your pardon?"

"Where are you from?"

He paused and looked at her for a tense moment. "What makes you ask that?"

"I…I don't know. When I told you how much I love Seattle, you claimed that was because it was home. Now I'm curious where home is for you."

His eyes took on a distant look. "The world—I've taken jobs just about everywhere now. The Middle East, South America, Australia, Europe."

"But where do you kick off your boots and put up your feet?"

"Wherever I happen to be," he explained.

"But—"

"I left what most others would consider home several years ago. I didn't ever intend to go back."

"Oh, Josh, that's so sad." Her voice sounded as if she'd whispered into a microphone, low and vibrating.

"Amy…" He paused, then chuckled softly. "It wasn't any big tragedy." Burying his hands in his pockets, he strolled away, effectively ending the conversation. He paused and waited on the pathway for her to join him.

Glancing at the time, Amy sighed. "I've got to get back to the house," she said with reluctance.

"Tell me what you're going to do tonight."

"Nothing much," she hedged. "Watch a little television probably, read some—"

"I don't mean that, and you know it."

"All right, all right, I'm going to talk to my father."

"And then tomorrow you're going to meet me at noon at the seafood stand and tell me what happened."

"I am?"

"That's exactly what you're going to do."

Her heart started to pound like an overworked piston in her chest, but that could have been because she would soon be confronting her father, and her success rate with making dragons purr was rather low at the moment. But the reaction could well have been due to the fact that she would be meeting Josh again.

"Any questions?" he asked.

"One." She paused and looked up at him, her eyes wide and appealing. "Will you marry me?"

"No."

"I was afraid of that."

Two

Manuela had served the last of the evening meal before Amy had the courage to broach the subject with her father. She looked at him, watching him closely, wanting to gauge his mood before she unloaded her mind. His disposition seemed congenial enough, but it was difficult to tell exactly how he would respond to her news.

"Did you have a pleasant afternoon?" Harold asked his daughter, glancing at her.

His unexpected question thumped her out of her musings. "Yes...I took a stroll along the waterfront."

"Good," he said forcefully, and nodded once. Harold Johnson took a bite of his shrimp-stuffed sole. He was nearly sixty-five and in his prime. His hair had gone completely white in the past few years, but his features were ageless, as sharp and penetrating as Amy could ever remember. He watched what he ate, was physically and mentally fit and lived life to the fullest. Nothing had ever been done by half measure. Harold Johnson was an all-or-nothing man. There were few compromises in attitude, health or personality.

He was the type of man who, when he saw something he wanted, went after it with everything he had. He would never accept defeat, only setbacks. He claimed his greatest achievements had been the result of patience. If ever he would need to call upon that virtue, it was now, Amy mused. She loved him just the way he was and prayed he could accept her for who she was, as well.

"Ms. Wetherell said you stopped in to see me," he added, when he'd finished his bite of fish.

"You were in a meeting," she answered lamely.

Her father's responding nod was eager. "An excellent one as it turned out, too. I told a group of executives in five minutes how they can outsell, outmanage and outmotivate the competition."

"You said all that in five minutes?"

"Less," he claimed, warming to his subject. "Mark my words, Amy, because you're going to be needing them soon enough yourself."

"Dad—"

"The first thing you've got to do is set your goals— you won't get any place in this world if you don't know where you're headed. Then visualize yourself in that role."

"Dad—"

He held up his hand to stop her. "And lastly, and this is probably the most important aspect of success, you must learn to deny the power of the adverse. Now you notice, I didn't say you should deny the negative, because there's plenty of that in our world. But we can't allow ourselves the luxury of thinking adversity can get control over us. Because the plain and simple truth is this—misfortune has power only when we allow it to. Do you understand what I'm saying?"

Amy nodded, wondering if she would ever get a word in edgewise and, if she did, how she could possibly say what she needed to tell him.

"You come to the office tomorrow," her father went on to say, smiling smugly. "I've got something of a surprise for you. I was saving it for later, but I want you to see it now."

"What's that?"

"Your own office. I've hired one of those fancy interior decorators and I'm having the space redesigned. Nothing but the best for my little girl. New carpet, the finest furniture, the latest technology, the whole nine yards. Once that's completed, I want you working with me and the others. Together, you and I are going to make a difference in this country—a big one." He paused and set aside his fork. When he looked up, his gaze was warm and proud. "I've been waiting for this day for nearly twenty years. I don't mind telling you how proud I am of you, Amy Adele. You're as pretty as your mother, and you've got her brains, too. Having you at my side will almost be like having Mary back again."

"Oh, Dad…" He was making this so much more difficult.

"These years that you've been away at school have been hard ones. You're the sunshine of my life, Amy, just the way your mother always was."

"I'd like to be more like her," she whispered, knowing her father would never understand what she meant. Her mother had always been behind the scenes, acting as a sounding board and offering moral support. That was where Amy longed to be, as well.

Her father reached for his wineglass. "You're more and more like Mary every day."

"Mom didn't work at the office though, did she?"

"No, of course not, but don't you discount her worth to me. It was your mother's support, love and encouragement that gave me the courage to accomplish everything I have done over the years. Never in all that time did Mary and I dream we'd come so far or achieve so much."

"I meant what I said about being more like her," Amy tried once again. "Mom…was more of a background figure in your life and I…think that's the role I should play, too."

"Nonsense! You belong at my side."

"Dad, oh, please…" Her voice trembled like loose change in an oversize pocket. "You just finished telling me how important it was to visualize yourself in a certain role, and I'm sorry, but I can't see myself cooped up in an office day in and day out. It just isn't me. I—"

"You can't what?"

"See myself as an important part of Johnson Industries," she blurted out in one giant breath.

Her announcement was followed by a short silence.

"I can understand that," Harold said.

"You can?"

"Of course. It's little wonder when all you've done so far is book learning," her father continued confidently. "Business isn't sitting in some stuffy classroom listening to a know-it-all professor spouting off his views. It's digging in with both hands and pulling out something viable and profitable that's going to affect people's lives for the better."

"But I'm not sure that's what I want."

"Of course you do!" he countered sharply. "You wouldn't be a Johnson if you didn't."

"What about Mom, and the support she gave you? Couldn't I start off like that…I mean…be a sounding board for you and a helpmate in other ways?"

"Years ago that was all you could have done, but times have changed," her father argued. "Women have fought for their rightful place in the corporate world. For the first time in history women are getting the recognition they deserve. You're my daughter, my only child—everything I've managed to accumulate will some day belong to you."

"But—"

"Now, I think I understand what you're saying. I should have thought of this myself. You're tired. Exhausted from your studies. You've worked hard, and you deserve a break. I wasn't thinking when I suggested you start working with me so soon after graduation."

"Dad, I'm not *that* tired."

"Yes, you are, only you don't realize it. Now I want you to take a vacation. Fly to Europe and soak up the sun on those fancy beaches. Then in September we'll talk again."

"Vacationing in Europe isn't going to change how I feel," she murmured sadly, her gaze lowered. The lump in her throat felt as large as a grapefruit. She loved her father , and it was killing her to disappoint him like this.

"We aren't going to talk about your working until

September. I apologize, Amy, I should have realized you needed a holiday. It's just that I'm a bit anxious to have you with me—it's been my dream all these years and I've been selfish not to consider the fact you're in need of a little time to yourself."

"Dad, please listen."

"No need to listen," he said, effectively cutting her off. "I just said we'd talk about it in the fall."

It took everything within Amy just to respond to him with a simple nod.

"You don't understand," Amy told Josh the following afternoon. "Before I could say a word, Dad started telling me how I was the sunshine of his life and how he'd waited twenty years for this day. What was I supposed to do?"

"I take it you didn't tell him?"

"I did—in a way."

"Only he didn't listen?"

Her nod was slow and reluctant. "It's obvious you've met my father, or at least someone like him. I don't blame Dad—this isn't exactly what he wanted to hear. The best I could do was to admit I couldn't see myself working with him in the office. Naturally, he didn't want to accept that, so he suggested I take the rest of the summer off to unwind after my studies."

"That's not such a bad idea. You probably shouldn't have expected anything more. Frankly, I think you did very well."

"You do?" she asked excitedly, but her mood quickly deflated. "Then why do I feel so rotten?"

"It's not going to get any easier. Last night was difficult, but at least you've gotten yourself a two-month reprieve. Perhaps, in the coming weeks, you'll come up with some way of making him understand."

Amy lowered her gaze and nodded. "Maybe." She raised the cup to her mouth and took a sip of coffee. "What about you, Josh? Did you hear about the government clearance?"

"No—nothing." His voice was filled with resignation.

"I know it's selfish of me," she admitted with a soft smile, "but I'm glad."

"It's easy enough for you to feel that way, you're not the one sitting on your butt waiting."

They exchanged smiles, and Josh brushed a stray strand of hair from her cheek. His fingers lingered as his eyes held hers.

"I'm grateful you came up and asked to share that table with me," Amy admitted. "I was feeling so low and miserable and talking to you has helped."

A reluctant silence followed, before he said, "Actually, I'd been watching you for some time."

"You had?"

Josh nodded. "I waited around for ten minutes to see if someone was going to join you before I approached the table. I was pleased you were alone."

"I wish there was more time for us to get to know each other," she whispered, surprised by how low and sultry her voice sounded.

"No," he countered bluntly, "in some ways it's for the best."

They stood at the end of the pier behind a long row of tourist shops, and Amy walked away, confused and uncertain. She didn't understand Josh. There wasn't anyone else nearby, and when she turned around and looked up, prepared to argue with him, she was taken aback to realize how close they were to one another—only a scant inch or two separated them.

Josh took the coffee from her hand and set it aside. Then he settled his hands on top of her shoulders, and his spellbinding gaze was stronger than the force of her will. His eyes searched hers for a long moment. She knew then that he intended to kiss her, and her immediate response was pleasure and anticipation. All morning, she'd been thinking about meeting Josh again and her heart had leaped with an eagerness she couldn't explain.

With unhurried ease, he lowered his head to settle his mouth over hers. He was surprisingly gentle. The kiss was slow and thorough, as if rushing something this sweet would spoil it. Amy sighed, and her lips parted softly, inviting him to kiss her again. Josh complied, and when he'd finished, a low moan escaped from deep within his throat.

"I was afraid of that," he said, on the ragged end of a sigh.

"Of what?"

"You taste like cotton candy...much too sweet."

Amy felt a little breathless, a little shaken and a whole lot confused. In one breath Josh had stated that it was better if they didn't get to know each other any better, and in the next he'd kissed her. Apparently, his mind was just as muddled as hers was.

"Amy, listen—"

"You don't like the taste of cotton candy?" she interrupted, her eyes still closed.

"I like it too much."

"Then maybe we should try kissing one more time… you know…as an experiment."

"That might be a bad idea," Josh countered.

"Why?"

"Trust me, it just could."

"Okay," she murmured, disappointed. He placed his fingertips to the vein that pounded in her throat and his thumb stroked it several times as if he couldn't help touching her.

"On second thought," he whispered, a little breathlessly, "maybe that wouldn't be such a big mistake after all." Once more his mouth settled over hers. His kiss was a leisurely exercise as his lips worked from one side of her lips to the other. The heat he generated within her was enough to melt concrete.

He was so tender, so patient, as if he understood and accepted her lack of experience and had made allowances for it. Timidly, Amy slid her hands up his chest and clasped them behind his neck, and when she leaned into him, her breasts brushed against him. He must have felt them through her thin shirt because he moaned and reluctantly put some space between them.

Amy struggled to breathe normally as she dropped her hands.

"You taste good, too," she admitted. That had to be the understatement of the year. Her knees felt weak, and her heart—well, her heart was another story entirely. It seemed as though it was about to burst out of her chest, it was pounding so hard and fast.

Josh draped his wrists over her shoulders and supported his forehead against hers. For a long time he didn't say a word.

"I've got to get back to the hotel. I have a meeting in half an hour."

Amy nodded; she was disappointed, but she understood.

"Can I see you tomorrow?"

"Yes. What time?" How breathless she sounded. How eager.

"Dinner?"

"Okay."

He suggested a time and place and then left her. Amy stood at the end of the pier, her gaze following Josh for as long as he was within sight, then she turned to face the water, letting the breeze off the churning green waters cool her senses.

With his hands buried deep in his pants pockets, Josh stood at the window of his hotel room and gazed out at the animated city below. His thoughts were heavy, confused.

He didn't know why he was so strongly attracted to Amy Johnson, and then again he did.

All right, he admitted gruffly to himself, she was different. Her openness had caught him off guard. From the first moment he'd seen her, something had stopped him. She had looked so miserable, so troubled. He wasn't in the business of counseling fair maidens, especially blond-haired, blue-eyed ones. Even now he was shocked at the way he'd stood and waited for someone to join her and then did so himself when he was certain she was alone. Somehow, the thought of her being friendless and troubled bothered him more than he could explain, even to himself.

It wasn't his style to play the part of a rescuer. Life

was complicated enough without him taking on someone else's problems. He'd convinced himself the best
course of action was to turn and walk away.

Then she had looked straight at him, and her slate-
blue eyes had been wide with appeal. He had realized
almost immediately that although she had been staring
in his direction, she wasn't seeing him. Perhaps it was
then that he recognized the look she wore. Resignation
and defeat flickered from her gaze. It was like looking
in a mirror and viewing his reflection from years past.

In Amy he saw a part of himself that he had struggled to put behind him, to bury forever. And there it
was, a look in a lovely woman's eyes, and he couldn't
refuse her. He waited for a moment, not knowing what
to do, if anything, then he had ordered the fish and
chips and approached her table.

Now the travel clearance he had been waiting for
had arrived. For the past fourteen days, he had been
looking for government approval before he headed for
the oil-rich fields of Saudi Arabia. By all rights, he
should be taking the first available flight out of Seattle. He should forget he had even met Amy Johnson,
with the blue angel eyes and the soft, sweet mouth. She
wasn't the first woman to attract him, but she was the
first to touch a deep part of himself that he'd assumed
was beyond reach.

In many ways Josh saw Amy as a complete opposite
to himself. She was young and vulnerable. The world
hadn't hardened her yet, life hadn't knocked her off
her feet and walked over her. Her freshness had been
retained, and her honesty was evident in every word
she spoke.

Yet, in as many ways as they were different there
was an equal number that made them similar. Several

years back, Josh had faced an almost identical problem to Amy's. He'd loved his father, too, longed to please him, had been willing to do anything to gain Chance Powell's approval.

It was his father's betrayal that had crippled him.

For Amy's sake, Josh prayed matters would resolve themselves differently for her and her father than they had for him and his own. He couldn't bear the thought of Amy forced to face the world alone.

Moving away from the view of downtown Seattle, Josh sat at the end of his mattress, where his suitcase rested. The problem was, he didn't want to leave Amy. His mistake had been kissing her. It was one thing to wonder what she would feel like in his arms, and something else entirely to have actually experienced her softness.

When he had suggested she tell him what had happened once she talked to her father, he had promised himself it would be the last time. Then he had kissed her, and even before he realized what he had been saying, he had suggested dinner. She had smiled at the invitation, and when she spoke, she had sounded eager to see him again.

Only he wouldn't be there. Josh had decided not to show up for their dinner date. It wouldn't take Amy long to figure out that his visa had been approved and he'd had to leave. He was being cruel in an effort to be kind. Funny, the thought of disappointing her troubled him more than anything he had done in a good long while.

"Amy," her father called, as she rushed down the curved stairway. "Why are you running like a wild animal through this house?"

"Sorry, Dad, I'm late," she said with a laugh, because he tended to exaggerate. She hadn't been running, only hurrying. She didn't want to keep Josh waiting.

"Late for what?"

"My date."

"You didn't mention anything about a dinner date earlier."

"I did, at breakfast."

Her father snorted softly. "I don't remember you saying a word. Who is this man you're seeing? Is he anyone I know?"

"No." She quickly surveyed herself in the hall mirror and, pleased with the result, reached for her jacket.

"Who is this young man?" her father repeated.

"Josh Powell."

"Powell…Powell," Harold echoed. "I can't recall knowing any Powells."

"I met him, Dad, you didn't."

"Tell me about him."

"Dad, I'm already five minutes behind schedule." She grabbed her purse and dutifully kissed him on the cheek.

"You don't want me to know about him? This doesn't sound the least bit like you, Amy. You've dated several young men before, but you've always told me something about them. Now you don't have the time to talk about him to your own father?"

"Dad." She groaned, then realized what he said was partially true. She was afraid he wouldn't approve of her seeing someone like Josh and hoped to avoid the confrontation—a recurring problem with her of late.

Dragging in a deep breath, she turned to face Harold Johnson. "I met Josh on the waterfront the other day. He's visiting Seattle."

"A tourist?"

She nodded, hoping that would satisfy him.

"How long will he be here?"

"I...don't know."

Her father reached for a Havana cigar and stared at the end of it as if that would supply the answers for him. "What aren't you telling me?"

It was all she could do not to groan. She was as readable as a first-grade primer when it came to her father in certain areas, while in others he had a blind eye. "Josh works for one of the oil companies—he didn't mention which one so don't think I'm hiding that. He's waiting for his visa to be approved before he leaves."

"And when will that be?"

"Anytime."

Her father nodded, still gazing at his fat cigar.

"Well?" She threw the question at him. "Aren't you going to tell me not to see him, that he's little more than a drifter and that I'm probably making a big mistake? Josh certainly doesn't sound like the kind of man you'd want me to become involved with."

"No. I'm not going to say a word."

Amy paused to study him. "You're not?"

"I raised you right. If you can't judge a man's character by now, you'll never be able to."

Amy was too shocked to say anything.

"So you like this oil worker?"

"Very much," she whispered.

A smile came over Harold as he reached for a gold lighter. The flames licked at the end of the cigar and he took two deep puffs before he added, "Frankly, I'm not surprised to discover you met someone. Your eyes are as bright as sparklers on the Fourth of July, and you can't get out of this house fast enough."

"I'd leave now if one nosy old man wasn't holding me up by asking me a bunch of silly questions."

"Go on now, and have a good time," he said with a chuckle. "I won't wait up for you."

"Good."

Her father was still chuckling when Amy hurried down the front steps to her car. She felt wonderful. Just when she was convinced her life was at its lowest ebb, she'd met Josh. He was a cool voice of reason that had guided her through the thick fog of her doubts and worries. She had opened up to him in ways she hadn't with others, and in doing so, she had unexpectedly discovered a rare kind of friend. His kiss had stirred up sensations long dormant, and she held those emotions to her chest, savoring them until she was able to see him again.

Fifteen minutes after she left home, Amy walked into the French restaurant near the Pike Place Market. A quick survey of the dim interior confirmed that Josh hadn't arrived yet.

Her heart raced with excitement. She longed for him to kiss her once more, just so she'd know the first time had been real and that she hadn't built it up in her mind.

"May I help you?" the maître d' asked when she stepped into the room.

"I'm meeting someone," Amy explained, taking a seat in the tiny foyer. "I'm sure he'll be along any minute."

The man nodded politely and returned to his station. He paused, glanced in her direction and picked up a white sheet of paper. "Would your name happen to be Amy Johnson?"

"Yes," she said and straightened.

"Mr. Powell phoned earlier with his regrets. It seems he's been called out of town."

Three

"Do you mean he's left?" Amy's voice rose half an octave with the question. A numb feeling worked its way from her heart to the ends of her fingertips.

The maître d' casually shrugged his thin shoulders. "All I know is what the message says."

He handed it to her, and Amy gripped the white slip and glared at the few words that seemed so inadequate. "I see," she murmured. They hadn't exchanged phone numbers so there'd been no way for him to contact her one last time and let her know his clearance had arrived.

"Would you like a table for one?" the maître d' pressed.

Amy glanced at the angular man and slowly shook her head. "No. Thanks." Her appetite vanished the moment she realized Josh wouldn't be joining her.

The man offered her a weak smile as she headed for the door. "Better luck next time."

"Thank you." The evening had turned exceptionally dark, and when Amy glanced toward the sky, she noted that thick gray thunderclouds had moved in. "Just in time," she mumbled toward the heavens. "I didn't think it was ever going to rain again, and if I was ever in the mood for it, it's now."

With her hands buried in the pockets of her long jacket, she started toward her car, which was parked in the lot across the street.

So Josh was gone. He had zoomed in and out of her life with a speed that had left her spinning in its aftermath, and in the process he had touched her in ways that even now she didn't completely understand.

She recalled the first time she had seen him standing above her, holding an order of fish and chips, wanting to know if he could share the picnic table with her. The look in his expressive dark eyes continued to warm her two days later.

Alone now, she stood at the curb, waiting for the light to change, when she heard her name carried in the wind. Whirling around, she noticed someone running toward her with his hand raised. Her heart galloped to her throat when she realized it was Josh. Briefly, she closed her eyes and murmured a silent prayer of thanksgiving. Turning abruptly, she started walking toward him, too happy to care that it had started to rain.

Josh was breathless by the time they met. He stopped jogging three steps away from her, and when he reached her, he wrapped his powerful arms all the way around her waist, half lifting her from the sidewalk.

His hold was so tight that for a second Amy couldn't breathe, but it didn't matter. Happiness erupted from her, and it was all she could do not to cover his face with kisses.

"What happened?" she cried when her feet were back on the ground.

The rain was coming down in sheets by this time, and securing his arm around her shoulders, Josh led her into the foyer of the restaurant.

"Ah," the maître d' said, looking pleased. "So your friend managed to meet you after all." He lifted two oblong menus from the holder on the side of the desk and motioned toward the dining room. "This way." His voice took on a formal tone and relayed a heavy French accent that had been noticeably absent earlier.

Once they were seated and presented with the opened menus as if there was insider information from Wall Street to be mindfully studied, Amy looked over to Josh. "What happened?" she asked again. "I thought you'd left town."

His smiling eyes met hers above the menu. "I'm still here."

"Obviously!" She was far more interested in talking to him than scanning the menu. Their waiter arrived and introduced himself as Darrel. Holding his hands prayerfully, he recited the specials of the day, poured their water and generally made a nuisance of himself. By the time he left their table, Amy was growing restless. "Your clearance came through?"

"Yesterday afternoon."

"Then you *are* leaving. When?"

He glanced at his watch as the waiter approached their table once more. "In a few hours."

"Hours," she cried, and was embarrassed when the conversations around them abruptly halted and several heads turned in her direction. Feeling the heat creep into her cheeks, she felt obligated to explain. "I...I wasn't talking about our dinner."

A couple of heads nodded and the talk resumed.

"Would you care to place your order?" Darrel inquired, his eyes darting from Amy to Josh and back again.

"No," she said forcefully. "Could you give us ten more minutes?"

"Of course." He dipped his head slightly and excused himself, looking mildly irritated.

Amy smoothed the white linen napkin onto her lap as the realization hit her that if Josh was scheduled to depart in several hours, then he must have decided earlier not to meet her. But for some unknown reason, he'd changed his mind. "What made you decide to see me?" she asked starkly.

Josh's eyes clashed with hers, and a breathless moment passed before he answered her. "I couldn't stay away."

His answer was honest enough, but it did little to explain his feelings. "But why? I mean why did you want to leave Seattle without saying goodbye?"

"Oh, Amy." He said her name on the end of a troubled sigh, as if he didn't know the answer himself. "It would have been best, I still believe that, but heaven help us both, here I am."

The look in his eyes caused her to grow hot inside, and she reached for her glass, tasting the cool lemon-flavored water.

"I knew the minute I kissed you I was in trouble." He was frowning as he said it, as though he couldn't help regretting that moment.

"Despite what you think, our kissing wasn't a mistake," she said softly, smiling, "It was fate."

"In any case, I'm flying out of Sea-Tac in a little less than seven hours."

Amy's eyes sparked with eagerness as she leaned toward him. "You mean, we have seven whole hours?"

"Yes." Josh didn't seem to share her excitement.

She set her menu aside. "Are you really hungry?"

Josh's gaze narrowed. "I'm…not sure. Why are you looking at me like that?"

"Because if we've got seven hours, I don't think we should waste them sitting in some elegant French restaurant with a waiter named Darrel breathing down our necks."

"What do you suggest?"

"Walking, talking…kissing."

Josh's Adam's apple moved up his throat as his eyes bored straight into hers. "I don't think so… Besides, it's raining." He dismissed her idea with an abrupt look of impatience.

Darrel returned with a linen cloth draped over his forearm, looking more like an English butler than ever.

"I'll have the lamp chops," Josh announced gruffly, handing him the menu. "Rare."

"Escalope de veau florentine," Amy said when their waiter looked expectantly in her direction. She would rather have spent these last remaining hours alone with Josh, but he was apparently going out of his way to avoid that.

Twice now, he'd claimed that kissing her had been problematic, and yet she knew he'd enjoyed the exchange as much as she. In fact he looked downright irritated with himself for having changed his mind about coming this evening. But he'd professed that he couldn't stay away. He was strongly attracted to her, and he didn't like it one bit.

"Amy, would you kindly stop looking at me like that?"

"Like what?" she asked, genuinely confused.

"You're staring at me with my grandmother would call 'bedroom eyes.'"

He was frowning so hard that she laughed out loud. "I am?"

He nodded, looking serious. "Do you realize I'm little more than a drifter? I could be a mass murderer for all you know."

"But you're not." Their salads arrived and she dipped her fork into the crisp greens.

"The fact that I wander from job to job *should* concern you."

"Why?" She didn't understand his reasoning.

"Because just like that—" he snapped his fingers to emphasize his point "—I'm going to be in and out of your life—I won't see you again after tonight. I don't intend on returning to Seattle. It's a nice place to visit, but I've seen everything I care to, and there isn't any reason for me to stop this way again."

"All right, then let's enjoy the time we have."

He stabbed his salad with a vengeance. "I don't know about you, but I'm having a fantastic time right here and now."

"Josh," she whispered. "Why are you so furious?"

"Because." He stopped and inhaled sharply. "The problem is, I'm experiencing a lot of emotions for you that I have no right feeling. I should never have come here tonight, just the way I should never have kissed you. You're young and sweet, and most likely a virgin."

Despite herself, Amy blushed.

"I knew it," he muttered, setting his salad fork aside and sadly shaking his head. "I just knew it."

"That's bad?"

"Yes," he grumbled, looking more put out than ever. "Don't you understand?"

"Apparently not. I think we should appreciate what we feel for each other and not worry about anything else."

"You make it sound so simple."

"And you're complicating everything. You were there for me when I needed a friend. I think you're marvelous, and I'm happy to have met you. If we've only got seven hours—" she paused and, after glancing at her watch, amending the time "—six and a half hours left together, then so be it. I can accept that. When you're gone, I'll think fondly of you and our brief interlude. I don't expect anything more from you, Josh, so quit worrying."

He didn't look any less disturbed, but he returned to his salad, centering his concentration there as if this was his last meal and he was determined to enjoy it.

They barely spoke after their entrées arrived. Amy's veal was excellent, and she assumed that Josh's lamb was equally good.

When Darrel carried their plates away, Josh ordered coffee for them both. When the bill arrived, he paid it, but they didn't linger over their coffee.

"The dinner was very good," Amy said, striving to guide them naturally into conversation. "I'm glad you came back, Josh. Thank you."

He looked as if he was tempted to smile. "I've been rotten company. I apologize."

"Saying goodbye is never easy."

"It has been until now," he said, his eyes locking with hers. "You're a special lady, Amy Johnson, don't sell yourself short. Understand?"

Amy wasn't sure that she did. "I won't," she answered.

"You're far more capable than you give yourself credit for. I don't think your father is as blind as you believe. Once you're in the family business and get your feet wet, you may be surprised by how well you do."

"Et tu, Brute?"

Josh chuckled. "Do you want any more coffee?"

She shook her head.

Josh helped her out of her chair and they left the restaurant.

The rain had stopped for the moment, and a few brave stars poked out from behind a thick cluster of threatening clouds.

With her hands in her pockets, Amy stood in front of the restaurant. "Do you want to say goodbye now?" He didn't answer her right away and, disheartened, Amy read that as answer enough. Slowly, she raised her hand to his face and held it against his clean-shaven cheek. "God speed, Joshua Powell." She was about to turn away when he took hold of her wrist and closed his eyes.

"No," he admitted tightly. "I don't want to say goodbye just yet."

"What would you like to do?"

He chuckled. "The answer would make you blush. Let's walk."

He looped her hand in the crook of his elbow and pressed his fingers over her own. Then he led the way down the sidewalk, their destination unknown, at least to her. His natural stride was lengthy, but Amy managed to keep pace with him without difficulty. He didn't seem inclined to talk, which was fine, since there wasn't anything special she wanted to say. It was such a joy just to spend this time with him, to be close to him, knowing that within a matter of hours, he would be gone forever from her life.

After the first couple of blocks, he paused and turned to her. His eyes were wide and restless as they roamed her features, as though setting them to memory.

"Do you want to talk?" she asked, looking around for a place for them to sit down and chat. The area was shadowy, and most of the small businesses had closed for the day. The only illumination available was a dim streetlight situated at the end of the block.

He shook his head. "No," he said evenly, his gaze effectively holding hers. "I want to kiss you."

Amy grinned. "I was hoping you'd say that."

"We shouldn't."

"Oh, I agree one hundred percent. If it was cotton candy the first time, there's no telling what we'll discover the second. Caramel apples? Hot buttered popcorn? Or worst of all—"

He chuckled and silenced her by expertly fitting his mouth over hers. His kiss was so unbelievably tender that it caused her to shiver. His grip tightened, bringing her more fully into the circle of his arms. Amy linked her hands to the base of his neck, leaning into him and letting him absorb the bulk of her weight. She strained upward, standing on the tips of her toes, naturally blossoming open to him the way a flower does to the summer sun.

When they broke apart, they were both trembling.

It had started to rain again, but neither of them seemed to notice. Josh threaded his fingers through her hair as he kissed her once more, rocking his lips slowly back and forth, creating a whole new range of delicious sensations with each small movement.

He shuddered when he finished. "You're much too sweet," he whispered, taking a long series of biting kisses, teasing her with his lips and his tongue.

"So you've said…just don't stop."

"I won't," he promised, and proceeded to show her exactly how much he enjoyed kissing her.

A low moan escaped, and Amy was surprised when she realized the sound had come from her.

"You shouldn't be so warm and giving," Josh continued. He held her close as if loosening his grip would endanger her life.

Amy felt her knees about ready to give. She was a rag doll in his arms. "Josh," she pleaded, caressing the sides of his face and the sharp contours of his jawline.

He continued to mold her softness to him and braced his forehead against hers while he drew in several deep breaths. Amy couldn't stop touching him; it helped root her in reality. Her hands cherished his face. She ran her fingertips up and down his jaw, trying to put the feel of him into her memory, hoping these few short moments would last her for all the time that would follow.

"It's raining," Josh told her.

"I know."

"Cats and dogs."

She smiled.

"You're drenched."

"The only thing I feel is your heart." She flattened her hand over his chest and dropped her lashes at the sturdy accelerated pulse she felt beneath her fingertips.

"If you don't get dry, you could catch cold," he warned as if he were searching for an excuse to send her away.

"I'll chance it."

"Amy, I can't let you do that." He slipped his arm around her shoulders and guided her east, toward the business-packed section of the downtown area. "I'm taking you to my hotel room. You're going to dry yourself off, and then I'm going to give you a sweater of mine."

"Josh…"

"From there, I'll walk you to your car. We'll be in and out of that hotel room in three minutes flat. Understand?"

Her eyes felt huge. He didn't trust himself to be alone with her in his room, and the thought warmed her from the inside out. Amy didn't need his sweater or a towel or anything else, but she wasn't about to tell him that.

By the time they reached the lobby of his hotel, her hair was so wet that it was dripping on the carpet. She was certain she resembled a drowned muskrat.

Josh's room was on the eighteenth floor. He opened the door for her and switched on the light. The suite was furnished with a king-size bed, chair, television and long dresser. His airline ticket rested on the dresser top, and her gaze was automatically drawn to that. The ticket forcefully reminded her that Josh would soon be out of her life. The drapes were open, and the view of the Seattle skyline was sweeping and panoramic.

"This is nice," she said, smiling at him.

"Here." He handed her a thick towel, which she used to wipe the moisture from her face and hair.

"What about you?" she asked, when she'd finished.

He stood as far away from her as he possibly could and still remain in the same room. His eyes seemed to be everywhere but on her.

"I'm fine." He scooted past her, keeping well out of her way. His efforts to avoid brushing against her were just short of comical. He seemed to breathe again once he was safely out of harm's way. From the way he was acting, one would suspect she carried bubonic plague. He opened the closet and took out a long-sleeved sweater. "There's a mirror in the bathroom if you need it."

She actually did want to run a comb through her hair and moved into the other room.

"Do you remember the other day when you asked me if I didn't go in to my father's business what I wanted to do instead?"

"I remember." His voice sounded a long way off, as though he was on the other side of the room.

"I've given the question some thought in the last few days."

"What have you come up with?"

She stuck her head around the door. She was right; Josh stood with his back to her in front of the windows, although she doubted that he was appreciating the view. "If I tell you, do you promise not to laugh?"

"I'll try."

She eased his sweater over her head and smoothed

it around her hips, then gingerly stepped into the room, hands dangling awkwardly at her sides. "In light of all the advancements in the feminist movement, this is going to sound ridiculous."

"Try me." He folded his arms over his broad chest and waited.

"More than anything, I'd like to be a wife and a stay-at-home mother." She watched him carefully, half expecting him to find something humorous in her confession. Instead, his gaze gentled and he smiled.

"I treasure the memories of my mother," she continued. "She was so wonderful to me and Dad, so loving and supportive of everything we did. I've already explained my father's personality, so you know what he's like. Mom was the glue that held our family together. Her love was the foundation that guided him in those early years. I don't know if she ever visited his office, in fact, I rather doubt that she did, and yet he discussed every decision with her. She was his support system, his rock. She was never in the limelight, but she was a vital part of Dad's life, and his business."

"You want to be like her?"

Amy nodded. "Only I'm more greedy. I want a house full of children, too."

Josh's gaze moved deliberately to his watch. "I think we'd better go," he said, sounding oddly breathless.

"Josh?"

He stiffened. "I promised you we'd be in and out of here in a matter of minutes. Remember?"

"I'd like to stay."

"No," he said forcefully, shaking his head. "Amy, please, try to understand. Being alone with you is temptation enough—don't make it any more difficult."

"What about the sweater?" She ran her fingers down the length of the sleeves. "Won't you want it back?"

"Keep it. Where I'm headed it's going to be a hundred degrees in the shade. Trust me, I'm not going to miss it."

"But—"

"Amy!" Her name was a husky rumble low in his chest. "Unless you'd like to start that family you're talking about right now, I suggest we get out of here."

"Soon," she told him firmly, refusing to give in to the shock value of his statement.

Twin brows arched. "Soon?" he repeated incredulously.

"Come here." Her back was pressed against the door, and her heart was pounding so hard that it had long since drowned out what reason remained to her. She had never been so bold with a man in her life, but she knew if she was ever going to act, the time was now. Otherwise, Josh was going to politely walk her to her car, kiss her on the cheek and wish her a good life and then casually stroll away from her and out of her world.

"Amy." His mouth thinned with impatience.

"Say goodbye to me here," she said, smiling, then she motioned with her index finger for him to come to her.

He shoved his hands into his jeans pockets as if he didn't trust them to keep still at his sides. He paused and cleared his throat. "It really is time we left."

"Fine. All I'm asking is for you to say our farewells here. It will be much better than in a parking lot outside the restaurant, don't you think?"

"No." The lone word was harsh and low.

She shrugged and hoped she looked regretful. "All

right," she murmured and sighed. "If you won't come to me, then I guess I'll have to go to you."

Josh looked shocked by this and held out his hand as if he were stopping traffic.

The action did more to amuse her than keep her at bay. "I'm going to say goodbye to you, Joshua Powell. And I'm warning you right now, it's going to be a kiss you'll remember for a good long while."

Everything about Josh told her how much he wanted her. From the moment they had stepped into his room the tension between them had been electric. She didn't understand why he was putting up such a fight. For her part, she was astonished by her own actions. Until she had met Josh, she had always been the timid, reserved one in a relationship. Two minutes alone with him and she had turned into a hellcat. She wasn't sure what had caused the transformation.

"Amy, please, you aren't making this easy," Josh muttered. "We're playing with a lighted fuse here, don't you understand that? If I kiss you, sweetheart, I promise you it won't stop there. Before either of us will know how it happened, you're going to be out of that dress and my hands are going to be places where no one else has ever touched you. Understand?"

She felt the blood drain out of her face as quickly as if someone had pulled a drain from a sink. Blindly, she nodded. Still, it didn't stop her from easing her way toward him.

Josh groaned. "I knew it was a mistake to bring you up here." His face was tight, his eyes dark and brilliant. "We're going to end up making love, and you're going to give me something I don't want. Save it for your husband, sweetheart, he'll appreciate it more than I will."

Her heart went crazy. It felt like a herd of charging elephants was stampeding inside her chest. She moistened her lips, and whatever audacity had propelled her into this uncharacteristic role abruptly left her at the threat in his words. Pausing, she drew in a deep, calming breath and forced a smile.

"Goodbye, Josh," she whispered. With that, she turned and bolted for the door.

He caught her shoulder and catapulted her around and into his chest before she made it another step. He cursed under his breath and locked her in his arms, rubbing his chin back and forth over the crown of her head in a caressing action, silently apologizing for shocking her.

"Oh, Amy," he groaned, "perhaps you're right. Maybe it *is* fate." She felt his warm breath against the hollow beneath her right ear.

Her head fell back in a silent plea, and he began spreading warm kisses over the delicate curve of her neck. With his hands holding each side of her face, he ran his lips along the line of her jaw, his open mouth moist and passionate. When she was sure he meant to torment her for hours before giving her what she craved, he lowered his mouth to hers, softly, tenderly in a kiss that was as gentle as the flutter of a hummingbird's wings. A welcoming rasping sound tumbled from her lips.

He made a low, protesting noise of his own as his lips caressed hers, tasted her, savored her, his mouth so hot and compelling that she felt singed all the way to the soles of her feet. When they broke apart, they were both breathless.

"Amy...I tried to tell you."

"Shh." She kissed him to silence his objections. She had no regrets and longed to erase his. "I want you to touch me...it feels so good when you do."

"Oh, angel, you shouldn't say things like that to a man."

"Not any man," she whispered, "only you."

Josh inhaled a sharp breath. "That doesn't make it any better."

"Why don't you just shut up and kiss me again?"

"Because," he growled, "I want so much more." He ground his mouth over hers as if to punish her for making him desire her so much.

Amy bit into her lower lip at the powerful surge of sensations that assaulted her like a tidal wave. Before she knew what was happening, he had removed the sweater he had given her to wear. His fingers were poised at the zipper at the back of her dress when he paused, his breathing labored. Then, with a supreme effort, he brought his strong loving hands to either side of her face, stroking her satiny cheeks with the pads of his thumbs.

"It's time to stop, Amy. I meant what I said about saving yourself for your husband. I won't be coming back to Seattle."

She dipped her head and nodded, accepting his words. "Yes, I know." Gently she raised her lips to his and kissed him goodbye. But she kept her promise. She made sure it was a kiss Joshua Powell would well remember.

Josh secured the strap of his flight bag to his shoulder and glanced a second time at his watch. He still had thirty minutes before he could board the plane that would carry him to his destination in Kadiri. He had been filled with excitement, eager for the challenge that awaited him in this Middle Eastern country, and now he would have gladly forfeited his life savings for an excuse to remain in Seattle.

His mind was filled with doubts. He had said good-bye to Amy several hours earlier and already he was being eaten alive, caught between the longing to see her again and the equally strong desire to forget they had ever met.

His biggest mistake had been trusting himself alone with her in his hotel room. The temptation had been too much for him, and she certainly hadn't helped matters any. The woman was a natural-born temptress, and she didn't even know it. She couldn't so much as walk across the room without making him want her. All his life, he would remember her leaning against his door and motioning for him to come to her with her index finger. She was so obviously new to the game that her efforts should have been more humorous than exciting. Unfortunately, everything about her excited him.

To complicate matters, she was innocent. When she started talking about building a secure home life for her husband and wanting children, he knew that she was completely out of his league. They were as different as fresh milk and aged Scotch. She was hot dogs and baseball and freshly diapered babies. And he was rented rooms, a dog-eared passport and axle grease.

He had to bite his tongue to keep from asking for her number. He didn't often think of himself as noble, but he did now. The sooner he left Amy, the sooner he could return to his disorderly vagabond lifestyle.

However, Josh was confident of one thing—it would be a long time before he forgot her.

As Josh stood in the security line at Sea-Tac Airport he checked the flight time and gate number on his ticket.

"Josh."

He jerked around to discover Amy hurrying down the concourse toward him. For one wild second, Josh didn't know if he should be pleased or not.

It didn't take him long to decide.

Four

"Amy." Josh rushed out of the line at security and gripped her shoulders as his eyes scanned hers. "What are you doing here?" She was still breathless and it took her several moments to speak. "I know I shouldn't... have come, but I couldn't stay home and...and let it all end so abruptly."

"Amy, listen to me—"

"I know." She pressed the tips of her fingers over his lips, not wanting him to speak. He couldn't say anything that she hadn't already told herself a dozen times or more. "I'm doing everything wrong, but I couldn't bear to just let you walk out of my life without—"

"We already said goodbye."

"I know that, too," she protested.

"How'd you know where to find me?"

"I saw your airline ticket on the dresser, and once I knew which airline, it wasn't difficult to figure out which secrurity checkpoint you'd be going through. Oh, Josh, I'm sorry if this embarrasses you." She was so confused, hot and cold at the same time. Hot from his kisses and cold with apprehension. She was making a complete idiot of herself, but after weighing her options, she'd done the only thing she could.

"Here," she said, thrusting an envelope toward him.

"What's this?"

"In case you change your mind."

"About what?" His brow condensed with the question.

"About ever wanting to see me again. It's my contact information, and for good measure I threw in a flattering photo of myself, but it was taken several years ago when my hair was shorter and...well, it's not much, but it's the best I have."

He chuckled and hauled her into his arms, squeezing her close.

"You don't have to email me," she told him, her voice steady with conviction.

"I probably won't."

"That's fine...well, it isn't, but I can accept that."

"Good."

He didn't seem inclined to release her, but buried his face in her neck and drew in a short breath. "Your scent is going to haunt me," he grumbled. "I'm going halfway around the world and all I'll think about is you."

"Good." Her smile was weak at best. She'd done everything she could by pitching the ball to him. If and when he decided to swing at it, she would be ready.

The security guard tapped him on the shoulder. "Are you going or not, cause you're blocking the line." Moving over slightly, Josh wrapped her in a warm embrace, he brushed his hand across her cheek, his touch was tender, as though he was caressing a newborn baby. "I have to go," he said, his voice low and gravelly.

"Yes, I know." Gently she smoothed his sweater at

his shoulders and offered him a feeble smile. "Enjoy the Middle East," she said, "but stay away from those belly dancers."

Amy dropped her arms and stuffed her hands inside her pockets for fear she would do something more to embarrass them both. Something silly like reaching out and asking him not to leave, or pleading with him to at least contact her.

She did her utmost to beam him a polished smile. If he was going to hold on to the memory of her, she wanted to stand tall and dignified and give him a smile that would make Miss America proud. "Have a safe trip."

He nodded, turned and took two steps away from her.

Panic filled Amy—there was one last thing she had to say. "Josh." At the sound of her voice, he abruptly turned back. "Thank you…for everything."

He offered her a weak smile.

She nodded, because saying anything more would have been impossible. She kept her head tilted at a proud angle, determined to send him off with a smile.

"Amy." Her name was a low growl as Josh dropped his flight bag and stepped toward her.

"Go on," she cried. "You'll miss your plane."

He was at her side so fast she didn't have time to think or act. He hauled her into his arms and kissed her with a hunger and need that were enough to convince her she would never find another man who made her feel the things this one did. His wild kiss was ardent, but all too brief to suit either of them.

Josh pulled himself away from her with some effort, picked up his bag and headed into the security checkpoint. Amy stood frozen to the spot he'd left her, following him with her eyes, until he was out of sight, her head demanding that she forget Joshua Powell and her heart claiming it was impossibile.

Harold Johnson was sitting in the library smoking a cigar when Amy quietly let herself into the house. The lights from the crack beneath the door alerted her to the fact her father was up and waiting for her return.

"Hi," she said, letting herself into the room. She sat in the wingback leather chair beside him and peeled off her coat. Slipping off her shoes, she tucked her feet beneath her and rested her eyes.

"You're back."

She nodded. "I saw Josh off at the airport. I gave him all my contact information and for good measure a photo of myself."

"Smart idea."

"According to Josh it was a mistake. I can't understand why he thinks that way, but he does. He made it clear he has no intention of keeping in touch."

"Can you accept that?"

To Amy's way of thinking, she didn't have a choice. "I'll have to."

Her father's low chuckle was something of a surprise. "I don't mind telling you that your interest in this young man is poetic justice."

"Why's that?"

"All these years, there've been boys buzzing around this house like bees in early summer, but you didn't pay a one of them a moment's heed. For all the interest you showed, they could have been made of marble."

"None of them was anything like Josh."

"What makes this one so different?" her father asked, chewing on the end of his cigar.

Amy swore he ate more of it than he smoked. "I don't know what to tell you. Josh is forthright and honest—to a fault sometimes. He's the type of man I'd want by my side if anything was ever to go wrong. He wouldn't back away from a fight, but he'd do everything within his power to see that matters didn't get that far."

"I'd like him, then."

"I know you would, Dad, you wouldn't be able to stop yourself. He's direct and sincere."

"Pleasant to look at, I suspect."

She smiled and nodded. "He wears his hair a little longer than what you'd like, though."

"Hair doesn't make the man." Harold Johnson puffed at the cigar and reached for his glass of milk.

"What are you doing up this late?" she asked after a moment of comfortable silence.

"After we talked when you came home from dinner, I heard you roaming around your bedroom for an hour or two, pacing back and forth loud enough to wake the birds. About the time I decided to find out what was troubling you, I heard you leave. Since I was awake, I decided to read a bit, and by the time I noticed the hour, it wasn't worth going back to bed."

"I'm sorry I kept you awake."

"No problem." He paused and yawned loudly, covering his mouth with the back of his hand. "Maybe I *will* try to get in an hour or two of rest before heading for the office."

"Good idea." Amy hadn't realized how exhausted she was until her father mentioned it.

They walked up the stairs together and she kissed his cheek when she reached her bedroom door. "Sally and I are playing tennis tomorrow morning, and then I'm doing some volunteer work at the homeless center later in the afternoon. You didn't need me for anything, did you?"

"No. But I thought you were going to take the summer off?"

"I am," she said, and yawned. "Trust me, Dad, tennis is hard work."

Josh had never been fond of camels. They smelled worse than rotting sewage, were ill-tempered and more stubborn than mules. The beasts were the first thing Josh saw as he stepped off his small plane that had delivered him to the oil fields. He had the distinct impression this country was filled with them. And soldiers. Each and every one of them seemed to be carting a machine gun. A cantankerous camel strolled across the runway followed by two shouting men waving sticks and cursing in Arabic.

Joel Perkins, Josh's direct superior and best friend, was supposed to meet him in the crowded Kadiri airport. Kadiri was a small town rich in oil. The company that employed Josh had recently signed a contract for oil exploration and drilling with the Saudi government.

It was like stepping back in time when Josh stepped off the plane. The terminal, if the building could be termed that, was filled with animals and produce and so crowded that Josh could barely move.

Ten minutes in this part of the country and already his clothes were plastered to his skin; the temperature must have been over a hundred degrees inside, and no telling what it was in the direct sunlight.

At six foot four, Joel Perkins was head and shoulders above most everyone, so it was easy enough for Josh to spot his friend. Making his way over to him, however, was another matter entirely.

"Excuse me," Josh said twenty times as he scooted around caged chickens, crying children and several robed men.

"Good to see you," Joel greeted him, and slapped his hand across Josh's back. "How was the flight?"

"From Seattle to Paris was a piece of cake. From Paris to Kadiri…you don't want to hear about it, trust me."

Joel laughed. "But you're here now and safe."

"No thanks to that World War II wreck of a plane that just landed."

"As you can see, the taxis are out of service," Joel explained. "We're going to have to ride into the city on these."

Josh took one look at the ugliest-looking camel he had ever encountered and let out an expletive that would have curled Amy's hair. He stopped abruptly. Every thought that drifted through his mind was in some way connected to her. He hadn't stopped thinking of her for a single minute. Every time he closed his eyes, it was her lips that smiled at him, her blue eyes that flashed with eagerness, her arms that reached toward him.

What he had said to her about her scent haunting him had been prophetic. In fact, he had strolled along the streets of Paris until he had found a small fragrance shop. It took him an hour to discover the perfume that reminded him of her. Feeling like a fool for having wasted the proprietor's time, he ended up buying a bottle. He didn't know what he was going to do with it. Mail it to his seventy-year-old Aunt Hazel?

"What's the matter?" Joel asked. "Has the heat gotten to you already?"

"No," Josh said. "A woman has."

Joel's eyes revealed his surprise. "A woman? Where?"

"Seattle."

Joel laughed.

"What's so funny?" Josh demanded.

"You. It does me good to see you aren't as immune as you'd like others to believe."

Josh muttered under his breath, regretting saying anything about Amy to his friend.

Joel slapped him across the back as his eyes grew dark and serious. "Are you going to do anything about it?"

Josh didn't need to think before he answered. "Not a damn thing."

Joel expelled his breath in a slow exercise. "Good. You had me worried there for a minute."

A week later, Josh had changed Joel Perkins's mind.

Exhausted, Amy let herself in the back door of her home. Her face was red, and she wiped it dry with the small white towel draped around her neck. Her tennis racket was in one hand, and after securing it under her arm, she poured herself a tall glass of iced tea.

"Manuela, is the mail here?"

"Nothing for you, Miss Amy," the Spanish-American housekeeper informed her.

Amy tried to swallow the disappointment, but it was growing increasingly difficult. Josh had been gone nearly two weeks, and she'd hoped to hear from him before now. No emails, no messages. She'd hoped he at least might write. Nothing yet and she was beginning to believe she wouldn't hear from him. The thought deeply depressed her.

Her phone rang, as she went to answer it she noted that the display read private. "Hello," she said, walking out of the kitchen. Her words were followed by an eerie hum. Amy blinked and was about to disconnect when someone spoke.

"Amy, is that you?"

Her heart raced into her throat. "Josh?"

"What time is it there? I wasn't sure of the time difference and I hope it isn't the middle of the night."

"It's not. It's three in the afternoon."

He sounded so different. So far away, but that didn't detract from the exhilaration she was experiencing from hearing the sound of his voice.

"I'm so glad you called," she said softly, slumping into her father's desk chair. "I've been miserable, wondering if you ever would. I'd just about given up hope."

"It was Joel's idea."

"Joel?"

"He's a friend of mine. He claimed that if I didn't call you, he would. Said I had my mind on you when I should be thinking about business. I guess he's right."

"If he were close by, I'd kiss him."

"If you're going to kiss anyone, Amy Johnson, it's me, understand?"

"Yes, sir."

"What's the weather like?"

"Seventy-five and balmy. I just finished playing two sets of tennis. I've been doing a lot of that lately... If I'm exhausted, then I don't think of you so much. What's the weather like in Kadiri?"

"You don't want to know. A hundred and five about ten this morning."

"Oh, Josh. Are you going to be all right?"

"Probably not, but I'll live." There was some commotion and then Josh came back on the line. "Joel's here, and he said I should email you."

Her heartbeat slowed before she asked, "Is that what you want?"

An eternity passed before he responded. "I don't know what I want anymore. At one time everything was clear to me, but after two weeks, I'm willing to admit I was a fool to think I could forget you. Yes, Amy, I'll be in touch. I'll try and get a message off to you now and again, but I'm not making any promises."

"I understand."

"Listen, I put something in the mail for you the other day, but it'll take a week or more before it arrives— if it ever does. The way everything else goes around here, I doubt that it'll make it through customs intact."

"Something from Kadiri?"

"No, actually, I picked this up in Paris."

"Oh, Josh, you were thinking of me in Paris?"

"That's the problem, I never stopped thinking about you." Once more there was a quick exchange of muffled words before Josh came back on the line. "Joel seemed to think it's important for you to know that I haven't been the best company the last couple of weeks."

Amy closed her eyes, savoring these moments. "Thank Joel for letting me know."

"Be sure and tell me if that package arrives. If it does, there's something else I'd like to send you, something from Kadiri." His words were followed by heavy static.

"Josh. Josh," she cried, certain she'd lost him.

"I'm here, but I can't say for how much longer."

"This is probably costing you a fortune."

"Don't worry about it. Joel's springing for the call."

A faint laugh could be heard in the distance, and Amy smiled, knowing already that she was going to like Josh's friend.

"As soon as you contact me I'll email you back, I promise." It was on the tip of her tongue to tell him how much she had thought about him and missed him since he'd left. Twice now, she had gone down to the waterfront and stood at the end of the pier where he had first kissed her, hoping to recapture those precious moments.

"I swear living in Kadiri is like stepping into the eighteenth century. This phone is the only one within a hundred miles, so there isn't any way to reach me."

"I understand."

"Amy, listen." Josh's voice was filled with regret. "I've got to go. Joel's apparently bribed a government official to use this phone, and we're about to get kicked out of here."

"Oh, Josh, do be careful."

"Honey," he said, and laughed. "I was born careful."

At that precise moment, the line was severed.

Amy sat down at the dinner table across from her father and smoothed the napkin across her lap, feeling warm and happy.

"So you got another email from Josh today?"

"Yes," she said, glancing up. "How'd you know?"

"You mean other than that silly grin you've been wearing all afternoon? Besides, you haven't played tennis all week, and before his phone call, you spent more time on the tennis courts than you did at home."

Amy reached for the lean pork roast and speared herself an end cut. "I don't know what tennis has to do with Joshua Powell."

Her father snickered softly. He knew her too well for her to disguise her feelings.

"Little things say a lot, remember that when you start working at the end of the summer. That small piece of advice will serve you well."

"I will," she murmured, handing him the meat platter, avoiding his gaze.

"Now," her father said forcefully, "when am I going to meet this young man of yours?"

"I…I don't know, Dad. Josh hasn't written a word about when he's leaving Kadiri. He could be there for several months—perhaps longer. I have no way of knowing."

Her father set the meat platter aside, then paused and rested his elbows on the table, clasping his hands together. "How do you feel about that?"

"I don't understand."

"I notice you're not dating anyone. Fact is, you've been living like a nun. Don't you think it's time to start socializing a little?"

"No." Her mind was too full of Josh to consider going out with another man, although she was routinely asked. Not once in all the weeks since Josh had left Seattle had the thought of dating anyone else entered her mind.

Harold Johnson brooded during the remainder of their meal. Amy knew that look well. It preceded a father-to-daughter chat in which he would tell her something "for her own good." This time she was certain the heart-to-heart talk would have to do with Josh.

Amy didn't have a single argument prepared. Harold was absolutely right, she barely knew Joshua Powell. She'd seen him a grand total of three times—four if she counted the fact they'd met twice that first day and five if she included her harried trip to the airport. It wouldn't have mattered if she'd seen him every day for six months, though. But her father wouldn't understand that. As far as Amy was concerned, she knew everything important that she needed to know about him.

When their talk was over, Amy went to her room, took out her computer and read the email she'd received and sat on the bed.

Dear Amy,

I opened your email this morning. There are no words to tell you how pleased I was to see it. It seems weeks since we talked on the phone, and with Joel standing over me, it was difficult to tell you the things that have been going through my head. Now, as I sit down to type, I realize it isn't any easier to find the words. I never was much good with this sort of thing. I work well with numbers and with my hands, but when it comes to expressing my feelings, I'm at a loss.

I suppose I should admit how glad I was to see you at the airport. As I headed to the airport to catch my flight I told myself it was best to make a clean break.

Then, all of a sudden, you were there and despite everything, I was thrilled you came. I still can't believe you came and how you knew when and where to find me. Anyways like I said before, I'm not much good at this. Email me back when you can.

Love, Josh

Needing to think about her response, Amy waited a day to reply.

Dearest Josh,
The perfume arrived in today's mail. The fragrance is perfect for me. Where did you ever find it? The minute I opened the package, I dabbed some behind my ear and closed my eyes, imagining you were here with me. I know it sounds silly, but I felt so close to you at that moment, as if it was your fingers spreading the fragrance at my pulse points, holding me close. Thank you.

Today was a traumatic one for me. Dad brought me in to work with him to show me how he'd had an office completely remodeled for me. It was so plush, so...I don't know, elaborate. Everything was done in a dark wood, mahogany I think. I swear the desk had to be six feet long. I don't suppose this means that much unless you've ever seen my dad's office. He's used the same furniture for twenty years...same office assistant, too. At any rate, everything about my dad's office shouts humble beginnings, hard work and frugality. He should be the one with the fancy furniture—not me. I swear the guilt was more than I could bear.

It made me realize that the clock is ticking and I won't be able to delay telling him my feelings much longer. I've got to tell him...only I don't know how. I wish you were here. You made me feel so confident that I'm doing the right thing. I don't feel that anymore. Now all I am is confused and alone.

Love, Amy

P.S. You haven't been seeing any belly dancers, have you?

Dearest Angel Eyes,

I swear this country is the closest thing to hell on earth. The heat is like nothing I've ever known. Last night, for the first time since I arrived, Joel and I went swimming. We were splashing around like a couple of five-year-olds. The whole time I was wishing it was you with me instead of Joel.

Later I lay on the sand and stared at the sky. The stars were so bright, they seemed to droop right out of the heavens. I had the feeling if I reached up I could snatch one right out of the sky. First chance I get I rush to my computer at the end of the day and I'm happy as a kid in a candy store when an email arrives from you. Then the next thing I know I'm gazing at the stars, wondering if you're staring at them, too. What have you done to me, Amy Johnson?

Joel keeps feeding me warnings. He tells me a woman can be too much of a distraction, and that I've got to keep my head screwed on straight. He's right. We're not exactly here on a picnic. Don't worry about me, if I'm anything it's cautious.

I put a surprise in the mail for you today. This is straight from the streets of Kadiri. Let me know when it arrives.

Love, Josh

P.S. No, I haven't seen any belly dancers. What about you? Any guys from the country club wanting you for doubles on the tennis courts?

My dearest Josh,
I love seeing the picture of you and Joel. You look so tan and so handsome. It made me miss you all the more. I sat down and studied the photo for so long the image started to blur. I miss you so much, it seems that we barely had a chance to know each other and then you were gone. Don't mind me for complaining. I'm in a blue funk today. Dad took me to lunch so I could meet the others from the office and when I jumped on the computer I saw your email.

It made me wish I could sit down and talk to you.

By the way, Joel's so tall. I'm pleased he's there with you. Thanks, too, for your vote of confidence in handling this situation with Dad. He seems oblivious to my feelings. Come September, I probably will move into my fancy new office because I can't honestly see myself confronting him. My fate is sealed.

Your Angel Eyes

It was one of those glorious summer afternoons that blesses the Pacific Northwest every August. Unable to resist the sun, Amy was venting her energy by doing laps in the pool.

"Miss Amy, Miss Amy!"

Manuela came running toward the pool, her hands flying. She stopped, breathless, and a flurry of Spanish erupted from her so fast and furiously that even after two years of studying the language, Amy couldn't make out a single word.

"Manuela," she protested, stepping out of the pool. She reached for her towel. "What are you saying?"

"You left your phone on the counter...long distance...man say hurry."

Amy's heart did a tiny flip-flop. "Is it Josh?"

The housekeeper's hands gestured to the sky as she broke into her native tongue again.

"Never mind," Amy cried, running toward the phone in her hand. "Josh...Josh, are you still there?"

"Amy? Who answered the phone? I couldn't understand a word she said."

"That's Manuela. I'm sorry it took me so long. How are you? Oh, Josh, I miss you so much."

"I miss you, too, angel. I read your email from yesterday, and I haven't been able to stop thinking about you since."

"I was in such a depressed state when I wrote that... I should never have pressed the Send button."

"I'm glad you did. Now, tell me what's happening between you and your father."

"Josh, I can't—not over the phone."

"You're going to work for him?"

"I can't see any way out of it. Are you going to think me a coward?"

"My Angel Eyes? Never."

"I figured the least I could do was give it a try. I don't hold out much hope, but who knows, I might shock everyone and actually be successful."

"You sound in better spirits."

"I am...now. Oh, before I forget, the traditional dress from Kadiri arrived, and I love it. It's so colorful and cool. What did you say the women call it again?"

"Btu-btu."

"I wore it all last night, and the whole time I had this incredible urge to walk around the house pounding drums and singing 'Kumbah Ya.'"

Josh laughed, and the sound did more to elevate Amy's mood than anything in two long months.

"Amy, listen, I've only got a few more minutes. We were able to get use of the phone again, but I don't know how long it's good for so if we're cut off again, don't worry."

She nodded before she realized he couldn't see her gesture of understanding. She closed her eyes to keep the ready emotion cornered. "I can't tell you how good it is to hear your voice."

"Yours, too, Angel Eyes."

She laughed. "I loved the picture of you and Joel. Thank you so much for sending it. You look even better than I remember."

"I'm coming back to Seattle."

Amy's head snapped up. "When? Oh, Josh, you don't know how many times I prayed you would."

"Don't get so excited, it won't be until December."

"December," she repeated. "I can wait another five months…easy. How about you?"

"I swear to you, Amy, I don't know anymore. I've never felt about a woman the way I do about you. Half the time I'm so confused by what's happening between us that I can't understand how this company can pay me the money it does. Joel keeps threatening to fire me; he claims he doesn't need anyone as lovesick as me on his crew."

Lovesick. It was the closest Josh had ever come to admitting what he felt for her.

"Hold on a minute," Josh shouted. He came back on

the line almost immediately. "Honey, I've got to go. I'm thinking about you, angel—"

"Josh…Josh," she cried, "listen to me. I love you."

But the line had already gone dead.

A man could only take so much, Josh reasoned as he walked among the huge drilling structures that had been brought into Kadiri by SunTech Oil. Joel, acting as general foreman, had left his instructions with Josh, but Josh had been running into one confounding problem after another all morning. There wasn't any help for it. Josh was going to have to find Joel and discuss the situation.

It was as he was walking across the compound that he heard the first explosion. The force of it was powerful enough to hurl him helplessly to the ground.

By the time he gathered his wits, men had panicked and were running, knocking each other down, fighting their way toward the gates.

"Joel," Josh cried when he didn't see his friend. Josh searched the frantic, running crowd, but battling through the workers was as difficult as swimming up a waterfall.

"Joel," Josh shouted a second time, then grabbed a man he recognized by the collar. "Where's Joel Perkins?"

The trembling man pointed toward the building that was belching smoke and spitting out flames from two sides. Something drove Josh forward. Whatever it was had nothing to do with sanity or reason or anything else. The only conscious thought Josh had was the brutal determination to go inside and bring out his friend.

Two men tried to stop him, screaming a word that

Josh found unintelligible. Covering his mouth with a wet cloth, Josh shoved them both aside with a super-human strength, then, without thought, stormed into the building.

He recognized two things almost immediately. The first was that Joel Perkins was dead. The second was more devastating than the first. The building was going to explode, and there was nothing he could do to get himself out alive.

Five

"Amy."

Her father's gentle voice stirred her from a light sleep. She rolled over onto her back to discover him sitting on the edge of her bed, dressed in his plaid robe, his brow puckered in a dark frown. He'd turned on her bedside lamp to its lowest setting.

"Dad?" she asked, softly. "What is it?"

His eyes pooled with regret, and instantly she knew.

"It's Josh, isn't it?"

Her father nodded. "The call came an hour ago."

He'd waited an hour. A full hour? Struggling into a sitting position, she brushed the hair from her temples, her hands trembling. She hadn't heard from him in almost two weeks and had already started to worry. Her heart had told her something was wrong.

"Tell me," she whispered. Her tongue felt thick and uncooperative, but she had to know even if it meant she'd lost him forever. "What's happened?"

Harold Johnson placed his hands on her shoulders. "He's been seriously injured. There was an accident, an explosion. Five men were killed. Josh wasn't hurt in the initial explosion, but he went back for his friend. Apparently, he was too late; his friend was already dead."

Amy covered her mouth with her palm and took in deep, even breaths in an effort to curtail the growing alarm that churned in her like the huge blades of a windmill, stirring up dread and fear. "But he's alive."

"Yes, baby, he's alive, but just barely. I can't even tell you the extent of his injuries, only that they're life threatening."

Fear coated her throat. "How did SunTech Oil know to contact me?" Whatever the reason, she thanked God they had. Otherwise, she might never have known.

Her father gently brushed the hair from her brow, his eyes tender and concerned. "Josh listed you as his beneficiary in case of his death. Since he hadn't written down anyone as next of kin, yours was the only name they had. I can't tell you any more than that. The line was terrible, and it was difficult to understand anything of what the official was saying."

Without waiting for anything more, Amy tossed back the covers. "I'm going to him."

Her father shook his head meaningfully. "Somehow I knew you'd say that."

"Then I suppose you also knew I'd want the next flight out of here for Kadiri?" She paused and thought for a moment. "What about a visa?"

"As a matter of fact, I thought of both those things," he admitted, chuckling softly. "There's a connecting plane in Paris, but the only flight into Kadiri flies on Wednesdays."

"But that means I'll have to wait an entire week." She used her thumb and index finger to cup her chin and frowned. "Then I'll get to Paris and hire a private plane to fly me into Saudi Arabia. If I have to, I'll walk from there."

"That won't be necessary," Harold told her.

"Why not?" She whirled around, not understanding.

"You can take the company jet. I'm not sending you off to that part of the world without a means of getting you out of there."

Despite the severity of the situation she smiled, tears glistening in her eyes. "Thank you, Dad."

"And while I was at it, I talked to a friend of mine in the State Department. You've been granted a six-week visa, but you won't be able to stay any longer—our relations with the Middle East are strained at best. Get in and out of there as fast as you can. Understand?"

Her mind was buzzing. "Is there anything else I need to know?"

"Yes," Harold said firmly. "When you come home, I want Josh with you."

When Josh awoke, the first thing that met him was pain so ruthless and severe that for a moment he couldn't breathe. He groaned and dragged in a deep breath, trying to come to terms with the fact that he was alive and not knowing how much longer he wanted to live if being alive meant this excruciating pain. Blissfully, he returned to unconsciousness.

The second time, he was greeted with the same agony, only this time there was a scent of jasmine in the air. Josh struggled to hold on to consciousness. The flower brought Amy to the forefront of his mind. His last thoughts before the building exploded had been of his Angel Eyes, and regret had filled him at the thought of never seeing her again. Perhaps it had been that thought that had persuaded death to give him a second chance. Whatever it was, Josh was grateful. At least, he thought he was, until the pain thrust him into a dark world where he felt nothing.

Time lost meaning. Days, weeks, months could have silently slipped past without him ever realizing it. All he experienced were brief glimpses of consciousness, followed by blackouts for which he was always grateful, because they released him from the pain.

The scent of jasmine was in the wind whenever he awoke. He struggled to breathe it into his lungs because it helped him remember Amy. He held on to her image as long as he could, picturing her as she stood at the airport, determined to send him off with a smile. So proud. So lovely—with soulful eyes an angel would envy. It was then that he had started thinking of her as Angel Eyes.

The sound of someone entering his room disturbed his deep sleep. He heard voices—he had several times. They disturbed him when all he wanted to do was sleep. Only this time, one soft, feminine voice sounded so much like Amy. He must have died. But if this was heaven, then why the pain?

"No," he cried, but his shout of protest was little more than a whisper. It wasn't fair that he should fall in love for the first time and then die. Life wasn't fair, he'd known that from the moment he walked out of his father's office, but somehow he'd always thought death would be…

"Josh," Amy whispered, certain she'd heard him speak. It had been little more than a groan, but it had given her hope. "I'm here," she told him, clasping his hand in her own and pressing it to her cheek. "I love you. Do you understand?"

"Miss Johnson," Dr. Kilroy, Josh's English doctor, said with heavy reluctance. "I don't think he can hear you; the injuries to his body have been catastrophic. I don't think your friend is going to make it. We've only given him a fifty percent chance to live."

"Yes, I know."

"He's been unconscious for nearly three weeks."

"I know that, too."

"Please, you aren't helping him by staying at the hospital day and night. Perhaps if you returned to your hotel room and got a decent night's sleep."

"You'll have to get used to my presence, Doctor, because I'm not budging." She turned toward the bed and swallowed back the alarm, as she had every time her gaze rested on Josh. His injuries were multiple, including second-degree burns on his arms, a broken leg, cracked ribs, a bruised kidney and other internal damage, not to mention a severe concussion. Mercifully, he'd been unconscious from the moment she arrived, which had been five days earlier. Not once had she left his side for more than a few minutes. She talked to him, read to him and wiped the perspiration from his brow, touching him often, hoping her presence would relay her love.

The weak sound he'd made just a moment before was the first indication she'd had that he was awake.

"Miss Johnson, please," Dr. Kilroy continued.

"Doctor, I'm not leaving this hospital," she returned sternly.

"Very well," he acquiesced and left the room.

"Josh." She whispered his name and lightly ran her

hand across his forehead. "I'm here." His eyes were bandaged, but Dr. Kilroy had assured her Josh hadn't been blinded in the accident.

Another soft cry parted his lips, one so unbelievably weak that she had to strain to hear it. Cautiously, she leaned over the hospital bed and placed her ear as close to his mouth as she could.

"Angel Eyes? Jasmine?"

"At your service," she said, choking back the tears. She didn't know who Jasmine was, but she wasn't going to let a little thing like another woman disturb her now. "You're awake?" It was a stupid question. Of course he was.

"Dead?"

It took her a moment to understand his question. "No, you're very much alive."

"Where?"

"We're here in Kadiri."

Gently, he shook his head and then grimaced. The action must have caused him severe pain. She could tell that talking was an effort for him, but there wasn't anything more she could do to help.

"Where?" he repeated. "Hell? Heaven?"

"Earth," she told him, but if he heard her, he didn't give any indication.

She ran for the nurse but by the time they arrived at the room Josh was unconscious again.

Another twenty-four hours passed before she was able to communicate with him a second time. She had been sitting at his bedside, reading. Since his eyes were wrapped it was impossible to tell if he was asleep or awake, but something alerted her to the fact that he had regained consciousness.

"It's Amy," she said softly, taking his hand and rubbing his knuckles gently. "Here, touch my face."

Very slowly he slid his thumb across the high arch of her cheek. Amy was so excited that it was impossible to sit still. She kissed the inside of his palm. "I love you, Joshua Powell, and I swear I'll never forgive you if you up and die on me now."

A hint of a smile cracked his dry lips. "Earth," he said and his head rolled to the side as he slipped into unconsciousness.

"Dad," Amy shouted into the heavy black telephone receiver. It made her appreciate the effort Josh had made to contact her by phone, not once but twice.

"Amy, is that you?"

She could almost see her father throwing back his covers and sitting on the edge of his mattress. By now, he would have reached for his glasses and turned on the bedside lamp.

"It's me," she cried. "Can you hear me all right?"

"Just barely. How's Josh doing?"

"Better, I think. The English doctor SunTech Oil flew in says he's showing some signs of improvement. He knows he's alive, at any rate. He's said 'earth' twice now."

"What?"

Amy laughed. "It's too difficult to explain."

"Are you taking care of yourself?"

"Yes…don't worry about me."

"Amy." Her father paused and continued in his most parental voice. "What's wrong?"

"Wrong?" she repeated. "What could possibly be wrong? Oh, you mean other than the fact I've flown halfway around the world to be at the deathbed of the man I love?"

"You just told me Josh is improving."

"He is. It's just that…oh, nothing, Dad, everything is fine. Just fine."

"Don't try to feed me that. There's something troubling you. Whatever it is—I can hear it in your voice even if you *are* eight thousand miles away. You can't fool me, sweetheart. Tell me what's up."

Amy bit her lower lip and brushed the tears from her eyes. "Josh keeps asking for another woman. Someone named Jasmine. He's said her name three or four times now, and he seems to think I'm her."

"You're jealous?"

"Yes. I don't even know who she is, but I swear I could rip her eyes out." No doubt she'd shocked her dear father, but she couldn't help it. After spending all this time with Josh, praying he would live, nursing his injuries, loving him, it was a grievous blow to her ego to have him confuse her with another woman.

"Do you want to come home now?"

"Josh can't travel."

"Leave him."

Amy realized the suggestion was given for shock value, but it had the desired effect. "I love him, Dad. I'm here for the long haul. Whoever this Jasmine woman is, she's got a fight on her hands if she thinks I'm giving Josh up quite so easily."

Her father chuckled, and Amy felt rejuvenated by the sound. It had taken her the better part of three hours to place the call to Seattle, but the time and effort had been well-spent.

"Take care of yourself, Amy Adele."

"Yes, Dad, I will. You, too."

When she returned to Josh's room, she found a nurse and Dr. Kilroy with him. He was apparently in a good deal of pain and was restlessly rolling his head back and forth. Amy walked over to his bedside and clasped his hand between her own.

"Josh," she said. "Can you tell me what's wrong? How can we help you?"

His fingers curled around hers and he heaved a sigh, then apparently drifted into unconsciousness.

"What happened?" Amy asked.

The doctor lifted the patient's chart and made several notations. "I can't be sure. He apparently awoke soon after you left the room and was distressed. He mumbled something, but neither the nurse nor I could understand what he was trying to say. It's apparent, however, that you have a calming effect upon him."

It wasn't until later that night that Josh awoke again. Amy was sitting at his bedside reading. She heard him stir and set her novel aside, standing at his bedside.

"I'm here, Josh."

His hand moved and she laced her fingers with his, raising his hand to touch her face to prove she was there and real and not a disembodied voice in the distance.

"Joel's dead," he said in a husky murmur.

"Yes, I know," she whispered, and her voice caught. Instinctively, she understood that his uneasiness earlier in the afternoon had been the moment he realized his friend had been killed in the explosion.

"I'm so sorry." A tear crept from the corner of her eye and ran down the side of her face. He must have felt the dampness because he lifted his free hand and blindly groped for her nape, forcing her head down to his level. Then he buried his face in the curve of her neck and held her with what she was certain was all the strength he possessed. Soon his shoulders started shaking, and sobs overtook him.

Amy wept, too. For the life that was gone, for the man she never knew, for the dear friend Josh had tried to save and had lost.

She fell asleep that night with her head resting on her arms, which she'd folded over the edge of the mattress. She awoke to feel Josh caressing her hair.

"Good morning," she whispered, straightening.

"Thank you," he returned, his voice still incredibly weak.

No explanation was needed. Josh was telling her how grateful he was that she'd been with him while he worked out his grief for his friend.

She yawned, arching her back and lifting her arms high above her head. "Are you in a lot of pain?"

"Would you kiss me and make it better if I said I was?"

"Yes," she answered, smiling.

"Amy," he said, his voice growing serious. "You shouldn't be here. I don't know how it's possible, you being here. It took me weeks to get my visa remember?"

"I remember." She bent over and kissed his brow.

"Leave while you can."

"Sorry, I can't do that." She pressed a warm kiss along the side of his mouth. "Feel better yet?"

"Amy, please." He gripped her wrist with what little strength he had. "I'm going to be fine...you've got to get out of here. Understand?"

"Of course."

"I thought your father had better sense than this. You should never have come."

"Josh, you don't need to worry about me."

"I do...Amy, please."

She could tell the argument was draining his strength. "All right," she lied. "I'll make arrangements to leave tomorrow."

"Promise me."

"I...promise."

Amy could see the tension ease out of him. "Thank you, Angel Eyes."

He seemed to rest after that. Amy felt mildly guilty for the lie, but she couldn't see any way around it.

The following day when Josh awoke, he seemed to know instinctively that she was there. "Amy?"

"I'm here."

"No! You promised. What happened?"

"Kadiri Airlines only flies on Wednesday."

"What day is it?"

"I don't know, I lost track." Another white lie. But the minute he learned it was Tuesday, he would get upset and she didn't want to risk that.

"Find out."

"Dr. Kilroy said he was going to remove the bandages from your eyes today. You don't expect me to leave without giving you at least one opportunity to see me, do you?"

"I'm dying for a glimpse of you," he confessed reluctantly.

"Then I'd better make it worth your while. I have an appointment to get my hair done at eleven." There wasn't a beauty salon within five hundred miles of Kadiri. Josh had to know that.

"Any chance of getting me a toothbrush and crank-
ing up the head of this bed?"

"I'll see what I can do."

It took Amy fifteen minutes to locate a new toothbrush and some toothpaste. Josh was asleep when she
returned, but he awoke an hour later. She helped him
brush his teeth while he complained about the taste of
Kadiri water. She didn't have the heart to tell him he
was brushing with flat soda water.

By the time they'd completed the task, Dr. Kilroy
entered the room. The man reminded her of a British
Buddy Holly. He turned off the lights and removed
the bandages while Amy stood breathlessly waiting.

The minute the white gauze was unraveled from
Josh's head, he squinted and rotated his head to where
Amy was standing. He held out his hand to her. "I
swear, you've never looked more beautiful."

Knowing that after weeks of having his eyes covered, she couldn't be anything more than a wide blur
against the wall, she walked to his side and wrapped
her arms around his neck. "Joshua Powell, you don't
lie worth beans."

He curved his hand around her neck and he directed
her mouth down to his. "I've waited three long months
to kiss you, don't argue with me."

Amy had no intention of doing anything of the sort.

Josh moved his mouth over hers with a fierce kind
of tenderness, a deep, hungering kiss that developed
when one had come so terribly close to losing all that
was important, including life itself. He shaped and fit-
ted her soft lips to his own, drinking in her love and
her strength.

Dr. Kilroy nervously cleared his throat, mumbled

something about seeing his other patients and quickly vacated the room. Amy was grateful.

"Josh," she whispered while he continued nibbling at her lips, catching her lower lip between his teeth and tugging at it sensuously before he lay back and rested his head on the pillow. Still he didn't fully release her. He closed his eyes and his smile was slanted, full and possessive.

"Angel Eyes," he whispered. "I can't tell you how good it feels to kiss you again."

"Yes," she agreed, her own voice pathetically weak.

He brought his hand back to her nape, stroking and caressing, directing her mouth back to his own. Amy held back, fearing too much contact would cause him pain.

"I'm afraid I'll hurt you," she whispered.

"I'll let you know if you do."

"But, Josh—"

"Are you going to fight with me?"

Their mouths were so close that their breaths merged. Amy could deny him nothing. "No…"

"Good."

He touched his tongue to her lips, gently coaxing them open, and then she complied to his unspoken request.

Shudders of excitement braided their way along her backbone, and her heart was hammering like a machine gun inside her chest. When she flattened her palms against Josh's chest, she noted that his heart was beating equally strongly. The movement was reassuring.

Taking in a deep breath, Josh ended the kiss and rested his forehead against hers. Their mouths were moist and ready, their breaths mingling.

"Go back to Seattle, Amy," he pleaded, running his hands through her hair.

"One kiss and you're dismissing me already?"

"I want you home and safe."

"I'm safe with you."

He chuckled lightly. "Honey, you're in more danger than you ever dreamed. Is that door open or closed?"

"Open."

He muttered a curse.

She dipped her mouth to his and kissed him long and slow, taking delight in sensuously rubbing her mouth back and forth over his, creating a slick friction that was enough to take the starch from her knees. By the time they broke apart, she was so weak, she'd slumped against the side of the bed.

"Maybe...I should close it," she said, once she'd found her voice.

"No...leave it open," he said with a sigh as he ran his palms in wide circles across her back as though he had to keep touching her to make sure she was real. "Amy, please, you've got to listen to me."

"I can't," she told him, "because all you want to do is send me away." She leaned forward and pressed her open mouth over his, showing him all that he had taught her in the ways of subtle seduction. "Here," she whispered. "Feel my heart." She pulled one of his hands from her back and pressed it to her chest.

"Amy!" He sucked in a wobbly breath.

"Josh, I love you," she said, kissing him once more, teasing him with the tip of her tongue.

"No...you shouldn't...you can't."

"But I do."

He closed his eyes to deny her words, but he couldn't

keep his body from responding. He moved his hand and lovingly cupped her chin, then brushed the edges of her mouth. "I can't get over how good it feels to hold you again."

She leaned into his embrace, experiencing a grateful surge of thanksgiving that he was alive and on the mend.

"You promised me you were going to leave," he reminded her quietly.

"Yes, I know."

"Are you going back on your word?"

"No." Eventually she would fly out of Kadiri, but when she did, Josh would be with her. Only he didn't know that yet.

"Good. Now kiss me once more for good measure and then get out of here. I don't want to see you again until I'm in Seattle."

"Josh," she argued. "That could be weeks—"

"Honey, will you stop worrying?" He was exhausted. Resting his head against the pillow, he closed his eyes.

It took him all of two seconds to fall asleep. Carefully, Amy lowered the head of his bed, then tenderly kissed his forehead before silently slipping out of the room.

Amy felt better after she'd showered and eaten. From the moment her father had come to her bedside that fateful night all those weeks ago, she hadn't done anything more than nibble at a meal.

She slept better than she had in a month. Waking bright and early the following morning, she dressed in the traditional Kadiri dress Josh had mailed her and walked down to the public market. With her blond hair and blue eyes, she stuck out like a bandaged thumb. Small children gathered around her, and, laughing, she handed out pieces of candy. The eyes of the soldiers, with rifles looped over their shoulders, anxiously followed her, but she wasn't frightened. There wasn't any reason to be.

Amy bought some fresh fruit and a colorful necklace and a few other items, then lazily returned to the hospital.

"How's Josh this morning?" she asked Dr. Kilroy when they met in the hallway.

The doctor looked surprised to see her. "He's recovering, but unfortunately his disposition doesn't seem to be making the same improvement."

"Why not?"

The thin British man studied her closely. "I thought you'd left the country."

Amy smiled. "Obviously, I haven't."

"But Mr. Powell seems to be under the impression that you're back in America."

"I let him think that. When I leave Kadiri, he'll be with me."

Dr. Kilroy lifted his thick, black-framed glasses and pinched the bridge of his nose. "Personally, I don't want to be the one who tells him."

"You won't have to be."

"Oh." He paused.

"I'm going that way myself. Is there anything else you'd like me to tell him?"

Dr. Kilroy chuckled, and Amy had the impression that he was a man who rarely laughed.

"No, but I wish you the best of luck with your friend, Miss Johnson. I fear you're going to need it."

With a smile on her lips, Amy marched down the hall and tapped lightly against Josh's door. She didn't wait for a response, but pushed it open and let herself inside.

"I told you, I don't want any breakfast," Josh grumbled, his face turned toward the wall. The drapes were drawn and the room was dark.

"That's unfortunate, since I personally went out and bought you some fresh fruit."

"Amy." He jerked his head around, wincing in pain. "What are you still doing here?"

Six

"What does it look like I'm doing here?" Amy answered, gingerly stepping all the way into the room. "I brought you some fresh fruit."

Josh closed his eyes against what appeared to be mounting frustration. "Please, don't tell me you bought that in the public market."

"All right," she answered matter of factly. She brought out a small plastic knife and scored the large orange-shaped fruit. It looked like a cross between an orange and a grapefruit, but when she'd asked about it, the native woman she'd bought it from apparently hadn't understood the question.

"You *did* go the market, didn't you?" Josh pressed.

"You claimed I wasn't supposed to tell you." She peeled away the thick, grainy skin from the succulent fruit then licked the juice from the tips of her fingers.

"You went anyway."

"Honestly, Josh, I was perfectly safe. There were people all around me. Nothing happened, so kindly quit harping about it. Here." She handed him a slice, hoping that would buy peace. "I don't know what it's called. I asked several people, but no one seemed to understand." She smiled at the memory of her antics, her attempts to communicate with her hands, which were no doubt humorous to anyone watching.

Josh accepted the slice. "It's an orange."

"An *orange?* You mean I flew halfway around the world and thought I was buying some exotic fruit only to discover it's an orange? But it's so big."

"They grow that way here."

She found that amusing even if Josh didn't. She continued to peel away the skin and divided the sections between them. After savoring three or four of the sweet-tasting slices, she noted that Josh hadn't sampled a single one of his.

"You promised me you were leaving Kadiri," he said, his words sharp with impatience. His eyes were dark and filled with frustrated concern.

"I am."

"When?"

She sighed and crossed her long legs. "When you're ready to travel, which according to Dr. Kilroy won't be for another two weeks, perhaps longer. Josh, please try to understand, you've received several serious injuries. It's going to take time, so you might as well be tolerant."

"Amy—"

"Nothing you can say or do is going to change my mind, Joshua Powell. Nothing. So you might as well be gracious enough to accept that I'm not leaving Kadiri unless you're with me."

Joshua shut his eyes so tightly that barbed crow's feet marked the edges of his eyes. "How in the name of heaven did you get to be so stubborn?"

"I don't know." She wiped the juice from her chin with the back of her hand. "I'm usually not, at least I don't think I am, it's just that this is something I feel strongly about."

"So do I," he returned vehemently.

"Yes, I know. I guess there's only one solution."

"You're leaving!"

"Right," she agreed amicably enough. "But you're coming with me."

Amy could see that she was trying his patience to the limit. His tan jaw was pale with barely suppressed exasperation. If there had been anything she could do to comply with his demands, she would have done it, but Josh was as obstinate as she, only this time she was fortunate enough to have the upper hand. He couldn't very well force her out of the country.

In a burst of annoyance, Josh threw aside the sheet.

"Josh," she cried in alarm, leaping to her feet, "what are you doing?"

"Getting out of bed."

"But you can't…your leg's broken and you're hooked up to all these bottles. Josh, please, you're going to hurt yourself."

"You're not giving me any choice." The abrupt movements were obviously causing him a good deal of pain. His face went gray with it.

"Josh, please," she cried, his agony causing her own. Gently she pressed her hands against his shoulders, forcing him down. Josh's breathing was labored, and certain that he'd done something to harm himself, she hurried down the hall to find Dr. Kilroy.

The doctor returned with her to Josh's room. Almost immediately he gave Josh a shot to ease the pain and warned them both against such foolishness. Within minutes, Josh was asleep and resting relatively comfortably.

Amy felt terrible. When Dr. Kilroy invited her to have tea with him, she accepted, wiping the tearstains from her face.

"Josh seems to think my life is in imminent danger," she confessed. "He wants me out of the country." She stared into the steaming cup of tea, her gaze avoiding his. Even if the doctor agreed with Josh, she was bound and determined not to leave Kadiri unless Josh was at her side.

The good doctor, fortyish and graying, pushed his glasses up the bridge of his nose as if the action would guide his words. "Personally, I understand his concern. This is no place for an American woman on her own."

"But I just can't leave Josh here," she protested. "Are you sure it's going to be two more weeks before he can travel comfortably?"

"Three." He added a small amount of milk to his tea and stirred it in as if he were dissolving concrete. "It'll be at least that long, perhaps longer before he can sit for any length of time."

"What about laying down?"

"Oh, there wouldn't be any problem with that, but there aren't any airlines that provide hospital beds as a part of their flying options," he said dryly.

"But we could put a bed in my father's jet. I flew into Kadiri in a private plane," she rushed to explain. "It's at my disposal for the return trip as well."

Propping his elbows against the tabletop, Dr. Kilroy nodded slowly, thoughtfully. "That changes matters considerably. I think you might have stumbled upon a solution."

"But what about when we land in Seattle? Will Josh require further medical care?"

"Oh, yes. Your friend has been severely injured. Although the immediate danger has passed, it'll be several weeks—possibly months—before he'll be fully recovered. For the next two or three weeks it is critical he gets medical care only available at a hospital."

Amy knew the minute Josh was released from the Kadiri Hospital he wouldn't allow anyone to admit him to another one stateside.

"Josh isn't one to rest complacently in a hospital," she explained.

"I understand your concern. I fear Mr. Powell may try to rush his recovery, pushing himself. I only hope he realizes that he could do himself a good deal of harm that way."

"I could make arrangements for him to stay at my family home," she offered hopefully. "Would a full-time nurse be adequate to see to his needs? Naturally he'd be under a physician's care."

It didn't take the doctor long to decide. "Why, yes, I believe that could work quite well."

"Then consider it done. The plane's on standby and can be ready within twenty-four hours. Once we're airborne and we can contact Seattle, I'll have my father make all the necessary arrangements. A qualified nurse can meet us at the airport when we arrive."

"I can sedate Mr. Powell so the journey won't be too much of a strain on him…or anyone else," Dr. Kilroy added. It was agreed that a nurse would travel with them, although Amy would have preferred it if Dr. Kilroy could make the trip with them himself.

"I believe this will all work quite well." The British man looked pleased. "Now, both you and Mr. Powell can have what you want."

"Yes," Amy said, pleased by the unexpected turn of events.

When Josh awoke early in the afternoon, Amy was at his bedside. He opened his eyes, but when he saw her sitting next to him, he lowered his lids once more.

"Amy, please…"

"I'm flying out this evening, Josh, so don't be angry again."

His dark eyes shot open. "I thought you said Kadiri Airlines only flew on Wednesdays."

"They do. I'm going by private jet."

His lashes flew up to his hairline. "Private jet?"

"Before you find something else to complain about, I think you should know you're coming with me."

If he was shocked before it was nothing compared with the look of astonishment on his face now. "Amy… how…when…why?"

"One question at a time," she said, smiling softly and leaning over him to press her lips to his. "The how part is easy. Dr. Kilroy and I had a long talk. We're flying you to Seattle, hospital bed and all."

"Whose plane is this?"

"Dad's. Well, actually," she went on to explain, "it technically belongs to the company. He's just letting us use it because—"

"Hold on a minute," Josh said, raising his hand. "This jet belongs to your father's company?"

"Right."

His eyes slammed shut, and for one breathless moment he didn't say a word. When he opened them once more, his gaze held hers while several emotions flickered in and out of his eyes. Amy recognized shock, disbelief and a few other ones she wasn't sure she could identify.

"Josh, what is it?"

"Your father's name wouldn't happen to be Harold, would it?"

"Why, yes. How'd you know?" To the best of her knowledge she'd never mentioned her father's first name. But she hadn't been hiding it, either.

The harsh sound that followed could only be described as something between a laugh and a snicker. Slowly, Josh shook his head from side to side. "I don't believe it. And here I thought your father was just some poor devil who wanted to make you a part of a wholesale plumbing business."

Josh wasn't making the least bit of sense. Perhaps it was the medication, Amy reasoned. All she knew was that she didn't have time to argue with him, nor would there be ample opportunity for a lot of explanations. He looked so infuriated, and yet she was doing exactly what he wanted. She couldn't understand what was suddenly so terribly wrong.

The red flashing lights from the waiting ambulance were the first things Amy noted when they landed at Boeing field near Seattle some fifty hours later.

Amy was exhausted, emotionally and physically. The flight had been uncomfortable from the moment they'd taken off from the Kadiri Airport. Josh, although sedated, was restless and in a good deal of pain. Amy was the only one who seemed capable of calming him, so she'd stayed with him through the whole flight.

Harold Johnson was standing alongside the ambulance, looking dapper in his three-piece-suit. He hugged Amy close and assured her everything was ready and waiting for Josh at the house.

"Now what was this about me finding a nurse with the name of Brunhilde?" he asked, slipping his arm around her thin shoulders. "You were joking, weren't you? I'll have you know, Ms. Wetherell contacted five agencies, and the best we could come up with was a Bertha."

Amy chuckled, delighted that her father had taken her message so literally. "I just wanted to make sure you didn't hire someone young and pretty."

"Once you meet Mrs. White, I think you'll approve." Her father laughed with her. The worry lines around his mouth and eyes eased, and Amy realized her journey had caused him a good deal of concern, although he'd never let on. She loved him all the more for it.

"It's good to have you back, sweetheart."

"It's good to be back."

The ambulance crew were carrying Josh out of the plane on a gurney. "Just exactly where are you taking me?" he demanded.

"Josh." Amy smiled and hurried to his side. "Stop being such a poor patient."

"I'm not going back in any stuffy hospital. Understand?"

"Perfectly."

He seemed all the more flustered by her easy acquiescence. "Then where are they taking me?" His words faded as he was lifted into the interior of the ambulance.

"Home," she called after him.

"Whose home?"

The attendant closed one door at the rear of the ambulance and was reaching toward the second before Amy could respond to Josh's question.

"My home," she called after him.

"No you're not. I want a hotel room, understand? Amy, did you hear me?"

"Yes, I heard you."

The second door slammed shut. Before he could argue with her, the vehicle sped off into the night.

"It's good to be home," Amy said with an exhausted sigh. She slipped her arm around her father's trim waist and leaned her head against her strong shoulders. "By the way, that was Josh. In case you hadn't noticed, he isn't in the best of tempers. He doesn't seem to be a very good patient, but who can blame him after everything he's been through?" She lifted her gaze to her father's and sucked in a deep breath. "I almost lost him, Dad. It was so close."

"So he's being a poor patient," her father repeated, obviously trying to lighten her mood.

"Terrible. Mrs. White's going to have her hands full."

Harold Johnson took a puff of his cigar and chuckled softly. "I always hated being ordered to bed myself. I can't blame him. Fact is, I may have a good deal in common with this young man of yours."

Amy smiled, realizing how true this was. "I'm sure you do. It isn't any wonder I love him so much."

* * *

Josh awoke when the golden fingers of dawn slithered through the bedroom window, creeping like a fast-growing vine over the thick oyster-gray carpet and onto the edges of his bed. Every bone in his body ached. He'd assumed that by now he would have become accustomed to pain. He'd lived with it all these weeks, to the point that it had almost become his friend. At least when he was suffering, he knew he was alive. And if he was alive, then he would be able to see Amy again.

Amy.

He shut his eyes to thoughts of her. He'd been in love with her for months. She was warmth and sunshine, purity and generosity, and everything that was good. She was the kind of woman a man dreams of finding—sweet and innocent on the outside, but when he held her in his arms, she flowered with fire and ready passion, promising him untold delights.

Yet somehow Josh was going to have to dredge up the courage to turn his back and walk away from her.

If he was going to fall in love, he cried silently, then why did it have to be with Harold Johnson's daughter? The man was one of the wealthiest men in the entire country. His holdings stretched from New York to Los Angeles and several major cities in between; his name was synonymous with achievement and high-powered success.

Josh couldn't offer Amy this kind of life, and even if he could, he wouldn't. He had firsthand experience of what wealth did to a man. By age twenty-five, he had witnessed how selfishness and greed could corrupt a man's soul.

The love for money had driven a stake between Josh

and his own father, one so deep and so crippling that it would never be healed. Eight years had passed, and not once in all that time had Josh regretted leaving home. Chance Powell had stared Josh in the eye and claimed he had no son. Frankly, that information suited Josh well. He had no father, either. He shared nothing with the man who had sired him—nor did he wish to.

Josh's mother had died when he was in college, and his only other living relative was her sister, an elderly aunt in Boston whom he visited on rare occasions. His aunt Hazel was getting on in years, and she seemed to make it her mission in life to try to bridge the gap between father and son, but to no avail. They were both too proud. Both too stubborn.

"I see you're awake," Bertha White, his nurse, stated as she stepped into the room. She certainly dressed for the part, donning white scrubs with the dedication of a conquering army.

Josh made some appropriate sound in reply. As far as he was concerned, Bertha White should be wearing a helmet with horns and singing in an opera. She marched across his room with all the grace of a herd of buffalo and pulled open the blinds, flooding the room with sunlight. Josh noted that she hadn't bothered to ask him how he felt about letting the sun blind him. Somehow he doubted that she cared.

She fussed around his bedside, apparently so he would know she was earning her salary. She checked his vital signs, dutifully entering the statistics in his chart. Then she proceeded to poke and prod him in places he didn't even want to think about. To his surprise, she graciously gave him the opportunity to wash himself.

Josh appreciated that, even if he didn't much care for the woman, who was about as warm and comforting as a mud wrestler.

"You have a visitor," she informed him once he had finished.

"Who?" Josh feared it was Amy. It would be too difficult to deal with her now, when he felt weak and vulnerable. He didn't want to hurt her, but he wasn't sure he could do what he must without causing her pain.

"Mr. Johnson is here to see you," Bertha replied stiffly, and walked out of the room.

No sooner had she departed than Amy's father let himself in, looking very much the legend Josh knew him to be. The man's presence was commanding, Josh admitted willingly. He doubted that Harold Johnson ever walked anywhere without generating a good deal of attention. Everything about him spelled prosperity and accomplishment. This one man had achieved in twenty years what three normal men couldn't do in a lifetime.

"So you're Josh Powell," Amy's father stated, his eyes as blue as his daughter's and just as kind. "I would have introduced myself when you arrived last night, but you seemed to be in a bit of discomfort."

They shook hands, and Harold casually claimed the chair at Josh's bedside, as if he often spent part of his morning visiting a sickroom.

"I'll have you know I had nothing to do with this," Josh said somewhat defiantly, wishing there was some way he could climb out of his bed and meet Johnson man-to-man.

"Nothing to do with what?"

"Being here—I had no idea Amy planned to dump

me off in your backyard. Listen, I don't mean to sound like I'm ungrateful for everything you've done, but I'd like to make arrangements as soon as I can to recover elsewhere."

"Son, you're my guest."

"I would feel more comfortable someplace else," Josh insisted, gritting his teeth to a growing awareness of pain and an overabundance of pride.

"Is there a reason?" Harold didn't look unsettled by Josh's demands, only curious.

The effort to sit up was draining Josh of strength and conviction, which he struggled to disguise behind a gruff exterior. "You obviously don't know anything about me."

Harold withdrew a cigar from his inside jacket pocket and examined the end with a good deal of consideration. "My daughter certainly appears to think highly of you."

"Which doesn't say much, does it?"

"On the contrary," Harold argued. "It tells me everything I need to know."

"Then you'd better…" A sharp cramp thrust through his abdomen and he lay back and closed his eyes until it passed. "Suffice it to say, it would be best if I arranged for other accommodations. Amy should never have brought me here in the first place."

"My daughter didn't mean to offend you. In fact, I don't know if you've noticed, but she seems to have fallen head over heels in love with you."

"I noticed," Josh admitted dryly. Amy. Her name went through his mind like a hot blade. He had to leave her, couldn't her father understand that much? They were as different as the sun and the moon. As far apart as the two poles, and their dissimilarities were in ways that were impossible to bridge. Harold Johnson should be intelligent enough to recognize that with one look. Josh would have thought the man would be eager to be rid of him.

"You don't care for her?" Harold asked, chewing on the end of the cigar.

"Sir, you don't know anything about me," Josh said, taking in a calming breath. "I'm a drifter. I'm hardly suitable for your daughter. I don't want to hurt her, but I don't intend to lead her on, either."

"I see." He rubbed the side of his jaw in a thought-filled action.

It was apparent to Josh that Amy's father did nothing of the sort. "And another thing," Josh said, feeling it was important to say what was on his mind. "I can't understand how you could have let her fly to the Middle East because of me. Kadiri was no place for her."

"I agree one hundred percent. It took me an hour to come to terms with the fact she was going no matter what I said or did, so I made sure the road was paved for her."

"But how could you let her go and do a thing like that?" Josh demanded, still not understanding. Someone like Harold Johnson had connections, but even *his* protective arm could only stretch so far.

"I was afraid of being penalized for defensive holding," Harold said firmly.

Josh was certain he'd misunderstood. His confusion must have shown in his face, because the older man went on to explain.

"Amy's recently turned twenty-four years old and beyond the point where I can tell her what she can and can't do. If she wants to take off for the far corners of the world, there's little I can do to stop her. She knows it, and so do I. For that matter, if she's going to fall in love with you, it's not my place to tell her she's making a mistake. Either the girl's got sound judgment or she doesn't."

"I'm not good enough for her," Josh insisted.

The edges of the man's mouth lifted slightly at that. "Personally, I doubt that any man is. But I'll admit to being partial. Amy is, after all, my only child."

Josh closed his eyes, wanting to block out both the current pain and the one that was coming. If he stayed it would be inevitable. "I'm going to hurt her."

"Yes, son, I suspect you will."

"Then surely you realize why I need to get out of here, and the sooner the better."

"That's the only part I can't quite accept," Harold said slowly, his tone considerate. "As I understand it, you don't have any family close at hand?"

"None," Josh admitted reluctantly.

"Then perhaps you'd prefer several more weeks in a hospital?"

"No," Josh answered.

"Then you've made other arrangements that include a full-time nurse and—"

"No," Josh ground out harshly.

Harold Johnson's eyes filled with ill-concealed amusement.

"Your point is well taken," Josh admitted unwillingly. He didn't have a single argument that would hold up against the force of the other man's logic.

"Listen to me, son, you're welcome to remain here as long as you wish, and likewise, you're free to leave anytime you want. Neither Amy nor I would have it any other way."

"The expenses...?"

"We can discuss that later," Harold told him.

"No, we'll clear the air right now. I insist upon paying for all this...I want that understood."

"As you wish. Now, if you'll excuse me I'd better get into the office before my assistant comes looking for me."

"Of course." Josh wanted to dislike Amy's father. It would have made life a whole lot easier. If Harold Johnson had been anything like his own father, Josh would have moved the Panama Canal to get as far away from the Johnson family as humanly possible. Instead, he'd reluctantly discovered Amy's father was the kind of man he would have gladly counted as a friend.

"Sir, I don't want you to think I don't appreciate everything you've done." Josh felt obliged to explain. "It's just that this whole setup makes me uncomfortable."

"I can't say that I blame you. But you need to concentrate on getting well. You can worry about everything else later."

It commanded a good deal of effort for Josh to nod. Swirling pain wrapped its way around his body, tightening its grip on his ribs and his leg. Amy's father seemed to understand that Josh needed to rest.

"I'll be leaving you now."

"Sir." Josh half lifted his head in an effort to stop him. "If you could do one small favor for me, I'd greatly appreciate it."

"What's that?"

"Keep Amy away from me."

Harold Johnson's answering bellow of laughter was

loud enough to rattle the windows. "It's obvious you
don't know my daughter very well, young man. If I
couldn't prevent her from flying to Timbuktu and risking her fool neck to be at your side, what makes you
think I can keep her out of this sickroom?"

Josh felt an involuntary smile twitch at the corners
of his mouth. Harold was right. There was nothing Josh
could do to keep away Amy. But that wasn't the worst
of it. He wanted her with him, and he wasn't fooling
either of them by declaring otherwise.

He must have fallen asleep, because the next thing
Josh knew Bertha White was in his room, fussing
around the way she had earlier in the morning. Slowly,
he opened his eyes to discover the elderly woman dragging a table across the room with a luncheon tray on it.

A polite knock sounded on the door. "Ms. White."

"Yes?"

"Would it be all right if I came in now? I brought
my lunch so I could eat with Josh."

"No," Josh yelled, not waiting for the other woman
to answer. His nurse shot him a look that reminded
him of his sixth grade teacher, who Josh swore could
cuff his ears with a dirty look. "I don't feel like company," he explained.

"Come in, Miss Johnson," Mrs. White answered,
daring Josh to contradict her. "I've brought the table
over next to the bed so you can sit down here and enjoy
your visit."

"Thank you," Amy said softly.

Josh closed his eyes. Even her voice sounded musical. Almost like an angel's… He might as well accept
that he wasn't going to be able to resist her. Not now,
when he was too weak to think, much less argue.

Seven

"Hi," Amy said, sitting down at the table. She carried her lunch with her—a shrimp salad and a tall glass of iced tea. Try as he might, Josh couldn't tear his eyes away from her. If her voice sounded like an angel's, it didn't even begin to compare with the way she looked. Sweet heaven, she was lovely.

"Are you feeling any better?" she asked, her eyes filled with gentle concern.

Josh thought to answer her gruffly. If he was irritable and unpleasant, then she wouldn't want to spend time with him, but one flutter of soft blue eyes and the battle was lost.

"I'm doing just fine," he muttered, reluctantly accepting defeat. He couldn't seem to look away. She might as well have nailed him to a wall, that was how powerless he felt around her. Why did she have to be so sweet, so wonderful? Before she came to visit him, he'd tried to fortify his heart, build up his defenses. Some defenses! One glance and those defenses crumbled at his feet like clay.

"You're not fine," Amy countered swiftly, with a

hint of indignation. "At least, that's not what I heard. Mrs. White claimed you had a restless night and have been in a good deal of pain."

"I wouldn't believe everything Robo-nurse says if I were you."

Amy chuckled, then whispered, "She is a bit intimidating, isn't she?"

"Attila the Hun incarnate."

Josh momentarily closed his eyes to enjoy the sound of her merriment as it lapped over him like a gentle wave caressing the shoreline. How he loved it when Amy laughed.

She hesitated before spreading a napkin across the lap of her jeans. "I thought it was best if we cleared the air," she said, stabbing a fat pink shrimp with her fork. She carefully avoided his gaze. "You seemed so upset with me when Dad met us at the airport the other night. I didn't mean to take charge of your life, Josh, I honestly didn't. But I suppose that's how you felt, and I certainly can't blame you." She paused long enough to chew, but while she was eating, she waved her fork around like a conductor, as if her movements would explain what she was feeling.

"Amy, I understand."

"I don't think you do," she said, once she'd swallowed. "You wanted me out of Kadiri, and I saw the perfect chance to get us *both* out, and I grabbed it. There wasn't time to consult with you about arrangements. I'm sorry if bringing you here went against your wishes. I...I did the best I could under the circumstances." She stopped long enough to suck in a giant breath. "But you're right, I should have consulted with you. I want you to know I would have, except Dr. Kilroy had heavily sedated you, and he thought it best to keep you that way for the journey. Then when we arrived everything happened so fast, and you—"

"Amy, I understand," he said quickly, interrupting her when he had the chance.

"You do?"

"Yes."

The stiffness came out of her shoulders, like air rushing from a balloon as she relaxed and reached for another shrimp. His gaze followed her action, and when she lifted the fork, she paused and smiled at him. Her happiness was contagious and free-flowing. It assailed him in a whirlwind of sensations he'd desperately struggled to repress from the moment he learned she'd flown to Kadiri to be with him.

"Want one?" she asked, her voice low and a little shaky. Her lips were moist and slightly parted as she leaned forward and held the fork in front of his mouth.

Their eyes met, and obediently he opened his mouth for her to feed him the succulent shrimp. It shouldn't have been a sensuous deed, but his heart started beating hard and strong, and the achy, restless feeling of needing to hold and kiss her fueled his mind like dry timber on a raging fire.

He longed to touch her translucent skin and plow his fingers through the silky length of her hair. But most of all, he realized, he wanted her warm and naked beneath him, making soft sounds of pleasure in his ear, and with her long, smooth legs wrapped around his.

His stomach knotted painfully. He leaned back and closed his eyes to the image that saturated and governed his thoughts.

She was at his side immediately, her voice filled

with distress. "Should I get Mrs. White? Do you need something for the pain?"

The idea of a shot taking away the discomfort in his groin was humorous enough to curve up the edges of his mouth.

"Josh!" she blurted out. "You're smiling."

"I've got a pain, all right," he admitted, opening his eyes. He raised his hand, and trailed his fingertips across the arch of her cheek. "But it's one only you can ease."

"Tell me what to do. I want to help you. Oh, Josh, please, don't block me out. Not now, when we've been through so much together."

Gently, she planted her hands on his chest, as if that would convince him of her sincerity. Unfortunately, the action assured him of a good deal more. The ache within him intensified, and every second that she stared down on him with her bright angel eyes was adding heaps of coal to a fire that was already roaring with intensity.

"Honey, it's not that kind of pain." He set her hand on his groin.

Amy's eyes jolted with surprise and flickered several times as she came to terms with what he was saying.

Josh, unfortunately, was in for a surprise of his own. If he'd thought his action would cure what ailed him, then he was sadly mistaken. Instead, a shaft of desire stabbed through him with such magnitude that for a wild moment it was all he could do to breathe.

Amy's hand trembled, or perhaps he was the one shivering, he couldn't tell for sure. He released her wrist, but she kept her fingers exactly where they were, tormenting him in ways she couldn't even begin to understand.

"Josh," she whispered, her voice filled with wonder and excitement. "I want you, too…there's so much for you to teach me."

Her eyes reflected the painful longing Josh was experiencing. Knowing she was feeling the same urgency only increased his desire for her. He knew he could handle his own needs, but how was he going to be able to refuse hers?

"No," he cried desperately, his control already stretched beyond endurance. The need in him felt savage. The woman couldn't be *that* innocent not to realize she was driving him insane.

"Amy," he cried harshly, gripping her wrist once more. "Stop."

"It's…so hot," she whispered, her low words filled with wonder. "It makes me feel so…I don't know…so empty inside."

Josh had reached the point where reason no longer controlled him. All the arguments he'd built up against there ever being anything sexual between them vanished like mist under a noonday sun. He grasped her around the waist, half dragging her onto the bed beside him. Josh barely gave her time to adjust herself to the mattress before he kissed her, thrusting his fingers into her hair and sweeping his mouth over hers.

The kiss was hot and wild. Amy seemed to sense that he was giving her an example of what was soon to follow, and she slid her hand over his shoulder, digging her nails into the muscles there. Her untamed response was enough to send the blood shooting through him until he thought his head would explode with it.

He found her hipbone and scooted her as close as he could, then he gloried in the way she intuitively churned the lower half of her body against him.

"Amy" he groaned. "You don't know what you're doing to me."

She smiled, and her whole face glowed with joy as her soft, kittenlike sound was nearly his undoing. "You're wrong. I do know and I'm enjoying every second." Her hands were in his hair, encouraging him with soft, trembling sounds that came deep from the back of her throat.

The bliss was so sharp, so keen that for Josh it reached the point of pain. The ache in his loins was unbearable. It was either take her now or stop completely.

Josh didn't have long to consider his options. His shoulders were heaving when he buried his face in the gentle slope of her neck. It took him several seconds to compose himself, and even then he felt as shaky as a tree limb caught in a hurricane.

"Josh?" Amy's voice was filled with question. "What's wrong?"

Slowly, he lifted his head, struggling to maintain the last fragment of his control before it snapped completely. Gently, he kissed her lips, while he gently pushed her away, breaking their intimate hold on one another.

"Did I hurt you?" she asked, her voice low and warm, throbbing with concern.

Her question tugged at his heart, affecting Josh more than any in his life. He'd come within a hair's space of making love with her, driven to the edge of insanity by need and desire. His burning passion had dominated his every move. He might have frightened her, or worse, hurt her. The hot ache in him had been too strong to have taken the proper amount of care to be sure this first time was right. And Amy was concerned that she'd hurt *him*.

"Josh?" She repeated her question with his name, grazing his face with gentle, caressing fingers.

"I'm fine. Did I hurt you?"

"No...never. It was wonderful, but why did you stop?"

"Remember Robo-nurse?"

It was obvious that Amy had completely forgotten Bertha White by the startled look that flashed into her soft blue eyes. "Did she...is she back?"

"No, but she will be soon enough." Bertha was an excuse, Josh realized, a valid one, but she wasn't the reason he'd pulled away. He'd been about to lose all control, and heaven help him, he couldn't allow that to happen.

For two frustrating days, Amy's visits to Josh were limited to short ten-minute stays. Her father had her running errands for him. The charity bazaar she had worked on earlier that summer needed her for another project, and then Manuela had taken sick.

Everything seemed to be working against her being with Josh. It seemed every time she came, wanting to be alone with Josh, his nurse found an excuse to linger there. Amy wondered if he had put the older woman up to it. That was a silly thought, she realized, because he didn't seem to be any more fond of Bertha than Amy was.

Her thoughts were abuzz with questions. Every time her mind focused on the things Josh had done to her, the way he had held and kissed her, she grew warm and achy inside. The pleasure had been like nothing she had ever known, and once sampled, it created a need for more. She felt as though she had stood at the precipice, seeking something she couldn't name. Now that she had gazed upon such uncharted territory she was lost, filled with questions with no one to answer them.

It was late and dark and her father had retired for the evening. Amy lay in bed, restlessly trying to concentrate on a novel. The effort was useless, and she knew it. Every thought that entered her head had to do with Josh.

Throwing aside the sheets, she reached for her satin robe and searched out her slippers, which were hiding beneath her bed. Never in all her life had she done anything so bold as what she was about to do now.

She paused outside her bedroom door in the softly lit hallway and waited for reason to lead her back where she belonged. Nothing drove her backward. Instead she felt compelled to move forward.

Thankfully, at this time of night Bertha White would be sound asleep. As silently as possible Amy closed the door, then proceeded down the wide hallway to Josh's room.

The first thing she noticed was that his reading light was on. The sight relaxed her. She hadn't looked forward to waking him.

"Hello, Josh," she said as she silently stepped into the room. She closed the door, and when she turned around, she noticed that he was sitting up, gazing at her with dark, intense eyes.

"It's late," he announced starkly.

"Yes, I know. I couldn't sleep."

He eyed her wearily. "I was just about to turn out my light."

"I won't be a minute. It's just that I have a few questions for you, and I realize this is probably pretty embarrassing, but there isn't anyone else I can ask."

He closed his book, but she noticed that he didn't set it aside. In fact, he was holding it as if the hardbound novel would be enough of a barrier to keep her away.

"Questions about what?"

"The other day when we—"

"That was a mistake."

She swallowed tightly before continuing. "I don't know why you say that. Every time you so much as touch me, you claim it was a mistake. It's unbelievably frustrating."

A hint of a smile bounced against his eyes and mouth. "What do you want to know?" he asked, not unkindly. "And I'll do my level best to answer you."

"Without making a comment about the rightness or wrongness of what's happening between us?"

"All right," he agreed.

"Thank you." She pulled up a chair and sat, her gaze level with his own. Now that she had his full attention, she wasn't sure exactly where to start. Twice she opened her mouth, only to abruptly close it again, her muddled thoughts stumbling over themselves.

"I'm waiting," he said with a dash of impatience.

"Yes, well, this isn't exactly easy." She could feel a blush work its way up her face, and was confident she was about to make a complete idiot of herself. Briefly Amy had thought that if her mother had been alive, she could have asked her, but on second thought, she realized this was something one didn't discuss with one's mother.

"Amy," he questioned softly, "what is it?"

Her gaze was lowered, and the heat creeping up from her neck had blossomed into full color in her cheeks. She absently toyed with the satin ties at the neck of her robe.

"I...when we—you know—were on the bed together, you said something that has been on my mind ever since."

"What did I say?"

Josh sounded so calm, so...ordinary, as if he had this type of discussion with women every day of the week, as if he were a doctor discussing a medical procedure with his patient. Amy's heart was thundering in her ears so loudly she could barely form a coherent thought.

He prompted her again, and she wound the satin tie around her index finger so tightly she cut off the circulation. "You were trying to undo my blouse," she whispered, nearly choking on the words.

"And?"

"And you kissed me and held me in ways no other man ever has."

"I suspected as much."

"You see I attended a private girls school and there just wasn't much opportunity for this sort of...foreplay. I realize you must think me terribly naive and... gauche."

"I don't think anything of the sort. You're innocent, or at least you were until I got my hands on you." He frowned as he said it.

"Would you do it again...touch me the way you did before."

"Amy, no..."

"Please, I need to know these things and I want you to be the one to teach me."

"You don't know what you're asking."

"I do, Josh. I'm not completely innocent and I promise you I'm a quick learner."

He closed his eyes and groaned. "I'm all too aware of that fact already."

"It felt so good to have you touch me."

"It did for me, too." Josh's voice was low and hesitant.

"Will you do it again?" she asked, her voice so quiet she could barely hear herself. Boldly she raised her eyes to his, her heart beating wildly.

She stood and walked the few short steps to his bedside and laid open her robe. Josh sat there mesmerized, his face unreadable, but he didn't say or do anything to stop her. Her fingers were trembling as she slipped the robe from her shoulders. It fell silently at her feet. She made herself vulnerable to him in ways she was only beginning to comprehend. She was so pale, she realized, wishing now that she was tan and golden for him, instead of alabaster white.

"Amy."

Her name was little more than a rasp between his lips. "Like I explained earlier you don't know what you're asking." Of their own volition, it seemed, his fingers lightly brushed the smooth skin of her throat. Instantly, her tender skin there started to throb.

His touch, although featherlight, produced an immediate melting ache in her. She pulsed in places she'd never known existed until Josh had kissed and touched her.

"Please, Josh," she whispered. "I have to know." There was more she longed to ask, more she yearned to discover, but the words withered on the end of her tongue at the look of intense longing Josh gave her.

He reached for her waist and gently urged her forward until she was close enough for him to bury his face between her breasts. Abruptly, Josh stopped and jerked his head away. For several seconds he did nothing but draw in deep, lung-rasping breaths. "Enough," he said finally. Amy clung to him, not knowing how to tell him that he hadn't answered a single inquiry. Instead he'd created even more.

"I don't want you to stop," she moaned in bewilderment. She paused, hoping to clear her thoughts, then continued raggedly. "Josh, I want to make love with you. I want you to teach me to be a woman, your woman."

"No."

Her knees would no longer support her, and she sank onto the bed, sitting on the edge of the mattress. It was then that she realized that Josh was trembling, and the knowledge that she could make him want her so desperately filled her with a heady sense of power.

Reaching out to him, Amy wasn't about to let him push her away. Not again.

"No," he cried a second time, but with much less conviction. Even as he spoke he filled his palms with her breasts and made a low, rough sound of protest. "Amy…please." His voice vibrated between them, filled with urgency and helplessness. "Not like this… not in your father's house."

She sagged, drooping her head in frustration. Josh was right. They were both panting with the effort to resist each other as it was, and in a few seconds neither one of them would be able to stop. It took everything within her to quit now.

Amy blindly reached for her robe. She would have turned and vaulted from the room if Josh hadn't reached for her wrist, stalling her. Not for anything could she look him in the eye.

"Are you going to be all right?" he asked.

She nodded wildly, knowing it was a lie. She would never be the same again.

He swore quietly, and with a muffled deep gasp of pain sat upright in the bed and reached for her, hugging her close and burying his face in the gentle slope of her neck.

"Amy, listen to me; we've got to stop this horsing around before it kills the both of us."

"Josh," she whispered, her tone hesitant. "That's the problem. I don't want to stop. It feels so wonderful when you touch me, and I get all achy inside and out." Consternation and apprehension crept into her voice. "My behavior is embarrassing you, isn't it?"

"Me?"

"I mean, the last thing you need is me making all kinds of sexual demands on you. You're lucky to be alive. Here I am, like a kid who's recently discovered a wonderful toy and doesn't quite know how to make everything work."

"Believe me, honey, it's working."

"I'm sorry, Josh, I really am—"

He silenced her with a chaste kiss. "Go back to bed.

We can talk more about it in the morning, when both our heads are clear."

"Good night," she whispered, heaving a sigh.

"Good night." He kissed her once more and, with a reluctance that tore at her heart, he released her.

"Morning, Dad," Amy said as she seated herself at the table for breakfast the following morning.

Her father grumbled an inaudible reply, which wasn't anything like him. Harold Johnson had always been a morning person and boomed enthusiasm for each new day.

Amy hesitated, her thoughts in a whirl. Was it possible that her father had heard her sneak into Josh's room the night before? That thought was enough to produce a heated blush, and in an effort to disguise her discomfort, she hurriedly dished up her scrambled eggs and bacon.

Her father didn't say anything more for several minutes. Deciding it would be better to confront him with the truth than suffer this intolerable silence, Amy straightened her shoulders and clasped her hands in her lap.

"How's Josh doing?" Harold asked, reaching for the sugar bowl after pouring himself a cup of coffee.

"Better." She eyed him warily, trying to decide the best way to handle this awkward situation. Perhaps she should let him bring up the subject first.

"I talked to Mrs. White yesterday afternoon," she said with feigned cheerfulness, "and she said Josh is doing better than anyone expected."

"Good. Good."

Enthusiasm echoed in each word. Amy was absolutely positive that her father knew the reasons behind Josh's increasing strength. The crimson heat that had invaded her face earlier circled her ears like a lariat. She swallowed a bite of her toast, and it settled in her stomach like a lead ball.

"I had a chance to talk to Mrs. White this morning myself."

"You did?" she blurted out.

"Yes," he continued, eyeing her closely.

Amy did her level best to disguise her distress. She'd always been close to her father, and other than the business about him making her a part of Johnson Industries, she'd prided herself on being able to talk to him about anything.

"Amy, are you feeling all right?"

"Sure, Dad," she said energetically, knowing she wasn't going to be able to fool him.

He arched his brows and reached for his coffee, sipping at it while he continued studying her.

There was nothing left to do but blurt out the truth and clear the air before she suffocated in the tension. "You heard me last night, didn't you?"

"I beg your pardon?"

"Well, you needn't concern yourself, because nothing happened. Well, almost nothing, but not from lack of trying on my part. Josh was the perfect gentleman."

Her father stared at her with huge blue eyes. He certainly wasn't making this any easier on her. He continued to glare at her for several uneasy seconds until Amy felt compelled to explain further.

"It was late...and I couldn't sleep. I know that probably isn't a very good excuse, but I had a question that I wanted to ask Josh."

"You couldn't have asked me?"

Her startled eyes flew to him. "No!"

"Go on."

"How much more do you want to know? I already told you nothing happened."

"I believe the phrase you used a moment ago was 'almost nothing.'"

"I'm crazy about him, Dad, and I've never been in love before, and, well, it's difficult when you…feel that way about someone…if you know what I mean?"

"I believe I do."

"Good." She relaxed somewhat. Although her appetite had vanished the instant she realized her father was waiting to confront her about what had happened in Josh's room, she did an admirable job of finishing her breakfast.

"Mrs. White said Josh would be able to join us for dinner tonight."

Amy's happy gaze flew to her father. "That's wonderful."

"I thought you'd be pleased to hear it."

"I'll have Manuela prepare a special dinner."

Her father nodded. "Good idea." He downed the last of his coffee, glanced at his watch, then stood abruptly. "I've got to go to the office. Have a good day, sweetheart."

Amy raised her coffee cup to her lips and sipped. "Thanks. You, too."

"I will." He was halfway out of the dining room when he turned around. "Amy."

"Yes, Dad."

"I'm not exactly certain I should admit this. But I didn't hear a thing last night. I slept like a log."

Eight

"It's your move," Amy reminded Josh for the second time, growing restless. Just how long did it take to move a silly chess piece, anyway?

Josh nodded, frowning slightly as he studied the board that rested on the table between them.

Amy's gaze caught her father's and she rolled her eyes. Josh was the one who'd insisted they play chess following dinner. Harold Johnson shared a secret smile with her. He pretended to be reading when in fact he was closely watching their game.

Amy had never been much of a chess player; she didn't have the patience for it. As far as she was concerned, chess was a more difficult version of checkers, and she chose to play it that way. It never took her more than a few seconds to move her pieces. Josh, on the other hand, drove her crazy, analyzing each move she made, trying to figure out her strategy. Heaven knew she didn't have one, and no one was more shocked than she was when Josh announced that she'd placed him in checkmate. Good grief, she hadn't even noticed.

"You're an excellent player," he said, leaning back

and rubbing the side of his jaw. He continued to study the board as though he couldn't quite figure out how she'd done it. Amy hoped he would let her in on the secret once he figured it out; she was curious to find out herself.

Her father rose from his wingback leather chair and crossed the room to get a book from the mahogany cases that lined two walls. As soon as he was out of earshot, Amy glanced over to Josh.

"You haven't kissed me all week," she whispered heatedly.

Josh's anxious gaze flew to her father, then to her. "I don't plan to."

"Ever again?"

Josh frowned. "Not here."

"Why not?"

"Because!" He hesitated and glanced toward her father. "Can we discuss this another time?"

"No," she answered with equal fervor. "You're driving me crazy."

"Mr. Johnson," Josh said anxiously and cleared his throat when her father started toward his chair. "Could I interest you in a game of chess?"

"No thanks, son. Amy's the champion of our family, you're going to have to demand a rematch with her." He stopped and placed his hand over his mouth, then did a poor job of feigning a yawn. "The fact is, I was thinking of heading up to bed. I seem to be tired this evening."

"It's barely eight," Amy protested. She immediately regretted her outburst. With her father safely tucked away in his bedroom, she might be able to spend a few minutes alone with Josh, which was something she hadn't been able to do in days.

"Can't help it if I'm tired," Harold grumbled and, after bidding them both good night, he walked out of the room.

Amy waited a few moments until she was sure her father was completely up the stairs. "All right, Joshua Powell, kindly explain yourself."

"The subject's closed, Amy."

She bolted to her feet, her fists digging into her hipbones as she struggled to quell her irritation. "Subject? What subject?"

"You and me...kissing."

If his face hadn't been so twisted with determination and pride, she would have laughed outright. Unfortunately, Josh was dead serious.

"You don't want to kiss me anymore? At all?"

He tossed her a look that told her she should know otherwise by now. Reaching for his crutches, he struggled to his feet. The cast had been removed from his leg, but he still had trouble walking without support.

"Where are you going?" she demanded, growing more agitated by the minute.

"To bed."

"Oh, honestly," she cried. "There's no reason to wrestle your way up those stairs so early. If you're so desperate to escape me, then I'll leave."

"Amy..."

"No." She stopped him by holding up both hands. "There's no need to worry your stubborn little head about me taking a drive alone in the cold, dark city. There are plenty of places I can go, so sit down and enjoy yourself. You must be sick of that room upstairs."

With a proud thrust of her chin she marched out of the room and retrieved her purse. Glancing over her shoulder, she sighed and added, "There's no need to fret. Seattle has one of the lowest murder rates on the west coast." She had no idea if this was true or not, but it sounded good.

"Amy," he shouted, and followed her. His legs swung wide as he maneuvered his crutches around the corner of the hallway, nearly colliding with her.

She offered him a brave smile and pretended she wasn't the least bit disturbed by his attitude, when exactly the opposite was true. If he didn't want to kiss or hold her again then…then she would just have to accept it.

"Yes?" she asked, tightly clenching the car keys in her hand as though keeping them safely tucked between her fingers was the most important thing in her life.

For a long moment Josh did nothing but stare at her. A battle raged in his expression as if he was fighting himself. Whichever side won apparently didn't please him, because his shoulders sagged and he slowly shook his head. "Do you want company?"

"Are you suggesting you come along with me?"

His smile was off center. "What do you think?"

"I don't know anymore, Josh. You haven't been yourself all week. Do you think I'm so blind I haven't noticed how you've arranged it so we're never alone together anymore?"

"It's too much temptation," he argued heatedly. "We're in trouble here, Amy. We're so hot for each other it's a minor miracle that we don't burst into spontaneous combustion every time we touch."

"So you're making sure that doesn't happen again?"

"You've got that right," he returned forcefully. He was leaning heavily upon his crutches. He wiped a hand over his face as if to erase her image from his mind. "I don't like it any better than you do, Angel Eyes."

Somehow Amy doubted that. Her tight look must have said as much because Josh emitted a harsh groan.

"Do you have any idea how much I want to make love with you?" he asked her in a harsh whisper. "Every time you walk into the room, it's pure torment. Tonight at dinner, I swear I didn't take my eyes off your breasts the entire meal."

She smiled, not knowing how to answer him.

"Then you got up and walked away, and it was all I could do to keep from watching your sweet little tush swaying back and forth. I kept thinking how good it would be to place my hands there and hold you against me. Did you honestly believe I wanted seconds of dessert? The fact was, I didn't dare stand up."

"Oh, Josh." Her smile was watery with relief.

He held open his arms for her, and she walked into them the way a frightened child ducks into a family home, sensing security and safety. Using the wall to brace his shoulders, he set one crutch aside and reached for her, wrapping his arm around her waist. Slowly, he lowered his hand, lifting her toward him so he could press himself more intimately against her. "Josh…"

"Do you understand now?" he ground out, close to her ear.

"Yes," she whispered with a barely audible release of breath. She slipped her arms around his neck.

He stroked his thumb along the side of her neck and

inhaled a wobbly breath before he spoke again. "Now, what was it you were saying about going for a ride?"

"Ride?" she repeated in a daze.

"Yes, Amy, a ride, as in a motorized vehicle, preferably with all the windows down and the air conditioner on full blast so my blood will cool."

She pressed her forehead to his chin and smiled before reluctantly breaking away from him. Josh reached for his crutches and followed her through the kitchen and to the garage just beyond.

A few minutes later, with Amy driving and Josh sitting in the passenger seat, they headed down the long, curved driveway and onto the street, turning east toward Lake Washington.

"I love Seattle at night," Amy said, smiling at him. "There're so many bright lights, and the view of the water is fantastic."

"Where are you taking me?"

"Lover's Leap?" she teased.

"Try again."

"All right, it isn't exactly Lover's Leap, but it is a viewpoint that looks out onto the lake. It's been a while since I've been there, but from what I remember, it's worth the drive."

"And what exactly do you know about lookout points, Amy Johnson? I'd bet my entire life's savings that you've never been there with a man."

"Then you'd lose." She tossed him a saucy grin, then pulled her gaze to the roadway, her love for him so potent she felt giddy with it.

He eyed her skeptically. "Who?"

"Does it matter? All you need to know is that I was

there with a man. A handsome one, too, by anyone's standards."

"When?" he challenged.

"Well," she hesitated, not wanting to give her secret away quite so easily. "I don't exactly remember *when*. Let me suffice to say, it was several years back, when I was young and foolish."

"You're young and foolish now."

"Nevertheless, I was with a man. I believe you said you'd hand over your life savings to me." She laughed, her happiness bubbling over. "I'll take a check, but only with the proper identification."

"All right, if you're going to make this difficult, I'll guess. You were ten and your daddy was escorting you around town and stopped at this lookout point so you could view the city lights."

"How'd you guess that?" she asked, then clamped her mouth shut, realizing she'd given herself away. "I should make you pay for that, Joshua Powell."

He brushed his fingers against her nape, and when he spoke his voice was low and seductive. "I'm counting on it, Angel Eyes."

"You think once I park this car that I'm going to let you kiss me, don't you?"

Josh's laugh was full. "Baby, you're going to ask for it. Real nice, too."

Laughing, she eased the Mercedes to a stop at the end of the long, deserted street and turned off the headlights, then the ignition. The view was as magnificent as she remembered. More so, because she was sharing it with Josh. The city stretched out before them like a bolt of black satin, littered with shimmering lights that sparkled and gleamed like diamonds. Lake Washington was barely visible, but the electricity from the homes that bordered its shores traced the curling banks. The sky was cloudless and the moon full.

Amy expelled her breath and leaned her head back to gaze into the heavens. It was so peaceful, so quiet, the moment serene. It was a small wonder that this area hadn't been developed over the intervening years since she'd last been here. She was pleased that it remained unspoiled, because it would have ruined everything to have this lovely panorama defaced with long rows of expensive homes.

Josh was silent, apparently savoring the sight himself.

"All right," she whispered, her voice trembling a little with anticipation.

He turned to her, his mending leg stretched out in front of him in as comfortable a position the cramped quarters of the car could afford him. The crutches were balanced against the passenger door. "All right what?"

"You said I was going to have to ask for a kiss. I'm asking, Josh." She felt breathless, as if she'd just finished playing a set of tennis. "Please."

Josh went stock-still, and she could sense the tension in him as strongly as she could smell the fragrant grass that grew along the roadside.

"Heaven help me, Amy, I want to please you."

"You do, every time we touch."

He turned her in his arms, his kiss slow and sultry. So hot and sweet that her toes curled and she twisted, wanting to get as near to him as possible in the close confines. The console was a barrier between them, and the steering wheel prevented her from twisting more than just a little.

In their weeks together, Josh had taught her the fine art of kissing, his lessons exhaustive and detailed. Tonight, Amy was determined to prove to him what an avid student she had been. His shoulders heaved, and he drew in a sharp breath.

"Amy," he warned in a severe whisper, "you should never have gotten us started. Angel, don't you understand yet what this is eventually going to lead to—"

She pressed the tips of her fingers over his lips. "Why do you insist on arguing with me, Joshua Powell?" She didn't give him an opportunity to answer, but slid her hands up his shoulders and joined them at the base of his neck, lifting her mouth to his once more, unwilling to spend these precious moments alone debating a moot point.

Josh's kiss wasn't slow or sweet this time, but hot and urgent, so hungry that he drove the crown of her head against the headrest. He grasped the material of her skirt, bunching it up around her upper thighs as he slid his callused palm over her silk panties.

Her eyes snapped open with surprise at this new invasion. He wanted to shock her, prove to her that she was in over her head. What Josh didn't realize was that with all the other lessons he'd been giving her, she'd learned to swim. So well she wanted to try out for the Olympic team. Lifting her hips just a little to aid him, her knee came in sharp contact with the steering wheel, and she cried out softly.

"Damn."

"If you think that's bad, I've got a gear shift sticking in my ribs," he informed her between nibbling kisses. "I'm too old for this, Angel Eyes."

"I am, too," she whispered and teased him with her tongue.

"Maybe I'm not as old as I think," he amended at the end of a ragged sigh.

Amy smoothed the hair away from his face, spreading eager kisses wherever she could. "You know what I want?"

"Probably the same thing I do, but we aren't going to get it in this car."

"Honestly, Josh, you've got a one-track mind."

"Me!" he bellowed, then groaned and broke away from her to rub the ache from his right leg.

"Are you all right?" Amy asked, unable to bear the thought of Josh in pain.

"Let me put it this way," he said, a frown pleating his brow. "I don't want you to kiss it and make it better."

"Why not?" She tried to sound as offended as she felt.

"Because the ache in my leg is less than the one that console is giving my ribs. If this is to go any farther, then it won't be in this car."

"Agreed." Without another word, she snapped her seat belt into place, turned on the ignition and shifted the gears into Reverse. Her tires kicked up loose gravel and dirt as she backed into the street.

"*Now* where are you taking me?" Josh asked, chuckling.

"Don't ask."

"I was afraid of that," he muttered.

A half hour later, they turned off the road onto the driveway that led to her family home. She drove past the garage and the tennis courts and parked directly in front of the pool.

"What are we doing here?" he demanded, looking none too pleased.

"I tried to say something earlier," she reminded him, "but you kept interrupting me. I think we should go swimming."

He groaned and shut his eyes, obviously less than enthusiastic with her suggestion. "Swimming? In case you hadn't noticed it's October, and there's a definite nip in the air."

"The pool's heated. Eighty-two degrees, to be exact."

"I don't have a suit."

"There are several your size in the cabana."

Josh closed his fingers around the door handle. Slowly shaking his head, he opened the door and, using both hands, carefully swung out his right leg. "I have the distinct notion you have an argument for every one of my objections."

"I do." She climbed out of the car, and with her arm around his waist, she guided him toward the changing room and brought out several suits for him to choose from. She kissed him, then smiled at him. "The last one in the water is a rotten egg."

By the time Amy came out of the cabana, Josh was sitting at the edge of the deep end, his long legs dangling in the pool. He was right about there being a chill in the night air. She kept the thick towel securely wrapped around her shoulders as she walked over to join him, but she did this more for effect than to ward off the cold.

"Hello, rotten egg."

"Hi, there," she said, giving him a slow, sweet smile before letting the towel drop to her feet.

The minute she did, Josh gasped and his eyes seemed to pop out of their sockets. "Oh, no," he muttered, expelling his breath in a slow exercise.

"Do you like it?" she asked, whirling around in a wide circle for him to admire her itsy-bitsy string bikini.

"You mean, do I like what there is of it?"

She smiled, pleased to the soles of her feet by his response. "I picked it up in France last summer. Trust me, this one is modest compared to what some of the other women were wearing."

"Or not wearing," he commented dryly. "You'd be arrested if you showed up in that...thing on any beaches around here."

Holding her head high to appear as statuesque as possible, she smiled softly, turned and dipped her big toe into the pool to test the temperature. "I most certainly would *not* be arrested. Admired, perhaps, but not imprisoned."

His Adam's apple moved up and down his throat, but he didn't take his eyes off her. "Have you...worn this particular suit often?"

"No. There was never anyone I wanted to see me in it until now." With that, she stood at the edge of the pool, raised her arms high above her head and dove headlong into the turquoise blue waters, slicing the surface with her slender frame.

She surfaced, sputtering and angry. "Oh, dear."

"What's wrong?"

"You don't want to know." Before he could question her further, she dove under the clear blue water and held her breath for as long as she could.

When she broke the surface, gasping for breath, Josh

was in the pool beside her, treading water. He took one look at her and started to laugh.

"You lost your fancy bikini top," he cried, as if she hadn't noticed.

"I suppose you find this all very amusing," she said, blushing to the roots of her hair. To her horror, she discovered that women's breasts have the uncanny habit of floating. Trying to maintain as much dignity as possible, she pressed her splayed fingers over her breasts, flattening them to her torso. But she soon discovered that without her hands, she couldn't stay afloat. Her lips went below the waterline, and she drank in several mouthfuls before choking. Mortified, she abandoned the effort, deciding it was better to be immodest than to drown.

Josh was laughing, and it was all she could do not to dunk him. "The least you can do is try to help me find it."

"Not on your life. Fact is, this unfortunate incident is going to save me a good deal of time and trouble."

"Josh." She held out her hand. "I insist that you... keep your distance." She eyed him warily while clumsily working her way toward the shallow end of the pool.

"Look at that," he said, his gaze centering on her breasts, which were bobbing up and down at the surface as she tried to get away from him.

Her toes scraped the bottom of the pool, and once her feet were secure, she scrunched down, keeping just her head visible. She covered her face with both hands. "This is downright embarrassing, and all you can do is laugh."

"I'm sorry."

But he didn't sound the least bit petulant.

"I wanted you to see me in that bikini and swoon with desire. You were supposed to take one look at me and be so overcome with passion that you could hardly speak."

"I was."

"No, you weren't," she challenged. "In fact you looked angry, telling me I should be arrested."

"I didn't say that exactly."

"Close enough," she cried, her discontent gaining momentum. "I spent an extra ten minutes in the cabana spreading baby oil all over my body so I'd glisten for you, and did you notice? Oh, no, you—"

Before another word passed her lips, Josh had gripped her by the waist and carried her to the corner of the pool, securing her there and blocking any means of escape with his body. His outstretched arms gripped the edge of the pool.

Wide-eyed, she stared at him, the only light coming from the full moon and the dim blue lights below the water. "It isn't any big disaster," Josh told her.

"Oh, sure, you're not the one floating around with your private parts exposed. Trust me, it has a humbling effect."

She knew he was trying not to laugh, but it didn't help matters when the corners of his mouth started quivering. "Joshua Powell," she cried, bracing her hands against his shoulders and pushing for all she was worth. "I could just—"

"Kiss me." The teasing light had vanished and he lowered his gaze to the waterline. His eyes were dark and narrowed, and her breasts felt heavy and swollen just from the way he was looking at her.

Timidly, she slanted her mouth over his, barely brushing his lips with her own.

"Not like that," he protested, threading his fingers through her wet, blond hair. "Kiss me the way you did earlier in the car." His voice was low and velvety. "Oh, baby," he moaned, slipping his moist mouth back and forth over her own. "The things you do to me." Seemingly impatient, he took advantage of her parted lips, and kissed her thoroughly and leisurely. He kissed her as he never had before, tasting, relishing, savoring her in a hungry exchange that left them both breathless.

"Wrap your legs around my waist," he instructed, his words raspy with desire.

Without question she did as he asked. Slipping her hands over the smooth-powered muscles.

"Josh?"

"Yes, love."

She didn't know what she wanted to ask.

She slipped her arms around his neck and pressed her torso against the water-slickened planes of his chest.

"Are you...hungry?" she asked, her voice little more than a husky murmur.

His response was guttural. "You know that I am."

Her head spun with all the things he was doing to her, kissing her until she was senseless.

"Angel," he whimpered, "be still for just a moment."

"I can't," she cried breathlessly.

Her nails curled into his chest, but if the action caused him any pain, he gave no indication. The need to taste him dominated every thought as she ran the tip of her tongue around the circumference of his mouth. Her breasts were heaving when she collapsed on him.

"Oh, Josh, I never knew...I never knew." She was just regaining her breath when she heard the sound of voices and laughter advancing from the other side of the cabana.

Josh heard it as well and stiffened, tension filling his body. "Who's there?" he shouted, his body shielding Amy from view.

"Peter Stokes."

Josh's questioning gaze met Amy's. "He's our gardener's son," she explained in a whisper. "Dad told him he could come swimming anytime...but not now."

"The pool's occupied," Josh called out. "Come back tomorrow." A low grumble followed his words, but soon the sound of the voices faded.

The moment was ruined. They both accepted it with reluctance and regret. Josh kissed her forehead, and she snuggled against him. The water lapped against them, and they hugged each other, their bodies entwined.

"Next time, angel," he said, tucking his finger under her chin and raising her eyes to his. "We don't stop."

Nine

"About last night," Josh started, looking disgruntled and eager to talk.

"That's exactly what I want to talk to you about," Amy whispered fiercely as she joined him in the dining room the following morning. "It isn't there."

Manuela had just finished serving him a plate heaped high with hot pancakes. He waited until the housekeeper was out of the room before he spoke. "What isn't there?" Josh asked, pouring thick maple syrup over his breakfast.

"My bikini top," she returned, growing frustrated. "I went down to the pool early this morning…before anyone else could find it, and it *wasn't there*." She was certain her cheeks were the same color as the cranberry juice he was drinking. It had been too dark to search for it the night before, and so cold when they climbed out of the water that Josh had insisted they wait until morning.

"I'm sure it'll show up," he said nonchalantly.

"But it's not there now. What could have possibly happened to it?" Naturally, he was unconcerned. It wasn't *his* swimsuit that was missing. The fact that he was having so much trouble suppressing a smile wasn't helping matters, either.

"It's probably stuck in the pump."

"Don't be ridiculous," she countered, not appreciating his miserable attempt at humor. "The pump would never suck up anything that big."

"Trust me, honey. There wasn't enough material in that bikini to cover a baby's bottom. Personally, I don't want to be the one to explain to your father how it got there when he has to call in a plumber."

"Funny. Very funny."

She'd just pulled out a chair to sit across the table from him when the phone rang. She turned, prepared to answer, when the second ring was abruptly cut off.

"Manuela must have gotten it," she said, noting that Josh had set his fork aside as if he expected the call to be for him. Sure enough, a couple of moments later, the plump Mexican cook came rushing into the dining room. "The phone is for you, Mr. Josh," she said with a heavy accent.

Josh nodded, and he cast a glance in Amy's direction. She could have sworn his eyes held an apologetic look, which was ridiculous, since there was nothing to feel contrite about. He scooted away from the table and stood with the aid of his cane. Her gaze followed him, and she was surprised when he walked into the library and deliberately closed the door.

"Well," Amy muttered aloud, pouring herself a cup of coffee. So the man had secrets. To the best of her knowledge, Josh had never received or made a phone call the entire time he had spent with them. But then, she wasn't with him twenty-four hours a day, either.

An eternity passed before Josh returned—Amy was on her second cup of coffee—but she was determined to drink the entire pot if it took that long.

He was leaning heavily upon the cane, his progress slow as he made his way into the dining room. This time his eyes avoided hers.

"Your breakfast is cold," she said, standing behind her chair. "Would you like me to ask Manuela to make you another plate?"

"No, thanks," he said, and his frown deepened.

Amy strongly suspected his scowl had little or nothing to do with his cold breakfast.

"Is anything the matter?" She would have swallowed her tongue before she'd directly inquire about the phone call, but something was apparently troubling Josh, and she wanted to help if she could.

"No," he said.

He gave her a brief smile that was meant to hearten her, but didn't. His unwillingness to share, plus his determined scowl, heightened her curiosity. Then, in a heartbeat, Amy knew.

"That was Jasmine, wasn't it?" Until that moment she'd put the other woman completely out of her mind, refusing to acknowledge the possibility of Josh loving someone else. It shocked her now that she had been so blind.

"Jasmine?"

"In the hospital you murmured her name several times...apparently you had the two of us confused."

"Amy, I don't know anyone named Jasmine." His eyes held hers with reassuring steadiness.

"Then why would you repeat her name when you were only half-conscious?"

"Good grief, I don't know," he returned resolutely.

He looked like he was about to say something more, but Amy hurried on. "Then I don't need to worry about you leaving me for another woman?" She gave a small laugh, not understanding his mood. It was as if he had erected a concrete wall between them, and she had to shout to gain his attention.

"I'm not going to leave you for another woman." His eyes softened as they rested on her, then pooled with regret. "But I *am* leaving you."

He stated it so casually, as if he was discussing breakfast, as if it was something of little consequence in their lives. Amy felt a fist closing around her heart, the winds of his discontent whipping up unspoken fears.

"I'm sorry, Angel Eyes."

She didn't doubt his contrition was sincere. She closed her hands deliberately over the back of the dining room chair in front of her. "I...I don't think I understand."

"That was SunTech on the phone."

Amy swallowed tightly, debating whether she should say anything. The decision was made simultaneously with the thought. She had to! She couldn't silently stand by and do nothing.

"You couldn't possibly mean to suggest you're going back to work? Josh, you can't—you're not physically capable of it. Good grief, this is only the first day you haven't used your crutches."

"I'll be gone as soon as I've finished packing."

She blinked, noting that he hadn't bothered to respond to her objections. He never intended to discuss his plans with her. He told her, and she was to accept them.

"Where?" she asked, feeling sick to her stomach, her head and her heart numb.

"Texas."

She sighed with relief; Texas wasn't so far. "How long?" she asked next.

"What does it matter?"

"I...I'd like to know how long it will be before you can come back."

He tensed, his back as straight as a flagpole. "I won't be coming back."

"I see." He was closing himself off from her, blocking her out of his life as if she was nothing more than a passing fancy. The pain wrapped itself around her like ivy climbing up the base of a tree, choking out its life by degrees.

Without another word of explanation, Josh turned and started to walk away from her.

"You intend to forget you ever knew me, don't you?"

He paused in the doorway, his back to her, his shoulders stiff and proud. "No."

Amy didn't understand any of this. Only a few hours before he'd held her in his arms, loved her, laughed with her. And now...now, he was casually turning and strolling out of her life with little or no excuse. It didn't make any sense.

Several minutes passed before Amy had the strength to move. When she did, she vaulted past Josh as he slowly made his way up the stairs one at a time. Poised at the top, she forced a smile to her lips, although they trembled with barely suppressed emotion.

"You can't leave yet," she said with a saucy grin,

placing a hand on her hip and doing her best to look sophisticated and provocative. "We have some unfinished business. Remember?"

"No, we don't."

"Josh, you're the one who claimed that the next time we don't stop."

"There isn't going to be a next time."

He was so cold, so callous, so determined. Removing her hand from her hip, Amy planted it on her forehead, her thoughts rumbling in her mind, deep and dark. Lost. "I think I'm missing out on something here. Last night—"

Josh stopped her with a glare, telling her with his eyes what he said every time he touched her. *Last night was a mistake.*

"All right," she continued, undaunted. "Last night probably shouldn't have happened. But it did. It has in the past, and I was hoping—well, never mind, you know what I was hoping."

"Amy..."

"I want to know what's so different now? Why this morning instead of yesterday or the day before? It's as though you can't get away from me fast enough. Why? Did I do something to offend you? If so, I think we should talk about it and clear the air...instead of this."

He reached the top of the stairs, his gaze level with her own. He tried to disguise it, but Amy saw the pain in his eyes, the regret.

"The last thing I want to do is hurt you, Amy."

"Good, then don't."

He cupped her face in his hand and gazed deeply into her eyes as if to tell her that if there had been any way to avoid this, he would have chosen it. He dropped his hand and backed up two small steps. Once more, Amy noted how sluggish his movements were, but this time she guessed it wasn't his leg that was bothering him, but his heart. She looked into his eyes and saw so many things she was certain he meant to hide from her. Confusion. Guilt. Rationalization.

Without another word, he walked past her and to his room. Not knowing what else to do, she followed him.

"You can't tell me you don't love me," she said, stepping inside after him. Immediately, her eyes fell on the open suitcase sitting atop the bed and a sick, dizzying feeling assaulted her. Josh had intended to leave even before the phone call, otherwise his suitcase wouldn't be where it was. "You *do* love me," she repeated, more forcefully this time. "I know you do."

He didn't answer, apparently unwilling to admit his feelings either way.

"It's the money, isn't it? That ridiculous pride of yours is causing all this, and it's just plain stupid. I could care less if you have a dime to your name. I love you, and I'm not going to stop loving you for the next fifty years. If you're so eager to go to Texas, then fine, I'll go with you. I don't need a fancy house and a big car to be happy…not when I have you."

"You're not following me to Texas or anyplace else," he said harshly, his words coated with steel. "I want that understood right now." While he was speaking, he furiously stuffed clothes into the open piece of luggage, his movements abrupt and hurried.

Amy walked over to the window and gripped her hands behind her back, her long nails cutting into her palms. "If you are worried about Dad's—"

"It isn't the money," he said curtly.

"Then what is it?" she cried, losing patience.

He pressed his lips together, and a muscle leaped in his lean jaw.

"Josh," she cried. "I want to know. I have the right, at least. If you want to walk out of my life, then that's your business, but tell me why. I've got a right to know."

He closed his eyes and when he opened them again, they were filled with a new determination, a new strength. "It's you. We're completely different kinds of people. I told you when we met I had no roots, and that's exactly the way I like my life. I like jobs that take me around the world and offer fresh challenges. You need a man who's going to be a father to those babies you talked about once. And it's not going to be me, sweetheart."

She flinched at the harsh way he used the term of affection. Sucking in her breath, she tried again. "When two people love each other, they can learn to compromise. I don't want to chain you to Seattle. If you want to travel, then I'll go with you wherever you want."

"You?" He snickered once. "You're used to living the lifestyles of the rich and famous. Jetting off in your daddy's plane, shopping in Paris, skiing in Switzerland. Forget it, Amy. Within a month, you'd be bored out of your mind."

"Josh, how can you say that? Okay, I can understand why you'd think I'm a spoiled rich kid, and…and you're right, our lifestyles *are* different, but we're compatible in other ways," she rushed on, growing desperate. "You only have to think about what…what nearly happened in the pool to realize that."

He paused, and his short laugh revealed no amusement. "That's another thing," he said coldly. "You with your hot little body, looking for experience. I'm telling you right now, I'm not going to be the one to give it to you."

"You seemed willing enough last night," she countered, indignation overcoming the hurt his words caused.

He granted her that much with a cocky grin. "I thank the good Lord that your gardener's son showed up when he did, otherwise there could be more than one unpleasant complication to our venture into that pool."

"I'm not looking for experience, Josh, I'm looking for love."

"A twenty-four-year-old virgin always coats her first time with thoughts of love—it makes it easier to justify later. It isn't love we share, Amy, it's a healthy dose of good old-fashioned lust." He stuffed a shirt inside his suitcase so forcefully it was a miracle the luggage remained intact. "When it comes to making love, you're suffering from a little retarded growth. The problem is, you don't fully realize what you're asking for, and when you find out, it's going to shock you."

"You haven't shocked me."

"Trust me, I could."

He said this with a harshly indrawn breath that was sharp enough to make Amy recoil.

"Sex isn't romance, Angel Eyes, it's hot mouths and grinding hips and savage kisses. At least it is with me, and I'm not looking to initiate a novice."

"It seems we've done our share of…that."

"You wouldn't leave me alone, would you? I tried to stay out of your way. I went to great pains to be sure we wouldn't be alone together—to remove ourselves from the temptation. But you would have none of that—you threw yourself at me at every opportunity."

That was true enough, and Josh knew it.

"I'm a man, what was I supposed to do, ignore you? So I slipped a couple of times. I tried to ward you off, but you were so eager to lose your virginity, you refused to listen. Now the painful part comes, I was as much of a gentleman as I could be under the circumstances. It wasn't as if I didn't try." He slammed the lid of his suitcase closed, shaking the bed in the process.

A polite knock sounded at the door, and Josh turned slowly toward it. "Yes, what is it, Manuela?"

"Mr. Josh, there is taxi here for you."

"Thank you. Tell him I'll be down in a couple of minutes."

Amy blinked as fast as she could to keep the burning tears from spilling down her cheeks. "You're really leaving me, aren't you?" She was frozen with shock.

"I couldn't make it any more clear," Josh shouted. "You knew the score when I met you. I haven't lied to you, Amy, not once. Did you think I was joking when I told you I was walking out that door and I didn't plan on coming back? Accept it. Don't make this any more difficult than it already is."

"Go then," she whispered, pride coming to her rescue. "If you can live with the thought of another man holding and kissing me and making love with me then…go." *Go,* she cried silently, *before I beg you to stay.*

For a moment, Josh stood stock-still. Then he reached for his suitcase, closing his fingers viciously around the handle, and dragged it across the bed. He held it in one hand and his cane in the other. Without looking at her, he headed toward the stairs.

Amy stood where she was, tears raining down her face in a storm of fierce emotion. By the time the shock had started to dissipate and she ran to the head of the stairs, Josh was at the front door.

"Josh," she cried, bracing her hands against the railing.

He paused, but he didn't turn and look at her.

"Go ahead and walk out that door...I'm not going to do anything to stop you."

"That's encouraging."

She closed her eyes to the stabbing pain. "I...I just wanted you to know that you can have all the adventures you want and travel to every corner of the world and even...and even make love to a thousand women."

"I intend on doing exactly that."

He was facing her now, but the tears had blinded her and all she could make out was a watery image. "Live your life and I'll...I'll live mine, and we'll probably never see each other again, but...I swear to you... one day you're going to regret this." Her shoulders shook with sobs. "One day you're going to look back and think of all that you threw away and realize..." She paused, unable to go on, and wiped the moisture from her eyes.

"Can I go now?"

"Stop being so cruel."

"It's the only thing you'll accept," he shouted, his anger vibrating all the way up the stairs. He turned from her once more.

"Josh," she cried, her hands knotting into tight fists at her sides.

"Now what?"

The air between them crackled with electricity and the longest moment of her life passed before she could speak. "Don't come back," she told him. "Don't ever come back."

Josh rubbed his eyes with his thumb and index finger and sagged in the seat of the yellow cab.

"Where to, mister?"

"Sea-Tac Airport," Josh instructed. His insides felt like a bowl of overcooked oatmeal tossed in a campfire. Surviving the explosion had been nothing compared to saying goodbye to Amy. He would gladly have run into another burning building rather than walk away from her again. He had to leave, he had known that the minute he climbed out of the pool the night before. It was either get out of her life before their lovemaking went too far or marry her.

For both their sakes, he was leaving.

But it hadn't been easy. The memory of the way her eyes had clouded with pain would haunt him until the day he died. He shut his mind to the image of her standing at the top of the stairs. Her anguish had called to him in an age-old litany that would echo in his mind far beyond the grave.

What she said about him regretting leaving her had hit him like a blow to the solar plexus. He hadn't even been away five minutes, and the remorse struck him the way fire attacks dry timber.

She was right about him loving her, too. Josh hadn't tried to lie about his feelings. He couldn't have, because she knew. Unfortunately, loving her wouldn't make things right for them. It might have worked, they may have been able to build a life together, if she wasn't who she was—Harold Johnson's daughter. Even then Josh had his doubts. There was only one absolute in all this—he wasn't ever going to stop loving her. At least not in this lifetime.

"Hey, buddy, are you all right back there?" the cab driver asked over his shoulder. He was balding and friendly.

"I'm fine."

"You don't look so fine. You look like a man who's been done wrong by his woman. What's the matter, did she kick you out?"

Josh met the driver's question with angry silence.

"Listen, friend, if I were you, I wouldn't put up with it." His laugh was as coarse as his words.

Josh closed his eyes against fresh pain. Amy's words about another man making love to her had hit their mark. Bull's-eye. If he had anything to be pleased about, it was the fact that he had left her with her innocence intact. It had come so close in the pool. He had managed to leave her pure and sweet for some other man to initiate into lovemaking.

A blinding light flashed through his head, and the pain was so intense that he blinked several times against its unexpected onslaught.

"Hey, friend, I know a good lawyer if you need one. From the looks of it, you two got plenty of cold cash. That makes it tough. I know a lot of people who've got money, and from what I see, it sure as hell didn't buy happiness."

"I don't need a lawyer."

The taxi driver shook his head. "That's a mistake

too many men make, these days. They want to keep everything friendly for the kids' sake. You got kids?"

Josh's eyes drifted closed. Children. For a time there, soon after they had returned from Kadiri, Josh had dreamed of having children with her. He dreamed a good deal about making those babies, too. He smiled wryly. If he had learned anything in the months he had spent loving Amy, it was the ability to imagine the impossible. He would wrap those fantasies around him now the way his aunt Hazel tucked an afghan around her shoulders in the heart of winter.

"I got two boys myself," the driver continued, apparently unconcerned with the lack of response from his passenger. "They're mostly grown now, and I don't mind telling you they turned out all right. Whatever you do, buddy, don't let the wife take those kids away from you. Fight for 'em if you got to, but fight."

Josh was battling, all right, but the war he was waging was going on inside his head. It didn't take much imagination to picture Amy's stomach swollen with his child and the joy that would radiate from her eyes when she looked at him. Only there wouldn't be any children. Because there wouldn't be any Amy. At least not for him.

"Buddy, you sure you don't want the name of that lawyer? He's good. Real good."

"I'm sure."

The cab eased to a stop outside the airport terminal, and the chatty driver looped his arm around the back of the seat and twisted around to Josh. "Buddy, I don't mean to sound like a know-it-all, but running away isn't going to solve anything."

Josh dug out his wallet and pulled out a couple of bills. "This enough?"

"Plenty." The cabbie reached for his wallet. "No, sir, the airport is the last place in the world you should be," he muttered as he drew out a five-dollar bill.

Josh already had his hand on the door. He needed to escape before he realized how much sense this taxi driver was making. "Keep the change."

"Amy." Her father tapped gently against her bedroom door. "Sweetheart, are you all right?"

She sat with her back against the headboard, her knees drawn up. The room was dark. Maybe if she ignored him, her father would go away.

"Amy?"

She sniffled and reached for another tissue. "I'm fine," she called, hoping he would accept that and leave her alone. "Really, Dad, I'm okay." She wasn't in the mood for conversation or father-daughter talks or anything else. All she wanted was to curl up in a tight ball and bandage her wounds. The pain was still too raw to share with her father, although she loved him dearly.

Contrary to her wishes, he let himself into her room and automatically reached for the light switch. Amy squinted and covered her face. "Dad, please, I just want to be by myself for a while." It was then that she noticed the illuminated dial on her clock radio. "What are you doing home this time of day, anyway?"

"Josh phoned me from the airport on his way out of town."

"Why? So he could gloat?" she asked bitterly.

Harold Johnson sat on the edge of his daughter's bed and gently patted her shoulder. "No. He wanted to thank me for my hospitality and to say you probably needed someone about now. From the look of things, he was right."

"I'm doing quite nicely without him, so you don't need to worry." And she would—in a few months or a few years, she added mentally.

"I know you are, sweetheart."

She blew her nose and rubbed the back of her hand across her eyes. "He loves me...in my heart I know he does, and still he walked away."

"I don't doubt that, either."

"Then why?"

"I wish I knew."

"I...I don't think we'll ever know," she sobbed. "I hurt so much I want to hate him and then all I can think is that the...the least he could have done was marry me for my money."

Her father chuckled softly and gathered her in his arms. "Listen, baby, a wise man once stated that happiness broadens our hearts, but sorrow opens our souls."

"Then you can drive a truck through mine."

He held her close. "Try to accept the fact Josh chose to leave, for whatever reason. He's gone. He told me when he first came that was his intention."

"He didn't tell me," she moaned. "Dad, I love him so much. How am I ever going to let him go?"

"The pain will get better in time, I promise you."

"Maybe," she conceded, "but it doesn't seem possible right now." Knowing Josh didn't want to marry her was difficult enough, but refusing to make love with her made his rejection all the more difficult to bear.

"Come downstairs," her father coaxed. "Sitting in

your room with the drapes closed isn't helping anything."

She shook her head. "Maybe later."

"How about a trip? Take off with a friend for a while
and travel."

She shook her head and wiped a tear from her cheek.
"No, thanks. It isn't that I don't appreciate the offer, but
I wouldn't enjoy myself. At least not now."

"Okay, baby, I understand." Gently he kissed her
crown and stood.

"Dad," she called to him when he started to walk out
of her room. "Did Josh say...anything else?"

"Yes." His eyes settled on her and grew sad. "He
said goodbye."

The knot in her stomach twisted so tight that she
sucked in her breath to the surge of unexpected pain.
"Goodbye," she repeated, and closed her eyes.

The next morning, Amy's alarm clock rang at six,
rousing her from bed. She showered and dressed in
her best suit, primly tucking in her hair at her nape in
a loose chignon.

Her father was at the breakfast table when she joined
him. His eyes rounded with surprise when she walked
into the room.

"Good morning, Dad," she said, reaching for the
coffee. She didn't have Josh, but she had her father.
Harold Johnson had the courage of a giant and the
sensitive heart of a child. Just being with him would
help her find the way out of this bitter unhappiness.

"Amy." It looked as if he wasn't quite sure what to
say. "It's early for you, isn't it?"

"Not anymore. Now, before we head for the office, is there anything you want to fill me in on?"

For the first time Amy could remember, her father was completely speechless.

Ten

"There was a call for you earlier," Rusty Everett told Josh when he returned from lunch.

Josh's heart thudded heavily. "Did you catch the name?"

"Yeah, I wrote it down here someplace." Rusty, fifty and as Texan as they come, rummaged around his cluttered desk for several moments. "I don't know what I did with it. Whoever it was said they'd call back later."

"It didn't happen to be a woman, did it?" One that had the voice of an angel, Josh added silently. He'd gone out of his way to be sure Amy never wanted to see or talk to him again, and yet his heart couldn't stop longing for her.

"No, this was definitely a man."

"If you find the name, let me know."

"Right."

Leaning upon his cane, Josh made his way into the small office. Since he was still recovering from the explosion, Josh was pushing a pencil for SunTech. He didn't like being cooped up inside an office, but he didn't know if he should attribute this unyielding restlessness to the circumstances surrounding his employment or the gaping hole left in his life without Amy. He had the feeling he could be tanning on the lush white sands of a tropical paradise and still find plenty of cause for complaint.

As painful as it was to admit, there was only one place he wanted to be, and that was in Seattle with a certain angel. Instead, he was doing everything within his power to arrange a transfer to the farthest reaches of planet earth so he could escape her. The problem was, it probably wouldn't matter where he ran, his memories would always catch up with him.

He was wrong to have abruptly left her the way he did, to deliberately hurt her, but, unfortunately, he knew it was the right thing for them both, even if she didn't.

He'd been noble, but he'd behaved like a jerk.

He had to forget her, but his heart and his mind and his soul wouldn't let him.

Wiping a hand across his face, Josh leaned back in his chair and rubbed the ache from his right thigh. The pain in his leg was minute compared to the throbbing anguish that surrounded his heart.

With determination, Josh reached for the geological report he wanted to read, but his mind wasn't on oil exploration. It was on an angel who had turned his life upside down.

"Hey, Josh," Rusty called from the other room. "You've got a visitor."

Josh stood and nearly fell back into his chair in shock when Harold Johnson casually strolled into his office.

"Hello, Josh."

Amy's father greeted him as if they were sitting down to a pleasant meal together. "Mr. Johnson," Josh replied stiffly, ill at ease.

The two shook hands, eyeing each other. One confident, the other dubious, Josh noted. Without waiting for an invitation, Harold claimed the chair on the other side of the desk and crossed his legs as though he planned to sit and chat for a while. All he needed to complete the picture was a snifter of brandy and a Cuban cigar.

"What can I do for you?" Josh asked, doing his level best to keep his voice crisp and professional.

"Well, son," Harold said, and reached inside his suit jacket for the missing cigar. "I've come to talk to you about my daughter."

Vicious fingers clawed at Josh's stomach. "Don't. I made it clear to her, and to you, that whatever was between us is over."

"Just like that?"

"Just like that," Josh returned flatly, lying through clenched teeth.

A flame flickered at the end of the cigar, and Harold took several deep puffs, his full attention centered on the Havana Special. "She's doing an admirable job of suggesting the same thing."

Perhaps something was wrong. Maybe she had been hurt or was ill. Josh struggled to hide his growing concern. Amy's father wouldn't show up without a good reason.

"Is she all right?" Josh asked, unable to bear not knowing any longer.

Harold chuckled. "You'd be amazed at how well she's doing at pretending she never set eyes on you. She hasn't so much as mentioned your name since the day you left. She's cheerful, happy, enthusiastic. If I didn't know her so well, I could almost be fooled."

Relief brought down his guard. "She'll recover."

"Yes, I suspect so. She's keeping busy. The fact is, the girl surprised the dickens out of me the morning after you left. Bright and early she marched down the stairs, dressed in her best business suit, and claimed it was time she started earning her keep. Accounting never knew what hit them." The older man chuckled, sounding both delighted and proud.

If Amy's father had meant to shock him, he was doing an admirable job of it.

"The girl's got grit," Harold continued.

"Then why are you here?" Josh demanded.

"I came to see how you were doing, son."

"A phone call would have served as well."

"Tried that, but your friend there said you were out to lunch, and since I was in town, I thought I'd stop by so we could chat a bit before I flew home."

"How'd you know where to find me?"

Harold inhaled deeply on the cigar. "Were you in hiding?"

"Not exactly." But Josh hadn't let it be known where in Texas he was headed.

"I must say you're looking well."

"Thanks," Josh murmured. Most days he felt as though he wanted to hide under a rock. At least it would be dark and cold, and perhaps he could sleep without dreaming of Amy. The last thing he needed was a confrontation with her father, or to own up to the fact he was dying for news of her.

"Fact is, you look about as well as my daughter does."

Josh heaved a sigh and lowered his eyes to his paperwork, hoping Harold Johnson would take the hint.

"By the way," the older man said, a smile teasing the corners of his mouth, "you wouldn't happen to know anything about a swimsuit I found at the bottom of my pool the day you left, would you?"

It took a good deal to unsettle Josh, but in the course of five minutes Harold Johnson had done it twice. "I... Amy and I went swimming."

"Looks like one of you decided to skinny-dip," Harold added with an abrupt laugh.

His amusement bewildered Josh even more. "We... ah...I know it looks bad."

"That skimpy white thing must have belonged to my daughter, although I'll admit that I'd no idea she had such a garment."

"Sir, I want you to know I...I didn't..."

"You don't have to explain yourself, son. My daughter's a grown woman, and if nothing happened, it's not from any lack of trying on her part, I'll wager."

Josh hadn't blushed since he was a boy, but he found himself doing so now.

"She must have been a tempting morsel for you to walk away from like that."

Josh swallowed with difficulty and nodded. "She was."

Harold Johnson puffed long and hard on his cigar once more, then held it away from his face and examined the end of it as if he suspected it wasn't lit. When he spoke again, his voice was nonchalant. "I knew a Powell once."

Josh stiffened. "It's a common enough name."

"This Powell was a successful stockbroker with his

own firm situated on Wall Street. Ever hear of a fellow by the name of Chance Powell?"

A cold chill settled over Josh. "I've heard of him," he admitted cautiously.

"I thought you might have." Harold nodded, as if confirming the information he already knew. "He's one of the most successful brokers in the country. From what I understand he has offices in all fifty states now. There's been a real turnaround in his business in recent years. I understand he almost lost everything not too long ago, but he survived, and so did the business."

Josh didn't add anything to that. From the time he'd walked away from his father, he'd gone out of his way *not* to keep track of what was happening in his life, professional or otherwise.

"From what I know of him, he has only one child, a son."

If Harold was looking for someone to fill in the blanks, he was going to be disappointed. Josh sat with his back rigid, his mouth set in a thin line of impatience.

Harold chewed on the end of the cigar the way a child savors a candy sucker. "There was a write-up in the *Journal* several years back about Chance's son. I don't suppose you've heard of *him?*"

"I might have." Boldly Josh met the older man's stare, unwilling to give an inch.

"The article said the boy showed promise enough to be one of the brightest business minds this country has ever known. He graduated at the top of his class at MIT, took the business world by storm and revealed extraordinary insight. Then, without anyone ever learning exactly why, he packed up his bags and walked away from it all."

"He must have had his reasons."

Harold Johnson nodded. "I'm sure he did. They must have been good ones for him to walk away from a brilliant future."

"Perhaps he was never interested in money," Josh suggested.

"That's apparently so, because I learned that he served for several years as a volunteer for the Peace Corps." Harold Johnson held the cigar between his fingers and lowered his gaze as if deep in thought. "It's unfortunate that such a keen business mind is being wasted. Fact is, I wouldn't mind having him become part of my own firm. Don't know if he'd consider it, though. What do you think?"

"I'm sure he wouldn't," Josh returned calmly.

"That's too bad." Harold Johnson heaved a small sigh. "His life could be a good deal different if he wished. Instead—" he paused and scowled at Josh "—he's wasted his talents."

"Wasted? Do you believe helping the less fortunate was squandering my—his life?"

"Not at all. I'm sure he contributed a good deal during the years he served with the Peace Corps. But the boy apparently has an abundance of talent in other areas. It's a shame he isn't serving where he's best suited." He stared directly at Josh for a lengthy, uncomfortable moment. "It would seem to me that this young man has made a habit of walking away from challenges and opportunities."

"I think you may be judging him unfairly."

"Perhaps," Amy's father conceded.

Josh remained silent. He knew what the older man was saying, but he wanted none of it.

Harold continued to chew on his cigar, apparently appreciating the taste of the fine Cuban tobacco more than he enjoyed smoking it. "I met Chance Powell several years back, and frankly, I liked the man," Harold continued, seeming to approach this conversation from fresh grounds.

"Frankly," Josh echoed forcefully, "I don't."

The older man's eyes took on an obstinate look. "I'm sorry to hear that."

Josh made a show of looking at his watch, hoping his guest would take the hint and leave before the conversation escalated into an argument. Harold didn't, but that wasn't any real surprise for Josh.

"Do you often meddle in another man's life, or is this a recent hobby?" Josh asked, swallowing what he could of the sarcasm.

The sound of the older man's laughter filled the small office. "I have to admit, it's a recent preoccupation of mine."

"Why now?"

Harold leaned forward and extinguished his cigar, rubbing it with unnecessary force in the glass ashtray that rested on the corner of Josh's crowded desk. "What's between Chance Powell and his son is their business."

"I couldn't agree with you more. Then why are you bringing it up?"

Any humor that lingered in the older man's gaze vanished like sweet desserts in a room filled with children. "Because both you and Amy are about to make the biggest mistakes of your lives, and I'm finding it downright difficult to sit back and watch."

"What goes on between the two of us is our business."

"I'll grant you that much." Releasing his breath, Harold stood, his look apologetic. "You're right, of course, I had no right coming here. If Amy knew, she'd probably never forgive me."

Josh's tight features relaxed. "You needn't worry that I'll tell her."

"Good."

"She's a strong woman," Josh said, standing and shaking hands with a man he admired greatly. "From everything you said, she's already started to rebound. She'll be dating again soon."

The smile on his lips lent credence to his words, but the thought of Amy with another man did things to his heart Josh didn't even want to consider. It was far better that he never know.

"Before you realize it, Amy will have found herself a decent husband who will make her a good deal happier than I ever could," Josh said, managing to sound as though he meant it.

Harold Johnson rubbed the side of his jaw in measured strokes. "That's the problem. I fear she already has."

Amy sat in the office of the accounting supervisor for Johnson Industries. Lloyd Dickins would be joining her directly, and she took a few moments to glance around his neat and orderly office. Lloyd's furniture was in keeping with the man, she noted. His room was dominated by thick, bulky pieces that were so unlike her own ultramodern furnishings. A picture of Lloyd's wife with their family was displayed on the credenza, and judging by its frame, the picture was several years old. The one photograph was all there was to fill in the blanks of Dickins's life outside the company. Perhaps his need for privacy, his effort to keep the two worlds separate, was the reason Amy had taken such a liking to Lloyd. It was apparent her father shared her opinion.

Lloyd had welcomed Amy into the accounting department, although she was convinced he had his reservations. Frankly, she couldn't blame him. She was the boss's daughter and if she was going to eventually assume her father's position, albeit years in the future, she would need to know every aspect of managing the conglomerate.

"Sorry to keep you waiting," Lloyd mumbled as he sailed into the office.

Amy swore the man never walked. But he didn't exactly run, either. His movements were abrupt, hurried, and Amy supposed it was that which gave the impression he was continually rushing from one place to the other. He was tall and thin, his face dominated by a smile that was quick and unwavering.

"I've only been waiting a minute," she answered, dismissing his apology.

"Did you have the chance to read over the Emerson report?" he asked as he claimed the seat at his desk. He reached for the file, thumbing through the pages of the summary. The margins were filled with notes and comments.

"I read it last night and then again this morning."

Lloyd Dickins nodded, looking pleased. "You've been putting in a good deal of time on this project.

Quite honestly, Amy, I wasn't sure what to expect when your father told me you'd be joining my team. But after the last three weeks, I don't mind telling you, you've earned my respect."

"Thank you." She'd worked hard for this moment, and when the praise came, it felt good.

"Now," Lloyd said, leaning back in his chair, "tell me what you think?"

Amy spent the next twenty minutes doing exactly that. When she'd finished, Lloyd added his own comments and insights and then called for a meeting of their department for that afternoon.

When Amy returned to her office, there were several telephone messages waiting for her. She left Chad's note for last. Chad Morton worked in marketing and had been wonderful. He was charming and suave and endearing, and best of all, nothing like Josh. In fact, no two men could have been more dissimilar, which suited her just fine. If she was going to forget Josh, she would have to do it with someone who was his complete opposite.

Chad was the type of man who would be content to smoke a pipe in front of a fireplace for the remainder of his life. He was filet mignon, designer glasses and BMW personality.

"Chad, it's Amy." She spoke into the receiver. "I got your message."

"Hi, Angel Face."

Amy closed her eyes to the sudden and unexpected flash of pain. She was forced to bite her tongue to keep from asking him not to call her anything that had to do with angels. That had been Josh's line, and she was doing everything within her power to push every thought of him from her life.

"Are you free for dinner tonight?" Chad continued. "Brenn and James phoned and want to know if we can meet them at the country club at six. We can go to a club afterward."

"Sure," Amy responded quickly, "why not? It sounds like fun." Keeping busy, she'd discovered, was the key. If she wasn't learning everything she could about her father's business, she was throwing herself into social events with the energy of a debutante with a closet full of prom dresses.

Rarely did she spend time at home anymore. Every room was indelibly stamped with memories of Josh and the long weeks he had spent recovering there. She would have given anything to completely wipe out the time spent at his side, but simultaneously she held the memories tightly to her chest, treasuring each minute he'd been in her life.

She was mixed up, confused, hurting and pretending otherwise.

It seemed Josh had left his mark in each and every room of her home. She couldn't walk into the library and not feel an emptiness that stabbed deep into her soul.

Only when she ventured near the pool did she feel his presence stronger than his absence, and she left almost immediately, rather than have to deal with her rumbling emotions.

When Amy arrived home that evening, she was surprised to discover her father sitting in the library in front of the fireplace, his feet up and a blanket draped over his lap. It was so unusual to find him resting that the sight stopped her abruptly in the hallway.

"Dad," she said, stepping into the room. "When did you get back?" Still perplexed, but pleased to see him, she leaned over to affectionately kiss his cheek. He'd been away several days on a business trip and wasn't expected home until the following afternoon.

"I landed an hour ago," Harold answered, smiling softly at her.

Amy removed her coat and curled up in a chair beside him. "I didn't think you'd be home until tomorrow night. Chad phoned, and we're going out to dinner. You don't mind, do you?"

He didn't answer her for several elongated moments, as if he was searching for the right words. This, too, was unlike him, and Amy wondered at his mood.

"You're seeing a good deal of Chad Morton, aren't you? The two of you are gallivanting around town every night of the week, it seems. Things seem to be getting serious."

Amy sidestepped the question. As a matter of fact, she'd been thinking those same thoughts herself. She *had* been seeing a good deal of Chad. He'd asked her out the first day she started working at Johnson Industries, and they'd been together nearly every night since.

"Do you object?" she asked pointedly. "Chad would make an excellent husband. He comes from a good family, and seems nice enough."

"True, but you don't love him."

"Who said anything about love?" Amy asked, forcing a light laugh. As far as she was concerned, falling in love had been greatly overrated.

If she was going to become involved with a man she

would much rather it was with someone like Chad. He was about as exciting as one-coat paint, but irrefutably stable. If there was anything she needed in her life, it was someone she could depend on who would love her for the next fifty years without demands, without questions.

As an extra bonus, there would never be any threat of her falling head over heels for Chad Morton and making a fool of herself the way she had for Josh Powell. No, it wasn't love, but it was comfortable.

Her father reached for his brandy, and Amy poured herself a glass of white wine, savoring these few minutes alone with him. They seldom sat and talked anymore, but the fault was mainly her own. In fact, she had avoided moments such as this. Her biggest fear was that he would say something about Josh, and she wouldn't be able to deal with it.

"I may not love Chad, but he's nice," she answered simply, hoping that would appease the question burning in her father's deep blue eyes.

"Nice," Harold repeated, his smile sad and off-center. He made the word sound trivial and weak, as if he was describing the man himself.

"Chad works for you," she said as a means of admonishment.

"True enough."

"So how was the trip?" she asked, turning the course of the conversation. She hadn't said she would accept Chad's proposal when he offered it, only that she fully expected him to tender one soon. She hadn't made up her mind one way or the other on how she would answer such a question. A good deal would depend on what her father thought. Since the two men would be working closely together in the future, it would be best if they liked and respected each other...the way Josh and her father seemed to have felt.

Josh again. She closed her eyes to the thought of him, forgetting for the moment that he was out of her life and wouldn't be back.

Once more her father hesitated before answering her question. "The trip was interesting."

"Oh?" Rarely did her father hedge, but he seemed to be doing his fair share of it this evening.

His gaze pulled hers the same way a magnet attracts steel. "From Atlanta I flew down to Texas."

Amy rotated the crystal stem between her open palms, her heart perking like a brewing pot of coffee. Josh had claimed he was heading for Texas, but it was a big state and...

She blinked a couple of times, hoping desperately that she had misread her father, but one look from him confirmed her worst suspicion. Instantly, her throat went dry and her tongue felt as if it was glued to the roof of her mouth.

"You...talked to Josh, didn't you?"

Without the least bit of hesitation, Harold Johnson nodded, but his eyes were weary, as if he anticipated a confrontation.

Her lashes fluttered closed at the intense feelings of hurt and betrayal. "How could you?" she cried, bolting to her feet. Unable to stand still, she set the wineglass aside and started pacing the room, her movements crisp enough to impress the military.

"He put on a brave front—the same way you've been doing for the last three weeks."

Amy wasn't listening. "In all my life, I've never

questioned or doubted anything you've ever done. I love you…I trusted you." Her voice was trembling so badly that it was amazing he could even understand her. "How could you?"

"Amy, sit down, please."

"No!" she shouted. The sense of betrayal was so strong, she didn't think she could remain in the same room with him any longer. Through the years, Amy had always considered her father to be her most loyal friend. He was the safe port she steered toward in times of trouble. Since she was a child he'd been the one who pointed out the rainbow at the end of a cloudburst. He was the compass who directed the paths of her life.

Until this moment, she had never doubted anything he'd done for her.

"What possible reason could you have to contact Josh?" she demanded. "Were you looking to humiliate me more? Is that it? It's a wonder he didn't laugh in your face… Perhaps he did, in which case it would serve you right."

"Amy, sweetheart, that isn't the reason I saw Josh. You should know that."

Furious, she brushed away the tears that sprang so readily to her eyes and seared a wet trail down her cheeks. "I suppose you told him I was wasting away for want of him? No doubt you boosted his arrogance by claiming I'm still crazy about him…and that I'll probably never stop loving him."

"Amy, please—"

"Wasn't his leaving humiliation enough?" she shouted. "Who…gave you the right to rub salt in my wounds? Didn't you think I was hurting enough?" Without waiting for his reply, Amy stormed out of the library, so filled with righteous anger that she didn't stop until she was in her bedroom.

No more than a minute had passed before her father pounded on her door.

"Amy, please, just listen, would you?"

"No...just go away."

"But I need to explain. You're right, I probably shouldn't have gone to see Josh without talking with you about it first, but there was something I needed to discuss with him."

Although she remained furious, she opened her bedroom door and folded her arms across her chest. "What possible reason could you have to talk to Joshua Powell...if it didn't directly involve me?"

Her father stood just outside her door, a sheen of perspiration moistening his pale forehead and upper lip. He probably shouldn't have come racing up the stairs after her. He looked ashen, and his breathing was labored, but Amy chose to ignore that, too angry to care.

"Dad?" she repeated, bracing her hands against her hips. "Why did you talk to Josh?"

Her father's responding smile was weak at best. "I have a feeling you aren't going to like this, either." He hesitated and wiped a hand across his brow. "I went to offer him a job."

"You did what?" It demanded everything within Amy not to explode on the spot. She stood frozen for a moment, then buried her face in her hands.

"It isn't as bad as it seems, sweetheart. Joshua Powell is fully qualified. I was just looking to—"

"I know what you were trying to do," Amy cried. "You were looking to *buy* him for me!" Before it had been her voice that trembled. Now her entire body shook with outrage. Her knees didn't feel as if they were going to support her any longer.

But that didn't stop her from charging across the room to her closet and throwing open the doors with every ounce of strength she possessed. She dragged out her suitcases and slammed them across the bed.

"Amy, what are you doing?"

"Leaving. This house. Johnson Industries. And you."

Her calm, rational father looked completely undone. If he was colorless before, he went deathly pale now. "Sweetheart, there's no reason for you to move out." The look in his eyes was desperate. "There's no need to overreact... Josh turned down the offer."

The added humiliation was more than Amy could handle.

"Of course he did. He didn't want me before. What made you think he would now?" Without stopping, she emptied her drawers, tossing her clothes in the open suitcase, unable to escape fast enough.

"Amy, please, don't do anything rash."

"Rash?" she repeated, hiccuping on a sob. "I should have moved out years ago, but I was under the impression that we...shared something special...like trust, mutual respect...love. Until tonight, I believed you—"

"Amy."

Something in the strangled way he uttered her name alerted her to the fact something was wrong. Something was very, very wrong. She whirled around in time to see her father grip his chest, roll back his eyes and slump unconscious to the floor.

Eleven

Josh lowered the week-old *Wall Street Journal* and let the newspaper rest on his lap while his mind whirled with troubled concern. Mingling with his worries was an abundance of ideas, most of them maverick—but then he had been considered one in his time.

"What part of the world are you headed for now, dear?" his aunt Hazel inquired, her soft voice curious. She sat across the living room from him, her fingers pushing the knitting needles the way a secretary worked a keyboard. Her white hair was demurely pinned at the back of her head, and tiny wisps framed her oval face. Her features, although marked with age, were soft and gentle. Her outer beauty had faded years before, but the inner loveliness shone brighter each time he stopped to visit. Without much difficulty, Josh could picture Amy resembling his aunt in fifty or so years.

"I'm hoping to go back to Kadiri," he answered her, elbowing thoughts of Amy from his mind.

"Isn't that the place that's been in the news recently?" she asked, sounding worried. "There's so much unrest in this world. I have such a difficult time understanding why people can't get along with one another." She pointedly glanced in his direction, her hands resting in her lap as her tender brown eyes challenged him.

Over the years, Josh had become accustomed to his aunt inserting barbed remarks, thinly veiled, about his relationship with his father. Josh generally ignored them, pretending he didn't understand what she meant. He preferred to avoid a confrontation. As far as he was concerned, his aunt Hazel was his only relative, and he loved her dearly.

"What's that you're reading so intently?"

Josh's gaze fell to the newspaper. *"The Wall Street Journal."* Knowing his aunt would put the wrong connotation into the subject matter, since he normally avoided anything that had to do with the financial world, he hurried to explain. "I have a...friend, Harold Johnson, who owns and operates a large conglomerate. With all the traveling I do, it's difficult to keep in contact with him, so I keep tabs on him by occasionally checking to see how his stock is doing."

"And what does that tell you?"

"Several things."

"Like what, dear?" she asked conversationally.

Josh wasn't certain his aunt would understand all the ins and outs of the corporate world, so he explained it as best he could in simple terms. "Stock prices tell me how he's doing financially."

"I see. But you've been frowning for the last fifteen minutes. Is something wrong with your friend?"

Josh picked up the newspaper and made a ceremony

of folding it precisely in fourths. "His bond rating has just been lowered."

"That's not good?"

"No. There's an article here that states that Johnson Industries' stock price is currently depressed, which means the value has fallen below its assets. With several long-term bonds maturing, the cost of rolling them over may become prohibitive."

His aunt Hazel returned to her knitting. "Yes, but what does all that mean?"

Josh struggled to put it into terminology his aunt would understand. "Trouble, mostly. Basically it means that Johnson Industries is a prime candidate for a hostile takeover. He may be forced into selling the controlling interest of the business he's struggled to build over a lifetime to someone else."

"That doesn't seem fair. If a man works hard all his years to build up a business, it's not right that someone else can waltz right in and take over."

"Little in life is fair anymore," Josh said, unable to disguise his bitterness.

"Oh, Josh, honestly." His aunt rested her hands in her lap and slowly shook her head, pressing her lips together tightly. "You have become such a pessimist over the years. If I wasn't so glad to see you when you came to visit me, I'd take delight in shaking some sense into you."

Although his aunt was serious, Josh couldn't help laughing outright. "Harold's going to be just fine. He's a strong man with a lot of connections. The sharks are circling, but they'll soon start looking for weaker prey."

"Good. I hate the thought of your friend losing his business."

"So do I." Setting the newspaper aside, Josh closed his eyes, battling down the surge of long-forgotten excitement. The adrenaline had started to pound through his blood the minute he had picked up the *Wall Street Journal*. It had been years since he had allowed himself the luxury of remembering the life he'd left behind. Since the final showdown with his father, he had done everything he could to forget how much he loved plowing into problems with both hands, such as the one Johnson Industries was currently experiencing. Before he realized what he was doing, his mind was churning out ways to deal with this difficulty.

Releasing his breath, Josh closed his mind to the thought of offering any advice to Amy's father. The cord had been cut, and he couldn't turn back now.

"Your father is looking well," his aunt took obvious delight in informing him.

Josh ignored her. He didn't want to discuss Chance, and Aunt Hazel knew it, but she did her best to introduce the subject of his father as naturally as possible.

"He asked about you."

Josh scoffed before he thought better of it.

"He loves you, Josh," Hazel insisted sharply. "If the pair of you weren't so unbelievably proud, you could settle this unpleasantness in five minutes. But I swear, you're no better than he is."

The anger that shot through Josh was hot enough to boil his blood and, unable to stop his tongue, he blurted out, "I may not be a multimillionaire, but at least I'm not a crook. My father should be in prison right now, and you well know it. You both seem to think I was supposed to ignore the fact that Chance Powell is a liar and a cheat."

"Josh, please, I didn't mean to reopen painful wounds. It's just that I've seen you fly from one end of the world to the other in an effort to escape this difficulty with your father. I hardly know you anymore...I can't understand how you can turn away from everything that ever had any value to you."

The older woman looked pale, and Josh immediately regretted his outburst. "I'm sorry, Aunt Hazel, I shouldn't have raised my voice to you. Now, what was it you said you were cooking for dinner?"

"Crow," she told him, her eyes twinkling.

"I beg your pardon?"

She laughed softly and shook her head. "I seem to put my foot in my mouth every time I try to talk some sense into you. No matter what you do with the rest of your life, Joshua, I want you to know I'll always love you. You're the closest thing to a son I've ever had. Forgive an old woman for sticking her nose where it doesn't belong."

Josh set aside the paper and walked over to sit on the arm of her overstuffed chair. Then he leaned over and kissed her cheek. "If you can forgive me for my sharp tongue, we'll call it square."

That night, Josh wasn't able to sleep. He lay on the mattress with his hands supporting the back of his head and stared into empty space. Every time he closed his eyes, he saw Harold Johnson sitting across the desk from him, discussing his current financial difficulties. Amy's father was probably in the most delicate position of his business career. The sheer force of the older man's personality was enough to ward off all but the most bloodthirsty sharks. But Josh didn't know how long Harold could keep them at bay. For Amy's sake, he hoped nothing else would go wrong.

His first inclination had been to contact her father with a few suggestions. But Harold Johnson didn't need him, and for that matter, neither did Amy. According to her father, she was seriously dating someone else. In fact, he had claimed she would probably be wearing an engagement ring before long.

Josh hadn't asked any questions, although he would have given his right hand to have learned the name of the man who had swept her off her feet so soon after he had left. More than likely, Josh wouldn't have known the other man, and it wouldn't have mattered if he had.

When he had flown out of Seattle, Josh had hoped Amy would hurry and fall in love with someone else, so there was no reason for him to be unsettled now. This was exactly what he had wanted to happen. So it made no sense that he was being eaten alive with regrets and doubts.

The answer as to why was obvious. He was never going to stop loving Amy. For the first time since his conversation with her father, he was willing to admit what a fool he had been to have honestly believed he had meant it. Just the thought of her even *kissing* another man filled him with such anger that he clenched his fists with impotent rage.

If that wasn't bad enough, envisioning Amy making love with her newfound friend was akin to having his skin ripped off his body one strip at a time. The irony of this was that Amy had told him as much. She'd stood at the top of her stairs and shouted it to him, he recalled darkly. *If you can live with the thought of an-*

other man holding and kissing me and making love to me then...go.

Josh *had* walked away from her, but she had been right. The image of her in the arms of another man caused him more agony than his injuries from the explosion ever had.

Harold Johnson's words came back to haunt him, as well. They had been talking, and Amy's father had stared directly at him and claimed: *This young man has made a habit of walking away from challenges and opportunities.*

At the time it had been all Josh could do not to defend himself. He had let the comment slide rather than force an argument. Now the truth of the older man's words hit him hard, leaving him defenseless.

Josh couldn't deny that he had walked away from his father, turned his back on the life he had once enjoyed, and had been running ever since. Even his love for Amy hadn't been strong enough to force him to deal with that pain. Instead, he had left her and then been forced to deal with another more intense agony. His life felt like an empty shell, as if he were going through the motions, but rejecting all the benefits.

In his own cavalier way, he'd carelessly thrown away the very best thing that had ever happened to him.

Love. Amy's love.

Closing his eyes to the swell of regret, Josh lay in bed trying to decide what he was going to do about it. If anything.

He didn't know if he could casually walk into Amy's life after the way he had so brutally abandoned her. The answer was as difficult to face as the question had been.

Perhaps it would be best to leave her to what happiness she had found for herself.

Doubts pounded at him from every corner until he realized sleep would be impossible. Throwing back the blankets, he climbed out of bed, dressed and wandered into the living room. His aunt's bedroom door had been left slightly ajar, and he could hear her snoring softly in the background. Instead of being irritated, he was comforted by the knowledge that she was his family. He didn't visit her as often as he should, and he was determined to do so from now on.

Josh sat in the dark for several minutes, reviewing his options with Amy and her father. He needed time to carefully think matters through.

In the wee hours of the morning, he turned on the television, hoping to find a movie that would help him fall asleep. Instead, he fiddled until he found a station that broadcast twenty-four-hour financial news. The article in the *Wall Street Journal* was a week old. A great many things could have happened to Johnson Industries in seven days. It wasn't likely that he would learn anything, but he was curious nonetheless.

"Josh, what are you doing up at this time of night?" his aunt demanded, sounding very much like a mother scolding her twelve-year-old son. She stood and held the back of her hand over her mouth as she yawned. She was dressed in a lavender terry-cloth robe that was tightly cinched at the waist, and her soft hair was secured with a thin black net.

"I couldn't sleep."

"How about some warm milk? It always works for me."

"Only if you add some chocolate and join me."

His aunt chuckled and headed toward the kitchen. "Do you want a bedtime story while I'm at it?"

Josh grinned. "It wouldn't hurt."

She stuck her head around the corner. "That's what I thought you'd say."

Josh stood, prepared to follow her. He walked toward the television, intent on turning it off, when he heard the news. For one wild moment, he stood frozen in shock and disbelief.

"Aunt Hazel," he called once he found his voice. "You'd better cancel the hot chocolate."

"Whatever for?" she asked, but stopped abruptly when she turned and saw him. "Josh, what's happened? My dear boy, you're as pale as a ghost."

"It's my friend. The one I was telling you about earlier—he's had a heart attack and isn't expected to live."

For most of the evening, Josh had been debating what he should do. He had struggled with indecision and uncertainty, trying to decide if it would be best to leave well enough alone and let both Amy and her father go on with their lives. At the same time, he had begun to wonder if he could face life without his Angel Eyes at his side.

Now the matter had been taken out of his hands. There was only one option left to him, and that was to return. If Johnson Industries had been a prime candidate for a hostile takeover *before* Harold's heart attack, it was even more vulnerable now. Sharks always went after the weakest prey, and Johnson Industries lay before them with its throat exposed. Josh's skills might be rusty, but they were intact, and he knew he could help.

Amy would need him now, too. Father and daughter

had always been especially close, and losing Harold now would devastate her.

"Josh." His aunt interrupted his musings, her hand on his forearm. "What are you going to do?"

Josh's eyes brightened and he leaned forward to place a noisy kiss on his aunt's cheek. "What I should have done weeks ago—get married."

"Married? But to whom?" A pair of dark brown eyes rounded with surprise. Flustered, she patted her hair. "Actually, I don't care who it is as long as I get an invitation to the wedding."

Like a limp rag doll, Amy sat and stared at the wall outside her father's hospital room. He was in intensive care, and she was only allowed to see him for a few minutes every hour. She lived for those brief moments when she could hold his hand and gently reassure him of her love, hoping to lend him some strength. For three days he'd lain in a coma, unable to respond.

Not once in those long, tedious days had she left the hospital. Not to sleep, not to eat, not to change clothes. She feared the minute she left him, he would slip into death and she wouldn't be there to prevent it.

Hurried footsteps sounded on the polished floor of the hospital corridor, but she didn't turn to see who was coming. So many had sat by her side, staff requesting information, asking questions she didn't want to answer, friends and business associates. But Amy had sent them all away. Now she felt alone and terribly weary.

The footsteps slowed.

"Amy."

Her heart thudded to a stop. "Josh?" Before she was

entirely certain how it happened, she was securely tucked in his embrace, her arms wrapped around his neck and her face buried in his chest, breathing in his strength the way desert-dry soil drinks in the rain.

For the first time since her father's heart attack, she gave in to the luxury of tears. They poured from her eyes like water rushing over a dam. Her shoulders jerked with sobs, and she held on to Josh with every ounce of strength she possessed.

Josh's hands were in her hair, and his lips moved over her temple, whispering words she couldn't hear over the sound of her own weeping. It didn't matter; he was there, and she needed him. God had known and had sent him to her side.

"It's my fault," she wailed with a grief that came from the bottom of her soul, trying to explain what had happened. "Everything is my fault."

"No, angel, it isn't, I'm sure it couldn't be."

No one seemed to understand that. No one, and she was too weak to explain. Stepping back, she wiped the tears from her eyes, although it did little good because more poured down her face. "I caused this…I did…we were arguing and…and I was so angry, so hurt that I wanted to…move out and…that was when it happened."

Josh gripped her shoulders, and applying a light pressure, he lowered her into the chair. He squatted in front of her and took both her hands between his, rubbing them. It was then that Amy realized how cold she felt. Shivering and sniffling, she leaned forward enough to rest her forehead against the solid strength of his shoulder.

His arms were around her immediately.

"He's going to be all right," Josh assured her softly.

"No...he's going to die. I know he is, and I'll never be able to tell him how sorry I am."

"Amy," Josh said, gripping the sides of her head and raising her face. "Your father loves you so much, don't you think he already knows you're sorry?"

"I...I'm not sure anymore."

She swayed slightly and would have fallen if Josh hadn't caught her.

He murmured something she couldn't understand and firmly gripped her waist. "When was the last time you had anything to eat?"

She blinked, not remembering.

"Angel," he said gently, "you've got to take care of yourself, now more than ever. Your father needs to wake up and discover you standing over him with a bright smile on your face and your eyes full of love."

She nodded. That was exactly how she pictured the scene in her own mind, when she allowed herself to believe that he would come out of this alive.

"I'm taking you home."

"No." A protest rose automatically to her lips, and she shook her head with fierce determination.

"I'm going to have Manuela cook you something to eat and then I'm going to tuck you in bed and let you sleep. When you wake up, we'll talk. We have a good deal to discuss."

Something in the back of her head told Amy that she shouldn't be listening to Josh, that she shouldn't trust him. But she was so very tired, and much too exhausted to listen to the cool voice of reason.

She must have fallen asleep in the car on the way home from the hospital because the next thing she knew, they were parked outside her home and Josh was coming around to the passenger side to help her out.

He didn't allow her to walk, but gently lifted her into his arms as if she weighed less than a child and carried her in the front door.

"Manuela," he shouted.

The plump housekeeper came rushing into the entryway at the sound of Josh's voice. She took one look at him and mumbled something low and fervent in Spanish.

"Could you make something light for Amy and bring it to her room? She's on the verge of collapse."

"Right away," Manuela said, wiping her hands dry on her blue apron.

"I'm not hungry," Amy felt obliged to inform them. She would admit to feeling a little fragile and a whole lot sleepy, but she wasn't sick. The one they should be taking care of was her father. The thought of him lying so pale and so gravely ill in the hospital bed was enough to make her suck in her breath and start to sob softly.

"Mr. Josh," Manuela shouted, when Josh had carried Amy halfway up the stairs.

"What is it, Manuela?"

"I say many prayers you come back."

Amy wasn't sure she understood their conversation. The words floated around her like dense fog, few making sense. She lifted her head and turned to look at the housekeeper, but discovered that Manuela was already rushing toward the kitchen.

Josh entered her bedroom, set her on the edge of her bed and removed her shoes.

"I want a bath," she told him.

He left her sitting on the bed and started running the bathwater, then returned and looked through her chest of drawers until he found a nightgown. He gently led her toward the tub, as if she needed his assistance. Perhaps she did, because the thought of protesting didn't so much as enter her mind.

To her consternation, Amy had to have his help unbuttoning her blouse. She stood lifeless and listless as Josh helped remove her outer clothing.

A few minutes later, Manuela scurried into the bedroom, carrying a tray with her. Frowning and muttering something in her mother tongue, she pushed Josh out of the room and helped Amy finish undressing.

Josh was pacing when Amy reappeared. She had washed and blow-dried her hair, brushed her teeth and changed into the soft flannel pajamas covered with red kisses.

Instantly Josh was at her side, his strong arms encircling her waist.

"Do you feel better?" he inquired gently.

She nodded and noted the way his eyes slid to her lips and lingered there. He wanted to kiss her, she knew from the way his gaze narrowed. Her heart began to hammer when she realized how badly she wanted him to do exactly that. Unhurried, his action filled with purpose, Josh lowered his head.

His mouth was opened over hers. Amy sighed at the pleasure and wrapped her arms around his neck, glorying in the feel of him until he broke off the kiss. "Manuela brought you a bowl of soup," Josh insisted, leading her to the bed.

Like a lost sheep, Amy obediently followed him to where the dinner tray awaited her. Josh sat her down on the edge of the mattress and then placed the table and tray in front of her.

After three bites she was full. Josh coaxed her into taking that many more, but then she protested by closing her eyes and shaking her head.

Josh removed the tray and then pulled back the covers, prepared to tuck her into bed.

"Sleep," he said, leaning over and kissing her once more.

"Are you going away again?"

"No," he whispered, and brushed the hair from her temple.

She caught his hand and brought it to her lips. "Promise me you'll be here when I wake up...I need that, Josh."

"I promise."

Her eyes drifted shut. She heard him move toward the door and she knew that already he was breaking his word. The knowledge was like an unexpected slap in the face and she started to whimper without realizing the sounds were coming from her own throat.

Josh seemed to understand her pain. "I'm taking the tray down to the kitchen. I'll be back in a few minutes, angel, I promise."

Amy didn't believe him, but when she stirred a little while later, she discovered Josh sitting in a chair, leaning forward and intently studying her. His forearms were resting on his knees.

He reached out and ran his finger down the side of her face. "Close your eyes, baby," he urged gently. "You've only been asleep a little while."

Amy scooted as far as she could to the other side

of the mattress and patted the empty space at her side, inviting him to join her.

"Amy, no," he said, sucking in his breath. "I can't."

"I need you."

Josh sagged forward, indecision etched in bold lines across his tight features. "Oh, angel, the things you ask of me." He stood and sat next to her. "If I do sleep with you, I'll stay on top of the covers. Understand?"

She thought to protest, but hadn't the strength.

Slowly, Josh lowered his head to the pillow, his eyes gentle on her face, so filled with love and tenderness that her own filled with unexpected tears. One inglorious teardrop rolled from the corner of her eye and over the bridge of her nose, dropping onto the pillow.

Josh caught the second droplet with his index finger, his eyes holding hers.

"Oh, my sweet Amy," he whispered. "My life hasn't been the same from the moment I met you."

She tried to smile, but the result was little more than a pathetic movement of her lips. Closing her eyes, she raised her head just a little, anticipating his kiss.

"So this is how you're going to make me pay for my sins?" he whispered throatily.

Amy's eyes flickered open to discover him studying her with sobering intensity.

"Don't you realize how much I want to make love with you?" he breathed, and his tongue parted her lips for a deep, sensual kiss that left her shaken. She raised her hand and tucked it at the base of his neck, then kissed him back. Although she was starved for his touch, having him in bed with her didn't stir awake sexual sensations, only a deep sense of love and security.

He closed his hand possessively over her hip, dragging her as close as humanly possible against him on the mattress. He kissed her again.

Beneath the covers he slid his hand along her midriff. There was much she wanted to tell him, much she wanted to share. Questions she longed to ask but to her dismay, she was forced to stop in order to yawn.

He seemed to understand what she wanted. "We'll talk later," he promised. "But first close your eyes and rest."

She nodded, barely moving her head. Her lashes drifted downward, and before she knew what was happening, she was stumbling headlong on the path to slumber.

Sometime later Amy stirred. She blinked a couple of times, feeling disoriented and bemused, but when she realized that she was in her own bedroom, she sighed contentedly. The warm, cozy feeling lulled her, and her eyes drifted closed once more. It was then that she felt the large male hand slip wrapped around her middle.

With a small cry of dismay, her eyes flew open, and she lifted her head from the thick feather pillow. Josh was asleep at her side, and she pressed her hand over her mouth as the memories rolled into place, forming the missing parts of one gigantic puzzle.

"No," she cried, pushing at his shoulder in a flurry of anger and pain. "How dare you climb into my bed as though you have every right to be here."

Josh's dark eyes flashed open and he instantly frowned, obviously perplexed by her actions. He levered himself up on one elbow, studying her.

"Kindly leave," she muttered between clenched teeth, doing her best to control her anger.

"Angel Eyes, you invited me to join you, don't you remember?"

"No." She threw back the covers with enough force to pull the sheets free from between the mattress and box springs. To add to her dismay, she discovered that her nightgown had worked its way up her body and was hugging at her waist, exposing a lengthy expanse of leg, thigh and hip. In her rush to escape, she nearly stumbled over her own two feet.

"Will you please get out of my bedroom…or I'll… I'll be forced to phone the police."

"Amy?" Josh sat up and rubbed the sleep from his eyes as though he expected this to be a part of a bad dream. "Be reasonable."

"Leave," she said tersely, throwing open the door to be certain there could be no misunderstanding her request.

"Don't you remember?" he coaxed. "We kissed and held each other and you asked me to—"

"That was obviously a mistake, now get out," she blared, unconsciously using his own phrase. She wasn't in the mood to argue or discuss this—or anything else—rationally. All she knew was that the man she'd been desperately trying to forget was in her bed and looking very much as though he intended to stay right where he was.

Twelve

"Amy," Josh said, his voice calm and low, as though he was trying to reason with a deranged woman.

"Out," she cried, squeezing her eyes shut as if that would make him go away.

"All right," he returned, eyeing her dubiously. "If that's what you really want."

The audacity of the man was phenomenal. "It's what I *really* want," she repeated, doing her level best to maintain her dignity.

Josh didn't seem to be in any big rush. He sat on the end of the bed and rubbed his hand down his face before he reached for his shoes. It demanded everything within Amy not to openly admire his brazen good looks. It astonished her that she could have forgotten how easy on the eyes Josh was. Even now, when his expression was impassive, she was struck by the angled lines of his features, as sharp as a blade, more so now as he struggled not to reveal his thoughts.

He stood, but the movement was marked with reluctance. "Can we talk about this first?"

"No," she said, thrusting out her chin defiantly.

"Amy—"

"There's nothing to discuss. I said everything the day you left."

"I was wrong," he admitted softly. "I'd give everything I own if I could turn back time and change what happened that morning. From the bottom of my heart, I'm sorry."

"Of course you were wrong," she cried, fighting the urge to forgive and forget. She couldn't trust Josh anymore. "I knew you'd figure it out sooner or later, but I told you then and I meant it—I don't want you back."

Manuela appeared, breathless from running up the stairs. "Miss Amy...Mr. Josh, the hospital is on phone."

In her eagerness to expel Josh from her room, Amy hadn't even heard it ring. "Oh no..." she murmured and raced across the room, nearly toppling the telephone from her nightstand in her eagerness.

"Yes?" she cried. "This is Amy Johnson." Nothing but silence greeted her. Frantically, she tried pushing on the phone lever, hoping to get a dial tone.

"I unplugged it," Josh explained and hurriedly replaced the jack in the wall. At her fierce look, he added, "I wanted you to rest undisturbed."

"This is Amy Johnson," she said thickly, her pulse doubling with anxiety and fear.

Immediately the crisp, clear voice of a hospital staff member came on the line. The instant Amy heard that her father was awake and resting comfortably, she slumped onto the mattress and covered her mouth with her hand as tears of relief swamped her eyes.

"Thank you, thank you," she repeated over and over before hanging up the phone.

"Dad's awake...he's apparently doing much better,"

she told Manuela, wiping the moisture from her face with the side of her hand. "He's asking for me."

"Thank the good Lord," Josh whispered.

Amy had forgotten he was there. "Please leave." She cast a pleading glance in Manuela's direction, hoping to gain the housekeeper's support in removing Josh from her bedroom.

"Mr. Chad come to see you," Manuela whispered, as though doing so would prevent Josh from hearing her. "I tell him you sleep."

"Thank you, I'll phone Mr. Morton when I get back from the hospital."

"I also tell him Mr. Josh is back to stay," Manuela said with a triumphant grin.

"If you'll both excuse me," Amy said pointedly, "I'd like to get dressed."

"Of course," Josh answered, as if there had never been a problem. He winked at her on his way out the door, and it was all Amy could do not to throw something after him.

She was trembling when she sat on the edge of her mattress. The emotions battling within her were so potent, she didn't know which one to respond to first. Relief mingled with unbridled joy that her father had taken a decided turn for the better.

The others weren't so easy to identify. Josh was here, making a dramatic entrance into her life when she was too wrapped up in grief and shock to react properly.

Instead, she'd fallen into his arms as though he was Captain America leaping to the rescue, and the memory infuriated her. He could just as easily turn and walk away from her again. She'd suffered through a good deal of heartrending pain to come to that conclusion. And once burned, she knew enough to stay away from the fire.

By the time she had dressed and walked down the stairs, Josh was nowhere to be seen. She searched the living room, then berated herself for looking for him. After all, she had been firm about wanting him to leave. His having left avoided an unpleasant confrontation.

No sooner had the thought passed through her mind when the front door opened and he walked into the house as brazen as could be.

Amy pretended not to see him and stepped into the dining room for a badly needed cup of coffee. She ignored the breakfast Manuela had brought in for her and casually sought her purse and car keys.

"You should eat something," Josh coaxed.

Amy turned and glared at him, but refused to become involved in a dispute over something as nonsensical as scrambled eggs and toast.

"I've got a rental car, if you're ready to go to the hospital now."

"I'll take my own," she informed him briskly.

Josh leaned across the table and reached for the toast on her plate. "Fine, but I assume it's still at the hospital."

Amy closed her eyes in frustration. "I'll take another vehicle then."

"Seems like a waste of gasoline since I'm going that way myself. Besides, how are you going to bring two cars home?"

"All right," she said from between clenched teeth. "Can we leave now?"

"Sure."

Amy told Manuela where she could be reached and walked out to Josh's car, which was parked in front of the house. She climbed inside without waiting for him to open the door for her and stiffly snapped her seat belt into place.

They were in the heavy morning traffic before either spoke again. And it was Josh who ventured into conversation first. "I can help you, Amy, if you'll let me."

"Help me," she repeated with a short, humorless laugh. "How? By slipping into my bed and forcing unwanted attentions on me?" She couldn't believe she had said that. It was so unfair, but she would swallow her tongue before she apologized.

Josh stiffened, but said nothing in his own defense, which made Amy feel even worse. She refused to allow herself to be vulnerable to this man again, least of all now, when she was so terribly alone.

"I'd like to make it up to you for the cruel way I acted," he murmured after a moment.

Her anger stretched like a tightrope between them, and he seemed to be the only one brave enough to bridge the gap.

Amy certainly wasn't. It angered her that Josh thought he could come back as easily as if he'd never been away, apparently expecting to pick up where they'd left off.

"I'd like to talk to your father," he said next.

"No," she said forcefully.

"Amy, there's a good deal you don't know. I could help in ways you don't understand, if you'll let me."

"No, thank you," she returned, her voice hard and inflexible, discounting any appreciation for his offer.

"Oh, Amy, have I hurt you so badly?"

She turned her head and glared out the side window, refusing to answer him. The fifteen-minute ride to the hospital seemed to take an hour. Josh turned into the parking lot, and she hoped he would drop her off at the entrance and drive away. When he pulled into a parking space and turned off the engine, she realized she wasn't going to get her wish.

Biting back a caustic comment, she opened the door and climbed out. Whether he followed her inside or not was his own business, she decided.

She groaned inwardly when the sound of his footsteps echoed behind her on the polished hospital floor. The ride in the elevator was tolerable only because there were several other people with them. Once they arrived on the eighth floor, Amy stopped at the nurses' station and gave her name.

"Ms. Johnson, I was the one who called you this morning," a tall redheaded nurse with a freckled face said. "Your father is looking much better."

"Could I see him, please?"

"Yes, of course, but only for a few minutes."

Amy nodded, understanding all too well how short those moments would be, and followed the nurse into the intensive-care unit.

Harold Johnson smiled feebly when she approached his bedside. Her gaze filled with fresh tears that she struggled to hide behind a brilliant smile. His color was better, and although he remained gravely ill, he was awake and able to communicate with her.

"This is an expensive way to vacation," she said, smiling through the emotion.

"Hi, sweetheart. I'm sorry if I frightened you."

Her fingers gripped his and squeezed tightly. "I'm the one who's sorry...more than you'll ever know. Every time I think about what happened, I blame myself."

A weak shake of his head dismissed her apology. He moistened his mouth and briefly closed his eyes. "I need you to do something."

"Anything."

His fingers tightened around hers, and the pressure was incredibly slight. "It won't be easy, baby...your pride will make it difficult."

"Dad, there isn't anything in this world I wouldn't do for you. Don't waste your strength apologizing. What do you need?"

"Find Joshua Powell for me."

Amy felt as if the floor had started to buckle beneath her feet. She gripped the railing at the side of his bed and dragged in a deep breath. "Josh? Why?"

"He can help."

"Oh, Daddy, I'm sure you mean well, but we don't need Josh." She forced a lightness into her voice, hoping that would reassure him.

"We need him," her father repeated, his voice barely audible.

"Of course, I'm willing to do whatever you want, but we've gotten along fine without him this far," she countered, doing her best to maintain her cheerful facade. Then it dawned on her. "You think *I* need him, don't you? Oh, Dad, I'm stronger than I look. You should know by now that I'm completely over him. Chad and I have a good thing going, and I'd hate to throw a wrench into that relationship by dragging Josh back."

"Amy," Harold said, his strength depleting quickly.

"I'm the one who has to talk to him. Please, do as I ask."

"All right," she agreed, her voice sagging with hesitation.

"Thank you." He closed his eyes then and was almost immediately asleep.

Reluctantly, Amy left his side, perplexed and worried. Josh was pacing the small area designated as a waiting room when she returned.

"How is he?"

"Better."

"Good," Josh said, looking encouraged. His gaze seemed to eat its way through her. "Did you tell him I was here?"

"No."

"You've got to, Amy. I can understand why you'd hesitate, but there are things you don't know or understand. I just might be able to do him some good."

She didn't know what to make of what was happening, but it was clear she was missing something important.

"We've got to talk. Let me buy you breakfast—we can sit down and have a rational discussion."

Amy accepted his invitation with ill grace. "All right, if you insist."

His mouth quirked up at the edges. "I do."

The hospital cafeteria was bustling with people. By the time they had ordered and carried their orange trays through the line, there was a vacant table by the window.

While Amy buttered her English muffin, Josh returned the trays. When he joined her, he seemed unusually quiet for someone who claimed he wanted to talk.

"Well?" she asked with marked impatience. "Say whatever it is that's so important, and be done with it."

"This isn't easy."

"What isn't, telling the truth?" she asked flippantly.

"I never lied to you, Amy. Never," he reinforced. "I'm afraid, however," he said sadly, "that what I'm going to tell you is probably going to hurt you even more."

"Oh? Do you have a wife and family securely tucked away somewhere?"

"You know that isn't true," he answered, his voice slightly elevated with anger. "I'm not a liar or a cheat."

"That's refreshing. What are you?"

"A former business executive. I was CEO for the largest conglomerate in the country for three years."

She raised her eyebrows, unimpressed. That he should mislead her about something like this didn't shock her. He had misrepresented himself before, and another violation of trust wasn't going to prejudice her one way or the other. "And I thought you were into oil. Fancy that."

"I was, or have been for the past several years. I left my former employer."

"Why?" She really didn't care, but if he was willing to tell her, then she would admit to being semi-curious as to the reason he found this admission to be such a traumatic one.

"That's not important," he said forcefully. "What is vital now is that I might be able to help your father save his company. These are dangerous times for him."

"He's not going to lose it," she returned confidently.

"Amy, I don't know how much you're aware of what's going on, but Johnson Industries is a prime candidate for a hostile takeover by any number of corporate raiders."

"I know that. But we've got the best minds in the country dealing with his finances. We don't need you."

"I've been there, I know how best to handle this type of situation."

She sighed expressively, giving the impression that she was bored with this whole conversation, which wasn't entirely false. "Personally, I think it's supremely arrogant of you to think you could waltz your way into my father's business and claim to be the cure of all our ills."

"Amy, please," he said, clearly growing frustrated with her.

Actually she didn't blame him. She wasn't making this easy for a reason. There were too many negative emotions tied to Josh for her to blithely accept his offer of assistance.

"The next time you see Harold, ask him about me," he suggested.

The mention of her father tightened Amy's stomach. It was apparent that Harold already knew, otherwise he wouldn't have pleaded with her to find Josh. Nor would he have offered Josh a position with the firm. But they both had kept Josh's past a secret from her. The pain of their deception cut deep and sharp. Her father she could forgive. But Josh had already hurt her so intensely that another wound inflicted upon one still open and raw only increased her emotional anguish.

Valiantly, she struggled to disguise it. What little appetite she possessed vanished. She pushed her muffin aside and checked her watch, pretending to be surprised by the time. With a flippant air, she excused herself and hurried from the cafeteria.

Blindly, she stumbled into the ladies' room and braced her trembling hands against the sink as she sucked in deep breaths in an effort to control the pain. The last thing she wanted was for Josh to know he still had the power to hurt her. The sense of betrayal by the two men she'd loved the most in her life grew sharper with every breath.

Running the water, Amy splashed her face and dried it with the rough paper towel. When she'd composed herself, she squared her shoulders and walked out of the room, intent on returning to the intensive care unit.

She stopped abruptly in the hallway when she noticed that Josh was leaning against the wall waiting for her. Her facade was paper-thin, and he was the last person she was ready to deal with at the moment.

"I suppose I should mention that my father asked me to find you when I spoke to him this morning," she said when she could talk.

Josh's dark eyes flickered with surprise and then relief. "Good."

"You might as well go to him now."

"No," he said firmly, and shook his head. "We need to clear the air between us first."

"That's not necessary," she returned flatly. "There isn't anything I want to say to you. Or hear from you. Or have to do with you."

He nodded and tucked his hands in his pants pockets as if he had to do something in order not to reach out to her. "I can understand that, but I can't accept it." He paused as two orderlies walked past them on their way into the cafeteria. "Perhaps now isn't the best time, but at least believe me when I say I love you."

Amy pretended to yawn.

Josh's eyes narrowed and his mouth thinned. "You're not fooling me, Amy, I know you feel the same thing for me."

"It wouldn't matter if I did," she answered calmly. "What I feel—or don't feel for you—doesn't change a thing. If you and my father believe you can help the company, then more power to you. If you're looking for my blessing, then you've got it. I'd bargain with the devil himself if it would help my father. Do what you need to do, then kindly get out of my life."

Josh flinched as if she had struck him.

Amy didn't understand why he should be so shocked. "How many times do I have to tell you to leave me alone before you believe me?"

"Amy." He gripped her shoulders, the pressure hard and painful as he stared into her eyes. "Did I do this to you?"

"If anyone is at fault, I am. I fell in love with the wrong man, but I've learned my lesson," she told him bitterly. Boldly, she met his stare, but the hurt and doubt in his dark eyes were nearly her undoing. Without another word, she freed herself from his grasp and headed toward the elevator.

Josh followed her, and they rode up to the eighth floor in an uncomfortable silence. She approached the nurses' station and explained that her father had requested to talk to Josh.

She had turned away, prepared to leave the hospital, when the elevator doors opened and Chad Morton stepped out.

"Amy," he cried, as if he expected her to vanish into thin air before he reached her. "I've been trying to see you for two days."

"I'm sorry," she said, accepting his warm embrace.

"I stopped off at the hospital yesterday, but I was told you'd gone home. When I drove to the house, Manuela explained that you were asleep."

"Yes, I…I was exhausted. In fact, I wasn't myself," she said pointedly for Josh's benefit.

"With little wonder. You'd been here every minute since your father's heart attack. If you hadn't gone home, I would have taken you there myself."

Amy could feel Josh's stare penetrate her shoulder blades, but she ignored him. "I was just leaving," she explained. "I thought I'd check in at the office this morning."

Chad's frown darkened his face. "I…I don't think that would be a good idea."

"Why not?"

It was clear that Chad was uncomfortable. His gaze shifted to the floor, and he buried his hands in his pockets. "The office is a madhouse with the news and… and, well, frankly, there's a good deal of speculation going around—"

"Speculation?" she asked. "About what?"

"The takeover."

"What are you talking about?" She'd known that their situation was a prime one for a hostile takeover— in theory at least—but the reality of it caused her face to pale.

Chad looked as though he would give his right arm not be the one to tell her this. He hesitated and drew in a breath. "Johnson shares had gone up three dollars by the time Wall Street closed yesterday. Benson's moved in."

George Benson was a well-known corporate raider, the worst of the lot, from what little Amy knew. His reputation was that of a greedy, harsh man who bought out companies and then proceeded to bleed them dry with little or no compassion.

Amy closed her eyes for a moment, trying to maintain a modicum of control. "Whatever you do, you mustn't tell my father any of this."

"He already knows," Josh said starkly from behind her. "Otherwise, he wouldn't have asked for me."

Chad's troubled gaze narrowed as it swung to Josh. "Who is this?" he asked Amy.

Purposely, she turned and stared at Josh. "A friend of my father's." With that she turned and walked away.

Josh lost track of time. He and Lloyd Dickins had pored over the company's financial records until they were both seeing double. They needed a good deal of money, and they needed it fast. George Benson had seen to it that they were unable to borrow the necessary funds, and he had also managed to close off the means of selling some collateral, even if it meant at a loss. Every corner he turned, Josh was confronted by the financial giant who loomed over Johnson Industries like black death. Harold Johnson's company was a fat plum, and Benson wasn't about to let this one fall through his greedy little fingers.

"Are we going to be able to do it?" Lloyd Dickins asked, eyeing Josh speculatively.

Josh leaned back in his chair, pinched the bridge of his nose and sadly shook his head. "I don't see how."

"There's got to be some way."

"Everything we've tried hasn't done a bit of good."

"Who does George Benson think he is, anyway?" Lloyd flared. "God?"

"At the moment, he's got us down with our hands tied behind our backs," Josh admitted reluctantly. The pencil he was holding snapped in half. He hadn't realized his hold had been so tight.

"The meeting of the board of directors is Friday. We're going to have to come up with some answers by then."

"We will." But the confidence in Josh's voice sounded shaky at best. He had run out of suggestions. Years before, his ideas had been considered revolutionary. He never *had* been one to move with the crowd, nor did he base his decisions on what everyone else was doing around him. He had discovered early on that if he started looking to his colleagues before making a move he would surrender his leading edge to his business peers. That realization had carried him far. But he had been out of the scene for too many years. His instincts had been blunted, his mind baffled by the changes. Yet he had loved every minute of this. It was as if he was playing a good game of chess—only this time the stakes were higher than anything he had ever wagered. He couldn't lose.

"I think I'll go home and sleep on it," Lloyd murmured, yawning loudly. "I'm so rummy now I can't think straight."

"Go ahead. I'll look over these figures one more time and see what I can come up with."

Lloyd nodded. "I'll see you in the morning." He hesitated, then chuckled, the sound rusty and discordant. "Looks like it *is* morning. Before much longer this place is going to be hopping, but as long as it isn't with Benson's people, I'll be content."

Josh grinned, but the ability to laugh had left him several hours ago. A feeling of impending doom was pounding at him like a prizefighter's fist, each blow driving him farther and farther until his back was pressed against the wall.

There had to be a way…for Amy and her father's sake, he needed to find one. With a determination born of desperation, he went over the numbers one last time.

"What are you doing here?"

Amy's voice cracked against his ears like a horsewhip. His eyes flew open, and he blinked several times against the bright light. He must have dozed off, he realized. With his elbows braced against the table, he rubbed the sleep from his face. "What time is it?"

"Almost seven."

"Isn't it a little early for you?" he asked, checking his watch, blinking until his eyes focused on the dial.

"I…I had something I needed to check on. You look absolutely terrible," she said, sounding very much like a prim schoolteacher taking a student to task. "You'd better go to your hotel and get some sleep before you pass out."

"I will in a minute," Josh answered, hiding a smile. Her concern was the first indication she still loved him that she'd shown since the morning she awoke with him in her bed. That had been…what? Two weeks ago? The days had merged in his mind, and he wasn't entirely certain of the date even now.

"Josh, you're going to make yourself sick."

"Would you care?"

"No...but it would make my father feel guilty when I tell him, and he's got enough to worry about."

"Speaking of Harold, how's he doing?"

"Much better."

"Good."

Amy remained on the other side of the room. Josh gestured toward the empty chair beside him. "Sit down and talk to me a minute while I gather my wits."

"Your wits are gathered enough."

"Come on, Amy, I'm not the enemy."

Her returning look said she disagreed.

"All right," he said, standing, "walk me to the elevator then."

"I'm not sure I should...you know the way. What do you need me for?" She held herself stiffly, as far on the other side of the office as she could get and still be in the same room with him.

"Moral support. I'm exhausted and hungry and too tired to argue. Besides, I have a meeting at nine. It's hardly worth going to the hotel."

"My dad has a sofa in his office...you could rest there for an hour or so," she said, watching him closely.

Josh hesitated, thinking he'd much rather spend the time holding and kissing her. "I could," he agreed. "But I wouldn't rest well alone." Boldly his eyes held hers. "The fact is, I need you."

"You can forget it, Joshua Powell," she said heatedly. She was blushing, very prettily, too, as she turned and walked out of Lloyd Dickins's office.

Josh followed her. When she stepped into her father's office, he dutifully closed the door.

"I...think there's a blanket around here somewhere."

She walked into a huge closet that contained supplies. Josh went in after her, resisting the temptation to slip his arms around her and drag her against him.

"Here's one," she said and when she turned around he was directly behind her, blocking any way of escape. Her startled eyes clashed with his. Josh loved her all the more as she drew herself up to her full height and set her chin at a proud, haughty angle. "Kindly let me go."

"I can't."

"Why not?" she demanded.

"Because there's something else I need far more than sleep."

She braced one hand against her hip, prepared to do battle. Only Josh didn't want to fight. Arguing was the last thing on his mind.

"What do you want, Joshua?" she asked.

"I already told you. We should start with a kiss, though, don't you think?"

Astonished, she glared at him. "You've got to be out of your mind if you think I'm going to let you treat me as though I was some brainless—"

Josh had no intention of listening to her tirade. Without waiting for her to pause to breathe, he clasped his hands around her waist and dragged her against his chest. She opened her mouth in outrage, and Josh took instant advantage.

Amy tried to resist him. Josh felt her fingernails curl into the material of his shirt as if she intended to push him away, but whatever her intent had been, she abruptly changed her mind. She may have objected to his touching her, but before she could stop herself, she was kissing him back and small moaning sounds were coming from her throat. Or was he the one making the noise?

"Oh…oh…"

At the startled gasp, Josh broke off the kiss and shielded Amy from probing eyes.

Ms. Wetherell, Harold Johnson's secretary, was standing in the office, looking so pale it was a wonder that she didn't keel over in a dead faint.

Thirteen

Matters weren't looking good for Johnson Industries. Amy didn't need to attend the long series of meetings with Josh and the department executives to know that. The gloomy looks of those around her told her everything she needed to know. Lloyd Dickins, usually so professional, had been short-tempered all week, snapping at everyone close to him. His movements were sluggish, as if he dreaded each day, so unlike the vivacious man whose company she'd come to enjoy.

Twice in the past two weeks, Amy had found Ms. Wetherell dabbing at her eyes with a spotless lace hankie. The grandmotherly woman who'd served her father for years seemed older and less like a dragon than ever.

Amy sincerely doubted that Josh had slept more than a handful of hours all week. For that matter, she hadn't either. In the evenings when she left the office, she headed directly for the hospital. Josh had made several visits there himself once her father was moved out of the intensive-care unit, but the older man always seemed cheered after Josh had stopped by. Amy knew

Josh wasn't telling Harold the whole truth, but, despite their differences, she approved and didn't intervene.

For her part, Amy had avoided being alone with Josh since that one incident when Ms. Wetherell had discovered them. She had learned early on that she couldn't trust Josh, but he taught her a second more painful lesson—*she couldn't trust herself around him.* Two seconds in his arms and all her resolve disappeared. Even now, days later, her face heated at the memory of the way she had opened to his impudent kisses.

"How's he doing?"

Amy straightened in her chair beside her father's hospital bed. Josh, the very object of her musings, entered the darkened room. "Fine. I think."

"He's sleeping?"

"Yes."

Josh claimed the chair next to her and rubbed a hand down his face as if to disguise the lines of worry, but he wasn't fooling her. Just seeing him caused her heart to throb with concern. He looked terrible. Sighing inwardly, Amy guessed that she probably wasn't in much better shape herself.

"When was the last time you had a decent night's sleep?" she couldn't help asking.

He tried to reassure her with a smile, but failed. "About the same time you did. Amy, I'm sorry to tell you this but it doesn't look good. You know as well as I do how poorly that meeting went with the board of directors this afternoon. We're fighting even more of an uphill battle than we first realized. Half are in favor of selling out now, thinking we might get a better price, and no one's willing to speculate what Benson will be offering next week."

"We…we can't let my father know."

Josh shrugged. "I don't know how we can keep it from him. He's too smart not to have figured it out. We've done everything we can to hide it, but I'm sure he knows."

Amy nodded, accepting the truth of Josh's statement. She was all too aware of the consequences of the takeover. It would kill her father as surely if George Benson was to shoot him through the heart. Johnson Industries was the blood that flowed through her father's veins. Without the business, his life would lack purpose and direction.

Josh must have read her thoughts. His hand reached for hers, and he squeezed her fingers reassuringly. "It's going to work out," he told her. "Don't worry."

"It looks like you're doing enough of that for the both of us."

He tried smiling again, this time succeeding. "There's too much at stake to give up. If I lose this company," he said, his eyes holding hers, "I lose you."

Amy's gaze fell to her lap as his words circled her mind like a lariat around the head of a steer. "You lost me a long time ago."

The air between them seemed to crackle with electricity. Amy could almost taste his defeat. So much was already riding on Josh's shoulders without her adding her head as a prize. Whatever happened happened. What was between them had nothing to do with that.

"I can't accept that."

"Maybe you should."

"You can't fool me, Amy. You love me."

"I did once," she admitted reluctantly, "but, as you

so often had told me in the past, that was a mistake. Chad and I—"

"Chad!" He spat out the name as if it were a piece of spoiled meat. "You can't honestly expect me to believe you're in love with that spineless pansy?"

A tense moment passed before she spoke again. "I think we'd best end this conversation before we both lose our tempers."

"No," he jeered. "We're going to have this out right now. I'm through playing games."

"Talk this out? Here and now?" she flared. "I refuse to discuss anything of importance with you in my father's hospital room."

"Fine. We'll leave."

"Fine," she countered, nearly leaping to her feet in her eagerness. She felt a little like a boxer jumping out from his corner at the beginning of a new round. Every minute she was with Joshua, he infuriated her more.

At a crisp pace, she followed him out of the hospital to the parking lot. "Where are we going?" she demanded, when he calmly unlocked the passenger side of his car door.

"Where do you suggest?" he asked, as casually as if he was seeking her preference for a restaurant.

"I couldn't care less." His collected manner only served to irritate her all the more. The least he could do was reveal a little emotion. For her part, she was brimming with it. It was all she could do not to throw her purse to the ground and go at him with both fists. The amount of emotion churning inside her was a shock.

"All right then, *I'll* decide." He motioned toward the open car door. "Get in."

"Not until I know where we're headed."

"I don't plan on kidnapping you."

"Where are we going?" she demanded a second time, certain her eyes must be sparking with outrage and fury.

"My hotel room."

Amy slapped her hands against her thighs. "Oh, brother," she cried. "Honestly, Josh, do I look that stupid? I simply can't believe you! There is no way in this green earth that I'd go to a hotel room with you."

He stood on the driver's side, the open door between them. "Why not?" he asked.

"You...you're planning to seduce me."

"Would I succeed?"

"Not likely."

Unconcerned, Josh shrugged. "Then what's the problem?"

"I..." She couldn't very well admit that he was too damn tempting for her own good.

"We're closer to my hotel than your house, and at least there we'll be afforded some privacy. I can't speak for you, but personally, I'd prefer to discuss this in a rational manner without half of Seattle listening in."

He had her there. Talk about taking the wind out of her sails! "All right, then, but I'd rather drive there in my own car."

"Fine." He climbed inside his vehicle, leaned across the plush interior and closed the passenger door, which he had opened seconds earlier for her.

The ride to the hotel took only a few minutes. There was a minor problem with parking, which was probably the reason Josh had suggested she ride with him. Since there wasn't any space on the street, she found a lot, paid the attendant and then met Josh in the lobby.

"Are you hungry?"

She was, but unwilling to admit it. The hotel was the same one where he had been staying when she had first met him. The realization did little to settle her taut nerves. "No."

"If you don't object, I'll order something from room service."

"Fine."

The air between them during the elevator ride was still and ominous, like the quiet before a tornado touches down.

Josh had his key ready by the time they reached his room. He unlocked the door and opened it for her to precede him. She stopped abruptly when she realized that even the *room* was identical to the one he'd had months earlier. How differently she'd felt about him then. Even then she'd been in love with him.

And now...well, now, she'd learned so many things. But most of those lessons had been painful. She'd come a long way from the naive college graduate she'd been then. Most of her maturing had come as a result of her relationship with Josh.

"This is the same room you had before," she said, without realizing she'd verbalized her thought.

"It looks the same, but I'm on a different floor," Josh agreed absentmindedly. He reached for the room-service menu and scanned its listings before heading toward the phone. "Are you sure I can't change your mind?"

"I'm sure." Her stomach growled in angry protest to the lie. Amy gave a brilliant performance of pretending the noise had come from someone other than herself.

Josh ordered what seemed like an exorbitant amount

of food and then turned toward her. "All right, let's get this over with."

"Right," she said, squaring her shoulders for the coming confrontation.

"Sit down." He motioned toward a chair that was angled in front of the window.

"If you don't mind, I'd like to stand."

"Fine." He claimed the chair for himself.

Amy had thought standing would give her an advantage. Not so. She felt even more intimidated by Josh than at any time in recent memory. Garnering what she could of her emotional fortitude, she squared her shoulders and met his look head on, asking no quarter and giving none herself.

"You wanted to say something to me," she prompted, when he didn't immediately pick up the conversation.

"Yes," Josh reiterated, looking composed and not the least bit irritated. "I don't want you seeing that mamma's boy again."

Amy snickered at the colossal nerve of the man. "You and what army are going to stop me?"

"I won't need an army. You're making a fool of him and an even bigger one of yourself. I love you, and you love me, and frankly, I'm tired of having you use Chad as an excuse every time we meet."

"I was hoping you'd get the message," she said, crossing her arms over her waist. "As for this business of my still loving you," she said, forcing a soft laugh, "any feeling I have for you died months ago."

"Don't lie, Amy, you do a piss-poor job of it. You always have."

"Not this time," she told him flatly. "In fact, I can remember the precise moment I stopped loving you,

Joshua Powell. It happened when you stepped inside a taxi that was parked outside my home. I...I stood there and watched as you drove away, and I swore to myself that I'd never allow a man to hurt me like that again."

Josh briefly closed his eyes and lowered his head. "Leaving you that day was the most difficult thing I'd ever done in my life, Amy. I said before that I'd give anything for it never to have happened. Unfortunately, it did."

"Do you honestly believe that a little contrition is going to change everything?"

Josh leaned back in the chair, and his shoulders sagged with fatigue. "I was hoping it would be a start."

"A few regrets aren't enough," she cried, and to her horror, she felt the tears stinging in the back of her eyes. Before they brimmed and Josh had a chance to see them, she turned and walked away from him.

"What do you want?" he demanded. "Blood?"

"Yes," she cried. "Much more than that...I want you out of my life. You...you seem to think that...that if you're able to help my father, that's going to wipe out everything that's happened before and that...I'll be willing to let bygones be bygones and we can marry and have two point five children and live happily-ever-after."

"Amy..."

"No, Josh," she cried, and turned around, stretching her arm out in front of her in an effort to ward him off. "I refuse to be some prize you're going to collect once this craziness with George Benson passes and my father recovers."

"It's not that."

"Then what is it?"

"I love you."

"That's not enough," she cried. "And as for my not seeing Chad Morton again…there's something you should know. I…plan on marrying Chad. He hasn't asked me yet, but he will, and when he does, I'll gladly accept his proposal."

"You don't love Chad," Josh cried, leaping from his chair. "I can't believe you'd do anything so stupid!"

"I may not love Chad the way I love—used to love you, but at least if he ever walks out on me it won't hurt nearly as badly. But then, Chad never would leave me—not the way you did at any rate."

"Amy, don't do anything crazy. Please, Angel Eyes, you'd be ruining our lives."

"Chad's wonderful to me."

Momentarily, Josh closed his eyes. "Give me a chance to make everything up to you."

"No." She shook her head wildly, backing away from him, taking tiny steps as he advanced toward her. "Chad's kindhearted and good."

"He'd bore you out of your mind in two weeks."

"He's honorable and gentle," she continued, holding his gaze.

"But what kind of lover would he be?"

Amy's shoulders sagged with defeat. Chad's kisses left her cold. Josh must have known it. A spark of triumph flashed from his eyes when she didn't immediately respond to his taunt.

"Answer me," he demanded, his eyes brightening.

Amy had backed away from him as far as she could. Her back was pressed to the wall.

"When Chad touches you, what do you feel?"

The lie died on the end of her tongue. She could

shout that she came alive in Chad Morton's arms, insist that he was an enviable lover, but it would do little good. Josh would recognize the lie and make her suffer for it.

Slowly, almost without her being aware of it, Josh lifted his hand and ran his fingertips down the side of her face. Her nerves sprang to life at his featherlight stroke, and she sharply inhaled her breath, unprepared for the onslaught of sensation his touch aroused.

"Does your Mr. BMW make you feel anything close to this?" he asked, his voice hushed and ultra-seductive.

It was a strain to keep from closing her eyes and giving in to the sensual awareness Josh brought to life within her. She raised her hands, prepared to push him away, but the instant they came into contact with the hard, muscular planes of his chest, they lost their purpose.

"I don't feel anything. Kindly take your hands off me."

Josh chuckled softly. "I'm not touching you, angel, you're the one with your hands on me. Oh, baby," he groaned, his amusement weaving its way through his words. "You put up such a fierce battle."

Mortified, Amy dropped her hands, but not before Josh flattened his against the wall and trapped her there, using his body to hold her in check.

Amy's immediate reaction was to struggle, pound his chest and demand that he release her. But the wild, almost primitive look in his eyes dragged all the denial out of her. His pulse throbbed at the base of his throat like a drum, hammering out her fate. He held himself almost completely rigid, but Amy could feel the entire length of him pulsating with tension.

It came to her then that if she didn't do something to stop him, he was going to make love with her. The taste of bitter defeat filled her throat. Once he became her lover, she would never be able to send him away.

Her breath clogged her throat and she bucked against him. Her eyes flew to his face, and he smiled.

"That's right, angel," he urged in a deep whisper. "You want me as much as I want you."

"No I don't," she murmured, but her protest was feeble at best.

He kissed her then. Slow and deep, as if they had all the time in the world. Against every dictate of her will, blistering excitement rushed through her and she moaned. Her small cry seemed to please him, and he kissed her again, and she welcomed his touch, wanting to weep with abject frustration at the treachery of her body.

His hands were at the front of her blouse.

Knowing his intention, Amy made one final plea. "Josh...no...please."

His shoulders and chest lifted with a sharp intake of breath.

The polite knock against the door startled them both. Josh tensed and sweat beaded his fervent face.

"Josh," she moaned, "the door...someone's at the door."

"This time we finish," he growled.

The knock came a second time. "Room service," the male voice boomed from the other side. "I have your order."

"Please," she begged, tears filling her eyes. "Let me go."

Reluctantly, he released her, and needing to escape

him, Amy fled into the bathroom. From inside she could hear Josh dealing with the man who delivered the meal. She ran her splayed fingers through her mussed hair, disgusted with herself that she'd allowed Josh to kiss and hold her. It shocked her how quickly she'd given in to him, how easily he could manipulate her.

"Amy. He's gone."

Leaning against the sink, she splashed cold water on her face and tried to interject sound reason into her badly shaken composure.

When she left the bathroom, it demanded every ounce of inner strength she possessed. As she knew he would be, Josh was waiting for her, prepared to continue as if nothing had happened.

She raised her shoulders and focused her gaze just past him, on the picture that hung over the king-size bed. "You proved your point," she said, shocked by how incredibly shaky her voice sounded.

"I hope to high heaven that's true. You're going to marry me, Amy."

"No," she said flatly. "Just because I respond to you physically...doesn't mean I love you, or that I'm willing to trust you with my heart. Not again, Josh, never again."

Before he could say or do anything that would change her mind, she grabbed her purse and left the room.

Amy spent the next four days with her father, purposefully avoiding Josh. In light of what had happened in his hotel room, she didn't know if she would ever be able to look him in the eye again. If the hotel staff hadn't decided to deliver his meal when they had, there was no telling how far their lovemaking would have progressed.

No, she reluctantly amended, she *did* know where it would have ended. With her in his bed, her eyes filled with adoration, her body sated with his lovemaking. Without question, she would have handed him her heart and her life and anything else he demanded.

"You haven't been yourself in days," Chad complained over lunch. "Is there anything I can do?"

No matter what Josh believed about the other man, Chad had been wonderful. He'd anticipated her every need. Amy didn't so much as have to ask. More often than not, he arrived at the hospital, insisting that he was taking her to lunch, or to dinner, or simply out for a breath of fresh air.

Rarely did he stay and talk to her father, and for his part, Harold Johnson didn't have much to say to the other man, either.

"How's everything at the office?" she asked, recognizing that she was really inquiring about Josh and angry with herself for needing to know.

"Not good," Chad admitted, dipping his fork into his avocado and alfalfa-sprout salad. "Several of the staff have turned in their resignations, wanting to find other positions while they can."

"Already?" Amy was alarmed, fearing her father's reaction to the news. She hoped Josh would shield him from most of the unpleasantness.

"When Powell left, most everyone realized it was a lost cause. I want you to know that I'll be here for however long you and your father need me."

"Josh left?" Amy cried, before she could school her reaction. A numb pain worked its way out from her heart, rippling over her abdomen. The paralyzing agony edged its way down her arms and legs until it was nearly impossible to breathe or move to function normally.

"He moved out yesterday," Chad added conversationally. "I'm surprised your father didn't say anything."

"Yes," she murmured, lowering her gaze. For several moments it was all she could do to keep from breaking down into bitter tears.

"Amy, are you all right?"

"No...I've got a terrible headache." She pressed her fingertips to her temple and offered him a smile.

"Let me take you home."

"No," she said, lightly shaking her head. "If you could just take me back to the hospital. I...my car is there."

"Of course."

An entire lifetime passed before Amy could leave the restaurant. On the ride to the hospital, she realized how subdued her father had been for the past twenty-four hours. Although his recovery was progressing at a fast pace, he seemed lethargic and listless that morning, but Amy had been too wrapped up in her own problems to probe. Now it all made sense.

When the going got tough, Josh packed his bags and walked out of their lives. He hadn't even bothered to say goodbye—at least not to her. Apparently, he hadn't been able to face her, and with little wonder. Harold had needed him, even if she didn't. But none of that had mattered to Josh. He had turned his back on them and their problems and simply walked away.

"Why didn't you tell me?" Amy demanded of her

father the moment they were alone. Tears threatened but she held them in check. "Josh left."

"I thought you knew."

"No." She wiped away the moisture that smeared her cheeks and took in a calming breath before forcing a brave front for her father's sake. "He didn't say a word to me."

"He'll be back," her father assured her, gently patting her hand. "Don't be angry with him, sweetheart, he did everything he could."

"I don't care if he ever comes back," she cried, unable to hold in the bitterness. "I never want to see him again. Ever."

"Amy…"

"I'll be married to Chad before Josh returns, I swear I will. I detest the man, I swear I hate him with everything that's in me." She had yet to recover from the first time he had deserted her, and then in their greatest hour of need, he had done it a second time. If her father lost Johnson Industries, and in all likelihood he would, then Amy would know exactly who to blame.

"There's nothing left that he could do," her father reasoned. "I don't blame him. He tried everything within his power to turn the tide, but it was too late. I should have realized it long before now—I was asking the impossible. Josh knew it, and still he tried to find a way out."

"But what about the company?"

"All is lost now, and there's nothing we can do but accept it."

Amy buried her face in her hands.

"We'll recover," her father said, and his voice cracked. He struggled for a moment to compose himself before he spoke again. "I may be down, but I'm not out."

"Oh, Daddy." She hugged him close, offering what comfort she could, but it was little when her own heart was crippled with the pain of Josh's desertion.

Fourteen

By the weekend, Amy came to believe in miracles. Knowing that her father was about to lose the conglomerate he had invested his entire life building, she had been prepared for the worst. What happened was something that only happened to those who believe in fairy tales and Santa Claus. At the eleventh hour, her father sold a small subsidiary company that he had purchased several years earlier. The company, specializing in plastics, had been an albatross and a money loser, but an unexpected bid had come in, offering an inflated price. Her father and the corporate attorneys leaped at the opportunity, signing quickly. Immediately afterward, Johnson Industries was able to pay off its bondholders, all within hours of its deadline. By the narrowest of margins, the company had been able to fend off George Benson and his takeover schemes.

The following week, her father was like a young man again. His spirits were so high that his doctors decided he could be released from the hospital the coming Friday.

"Good morning, beautiful," Harold greeted his

daughter when she stopped in to see him on her way to work Monday morning. "It's a beautiful day, isn't it, sweetheart?"

Not as far as Amy was concerned. Naturally, she was pleased with the way matters had turned out for her father, but everything else in her life had taken a sharp downward twist.

Carefully, she had placed a shield around her heart, thinking that would protect her from Josh and anything he might say or do. But she had been wrong. Having him desert her and her father when they needed him most hurt more the second time than it had the first.

Amy found it a constant struggle not to break down. She could weep at the most nonsensical matters. A romantic television commercial produced tears, as did a sad newspaper article or having to wait extra long in traffic. She could be standing in a grocery aisle and find a sudden, unexplainable urge to cry.

"It's rainy, cold and the weatherman said it might snow," she responded to her father's comment about it being a beautiful day, doing her best to maintain a cheerful facade and failing miserably.

"Amy?" Her father's soft blue eyes questioned her. "Do you want to talk about it?"

"No," she responded forcefully. It wouldn't do the least bit of good. Josh was out of their lives, and she couldn't be happier or more sad.

"Is it about Josh?"

Her jaw tightened so hard her back teeth ached. "What possible reason would I have to feel upset about Joshua Powell?" she asked, making his question sound almost comical.

"You love him, sweetheart."

"I may have at one time, but it's over. Lately...I think I could hate him." Those nonsensical tears she had been experiencing during the past two weeks rushed to the corners of her eyes like water spilling over a top-full barrel. Once more, she struggled to disguise them.

Narrowing his gaze, Harold Johnson motioned toward the chair. "Sit down, sweetheart, there's a story I want to tell you."

Instead, Amy walked to the window, her arms cradling her waist. "I've got to get to work. Perhaps another time."

"Nothing is more important than this tale. Now, sit down and don't argue with me. Don't you realize, I've got a bad heart?"

"Oh, Dad." She found herself chuckling.

"Sit." Once more he pointed toward the chair.

Amy did as he asked, bemused by his attitude.

"This story starts out several years back..."

"Is this a once-upon-a-time tale?"

"Hush," her father reprimanded. "Just listen. You can ask all the questions you want later."

"All right, all right," she said with ill grace.

"Okay, now where was I?" he mumbled, and stroked his chin while he apparently gathered his thoughts. "Ah, yes, I'd only gotten started.

"This is the story of a young man who graduated with top honors at a major university. He revealed an extraordinary talent for business, and word of him spread even before he'd received his MBA. I suspect he came by this naturally, since his own father was a well-known stockbroker. At any rate, this young man's ideas were revolutionary, but by heaven, he had a golden touch. Several corporations wanted him for their CEO. Before long he could name his own terms, and he did."

"Dad?" Amy had no idea where this story was leading, but she really didn't want to sit and listen to him ramble on about someone she wasn't even sure she knew. And if this was about Josh, she would rather not hear it. It couldn't change anything.

"Hush and listen," her father admonished. "This young man and his father were apparently very close and had been for years. To be frank, the father had something of a reputation for doing things just a tad shady. Nothing illegal, don't misunderstand me, but he took unnecessary risks. I sincerely doubt that the son was fully aware of this, although he must have guessed some of it was true. The son, however, defended his father at every turn."

Amy glanced at her watch, hoping her father got her message. If he did, it apparently didn't faze him.

"It seems that the son often sought his father's advice. I suppose this was only natural, being that they were close. By this time, the son was head of a major conglomerate, and if I said the name you'd recognize it immediately."

Amy yawned, wanting her father to arrive at the point of this long, rambling fable.

"No one is exactly certain what happened, but the conglomerate decided to sell off several of its smaller companies. The father, who you remember was a stockbroker, apparently got wind of the sale from the son and with such valuable inside information, made a killing in the market."

"But that's—"

"Unethical and illegal. What happened between the father and son afterward is anyone's guess. I suspect they parted ways over this issue. Whatever happened isn't my business, but I'm willing to speculate that there was no love lost between the two men in the aftermath of this scandal. The son resigned his position and disappeared for years."

"Can you blame him?"

"No," her father replied, his look thoughtful. "Although it was a terrible waste of talent. Few people even knew what had happened, but apparently he felt his credibility had been weakened. His faith in his father had been destroyed, no doubt, and that blow was the most crushing. My feeling is that he'd lived with the negative effects of having money for so many years that all he wanted was to wash his hands of it and build a new life for himself. He succeeded, too."

"Was he happy?"

"I can't say for certain, but I imagine he found plenty of fulfillment. He served in the Peace Corps for a couple of years and did other volunteer work. It didn't matter where he went, he was liked by all. It's been said that he never met a man who didn't like him."

"Does this story have a punch line?" Amy asked, amused.

"Yes, I'm getting to that. Let me ask you a couple of questions first."

"All right." She'd come this far, and although she hadn't been a willing listener, her father had managed to whet her appetite.

"I want you to put yourself into this young man's place. Can you imagine how difficult it would be for him to approach his father eight years after this estrangement?"

"I'm confident he wouldn't unless there was a good reason."

"He had one. He'd fallen in love."

"Love?" Amy echoed.

"He did it for the woman, and for her father, too, I suspect. He knew a way to help them, and although it cost him everything, he went to his father and asked for help."

"I see," Any said, and swallowed tightly.

"Amy." He paused and held his hand out to her. "The company that made the offer, the company that *saved* us, is owned by Chance Powell, Josh's father."

Amy felt as if she had received a blow to the head. A ringing sensation echoed in her ears, and the walls started to circle the room in a crazy merry-go-round effect. "Josh went to his father for us?"

"Yes, sweetheart. He sold his soul for you."

Although Amy had been to New York several times, she had never appreciated the Big Apple as much as she did on this trip. The city was alive with the sights and sounds of Christmas. Huge boughs of evergreens were strung across the entryways to several major stores. The city was ablaze with lights, had never shone brighter. A stroll through Central Park made Amy feel like a child again.

Gone was the ever-present need to cry, replaced instead with a giddy happiness that gifted her with a deep, abiding joy for the season she hadn't experienced since the time she was a child and the center of her parents' world.

With the address clenched tightly in her hand, Amy walked into the huge thirty-story building that housed Chance Powell's brokerage. After making a few pertinent inquiries, she rode the elevator to the floor where his office was situated.

Her gaze scanned the neat row of desks, but she didn't see Josh, which caused her spirits to sag just a little. She'd come to find him, and she wasn't about to leave until she'd done exactly that.

"I'm here to see Mr. Powell," Amy told the receptionist. "I don't have an appointment."

"Mr. Powell is a very busy man. If you want to talk to him, I'm afraid you'll have to schedule a time."

"Just tell him Amy Johnson is here...you might add that I'm Harold Johnson's daughter," she added for good measure, uncertain that Josh had even mentioned her name.

Reluctantly, the young woman did as Amy said. No sooner had she said Amy's name than the office door opened and Chance Powell himself appeared. The resemblance between father and son was striking. Naturally, Chance's looks were mature, his dark hair streaked with gray, but his eyes were so like Josh's that for a moment it felt as if she was staring at Josh himself.

"Hello, Amy," he said, clasping her hands in both of his. His gaze slid over her appreciatively. "Cancel my ten o'clock appointment," he said to the receptionist.

He led the way into his office and closed the door. "I wondered about you, you know."

"I suppose that's only natural." Amy sat in the chair across from his rich mahogany desk, prepared to say or do whatever she must to find Josh. "I don't know what Josh said to you, if he explained—"

"Oh, he said plenty," the older man murmured and chuckled, seemingly delighted about something.

"I need to find him," she said fervently, getting directly to the point.

"Need to?"

Amy ignored the question. "Do you know where he is?"

"Not at the moment."

"I see." Her hands tightened into a fist around the strap of her purse. "Can you tell me where I might start looking for him?" Her greatest fear was that he'd headed back to Kadiri or someplace else in the Middle East. It didn't matter, she would follow him to the ends of the earth if need be.

Chance Powell didn't seem inclined to give her any direct answers, although he had appeared eager enough to meet her. He scrutinized her closely, and he wore a silly half grin when he spoke. "My son always did have excellent taste. Do you intend to marry him?"

"Yes." She met his gaze head-on. "If he'll have me."

He laughed at that, boisterously. "Josh may be a good many things, but he isn't a fool."

"But I can't marry him until I can find him."

"Are you pregnant?"

Chance Powell was a man who came directly to the point, as well.

The color screamed in Amy's cheeks, and for a moment she couldn't find her tongue. "That's none of your business."

He laughed again, looking pleased, then slapped his hand against the top of his desk, scattering papers in several directions. "Hot damn!"

"Mr. Powell, please, can you tell me where I can find

Josh? This is a matter of life and death." His death, if he didn't quit playing these games with her. Perhaps she'd been a fool to believe that all she had to do was fly to New York, find Josh and tell him how much she loved him so they could live happily ever after. It had never entered her mind that his father wouldn't know where he was. Then again, he may well be aware of precisely where Josh was at that very moment and not plan to tell her.

"Do you have any water?" she said, feigning being ill. "My...stomach's been so upset lately."

"Morning sickness?"

She blushed demurely and resisted the temptation to place the back of her hand to her brow and sigh with a good deal of drama.

"Please excuse me for a moment," Chance said, standing.

"Of course."

A moment turned out to be five long minutes, and when the office door opened, it slammed against the opposite wall and then was abruptly hurled closed. The sound was forceful enough to startle Amy out of her chair.

Josh loomed over her like a ten-foot giant, looking more furious than she could ever remember seeing him. His eyes were almost savage. "What did you say to my father?"

"Hello, Josh," she said, offering him a smile he didn't return. Bracing her hands against the leather back of the chair, she used it as a shield between the two of them. The little speech she had so carefully prepared was completely lost. "I...I changed my mind about your offer. The answer is yes."

"Don't try to avoid the question," he shouted, advancing two steps toward her. "You told my father you're pregnant. We both know that's impossible."

He looked so good in a three-piece suit. So unlike the man who had asked to share a picnic table with her along the Seattle waterfront all those months ago. He had been wearing a fringed leather jacket then, and his hair had been in great need of a trim. Now…now he resembled a Wall Street executive, which was exactly what he was.

"What do you mean, you changed your mind?"

"I'm sorry I misled your father. I never came out directly and told him I was pregnant. But he didn't seem to want me to know where you were, and I had to find you."

"Why?"

He certainly wasn't making this easy on her. "Well, because…" She paused, drew in her breath and straightened her back, prepared for whatever followed. "Because I love you, Joshua Powell. I've reconsidered your marriage proposal, and I think it's a wonderful idea."

"The last I heard you were going to marry Chad Morton."

"Are you kidding? Don't you know a bluff when you hear one?"

He frowned. "Apparently not."

"I want to marry *you*. I have from the day you first kissed me on the Seattle waterfront and then claimed it had been a mistake. We've both made several of those over the past months, but it's time to set everything straight between us. I'm crazy about you, Joshua Powell. Your father may be disappointed, but the way I figure it, we could make him and my father grandparents in about nine months. Ten at the tops."

"Are you doing this out of gratitude?"

"Of course not," she said, as though the idea didn't even merit a response. "Out of love. Now please, stop looking at me as if you'd like to tear me limb from limb and come and hold me. I've been so miserable without you."

He closed his eyes, and his shoulders and chest sagged. "Oh, Amy…"

Unable to wait a moment longer, she walked into his arms the way a bird returns to its nest, without needing directions, recognizing home. A sense of supreme rightness filled her as she looped her arms around his neck and stood on her tiptoes. "I love you too, Angel Eyes," she said for him.

"I do, you know," he whispered, and his rigid control melted as he buried his face in her hair, rubbing his jaw back and forth against her temple as if drinking in her softness.

"There're going to be several children."

Fire hardened his dark eyes as he directed his mouth to hers in a kiss that should have toppled the entire thirty-story structure in which they stood. "How soon can we arrange a wedding?"

"Soon," she mumbled, her lips teasing his in a lengthy series of delicate, nibbling kisses. She caught his lower lip between her teeth and sucked at it gently.

Josh fit his hand over the back of her head as he took control of the kiss, slanting his mouth over hers with a hungry demand that depleted her of all strength. "You're playing with fire, angel," he warned softly, his dark eyes bright with passion.

She smiled up at him, her heart bursting with all the love she was experiencing. "I love it when you make dire predictions."

"Amy, I'm not kidding. Any more of that and you'll march to the altar a fallen angel."

She laughed softly. "Promises, promises."

Epilogue

"Amy?" Josh strolled in the back door of their home, expecting to find his pregnant wife either taking a nap or working in the nursery.

"I'm in the baby's room," he heard her shout from the top of the stairs.

Josh deposited his briefcase in the den, wondering why he even bothered to bring his laptop home. He had more entertaining ways of filling his evenings. Smiling, he mounted the stairs two at a time, while working loose the constricting silk tie at his neck. Even after five years, he still wasn't accustomed to wearing a suit.

Just as he suspected, he discovered Amy with a tiny paintbrush in her hand, sketching a field of wildflowers around several large forest creatures on the nursery wall.

"What do you think?" she asked proudly.

Josh's gaze softened as it rested on her. "And to think I married you without ever knowing your many talents." He stepped back and observed the scene she was so busy creating. "What makes you so certain this baby is a boy?"

Her smile was filled with unquestionable confidence. "A woman knows these things."

Josh chuckled. "As I recall, you were equally confident Cain would be a girl. It was darn embarrassing, bringing him home from the hospital dressed entirely in pink."

"He's since forgiven me."

"Perhaps so, but I haven't." He stepped behind her and flattened his hands over her nicely rounded abdomen. Her stomach was tight and hard, and his heart fluttered with excitement at the thought of his child growing within her. "I can think of a way for you to make it up to me, though," he whispered suggestively in her ear, then nibbled on her lobe. He felt her sag against him.

"Joshua Powell, it's broad daylight."

"So?"

"So…"

He could tell she was battling more with herself than arguing with him. Josh hadn't known what to expect once they were married. He had heard rumors about women who shied away from their husbands after they had spoken their vows. But in all the years he had been married to Amy, she had greeted his lovemaking with an eagerness that made him feel humble and truly loved.

"Where's Cain? Napping?"

"No…he went exploring with my father," she whispered.

"Then we're alone?" He stroked her breasts, and his loins tightened at how quickly her body reacted to his needs. No matter how many times they made love, it was never enough, and it never would be. When he was ninety, he would be looking for a few private moments to steal away with her.

"Yes, we're the only ones here," she told him, her voice trembling just a little.

"Good." He kissed the curve of her neck, and she relaxed against him. "Josh," she pleaded, breathless. "Let me clean the brush first."

He continued to nibble at her neck all the while, working on the elastic of her jeans.

"Josh," she begged. "Please," she moaned.

"I want to please you, angel, but you need to take care of that brush, remember."

"Oh, no, you don't," she cried softly. "You've got to take care of *me* first. You're the one who started this." Already she was removing her top, her fingers trembling, her hurried movements awkward. "I can't believe you," she cried, "in the middle of the day with Cain and my father due back any moment. We're acting like a couple of teenagers."

"You make me feel seventeen again," Josh murmured. He released her and started undressing himself.

Amy locked the door, then turned and leaned against it, her hands behind her back. "I thought men were supposed to lose their sexual appetite when their wives were pregnant."

Josh kicked off his shoes and removed his slacks. "Not me."

"I noticed."

He pinned her against the door, his forearms holding her head prisoner. "Do you have any complaints?"

"None," she whispered, framing his face lovingly with her hands. She kissed him, giving him her mouth

She looped her arms around his neck as she moved her body against him.

"I want you," he managed.

"Right here?" Her eyes widened as they met his. "Now?"

Amy closed her eyes, sagged against the door and sighed.

"You okay?"

"Oh, yes," she whispered.

By the time Josh had drifted back to earth, Amy was spreading kisses all over his face. He marveled at her, this woman who was his wife. She was more woman than any man deserved, an adventurous lover, a partner, a friend, the mother of his children, a keel that brought balance to his existence and filled his life with purpose.

Gently he helped her dress, taking time to kiss and caress her and tell her how much he loved her. Some things he had a difficult time saying, even now. Her love had taken all the bitterness from his life and replaced it with blessings too numerous to count.

As he bent over to retrieve his slacks, Josh placed a hand in the small of his back. "Remind me that I'm not seventeen the next time I suggest something like this."

"Not me," Amy murmured, tucking her arms around his neck and spreading kisses over his face. "That was too much fun. When can we do it again?"

"It may be sooner than you think."

Amy kissed him, and as he wrapped his arms around the slight thickening at her waist, he closed his eyes to the surge of love that engulfed him.

"Come on," she said with a sigh, reaching for her

paintbrush. "All this horsing around has made me hungry. How about some cream cheese and jalapeños spread over a bagel?"

"No, thanks." His stomach quivered at the thought.

"It's good, Josh. Honest."

He continued to hold her to his side as they headed down the stairs. "By the way, my father phoned this afternoon," he mentioned casually. "He said he'd like to come out and visit before the baby's born."

Amy smiled at him. "You don't object?"

"No. It'll be good to see him. I think he'd like to be here for the baby's arrival."

"I think I'd like that, too," Amy said.

Josh nodded. He had settled his differences with his father shortly before he had married Amy. Loving her had taught him the necessity of bridging the gap. His father had made a mistake based on greed and pride, and that error had cost them both dearly. But Chance deeply regretted his actions, and had for years.

In his own way, Josh's father had tried reaching out to Josh through his sister-in-law, but he had never been able to openly confront Josh. However, when Josh had come to him, needing his help, Chance had been given the golden opportunity to make up to his son for the wrong he had done years earlier.

Amy set a roast in the oven and reached for an orange, choosing that over the weird food combination she'd mentioned earlier.

"Mommy, Mommy." Three-year-old Cain crashed through the back door and raced across the kitchen, his stubby legs pumping for all he was worth. "Grandpa and I saw a robin and a rabbit and a...a worm."

Josh waylaid his son, catching him under the arms

and swinging him high above his head. "Where's Grandpa?"

"He said Mommy wouldn't want the worm inside the house so he put it back in the garden. Did you know worms live in the dirt and have babies and everything?"

"No kidding?" Amy asked, pretending to be surprised.

Harold Johnson came into the kitchen next, his face bright with a smile. "It looks like Cain gave you a run for your money, Dad," Amy said, kissing her father on the cheek. "I've got a roast in the oven, do you want to stay for dinner?"

"Can't," he said, dismissing the invitation. "I'm meeting the guys tonight for a game of pinochle." He stopped and looked at Josh. "Anything important happening at the office I should know about?"

"I can't think of anything offhand. Are you coming in on Tuesday for the board of directors' meeting?"

"Not if it conflicts with my golfing date."

"Honestly, Dad," Amy grumbled, washing her son's hands with a paper towel. "There was a time when nothing could keep you away from the business. Now you barely go into the office at all."

"Can't see any reason why I should. I've got the best CEO in the country. My business is thriving. Besides, I want to live long enough to enjoy my grandchildren. Isn't that right, Cain?"

"Right, Gramps." The toddler slapped his open palm against his grandfather's, then promptly yawned.

"Looks like you wore the boy out," Josh said, lifting Cain into his arms. The little boy laid his cheek on his father's shoulder.

"He'll go right down after dinner," Harold said, smiling broadly. "You two will have the evening alone." He winked at Josh and kissed Amy on the cheek. "You can thank me later," he whispered in her ear.

* * * * *